Croaked

an Edgar Rowdey Cape Cod Mystery

---

by Carol Verburg

www.Boom-Books.com

This story was born over lunch with my friends
Edward and Jack.
I started writing it to entertain them,
and finished it in affectionate memory of them
and Herbert.
Now it's for all of us who miss them.

NOTE: This is a work of fiction. None of the people, places, or situations in this book are intended to represent actual people, places, or situations.

Cover designed by Barbara Oplinger www.boplinger.com

ISBN 978-0-983435-50-1

Chapter One

If Lydia Vivaldi hadn't tried to read the Cape Cod Times Help Wanted ads while driving, she wouldn't have wound up on the side of 6A with a flat tire. Her yellow Morris Minor wouldn't have caught the eye of Alistair Pope, passing in his vintage Mercedes. Lydia wouldn't have joined Alistair at Leo's Back End for lunch; Leo wouldn't have hired her to replace his assistant cook, Sue, who had just stormed out in tears after Leo diluted her split-pea soup; and the murder rate in Quansett, Massachusetts, might have stayed at zero.

"Taste it!" Leo clunked down two cups. "On the house. Now tell me that's not perfect exactly how it is."

Lydia tasted. She was feeling dizzy–whether from not sleeping, skipping breakfast, or falling down a rabbit hole into Wonderland, she couldn't tell. Her mind groped for facts she could cling to. *Cape Cod is a sixty-mile peninsula which juts into the Atlantic Ocean south of Boston like a bent arm. The fingers are Provincetown, the elbow is Chatham, the armpit is Bourne. Quansett, on the biceps, dates to the late 1600s.*

That patchwork wall behind Leo must be the Back End's menu: squares of colored paper hand-printed with today's specials ("SPESHULS"). And this must be the Splat P Soop. Its problem (in Lydia's opinion) wasn't thickness but flavor. If you didn't mind losing the vegetarians, as Leo clearly didn't, why not throw in a ham hock?

"I ask you! Any thicker you'd have to eat it with a fork."

She fished unobtrusively, found only a few meaty shreds. If stinginess was what kept Leo so skinny, it hadn't affected his customers. Of the twenty or so people in this two-room cafe, only the kid behind the cash register could be called thin. The mountainous aproned woman slinging burgers in the kitchen outweighed even Alistair.

Winters are milder than in Boston, thanks to the Gulf Stream bearing sea-warmth up from Florida and bouncing off the Cape toward Portugal. Springs are shorter, autumns longer. Golf is commonly played till Thanksgiving.

Her fingernails had gotten the worst of her battle with the flat tire. Yesterday's sparkly green polish was half chipped off. Green, like the streaks in her hair. Like her eyes, on the off chance anyone ever noticed.

Lydia set down her spoon and removed her sunglasses.

A stranger wouldn't even guess this place was here. She hadn't noticed it a year ago, on her first and only visit to Cape Cod. Its name she hoped was geographical: Leo's Back End stood at the far edge of a long parking lot behind a cluster of shops up on Main Street. She'd fallen in love at first sight with the dollhouse village of Quansett: ancient oaks and stone fences, gray-shingled shoebox houses, white porch railings, windowboxes overflowing with red geraniums and striped petunias–

No beach worth mentioning, Alistair Pope warned her, slowing his Mercedes. The nearest shopping mall is five miles away in Hyannis. Welcome to downtown: the post office, the drugstore, the firehouse, the Whistling Pig Tea Shoppe, the Frigate Bookstore, the town library, and one cluster of retail and office spaces. That's why we have the highest proportion of year-rounders on the Cape. Lunch is a social highlight.

Everybody in here did seem to know each other. Was it always this down-homey? Or had she arrived just in time–with Memorial Day over and June starting tomorrow–for one last Norman Rockwell moment before school let out and vacationers flooded over the bridge demanding lobster rolls?

No lobster on Leo's bulletin-board menu. Under Alistair's guidance Lydia took a slip to write down her order. Did he recommend anything? Her knight-errant smiled, shook his head. "It's a crap shoot." And added, "You don't come to Leo's for the food."

Back at her car he'd been more talkative. "I can see you've got this undah control," he'd begun graciously, "but I'm a Maw-ris fan from way back and it would be an aw-nah to assist you." His Massachusetts drawl recalled Jack Kennedy, although Alis-tayah had several years and at least fifty pounds on the late president. "I live just up the road. Pre-Civil War farmhouse, zealously guarded by our Historical Commission. You can stable horses in your back yard, but don't try to change your mailbox or paint your front door without a lawyer."

He'd kept up the flow of conversation while they worked, as if to reassure her of his intentions. What year was this beauty? Still the original engine? That was quite a load she'd packed in there. No wonder her tire blew. Moving to the Cape for the summer?

Lydia glanced at the suitcases piled beside the open trunk, the boxes crammed with books and clothes, lamps and plants, in the back seat. "Maybe. There's somebody I kind of need to find."

A raised eyebrow told her he wondered if he might be that somebody. Not a can of worms she cared to open.

He hadn't asked her the obvious question: "Is that your real name?" She'd braced for it, prepared to zing back: "It is now!" Instead he'd rolled the syllables around in his mouth, *Lydia Vivaldi*, like a sip of fine wine, and smiled at her: "Pleased to meet you." Then pushed up his sleeves and bolted on the spare tire faster than she'd been able to pry off the hubcap.

Alistair laid their slips beside the cash register. With a hand on her elbow he steered her to a bin of flatware. Armed with forks, spoons, and mugs, they slid into a booth. His leg pressed against hers. Was this why he'd brought her to Leo's?–because it gave him so many chances to touch her?

And why, dammit, did each touch jolt her like a hot wire?

On first sight she'd pegged Alistair Pope as a NFW. Too old, too hefty, too retro-suburban. His wavy salt-and-pepper hair was combed across a thin spot on top, splayed over his collar on the sides. His army jacket looked like it hadn't been washed since the Vietnam war. Who wore rugby shirts anymore? tucked into threadbare jeans? She did like his gold earring: small and simple, with a question-mark curve and an etched design.

Was her heart so shredded, was her betrayed body so starved, that any doofus off the street could get to her?

No. There was something about Alistair Pope–a presence, a magnetism she couldn't pin down. His eyes? Amused, curious, intelligent, flirtatious. His mouth? Wide and expressive, with a cryptic smile. When he spoke, husky and confiding, you felt he recognized qualities in you that no one else could see.

A big man with strong hands. Wrapped in those arms, you'd feel safe.

No wedding ring. Divorced? Maybe he'd bought the Mercedes to celebrate.

Maybe after lunch–

"Is this fella bothering you, young lady?"

A tall concave presence loomed beside their table. Lydia looked up at an electric shock of ice-white hair and eyebrows over icicle-sharp blue eyes.

Then: "Taste this!" And she and Alistair listened, with suitable expressions of sympathy, to the tale of the traitorous sous-chef.

Across the room, Edgar Rowdey skimmed the Cape Cod Times obituaries. Not (as a reviewer had once speculated) because he made his living from death. Yes, his miniature black-and-white books did follow one odd character after another through a dismal set of perils to a grotesque end. Edgar Rowdey's interest, however, was not in death per se. What fascinated him was people's reactions to death.

Take that poor girl last month. DeAnne Ropes.

Local Artist Tragedy, the Times had trumpeted. Even if you'd never actually spoken to her, you could hardly be unmoved. However! *Local artist?* DeAnne had spent one semester taking art classes up in Cambridge before retreating over the bridge. Her job for the retired Broadway-musical team of Song and Penn was to answer their phones, open their mail, make coffee, and walk their dog, Arson. *Tragedy*? In such a retirement haven as the Cape, perhaps the Times slapped that label on any fatality before age 70. Still! Why not call her death *untimely* or *premature?* Why not *shocking?* There's the film crew waiting for her at the Whistling Pig, toasting the end of their shoot while DeAnne closes the studio, and suddenly medics are rolling her out on a stretcher. What about (for instance) *ironic?* Her parents drag her home to find a suitable job and/or husband, and the Barnstable County medical examiner rewrites her résumé: Caucasian female, age 22, height five four, weight one thirty-nine, hair black, eyes brown, not a virgin but with no recent sexual activity. What about *heartbreaking?* After four months of doing as little work as possible, DeAnne decides to take down a heavy curtain alone, overbalances and crashes to her death.

Carlo Song had looked positively ashen over lunch. The news had spread through Quansett by then; still, everyone at Leo's wanted details. Head first? Died instantly? Damn! Hell of a price to pay for being in a movie. Not even Hollywood, either, just that PBS thing of Al Pope's. Poor kid, couldn't stop talking about it–dreaming of fame, her parents telling Oprah about her childhood while she cruised around in designer gowns and stretch limos.

Carlo's Eggz Bennie congealed untouched on his plate. Caroline Penn had stayed home. Neither of them had slept. Headlights coming and going in the driveway all night. Gusts of blurred music from car radios. Reporters? Rubberneckers? Looking for what? In the morning they found their boxwood hedge abloom with plastic-wrapped bouquets, photos, notes, even teddy bears.

Edgar Rowdey had squelched an impulse to head straight for his drawing room and start a new picturebook: *Alack, A Lass, A Ladder.*

Over the month that followed, he'd watched as–ironically–one after another of DeAnne's dreams came half-true. A candlelight vigil was held outside Carlo and Caroline's studio. News teams from Provincetown to Boston interviewed her parents. So many people attended the funeral that St. Pius X had to open a side room. Before the ceremony, on closed-circuit TV, mourners watched DeAnne's family holidays, school picnics, senior prom, and her brief interview about working for Song and Penn. PBS urged Alistair Pope to include a clip in his documentary, and to wrap in time for their summer pledge drive. The police investigation, which had just wrapped last week, found no evidence that DeAnne Ropes's death could have been anything but a tragic accident.

Nothing in today's obituaries came close.

"Lydia, Leo. Leo, Lydia." Again Alistair's leg rested against hers. "Despite the evidence, Leo likes to think he runs this sorry excuse for an establishment."

"He can't stay away," Leo confided to Lydia. "Istair here can't get enough of our fine cuisine. And our distinguished guests. Present company included." He made her a small bow.

"We all only eat here because we feel sorry for him. Don't tell him, though. It would break his poor old heart."

"They ask me to keep him out because he lowers the tone. But I'm too soft."

They almost sound like they mean it, thought Lydia. Looking past them, she gave Leo a thumbs-up for decor. No fishing nets and lobster buoys on the pine-plank walls, just local paintings: a sailboat, a flower garden. Bright red, blue, green, and yellow table-tops on the booths. A yard-sale assortment of wooden tables and chairs in the middle, like an old neighborhood bar. No liquor, though. The sign outside said Open 7 AM to 2 PM Except Sunday.

Alistair and Leo were still sparring. "It's a toss-up which has a worse reputation, his so-called food or his so-called service."

That shifted Leo's wrath back to Sue. According to him, she alone was to blame for any problems at the Back End, including its marginal existence and his own white hairs. According to Alistair, she was a lousy cook anyway. According to them both, she had a maddening habit of disappearing whenever she wanted time off and coming back, all smiles, before Leo could replace her.

Lydia listened with the sensation of having been dropped from the sky into a trout stream with a fishing rod poised to cast.

"So?" Leo demanded. "Am I right?"

"It's thick enough," she said. "What it needs is more meat. It's kind of bland, don't you think?"

Far from being offended, he beamed. "Did you hear her? This is a gourmet you've got here." He patted her shoulder. "Why can't I ever find a soup chef with such a discerning palate?"

Their lunch arrived. Lydia said, "Funny you should mention it, but I came to the Cape to look for a cooking job."

Aha! Now Leo was the superstitious one. Coincidence nothing! This was Fate! The hand of destiny!

"Ahem," said Alistair through his sandwich.

"Shut up, you," said Leo. "Always claiming credit. Go answer your phone."

"Pointless." Alistair reached into his jacket, where a muffled doorbell was ringing. "No reception." He slid out of the booth.

Leo perched on his vacated bench. How about it? Try the job for a week, no obligation. Help out Dinah during breakfast, make the soup, prep for lunch, serve meals, and pitch in wherever needed. The pay wasn't huge, but neither were the hours.

Is this possible? wondered Lydia. Could the hand of destiny be cupping her in its palm for a change instead of flipping her the finger? A job! Friends! Maybe even health insurance! All this on the same day she'd thrown her things in the car and her keys in the mailbox, fleeing Greater Boston in a last-ditch attempt to escape the disaster her life had become.

"Have you got a place to stay?" Leo rose to make way for Alistair.

"I think so. A friend of mine moved back here from Cambridge last Christmas. Her folks live in Dennis."

Leo's smile went rigid, as if his face had frozen. A familiar unwelcome chill prickled the back of Lydia's neck.

"I came down partly to see her. She sent me a postcard . . . "

Alistair spoke lightly. "What's her name?"

"DeAnne Ropes." Silence. "You know her, don't you. What's the problem?"

"I'm sorry." Leo patted her shoulder. "Lydia, I'm so sorry."

Chapter Two

Well, well, Dinah Rowan thought as she slapped burgers on the grill. Pope scores again! Where the heck does he find 'em? This girl couldn't be much past thirty, and way too hip for a horny old snake like Al. Now he was showing her the menu, his hand on her back. What's the matter, Al, can't she read?

My prices are low, Leo liked to say, because I don't pay babysitters. You want to eat? Write up your own damn order. You want the table set? There's the cutlery. Soda machine, too. Be grateful we supply the grub and a place to park your back end.

Dinah swiveled to shred a purple cabbage with a cleaver. Back off, Al! She don't need your big paws all over her just to find a spoon.

Even Edgar Rowdey was watching them over his newspaper. No wonder: Al had been lobbying all winter to do a documentary on him, and sometimes would trot over the girl du jour like a dog fetching slippers. Or (more likely) just to show off.

What it showed (Dinah shoveled the cabbage into a bowl) was Al's lack of common sense. For one thing, Rowdey was as famous for living like a hermit as for his creepy stories and finicky draw-ings. For another, Al had shot himself in the foot when he tried to steal Rowdey's gardener, J.D. Thought he'd grow some vegetables and get a dish named after him on the Back End's menu, like the Row-deyberry Tarte. What Al failed to figure was that squash, tomatoes, and corn don't go wild in the sandy Cape soil like blue-berries and blackberries. Pope's plot failed, in both senses: J.D. turned him down, and Al barely could grow grass by himself.

Now, having plowed under his doomed garden, he pretended the whole thing never happened. Same as he pretended his name was Alistair when everybody knew he was plain Al, short for

Albert, short for Fat Albert, till he went off to college.

Rowdey was too much the gentleman to bust him. Or tell him where he could stuff his documentary; so Al hung on like a bull-dog, even though most of Quansett knew the Atlantic would have to freeze over before a camera crew ever crossed Edgar Rowdey's threshold.

With a precision that would make her the envy of bomber pilots if any should stray in from the base at Otis, Dinah flipped each burger in one swift swoop. Was Leo feeding soup to Al's girl? Hussy! He'd better get his buns over here before the burgers burned, with no Sue to man the toaster.

But it was Mudge who scrambled around the counter, all arms and legs. Hired as a part-time dishwasher, he'd expanded to all-purpose gap-filler. Right now he was cashier, which he liked because he got to honk the tip horn. Leo kept a bucket on the counter for his ill-paid staff. Spare change won a honk from a brass bicycle horn; folding green, a rousing clang from a firebell.

"Dinah!" Mudge grabbed buns; splayed them on the revolving toaster. "Did you hear?"

"What?"

"Leo's hired that girl to take Sue's job!"

It would have been beneath her to show shock. "Well. Can't really call it Sue's job when she didn't want it."

"She did, though. He named it Sue-Chef for her. She just–oh, you know. And he didn't even ask her!"

"Nor us."

"Nor us," he echoed.

As each browned bun fell from the toaster, Mudge forked it onto a paper plate and slid it to Dinah. He lived–impatiently–with his family in Mashpee, where his father was some kind of chief in the Wampanoag tribe. His mother, now dead, was rumored to have hitched a ride to the annual pow-wow one summer from Roxbury and stayed. Nobody but Leo and the bookkeeper knew how old he was. Dinah guessed over eighteen but under twenty-one.

"She ever done any cooking?"

"Up in Boston. One of those chi-chi places–Legal Seafood?"

"Better be Durgin Park if she wants to work here. Where's

himself?"

Leo always delivered the burgers personally, one in each hand, manually anchored to their plates: the Back End's famous Thumburger.

"Coming. He gave her back to Mr. Pope. He looks–both of 'em–kind of . . . "

"Thunderstruck?"

"Well," said Mudge. "Did you see her?"

"Don't *you* start!"

But Mudge, Dinah wagered, could hold his own. As tall and lean as Leo, Mudge had the potent edge of youth. He didn't go fetch women, retriever fashion, like the tireless and tiresome Pope; they came after him. As so would I, she admitted, if I was sixteen again. Never mind that he'd scare the bejesus out of you in a dark alley, with his look of a Cherokee in a John Wayne movie. It was his eyes you fell into, deep and dark as a kettle-hole pond. Bewitching eyes!–like a deer's, like a dog's, so that you felt you could tell him anything at all and he would understand and still trust you.

He was staring at that girl again. Those eyes of yours, she warned him silently, will get you in trouble some day!

Within a week she would recall this thought and wonder if she was psychic.

If you turn left out of Leo's, continue through Quansett center, and take a left onto Willow Street, you may notice a long, low L-shaped building with white vinyl siding, blue doors and shutters, and a faded sign: Blue Moon Motel. Vacancy. No Turnarounds Police Take Notice.

After Labor Day, when the tourists have gone home, the average Cape Cod motel has no jobs for the maids, busboys, launderers, and receptionists who gave its customers a carefree summer vacation. Workers who can't afford to head north, to the ski resorts, or south, to the Florida beaches, move into the empty motels and squeak through the winter on unemployment.

At nine o'clock on this last Wednesday evening in May, the

Blue Moon parking lot was sparsely scattered with cars. Beyond it, the swimming pool in its chicken-wire cage lay empty under a blue tarp. The office window was lit, although no one could be seen inside. Along the rest of the row an occasional slatted yellow window shone; an occasional TV muttered to itself, loud and incoherent.

In Room 5, Lydia Vivaldi spoke into her cell phone.

"This is so fucked."

She had muted the sound on her TV and sat cross-legged on her bed. Blankets enveloped her legs. Beside her on the floor lay an open pizza box. A street light slanting through the venetian blinds lit up the white cardboard circle under the pizza's remains like a half moon.

"What's my procedure here? Do I go see them? Do I call them? Or what?"

"Why do you have to do anything?"

"Because she was my friend, Karin! My business partner! She was their daughter, and she's dead! At the age of fucking twenty-two! From falling off a fucking ladder for christ's sake!"

"Well, but, Liz–"

"Lydia. Please."

"Lydia, then. Am I right?–they don't even know you exist."

"So that lets me off the hook?" Lydia shook her head. "I don't think so."

"Well, if you want to talk to them, I'm sure they'd be glad to meet you."

"To hear about DeAnne. Don't you think? Her life in Cambridge, her artwork, the Fix-It Chix and all that. The house."

"Yeah. I'm sure they'd appreciate that."

"She sent me a postcard, Karin. A month ago. She wanted to patch things up. What was wrong with me? I should have called her!"

"You would have. How could you know?"

"I don't even remember what she said! Something like Hey, sorry, things are great here–which at the time just pissed me off, with my life in a total train wreck–"

"Hey. Which was totally not your fault."

"–And now I can't find the friggin' thing. I just spent like an hour searching through every inch of my stuff."

"It's OK. Stop blaming yourself."

"How can I help it? Anyway, that's not– Oh, hell."

"What?"

"I don't get it! How could that happen to her? DeAnne! With her, you know, spatial sense? Coordination?"

"You said it was night, a smooth floor, she was wearing clogs. It could happen to anybody. Her foot slipped, or the ladder. She fell and hit her head. Right? You said that's what was in the police report."

"Yeah, well. That's what Leo said was in the police report. But I'm thinking, shouldn't I ask the cops? Do I, like, owe it to her? To make sure?"

"How do you owe anything to anybody on this? It's over. You're right, it sucks. But, you know, we just found out. Everybody else, like her family?–went through this a month ago. Whatever there was to do about it, they did. Case closed. They're like five weeks along in their grieving process. You want to open that up again?"

"Fuck. I don't know."

"No need to decide right now. Go back to sleep. Think it over when your head's clear."

"Right. You're absolutely right, Karin. Hey, how are things up there? You, I mean. And Ricky?"

"We're good. He found your note. That was quite the big shock."

"To him? Everybody?"

"Well, sure. Paul and MJ just about flipped. Christophe doesn't know yet. He's working a double shift."

"Well, say hi for me. Just to them, you know? Not–anybody else."

"Got it."

"I don't even want to hear if he's alive."

"Course not."

"In fact I hope he isn't. I hope the shithead fries in Hell, the sooner the better."

"Yup."

"And his little bimbo, too."

"Especially her."

"So if he asks you if I asked about him, the answer is no. I didn't."

"No, you definitely did not."

"Karin, are you sure you're OK with breaking the news about DeAnne?"

"Well, it's not like I've got a choice, do I? Yeah, I'll go knock on doors tonight. Whoever's here. Dinner kind of fell apart without you here to, you know, rally the troops."

"Tell them I'm a professional cook now. That ought to get some laughs."

"Take care of yourself, Liz. I mean, Lydia. And don't worry about her parents or the cops or whatever. Give yourself time to get settled. See how it goes."

"Thanks, Karin. You're a true friend."

"Keep in touch, OK?"

"You too."

But we won't, she thought as she hung up. Liz is over. Dead as ashes, like her pal DeAnne.

On a side street in Hyannis, Mudge Miles sat on a barstool. His right hand gripped a beer bottle; his left arm was slung around the waist of a girl he remembered was cute but whose name he'd forgotten. Talk ricocheted around him like pool balls. Mudge was (as he liked to think of it) multitasking: laughing, joshing his buddies, drinking, teasing the girl.

In the privacy of his brain, two thoughts buzzed like mosquitoes.

One: beer bored him. He drank it because everybody did, and it was a hell of a lot cheaper than the tequila shot he'd kicked off with. But who picked this piss as the default drink for men? Why couldn't a man order a sombrero, a Cape Codder, or a pina colada without getting laughed off his barstool?

If the girl pressed against his side had broken the rules, however, and asked what he was thinking about, Mudge would have said: my truck. That was a problem that verged on the eternal. It was a running joke among his buddies: Well, Mudge could pick us up in the truck, except she'll be broke down. Tonight he intended to leave the worthless piece of shit in Leo's parking lot. He'd hitched here from Mashpee; somebody would give him a ride back. Then, well past midnight, in beer-elevated spirits, plus some weed if he got lucky, he'd figure out how to get her running.

Or not. His father's girlfriend had snapped at him worse than usual this morning. She hated being woken up, he knew that, but the house was so small that he couldn't be as silent as he meant to. Some days she just yelled, some days she threatened. Today she'd ordered him to have his lazy good-for-nothing butt at the dinner table by 6:30 or don't come home at all. Which meant either sneak in after they were all asleep, or go home with this girl, or sleep in the truck. He'd thrown a couple of blankets in the back just in case.

You'd think she'd give him credit for holding down a steady job. Most of these guys were in and out of work like a revolving door, jumping from restaurant to gas station to construction to unemployment faster than they switched girlfriends. You'd think she'd be glad he was saving up for college. If it pissed her off that he didn't put money in the kitty, let her bitch at his dad. The education fund was his idea. Let her just tell Lincoln Miles to get off his high horse about being the family provider, and see whose lazy good-for-nothing butt got kicked out the damn door!

The girl was ruffling his hair, tickling his ear with her long fingernail. He grinned at her. Darla, that was it. He could see she was drunk. Cute, though. He felt a little drunk himself.

Not liking beer didn't–couldn't–mean you were gay. Did it? You'd know that about yourself, wouldn't you, by the time you were old enough to drink? If you were gay, you wouldn't get hot around girls, which Mudge definitely did. You'd want to grope guys, which he definitely didn't. Wouldn't you? Homosexuality wasn't something that could sneak up on a person, was it?–like the cancer that had killed his mother, or the Alzheimer's that put his grandmother in a home. Even if you didn't always want to spend the night with the girl. Even if you secretly thought the coolest thing you'd ever done in your life was create the semi-famous Rowdeyberry Tarte. There had to be straight dessert chefs somewhere, right? OK, sure, fancy restaurants and Provincetown and gays, everybody knew that; but it wasn't, like, built into your genes, was it?

Oh, screw it. Sex was too fucking complicated anyway. Somewhere it had gotten twisted, from too many rules to none. From where you couldn't do anything, to where somebody gets hurt no matter what you do. Like that girl who worked for Caroline and Carlo. DeAnne. Whenever he thought about her he felt guilty. Not that it could possibly be his fault what happened to her. They'd stopped seeing each other weeks before. Well, he'd stopped. She claimed to be fine with it, and after one awkward meeting at Leo's, she acted fine with it. The last time she came in for lunch, with the film crew, he couldn't tell if she was showing off or if she really thought somebody had turned that toad Alistair Pope into a handsome prince.

One of his buddies was into a shoving match at the far end of the bar with some redneck Irish asshole who'd made a loud comment about Indians and firewater. Darla nuzzled his neck. Mudge leaned past her and caught his friend Justin's eye. Two minds with the same thought.

Mudge fished out his wallet, disentangled himself from Darla, and braced for a cold cramped night in Leo's parking lot.

Chapter Three

The first day of June! Easing the Morris onto Route 6A, Lydia congratulated herself (since no one else was likely to) on being upright, dressed, clean, and functional at 6:45 AM. Now at last she could leave behind DeAnne Ropes, who'd haunted her all night. A new day! A fresh start! Time for simple, practical questions: Could she support herself as a sous-chef? Would she walk in the door to find Sue back and herself out? Would Alistair show up for breakfast?

Part of her hoped he would, part of her wished he wouldn't. She was curious to see him again, if only to find out what (if anything) he was up to, but she didn't want to go all distracted and klutzy while she was chopping vegetables.

Not much traffic at this hour. Colder than she'd expected. After an afternoon nap and a walk on the beach, she'd stayed up late, watching TV to drown out her turbulent thoughts; so once she finally got back to sleep, the alarm clock had beeped way too soon and catapulted her, shivering, into daylight.

Maybe she wouldn't have to stay at the Blue Moon much longer.

She'd asked Alistair over lunch what kinds of films he made. Documentaries, he said, mostly biographical. Was that as cool as it sounded? He'd laughed and described his day: Check e-mail, footage, and phone calls; mow lawn, go to lunch, and–the high point–help a stranded motorist change her tire. Did he have coworkers? A family, anyone around through all this? He smiled and said no, so go ahead and order dessert. Which she did: a remarkably tasty Choklit Moose cake. Toward the end of lunch she tried again: Was he, as they say, seeing anybody? His smile grew more enigmatic. He shook his head: "I gave that up."

Meaning, she presumed, he'd loved too passionately and plunged too deep into disillusion and despair to keep an open heart. That was a problem she totally understood.

Which did not mean (she reminded herself then and now) they should plunge right in with each other. Talk about out of the frying pan! Just because her drawbridge was still down, and he'd gallantly rescued her, and this wasn't Cambridge, didn't make him a knight in shining armor.

In fact why was she even thinking about him? She hardly knew the guy. They'd spent–what?–maybe an hour together?–most of it focused on Leo or the Morris.

Because they'd connected. The hand-of-fate meeting? The electricity when they touched? And look at the 180-degree turnaround he'd triggered in her luck!

Then there was DeAnne.

Not a bond you'd wish for, but powerful. To Lydia's frustration, Alistair had nothing to say about her death beyond the gist: filming, studio, ladder, accidental fall. Died instantly, Leo added. No pain. For Alistair apparently it hadn't been so painless–a nightmare aftermath of cops and cordons, accusatory parents, intrusive paparazzi, upset employees. As for DeAnne herself, he claimed to have been too busy and distracted to pay her much attention.

Lydia tried again as they finished lunch and hit the same wall of silence. Why, dammit? Did she look like a cop, or reporter? Would it kill him to cough up a recollection? Couldn't he see that for her this was a huge shock?

For whatever reason, after such a charged beginning their good-bys were abruptly formal. Midway through coffee Alistair announced that Edgar Rowdey was leaving and they needed to catch him. He'd hustled Lydia up to the cash register and out the door, but too late; Rowdey had gone. OK, big disappointment. Still, she'd expected more from him than a stiff hug in the parking lot, mini-kisses on both cheeks like the French, and a wave as they drove off in separate cars.

He did ask "When will I see you again?" but the irony was obvious. She'd given the obvious answer: "You know where to find me."

6:58 AM. No Mercedes in the parking lot. Those few cars must be the regulars Leo had said might show up before the Back End opened. He left a hidden key rather than come down from his apartment (classic, Lydia thought, living over the shop) just to make coffee for insomniacs.

Really, it would be bad, not good, to find Alistair here. You don't want a man who's up with the chickens, do you?

The breakfast rush was so overwhelming that Lydia didn't get a chance until mid-morning, when the kitchen crew paused for bagels, to notice how miffed she was that he'd never appeared.

She whisked eggs, she chopped celery, she rang up customers. Ten-fifteen. She sensibly made cream of broccoli soup instead of curried cauliflower. (Next time.) Around her Mudge raced like Ben-Hur's chariot and Dinah moved with the slow majesty of an ocean liner. Eleven-fifteen. Leo praised her soup extravagantly. She suggested they divide tomorrow's chili, one batch with meat and one without. Twelve-fifteen: rush hour again. Chop, fry, toast, garnish, serve. Still no Alistair.

Two-fifteen. As they peeled off their aprons, Lydia asked Leo the question she'd been formulating since the first egg hit the griddle. "Does your friend Mr. Pope usually eat here, or did I just meet him on a lucky day?"

Leo groaned, dramatizing how hard he'd worked, how his old bones ached. "Istair? You never know. Mostly he comes in to stalk Edgar here." His hand flicked out and grabbed the writer's arm. "Edgar, meet my new second cook. Edgar, Lydia Vivaldi. Lydia, Edgar Rowdey."

She'd noticed the balding, white-bearded man sitting alone at a center table with a book. Cup of Brockli Soop and a Tooner Sallid, was it? He'd been here for breakfast, too. The Ing Muff she remembered; the Scram Egz had left their mark down the front of his faded blue sweatshirt. So this was the friend Alistair had so urgently wanted her to meet, the famous author of intricate, spooky little books that had given her nightmares as a child. Not dead, or English, or ghoulish, as she'd assumed. What to say?

"Hi. Good to meet you."

He had an admirable handshake, firm and dry. "Welcome to

the madhouse," he drawled. "Your soup is a godsend, dear. Whatever you do, keep this skinflint here away from it, and please don't quit." And to Leo: "Treat her with respect, will you? You're lucky a real chef is willing to set foot in this place. Don't go sucking her dry and cast her aside like all the others."

Leo patted his arm. "My biggest fan," he told Lydia. "You can tell by how he talks to me." To Rowdey: "Why don't you keep your mouth shut if you can't say anything nice? Vicious brute."

Under their harsh words was an affection Lydia had missed in Leo's exchanges yesterday with Alistair. This, she perceived, was a real friendship. Alistair, although he'd picked up the Back End's conversational style, remained outside its inner circle.

She looked with more curiosity at Edgar Rowdey. Would she have recognized him as a man renowned for deadpan tales of violence? Not a chance. Of course there was the egg-stained sweatshirt. But his face too looked more kindly than dangerous. His full lips were rosy as a baby's cheeks. Sparse white hair, unruly beard, half-glasses sliding down his aquiline nose . . . and blue eyes: not piercingly blue, like Leo's, but changeably, like the ocean. Like the faded jeans he wore with his once-white sneakers.

"Do you live around here?" she asked him.

"Oh, yes."

"Just up the road. You can't miss it," said Leo. "Big old pile, looks like it's falling down in a heap. Same as the owner. Whoops! Sorry."

Rowdey ignored him. "And you?" he asked Lydia.

"So far, the Blue Moon Motel. Leo's promised to find me a place if I last out the week."

"Trust him no farther than you can throw him. Ta-ta," he told them both, and strolled off toward the parking lot.

Lydia watched him leave the path and cross the grass to the Back End's ornamental pond. On the far rim, where a branch from the giant beech tree beside the restaurant hung low over the water, he folded his arms and gazed into the pool.

The famous author. Possibly soon to be a friend of mine.

A surge of happiness washed over her. This is me, world! This is my new life!

"Gotta watch that fella," said Leo. "He's after my frogs."

"Your frogs?" Lydia had spotted only three goldfish among the water plants.

Leo nodded darkly. "He studied French in college. Probably wants the legs."

They moved to the kitchen to join the rest of the crew for a quick lunch of leftovers. Lydia helped Dinah store the remaining food while Leo and Mudge went over the day's receipts. The dishwasher, Bruno, who spoke neither English nor French as far as she could tell, washed the floor, wheeling a tin bucket with rollers, pumping vigorously with a rag mop. Stepping around him, Lydia spotted a familiar profile through the window. Half hidden by beech branches, like a satyr emerging from a sacred grove, stood Alistair Pope.

Would he come in? No, the door was locked.

Why was he here? To see her?

She didn't dare rush out on her first day. Anyhow, she didn't want to give him ideas. Or give Leo and the others any excuse for gossip. Surely nobody on earth had ever taken as long as Dinah to fasten a piece of plastic wrap around a bowl! Why didn't she get proper tubs with lids?

He was still there when Lydia, Dinah, and Mudge emerged, contemplating the frog pond with Edgar Rowdey. Greetings were exchanged. Dinah chaffed Alistair–whom she called Al–for missing lunch. He replied with an insult to her cooking that was too automatic to be offensive. Edgar Rowdey asked Mudge if he planned to make the Tarte again this summer. Mudge said you bet, if it was OK with him and Leo and Dinah. Dinah said it was fine with her as long as Al didn't get any. Alistair said that was harsh when he hadn't been getting any all winter. He didn't even glance at Lydia. It struck her that the Back End was its own kind of frog pond; but what this might mean, especially for him and her, she was too flustered to think.

After what seemed to her a very long and pointless chat, Dinah moved off to her blue Honda sedan and Mudge to his ancient multicolored pick-up truck.

"Mr. Rowdey," said Lydia. "Leo thinks you're after his

frogs."

"Oh, too true."

"Cuisses de grenouille?" said Alistair. "Revolting. But you must call him Edgar. Can't she? Since you've evidently been introduced."

"By all means," he murmured. "A pleasure." Speaking to the frog pond. "I must be off."

"But we haven't reached a conclusion," Alistair objected. He explained to Lydia: "How they get here. Where they go. Some days there are several, some days none."

She surveyed the little pond. Layers of slate and stones around it created plenty of sunning spots for frogs, in addition to the lily pads in the water. No frogs were visible.

"Do they hop off under the tree, or up into it?" Rowdey elaborated, miming with a gesture.

"Are there tiny caves in the rocks where they hide, like Al Qaeda?" Alistair one-upped.

"Or tunnels? leading to some distant unknown lake?"

"Or does Leo materialize them afresh every morning, like Moses?" Alistair flung up his arms. "Are they conceived in the clouds, heavenly tadpoles, to drop with the gentle rain upon the place beneath?"

Edgar Rowdey pushed up his glasses. "I must," he repeated, "be off."

"Well, off you go, then."

And off he shambled. Lydia and Alistair stood where they were, watching, not looking at each other, until Rowdey and his black VW station wagon–license plate WARDOG–had gone.

Lydia turned first. "Wardog?"

"One of his pseudonyms. E. Dyer Wardog, putative author of his breakout book, *Hidden Turnips*. Thirteen weeks on the Times best-seller list, banned in three cities, including Boston. Bid on by three movie studios who wanted to turn it into, I don't know, some kind of animated soft-porn comic thriller. That never happened, thank God, but the advance paid for his house." He faced her; held out both hands. "Lydia. Come and see the rest of our Elephant Tree."

She had never encountered a tree so enormous. Judging from its trunk, which truly was as gray, as wrinkled, and half as wide as an elephant, it must be older than Massachusetts. Branches taller than the Back End roof curved down to touch the ground and re-ascend. New leaves of vivid translucent chartreuse made a shimmering multilayered curtain above and around them. Within this magical bower, she and Alistair were completely concealed.

Staring upward, she felt his arms encircle her, his chest press against her back. Then they were kissing, mouths melting together, entwined in each other, kissing till the cows came home, till the mountains tumbled to the sea, till the stars fell from the sky like tadpoles, till Lydia forgot where she was or who she was and only barely, occasionally, remembered to breathe.

Then they were standing apart, panting; still touching, gasping for air. Her hands were on his waist. His hands stroked her neck, her cheek, her hair.

"I have to go," he said, with aching tenderness.

"You can't." Lydia pictured rolling with him on the damp brown leaf-strewn earth under the tree: Adam and Eve.

"I'm wretchedly late. For a meeting. This blasted film." He pulled her close again and covered her mouth with his.

Lydia caressed his ear and the small gold ring that hung from it. She felt him shudder against her and draw back. "Oh, god! Lydia! You're unbelievable. I can't stand it. Please. Let me see you again. Soon. Very soon."

He led her out into the world. It was so bright it hurt her eyes. Part of Lydia recalled that this was her workplace, as well as her boss's home, with windows looking onto this very parking lot. There was Mudge, too, or the bottom half of him, working under his truck. She thrust a hand through her hair, ineffectually, and prayed to the tadpoles in heaven that luck was still on her side.

Wallace Hicks looked at the clock. Quarter to three. Ken had been shut in his office with that man for almost half an hour. What could they be doing?

He thought of him as *that man* because that was what Dinah

Rowan had called him at lunch, so fiercely that Wally had to cough so as not to laugh. Really, it wasn't funny. No, it really *was* funny. The other customers at the counter pretended it wasn't, because they assumed Dinah's agitation was over his fame, or his race, or his presumptuousness, or all three: a huge black football star, driving a car that cost more than some people's homes, strolling into the Back End for the second time this week! But that (Wally knew) wasn't what bristled Dinah's hackles. Roosevelt Sherman was the only person in Quansett, man or woman, Irish or Wampanoag or Cape Verdean, who outweighed Dinah Rowan.

His first appearance, on Tuesday, counted as a celebrity sighting. The regulars at the front counter had nudged each other in a wave as he passed: *Isn't that . . . ?* Neighbors murmured as they wrote their slips or ladled their soup: *Hey, did you see . . . ?* Only two tourists were gauche enough to ask him for an autograph. When he departed, the normal lunchtime ebb and flow closed behind him like the Red Sea behind the Israelites.

But when he came back this morning, he might have been Moses parting the waves. *What's he doing here? Does he mean to stay? Where? Why? How long?* Fred Tiller actually walked up to Roosevelt Sherman's table and offered his card–whether hoping to funnel some of the man's riches into a Tiller Homes waterfront estate, or just to show off, no one was certain.

Wallace Hicks had explained to Mr. Sherman that the Frigate was not for sale. Yup, that sure was a realtor's sign in the window; but if he looked closer, he'd see BOOKS written in above FOR SALE. A marketing gimmick, that's all. No sirree, Mr. Boose and his bookstore were not in any kind of trouble. Those boxes in the parking lot would be unpacked and shelved real soon. The stacks in the aisles, too. What with folks tromping in and out all day, who had time? Oh, no no, he wasn't an owner, only an employee. One more local boy who'd crossed the bridge in search of adventure and come back years later like a bad penny. Found one of those Airstreams, like a little old silver blimp– Well, OK, sure. If Mr. Sherman insisted, he'd go ask when Mr. Boose might be free to speak to him.

For one instant Wally feared he'd overdone it. But no; the

man wasn't suspicious, just backing out for some elbow room. Reaching for his cell phone. What did he care about a long-haired, weatherbeaten bookstore clerk who'd returned to the scene of his childhood?

Thirty-two minutes.

According to Dinah, Roosevelt Sherman had turned around the Patriots almost single-handed. Wally didn't know about that. Yes, the man probably could could squash her like a bug. But it might not be a bad thing if he threw his weight into Quansett.

The bell jingled: customers.

"Caroline! Carlo! Good to see you."

Air kisses and handshakes were exchanged, although they had just said good-by at Leo's two hours ago.

And here came Gromit, tags jingling as he wagged up to greet his friends. Ken Boose hadn't wanted a dog in the shop, until he saw what a magnet Gromit was. Being a black lab, he offered an adoring welcome to everyone. Maybe two customers a month asked why he didn't look like his cartoon namesake. At least two customers a day confided that they used to have a dog exactly like that.

"What can I do for you folks this fine afternoon?" Wally led them inside, with Gromit close behind. "Sorry about all this mess. Ken keeps swearing he's gonna hire us some help, soon as he finds the time."

Carlo was nodding sympathetically. "Only he never finds the time."

"Mudge would be glad to help out, I'm sure," said Caroline Penn. "He could probably use the money."

"Get that truck of his fixed," Wally agreed. "Take out girls, whatever."

"Oh." Caroline's eyebrow arced into a Nike swoosh. "Speaking of girls! What about Leo's new sous-chef?"

"Wasn't that a surprise! What planet do you suppose she dropped from? Boston?"

"Unusual hair." Carlo scratched Gromit's ears. "Dinah seems pleased."

"More rings in one ear than I've got in my whole jewelry

box." Caroline's lobes glittered with hand-blown glass. "Wherever she's from, her broccoli soup is scrumptious."

"Is what's-her-name gone for good, then?"

"Sue. She generally comes back," said Carlo.

"Like a yo-yo," said Caroline. "It's a crime how she's taken advantage–"

From the office came the short whooping laugh they all recognized as Ken Boose's: hiu! hiu! hiu!

Caroline arched an inquiring eyebrow at Wally.

"Oh, gosh," he said. "Sorry, folks. Here I am shooting the breeze, when you must have come in here for a reason. A book? What can I get for you?"

"Ah, yes," said Carlo. Caroline continued to gaze with lizard-like intensity at the office door. "I'm having a birthday next weekend, and Caroline hoped– Well, you tell Wally what you want."

"Who's in there with him?" Caroline asked.

"Well now best wishes, Carlo!"

"Is that the football player Dinah was going on about?"

Wally sighed and conceded. For a moment they eavesdropped in unison; but there was nothing to hear.

"I won't push, Wally. If you'd rather not say."

"It appears he's a reader," Carlo said cheerfully.

"Not much to say." Wally leaned on his crystal-headed cane, which he carried mostly to reach books on high shelves. "Aside from yes, his name is Roosevelt Sherman and he used to play for the Pats. Came in here asked me a bunch of questions; wanted to see Ken. There you have it."

"Dinah said he's eaten lunch at Leo's twice this week. Reading the Cape Cod Times. The real estate section."

"Seeking an investment opportunity, perhaps," Carlo suggested. "Somewhere to put his winnings."

"Earnings," said Wally.

"Of course. No winnings in football."

"Unless he cheated." Caroline glanced hopefully at the door.

"Whereas we," said Carlo, "are seeking a more modest investment opportunity for our earnings, or winnings, namely a book. Caroline?"

What they sought was an early volume of Edgar Rowdey's that Caroline could have him sign for Carlo. Wally pointed out, to be fair, that if she asked Edgar he'd probably give her the book, and be happy to honor his friend's birthday. Caroline insisted that would be taking advantage; and after all, the Frigate *was* their beloved local bookstore.

Wally found the book–a first printing of *The Mute Soprano*–and rang it up. Carlo and Caroline took their leave. 3:15 PM. Ken Boose and Rosey Sherman still hadn't come out of the office. If I'm right, Wally thought, this is gonna rattle Quansett like an earthquake. They sure as heck better know what they're doing.

Chapter Four

Please. Let me see you again. Soon. Very soon.

Alistair Pope's plea throbbed in Lydia's brain the next morning as she parked her Morris Minor and walked up the path past the frog pond into Leo's Back End. No Mercedes. Fine. She didn't need him showing up when she was elbow-deep in pancake batter. "See you" didn't mean *see you,* after all. It meant be alone with you, wrap you in my arms–

Stop right there, Lydia.

Leo slapped her on the back when she came in. "Hey, soup chef! How's tricks?"

Dinah, to her astonishment, greeted her with a smile before barking at her to hurry up and get out the eggs.

Mudge gave her a big grin. Several of the customers, including Edgar Rowdey, remembered her name.

Buoyed by all this approval, Lydia forgot to check soup levels until after breakfast. Too late to round up the ingredients for curried cauliflower. Tomorrow! For now she replenished the clam chowder, and divided the chili before Leo could object.

Alistair didn't come for lunch. Edgar Rowdey did, and introduced her to the friends who shared his table: Caroline Penn and Carlo Song.

She'd seen them here yesterday, talking to Dinah and a lanky long-haired man at the counter, but hadn't known who they were. Just as well. If she'd met them right after she heard about DeAnne, she'd probably have either burst into tears or pelted them with questions.

Caroline ordered a Chix Sallid. She might, Lydia thought, be 50 or 70. Relaxed and elegant, she exuded New York like perfume: not a fingernail chipped, every platinum hair in place. Her embroidered silk jacket hinted at a sixth-generation tailor in some exotic Oriental port not yet plundered by tourists. Lydia wondered how she survived in Quansett.

Carlo, outwardly more prosaic in jeans, a sweater, and a bristly salt-and-pepper brush cut, won her heart by ordering a bowl of the meatless chili and thanking her warmly for inventing it. He and Caroline could have been twins (fraternal; his style was Soho, hers uptown), not visually so much as verbally. To each other they spoke in shorthand. Talking with Edgar Rowdey, they volleyed.

"How is your opera coming along?" he inquired.

"Caroline's slowing me down," said Carlo.

"He's obsessed with recitatifs this week. I'm slogging through the first-act arias."

"Far more difficult, I do admit."

"You're leaning away from Lloyd-Webber, then, and back to Verdi?"

"Oh, for heaven's sake, yes," said Caroline.

"Puccini might be closer," said Carlo. "I myself don't aspire to Verdi."

"I aspire to find a way out of giving two arias to the contralto. In a row, no less!"

"So far we can't avoid it," Carlo explained. "She appears out of the blue and seduces him, and then she shoots him."

"Two classic moments." Edgar Rowdey sympathized. "What can you do?"

"She'd be on and off like a light switch if she'd stop singing. Instead she's hogging the stage and clogging up the first act."

"Which like every first act already runs way too long. Lydia," Carlo twisted around in his chair to call after her. "Have I thanked you enough for this wonderful chili?"

Lunch ended without Lydia's finding out what opera they were talking about, much less learning anything related to DeAnne, and with no sign of Alistair.

Two-twenty PM. She lingered over her BLT. This was Friday: end of most people's work week. For all she knew, he might go off Cape on weekends.

Two-thirty. She volunteered to help Mudge clean the grill.

How could they find each other once she left here? He hadn't asked for her phone number, nor offered his.

Two-forty. An ideal time to do a vegetable inventory for tomorrow's soup.

"That man hasn't come back," Dinah remarked.

Lydia blushed. "What man?"

"The football player. What's-his-name. "

"Oh. Who was in here yesterday? What *is* his name?"

"Sherman, as I recall," said Dinah. "Roosevelt Sherman. Second time this week he come in. And if you ask me, he ain't after our gor-may cuisine."

"What's he after, then?"

"Time will tell," said Dinah pontifically. "You through there? I'll lock up."

Rosey Sherman crunched across the crushed-clamshell parking lot, sizing up his target.

The Frigate fronted on Main Street, also known as Route 6A, also known as Old King's Highway. That confusion, he thought, somebody should straighten out. How can you revitalize your village center if you can't agree what to call its central road?

The bookstore overflowed a two-story Victorian building whose tall plate-glass windows, pilastered doorway, and ornate architectural detailing stood out magnificently from its shingled saltbox neighbors. Excellent! A bookstore *should* be magnificent. Never mind that its painted trim had faded over the decades from purple, green, and gold to shades of gray. Never mind the sagging lean-to alongside it–grandly referred to by Ken Boose as a porte-cochere–or the dozens of cardboard cartons stacked underneath. Never mind the columns and pyramids of unsorted books that prevented a man of Rosey's girth from stepping more than a few feet into the shop. All these were problems money could solve. But to be in charge of knowledge, culture, entertainment, laughter, learning, delight–that was priceless.

He'd known for years he wanted to own a bookstore. His wife, Thea, said it was because he was fed up with people treating him like a big dumb ape. (Not that apes were dumb. Genetically, a chimpanzee was almost identical to a human; it loved its babies, used simple tools, and enjoyed jokes.) Rosey supposed that was a factor. Thea was also right that he wanted his kids to grow up in the same kind of town he did, where they could ride their bikes and catch fish and fireflies and learn the constellations and gather for fireworks on the Fourth of July and take the dog for a walk without a poop bag. To him, the reasons didn't matter. The Frigate was his dream, and he meant to make it come true.

So Rosey Sherman strolled through the parking lot pondering strategy.

Ken Boose had stated flat out that he had no intention of selling his shop. He'd owned it for fourteen years, and meant to run it till he died. From the moldy smell of the place you might imagine that event had already occurred. Rosey didn't tackle him directly. Instead, after a few polite questions about the Frigate's out-of-control inventory (a challenge he'd guessed, correctly, that Ken was touchy about), he inquired about safety. Was it true that two houses in this neighborhood had been burgled recently? Did that concern Ken at all? Had he thought about installing an alarm system?

Ken assured him the burglaries were a fluke and not a crime wave. Still, Rosey could see they'd rattled him. Rather than push, he chatted about his own plans for retirement: Solitude! freedom! White sandy beaches on an island untouched by winter. Hot sun, palm trees, bare feet. No more humidity, mosquitos, or poison ivy. Bikini-clad beauties playing volleyball. A deck chair with a tall drink and a stack of long-awaited reading: Proust's *Remembrance of Things Past*. Poetry. Patrick O'Brian's seafaring novels. Back issues of *The New Yorker*.

Now he would leave those images to simmer for a few days, while he prepared his lawyers to back them up. The goal was to make Ken Boose an offer not only too generous to refuse, but so streamlined that he could step right out of the Frigate–clutter, smell, dilapidation, thieves lurking behind every rosebush–into a worry-free future.

Not many cars here on this second afternoon of June. Rosey had kept glancing across the street while he treated Ken to lunch at the Whistling Pig (too much ruffled chintz, but unlike the Back End you got table service), and only counted eight vehicles in and out. The crushed clamshells were patchy from years of neglect. The locals loved the idea of the Frigate, but they bought most of their books online or at the chains in Hyannis. No problem. First you resurface the lot, unpack the cartons, weed through the inventory. Then give the building a facelift. Hang a new sign: carved wood in the shape of a ship, painted to match the facade. Serve coffee and pastries, start reading groups, story hours, book signings. A little entrepreneurship could bring this leaky old boat up to speed by Christmas.

Not single-handed, of course. Ken Boose's commitment to the Frigate included its hippie employee–what was his name? Hicks? Which was fine. Behind that ponytail and folksy manner he seemed sharp enough, and most likely knew the stock better than Ken did. Add a couple of bright youngsters–for instance, that cashier at the Back End . . .

Most of Rosey's buddies had retired from the game into hospitality: bars, restaurants, a hotel or two, even an escort service. Through them he'd lined up legal advisers. Beyond that he relied on his own judgment and Thea's. She'd be down this weekend to check out Quansett and its bookstore. If she too was charmed, he only had to close with Ken Boose before they could start house-hunting. Then on to paperwork, construction, and team-building. The Quansett grapevine, he had no doubt, would supply publicity.

Rosey pulled out his keys, pushed the button to unlock his Mercedes SUV. Not until he started backing up did he discover that both his passenger-side tires had been slashed.

Friday afternoon: week's end. The sun dipped at last into the treetops along Route 6A, turning the new leaves a vivid emerald. Mothers shepherded children off playing fields and into cars. Office workers told jokes, compared weekend plans, saved documents. Beach-walkers pulled on sweaters.

At the Whistling Pig, Caroline Penn and Carlo Song joined Edgar Rowdey, who sat reading at their usual corner table.

Until its proprietor died, the Whistling Pig was Quansett's only bar. When Jerry McNally's widow switched to tea and sandwiches, her customers rebelled. Now shelves of teapots, frilly curtains and tablecloths, and the sign over its purple front door proclaimed The Whistling Pig to be a Tea Shoppe; but a discreet box on the back of the menu confessed that beer, wine, and spirits were also available.

"Well, good evening." Carlo pulled out a white bent-wire chair for Caroline.

"Hul-lo." Edgar inserted his bookmark and stowed his book.

Caroline uttered a poignant sigh.

"She's had a trying day," Carlo explained.

"Still battling with the contrary contralto?"

After a moment Carlo said, "I don't believe she's speaking just now. Is Connie about?"

"I haven't seen her," said Edgar. "This would seem to be our waitress."

A slim red-haired young woman in a white ruffled cap and apron took their orders: sherry for Edgar, merlot for Carlo, a Bloody Mary for Caroline. "And a plate of your homemade mixed biscuits," Edgar finished.

"We ran into Cathy Stevens at the grocery store. Speaking of a trying day. She'd just had the police in again, combing for clues. No progress yet, apparently."

"I saw Eric at the bank," Edgar nodded. "For a man who just spent two weeks in Ibiza, he looked haggard. Said he hasn't done a thing since they got home but answer questions and buy a new computer. Piece their life back together."

Carlo picked a fuzz-ball off the arm of his sweater. "Have you thought of putting in an alarm?"

"Mercy no. Who'd break into my house? And you know they go off at the drop of a souffle. The cats would be permanently hysterical. Why, have you?"

"No, we're trusting to Arson. And the Fates." He glanced at the book upside-down on the table. "What are you reading?"

"Oh, nothing much. Spanish cave art. Altamira and so forth."

"Cave art. Aha."

The mixed biscuits arrived, and three flowered napkins.

"How goes the opera?" Edgar inquired.

"Rather well, considering. The showdown beside the tracks came out better than I dared hope. We will prevail, you know."

"I don't doubt it for a moment."

"Caroline is manning the barricades, or I should say womaning, with her usual brilliance."

"Inevitably."

Caroline spoke. "Oh, please do shut up, both of you." She glared evenly at each of them. "It isn't the contralto. It's this day. I only realized in the car. I didn't want to say while I was driving, for fear– Well, never mind. Here we are, aren't we? The thing is, it was a month ago today we lost DeAnne."

"Ah," said Carlo, inadequately.

"Oh, dear," said Edgar.

The waitress approached. Drinks were distributed. Carlo was the first to raise his glass. Caroline and Edgar clinked in a toast no one needed to announce.

"I've been in a foul mood all day, and I couldn't imagine why," Caroline said.

"She was so thrilled, poor girl," said Carlo. "Being in a movie. Even that puny effort of Alistair's. Edgar, you wouldn't have recognized her."

"She fizzed," Caroline agreed sadly. "Followed him around like a besotted puppy."

"Of all things, to fall off a ladder."

"Why did she, do you think?" asked Edgar.

There was a pause. "God only knows," said Caroline.

"She was only meant to collect coffee cups, and then join us here for drinks," said Carlo.

"Did the police . . . ?" Edgar's question trailed off.

"Oh, no."

"Not to us," Carlo amended. "Possibly to her family. But then–"

"Alistair took charge of all that," Caroline completed, pulling the celery stick from her drink. "Swept the whole thing under the rug, insofar as he could. The show must go on, et cetera. At one point he started to say 'She would have wanted it,' but mercifully he heard himself and stopped before I was forced to hit him."

"Awfully cold, I thought, after he'd spent the whole shoot flirting with her."

Caroline nodded. "Put at least two noses out of joint on the film crew. We half expected a brouhaha. But then it was all over so fast."

"I suspect he bullied the police," said Carlo. "You know how he can be."

"Oh, indeed."

"There was a tiny implication," said Caroline, "that if we didn't accept the accident theory, we'd have to suppose she flew off a ten-foot ladder to–well, for purposes of her own. Which of course was utter nonsense. Whatever you might think about her, she certainly was not suicidal."

"No," said Edgar. "Poor bunny." He selected a biscuit. "You did accept the accident theory?"

Caroline sighed. "We had to, after the investigation."

"Helen Wills was terribly cut up," Carlo recalled. "She was the one who found her."

"No she wasn't. It was Kevin Kelly."

"I beg to differ, Caroline. Helen happened to be driving by and stopped to see if the filming was still going on. She called Kevin right away because he's local and she's state, so it was his jurisdiction."

"That's true," Caroline acknowledged. "It was Kevin who came and told us. We were sitting right there," she pointed her celery stick at a large center table, "with Alistair and the crew."

"He took statements, and then Helen hauled us down to state police headquarters for interrogation," nodded Carlo.

Their waitress, on her way toward their table, stopped in midstride and blinked at them in alarm.

"It's all right, dear," Edgar assured her. "They're perfectly harmless."

Not apparently convinced, she spoke from where she stood. "Are you folks all set here?"

"Oh, no," said Carlo.

Caroline translated: "Another round, if you please."

The waitress collected their empty glasses and retreated.

"Now, Caroline, shall we tell Edgar about the opera?"

In a cramped corner of the Frigate, behind a waist-high wall of books, Wally Hicks leaned back in his computer chair.

"Man, you shittin' me? *You* are Pirandello?"

The man's eyes just about popping out of his head in ament.

They would be shelving plays. Or–back up–culling through the week's acquisitions. Anyhow, the man pulls out *Six Characters in Search of an Author*. Holds it up; gazes at the cover with affection and awe.

Wally supplies the subtlest of prompts: "You a fan?" Something like that. "You into Pirandello?"

"Into him?" the man exclaims. "Might as well ask if I'm into God!"

No, no. Way too hokey. "Sure am," is what he would say. Or, even better: "Not this Pirandello."

Wally, playing straight man again: "What do you mean?"

"The other one! The real live twenty-first century– You must have heard of him." He waits, but Wally doesn't cooperate. "The cyber-conscience of Cape Cod?"

Except he wouldn't put it so locally, coming from Foxborough. "The brains behind CodCast.net." More than brains, though. "The brilliant imagination" or (here we go!) "The mystery genius behind the greatest webcam in southeastern–" Oh, come on, Hicks, give yourself credit. "–in all of New England!"

"Really?" says Wally, his face still blank.

"I'm tellin' you, man. You think I'd have ever heard of Quansett if it wasn't for Pirandello? He's the greatest!"

And now, at last, Wally grants him a smile. Maybe even a little bow, if they're standing behind the book boxes. "Thank you."

And the man's eyes widen, and his jaw drops, and he says–

"Hello? Anybody here?"

Crap! Wally's chair flipped upright so fast his knee slammed into the desk. How'd he get back so quick? Stroll over to the Pig, order coffee, stroll back, should have taken twice this long.

"Coming!" he shouted.

His fingers hopscotched over the keys. No clues in the first hour's stills. He'd hoped to scan through the whole afternoon. Find his *in flagrante*, print it, and produce it for the man with a triumphant flourish, like a magician's rabbit.

Too late now. Wally grabbed his cane.

In the armchair on the other side of the wall of books, Ken Boose, sleepy as an owl, was blinking away his preprandial nap. Gromit snored beside him, hind leg twitching. Wally limped past them to the door. Can't have the man jumping ship before he even boards the Frigate.

Rosey Sherman stood beside his Mercedes in the section of the U-shaped parking lot known as Incoming. OK, Hicks. Prepare to launch Plan B.

"Mr. Sherman." He crunched across the clamshells.

"Rosey. And you're Wally, right? Cops not here yet?"

"This time of year, it generally takes a while. Small town, small police force. They'll add on a few more by Fourth of July."

The man nodded and sipped his coffee. Here goes, thought Wally

"Rosey, can I ask you something?"

"Sure."

"Does the name Pirandello mean anything to you?"

His eyebrows and lower lip went up. "Can't say as it does."

The silent hiss of an ego deflating like a punctured tire. "Then would I be right in guessing you're not familiar with CodCast-dot-net?"

"Nope. What is it?"

Sssssss. Pulling a rabbit out of a hat is a parlor trick, Wally reminded himself. True genius is producing the rabbit without the hat.

"Well now, it's a number of things, and maybe some other day you'd be interested in the full five-dollar tour; but right this minute?–if you'll wait right here, I suspect I can show you pretty quick who slashed your tires."

Chapter Five

"Thank you," Lydia breathed into the sky.

A night so long she'd thought it would never end; a dawn so gray she hated to burrow out of her blankets. The shower spurted scalding hot, then cold, then hot again. The grease stains she'd scrubbed out of her jeans had reappeared when they dried. But under the Blue Moon Motel sign, a scrawny rhododendron bush had erupted into bloom. Through a hole in the quilted clouds, one sunbeam poured down and lit it up–a vibrant, exuberant dollop of pink.

She stretched behind the steering wheel: neck, shoulders, back, legs. You're OK, Lydia. You made it out of Dodge. You have a job, birds are singing, flowers are blooming, the car runs, and daylight comes earlier every morning.

"Hey," Mudge called from the grill as she came through the Back End's front door. "How's it going?" Then, looking closer: "Are you OK?"

"Yes. Fine." She turned her back on him, fastening her apron. "Why? Am I having a bad hair day? Already? At six whatever-it-is AM?"

"No." Mudge sounded cautious. Lydia could feel his eyes still on her. "You just– Well, you look like you seen a ghost."

She tied the strings and swiveled. "Well, *you* look like you slept under a bridge."

Dinah lumbered in and slammed the door behind her. "Howdy howdy! What's with you two? Ten minutes till opening and hail hail, the gang's all here. Leo been handing out early-bird bonuses?"

"She's way too cheerful," Lydia said to Mudge. "Shall we shoot her?

"Coffee," Dinah commanded, sailing around the cash register into the kitchen like a docking freighter.

"Yeah, and you know why?" Mudge handed mugs to both of them. He and Dinah chorused: "It's *Saturday!*"

"I'll drink to that," Lydia clinked.

The regulars were filtering in now from the back room, wanting eggs, waffles, bacon, English muffins, refills on coffee. Within minutes the breakfast whirlpool had sucked Leo's kitchen crew into their usual morning frenzy. Only in a corner of Lydia's mind she silently told Mudge: *You were right. I did see a ghost.*

At first she'd thought it was another nightmare. All last week they'd struck between 3 and 5 AM, jerking her out of half-sleep into shivering dread. Stress! she'd rationalized. Too many load-bearing walls collapsing at the same time. First the Fix-It Chix, thank you very much DeAnne, flushing her income down the toilet; then the Morris's valve job which ate up her savings; then Mr. Dickhead Rat Bastard, plus their housemates' craven silence, who should have rallied behind her and kicked his ass out; and the last straw, Caffe Firenze, her longtime oasis, closed to become a Starbucks. Who wouldn't feel blindsided? Who wouldn't react with too much caffeine, too little sleep, too much booze, too little exercise, too much TV, too few meals? and pay for it with a barrage of nightmares?

After the last one she'd crawled out of bed and sat quaking, wrapped in a bedspread, clutching at wispy images. What had scared her so badly? Too late; it was gone. So let it go! she ordered herself. It was only a dream. It's over. You're OK. But in her heart she knew it wasn't and she wasn't. When the sun finally rose she stripped her bed, packed up her personal things, left the furniture, wrote a good-by note to her housemates and wrapped it around her keys.

Two hours later she'd run over a rock and met Alistair Pope.

That was Wednesday. This was Saturday.

Ridiculous.

She groped for her bedside bag. If insomnia strikes, strike back! This is why we have pills–a couple of Percocet left over from Joe's sprained ankle, a Vicodin from MJ's surgery . . .

Instead her fingers found thin cardboard.

She switched on the light. What . . . ?

A shiny photograph of two lobsters locked in claw-to-claw combat. Her and DeAnne. The lost postcard.

A shudder rose from her gut to her throat.

Sitting up, she turned it over. There was DeAnne's round ball-point handwriting, as familiar and strange as the front door of their house.

No date at the top. The postmark, smudged, looked like April 30.

Fuck. Two days before she died.

You couldn't possibly have known that, Lydia told herself fiercely. Any more than DeAnne could. The Morris in the shop, that remodeling job canceled, Mr. Dickhead Rat Bastard sneaking off I didn't yet suspect where– No, I sure as hell wasn't thinking straight. Least of all about her. My backstabbing ex-partner. The first domino. The last person I wanted to hear from with the rest of my life collapsing around me.

Fuck. Did I even read her message?

She held the card under the light.

Hi Liz, so sorry about everything! Hope you're not still bummed. I got a great job working for 2 ex-famous musicians!!! & now I'm in a movie!!! So PLEASE don't hate me cuz I'm really happy! Come visit! SOON! You can stay here free, & meet Caroline & Carlo (bosses), you won't believe their amazing studio, & amazing things happening! I'll tell you when I see you. So COME!!! xxx DeAnne

So sorry about everything. At the time it must have stung like salt in a wound. Like twisting the knife. When in fact, having moved out at Christmas, DeAnne had missed the whole chain of explosions she'd touched off.

She was sorry simply for leaving.

Fuck!

What if I'd understood that? What if I'd responded instead of blowing her off?

Wait, though. Lydia wrapped herself tighter in blankets. I didn't blow her off, did I? Obviously I read the card. Obviously it pissed me off. But I couldn't have just ignored it. *Come visit*–isn't that the reason I'm here now?

Not the only reason. The first instinct that had spurred her out of the house was for sanctuary. Where to go but Cape Cod?–where she'd lost her heart a year ago. Lost it to these strangers who'd carved her a niche in their collective life; then to Joe's family's gray-shingled beach house (a cottage, they called it–six bedrooms plus a lawn big enough for volleyball); to scrubby pines and mist-wreathed cranberry bogs, huge sky, long beaches and restless jade ocean; to the picturebook village of Quansett; and most intensely to Fletcher Hall, who'd whisked her off in his MG to see Provincetown and brought her back giddy, dazzled, happy to spend that night with him and all the nights that followed.

When DeAnne applied to move into the Cambridge house in September, her Cape roots tipped the scale.

By then Lydia (now sharing rooms with Fletcher) had risen from Joe's home-repair assistant to partner. "The fix-it chick," he called her. In October, with more work than the two of them could handle, Joe invited DeAnne to help out. He and Lydia (or, rather, Liz) already had agreed she'd take over the business when he left for Maine to build his yurt. By Thanksgiving, all three of them voted for DeAnne to stay on as Fix-It Chick #2.

I did answer that postcard, Lydia recollected. Not right away; and not exactly overflowing with bonhomie. But I couldn't let our friendship go down the tube with the rest of my life. After half a dozen false starts, rewrites and deletes, I sent her an e-mail. And when it bounced back as undeliverable, well, didn't that just prove you can't fucking count on anybody for a fucking thing?

She held up the picture to the bedside lamp. Two lobsters rampant, olive green, on a checkered tablecloth, red and white. Posed for the camera, no doubt; but green, not boiled orange. Still alive.

Could I have saved her? If I'd e-mailed sooner, or phoned, or dashed off to Cape Cod, could I have stopped her from falling off that ladder?

Not likely. Over the winter DeAnne had set up her own dominoes; which must have begun toppling (whether she knew it or not) before she wrote.

And now?

Why had a postcard that didn't turn up during an hour of searching reappeared in the middle of the night at the Blue Moon Motel?

In the murky illogic of predawn, it seemed like a fair question. Didn't believers in ghosts claim it was this kind of death–too young, too uncalled-for–that could keep a person hovering among the living? Had DeAnne planted the postcard in Lydia's bag, and woken her up to find it, as a way of . . . what?

Lydia spoke into the darkness. "What do you want from me?"

Huddled in her blankets, she listened. No answer.

Maybe she already was doing what she was supposed to do. This past week she'd made the right moves; of that she was certain. Coming here, taking the job at Leo's, even calling Karin with the news of DeAnne's death–each step radiated necessity, like turns of the dial on a combination lock.

But steps toward what? What was locked that it was her job to open?

Hadn't she done enough by escaping from Cambridge? Did Quansett require more from her than finding time between breakfast and lunch to make the soup?

"DeAnne? Are you there?"

Then she was blinking at her pillow, with daylight?–no, just the damn streetlamp–slanting through the venetian blinds. Alone. One foot numb with cold from poking out of the blankets. And another hour till Leo's opened.

Now, surrounded by noise and motion, Lydia sliced bagels, ladled out waffles, poured syrup into tiny jugs, blotted bacon on paper towels. Newcomers shouted greetings; customers clamored for their orders. Mudge honked the tip horn, which could barely be heard above the din. Dinah signaled for more eggs. Here came Leo, making his grand entrance.

Coincidence, she told herself, rinsing strawberries in a colander. Or, Fletcher would say, projection of unconscious guilt onto an emotionally loaded object. How am I to blame here? What I ever could do to help DeAnne, I did. Like give her a job; doesn't that count? Like tell her not to climb a tall ladder alone? And never, ever in clogs! Honest to god, what was she thinking?

"Hey." Mudge slithered past her with a bowl of eggs. "Almost time for more soup!"

"You know what? This is nuts." Pour strawberries onto cutting board; grab cleaver. "Totally insane!" Anchor cleaver tip on board. "Leo!" Whap-whap-whap-whap!

"Mudge!" shouted Dinah.

"We need to make some changes!"

Leo leaned across the counter as Mudge headed for the grill. "And a cheery good morning to you, too, killer."

Lydia flicked her dripping red fingers at him threateningly. "Watch out or you're next." Whap-whap-whap-whap!

"If you have a complaint, fill out a form and place it in the suggestion box. Hello there, Louise. Don't even think about getting that on my nice clean shirt." Back to Lydia: "If it's about the government, you can deliver it to Congressman Delaney over there with his Egz Bennie."

"Making the soup after breakfast, it's too rushed. Even if I had time to do it right, it can't simmer long enough. What I *should* do is make it the day before. Like, after closing."

"Oho." Leo lowered his concave frame onto a stool. "And I guess that means I should pay you extra for the time, is that right?"

"Yes!" Dinah shouted unexpectedly. "Damn right you should!"

"Who asked you? Go fry an egg!"

"What are we talking about?" Dinah retorted. "An hour? Lydia?"

"Yeah." Scooping the berries into a bowl. "Or less."

"Is that gonna break you, Leo, you old cheapskate? One more hour so the girl can create some cuisine here?"

The customers at the counter were listening with interest, winking and grinning at each other. Far from minding, Leo seemed pleased to offer them entertainment with their breakfast. "And then what?" he flung at Dinah. "You're next? You need another hour a day to make the meat loaf? Or, how about two more hours? Hah! Extortion!"

"Leo," called Mudge from the refrigerator. "We need–"

"Et tu, brute? What is this, a workers' revolt?"

"–Ketchup."

"Basement." Leo rose. "What are you looking at?" he asked the woman next to him. "Show's over. Eat your waffle before it gets cold. There's no use asking my brutally exploited, underpaid kitchen staff to reheat it."

He pointed a bony finger at Lydia. "*You* I'll speak to later. In my office."

Which filled her with dismay–her one-week trial, her miraculous new job, cut short?–until she remembered Leo didn't have an office.

Mudge hoisted the eggs to his shoulder and twirled the bowl before setting it down beside Dinah. "Brown eggs are fresh eggs in New England," Leo liked to pontificate. To which Dinah would reply: "But their shells are thinner." Brown or white, she regarded a broken egg as a sin against Yankee thrift and cosmic harmony. Even on calm days, spinning the egg bowl drew a growl. On three-ring-circus days like this one, he might provoke an eruption. Today she just snapped, "Put that down, dammit!" and went on whisking.

Good! That should vent some of the steam building up in this pressure-cooker kitchen.

He'd discovered this useful trick last winter. Dinah tended to holler at Sue, who didn't handle it well; and one day Mudge stepped in. Hadn't Dinah noticed that when pushed, Sue took off? which irked Leo and maddened Dinah and changed Mudge's job from semi-interesting to pure drudgery. So he tried a move he'd learned as a waiter in Barnstable High School's production of *Cabaret*. First with a plate of toast; and when that got Sue to smile, a tray of flatware; and when that made Dinah bark at him, a bowl full of eggs. He had yet to drop anything.

Lydia–well, too soon to tell; but so far, she was a huge improvement. Much better at cooking than Sue, easier to work with, and sharper enough to keep Dinah from picking on her. Plus she got along with Leo, even when she disagreed with him. Mudge intended to use every tool in his well-honed kit to keep her at the Back End.

Maybe a little too sharp? Or maybe he just needed a shower. That crack about sleeping under a bridge had hit too close for comfort.

"Hey." He nudged her as he slid past her, chopping celery, on his way to the cash register. "How about a drink when we get out of here? To celebrate!"

"Great idea." A smile came over her face–the first one he'd seen all morning. "Only," the smile fading, "there's something I've got to do first."

In daylight Lydia dismissed the idea that DeAnne had come back from the dead to deliver a postcard. First off, she didn't believe in ghosts. Second, she didn't believe in regrets. Once you start wishing the two of you had gotten a chance to patch up your friendship, you might as well go all the way and wish DeAnne had stayed in Cambridge, or hadn't taken the job with Carlo and Caroline, or (at the very least) hadn't climbed that damn ladder.

Still: when a lost message turns up among your pill bottles in the middle of the night, how can you ignore it?

Lydia reread DeAnne's posthumous invitation while she brushed her teeth. *Come visit.* Well, here I am. *You can stay here free.* No, but I can visit your parents. *Meet Caroline & Carlo (bosses), you won't believe their amazing studio*. (A) done; (B) I'll work on it.

6:45 AM on a Saturday was too early to call the Ropeses. Carlo and Caroline she could catch at lunch . . .

But Carlo and Caroline didn't come in for lunch.

Lydia lingered at Edgar Rowdey's table after delivering his Kofi JelO. Did he know if they were around? No, they'd gone to New York for the weekend. Something to do with Carlo's birthday. Or the opera. Or possibly the documentary?

Well, so much for that, thought Lydia; and realized Alistair Pope hadn't shown up either, surprise surprise.

The last customers left. Leftovers were shared, food was

stowed, dishes were washed, tables wiped, chairs flipped up so Bruno could scrub the floor. Leo handed out paychecks. "Miss Vivaldi." He curled an index finger. "This way, please."

Out they went to the parking lot. Leo opened the passenger door of his ancient white Cadillac.

"Where are we going?"

"I have something to show you."

Past the library, past the post office. He turned right at the town green, a modest triangle with a scattering of trees and the obligatory statue. Left around the triangle's point and into a driveway. (Or, more accurately, a short dirt track through a gap in an overgrown hedge.) Leo pulled onto the grass and stopped near a giant magnolia tree which half-hid the house beside it.

What was he up to, the mysterious old devil?

Whoever lived here–if anyone did–clearly didn't welcome company. From the street you could hardly see past the overgrown shrubbery and the vines that climbed the porch pillars and hung from the roof.

A haunted house?

Surely, please God, this isn't a seduction attempt!

"Follow me." Leo jingled a set of keys.

"Where are we going?" Lydia asked. "Who lives here?" Thinking: What the hell, if worse comes to worst I can take him.

"Over there," he pointed, "your friend Edgar Rowdey. Up here, you'll find out."

He led her up the slope beside the house and its looming tree, into tall grass, past a copse of lilacs.

So that was Edgar Rowdey's house! In spite of his sweatshirts and jeans, she'd assumed such a successful author must live in a style that matched his status. A multi-level steel-and-glass box, perhaps, or a contemporary log cabin on a lake. This antique gone to seed was an unsettling reminder of the hapless orphans, bludgeoned dukes, vengeful dowagers, and garrotted debutantes that had made him famous. It looked as old as Quansett. Through the vegetation she made out broad wooden stairs leading up to the front porch, sloped and silvery with age, which ran the whole width of the house. Long arches soared between its slender vine-choked columns. At the center, below a pair of dormers and a brick chimney, stood a door with octagonal panels and flaking paint, framed by narrow leaded-glass windows.

"Watch out for the snake."

Lydia halted. Leo pointed at a long row of rocks curving through the grass beside them, like an outline for a twisted stone wall.

They reached the top of the hill. Now what?

Fifty yards behind the house stood a gable-roofed outbuilding: barn? garage? Clad in weathered gray shingles, its front side comprised a high arched double wooden door and a fan window. Around the corner was a single door, glass over wood, with a stone stoop.

Leo turned and held out the keys.

"Madame, your new home. If you want to stick around. I can't be paying for a motel room *and* an extra hour a day to make soup. I'm not made of money, y'know. I'm an old man trying to get by. Uncertainty, it's bad for my heart. The doctor's always telling me–"

He kept talking, but Lydia, pushing past him, had stopped listening. There was nothing haunted or seedy about this cottage. One good-sized room, simply furnished, with a wooden ladder up to a sleeping loft. Over the bed, that fan window. Cream-colored walls, white woodwork, flowered curtains. Two windows in the left wall, looking onto a small meadow; two more opposite, screened by trees. At the far end, white cupboards with ornamental brackets, an ancient refrigerator and porcelain sink, a tiny gas stove. A breakfast nook with built-in table and benches.

"Leo!" she interrupted. "How did you do this? This is like–a dream come true!"

He simpered. "It's all in who you know."

"When do Snow White and the dwarfs come back and kick me out? Or are we talking Three Bears?" There was even a miniature wood-burning fireplace.

"You can thank our friend Edgar's niece. Mirella the botanist. He let her fix up the place when she got a job with the Natural History Museum up the road. Now she's in Bhutan, studying the native habitat of the rhododendron."

"Is she coming back?"

"Not till Labor Day. Do we have a deal?

"Yes! Yes! Are you kidding me?" Lydia opened the back door onto a small wooden deck. "A bribe like this? You better believe I'll stick around. Long as we can stand each other. Long as you keep paying me."

She could move in as soon as she liked. Sheets and towels were in a drawer under the bed. Dishes, appliances, and so forth she would find in the logical places. "Food, laundry, cable TV, you're on your own. Any questions, call your mother, call 911, just don't ask the man in the big house because he don't know a thing. He's a recluse. That's how they are. Knock on his door, he won't answer, or if he does, he'll bite your hand off."

OK, thought Lydia, although she couldn't picture mild-mannered, white-bearded Edgar Rowdey biting anything more formidable than an English muffin.

Back at Leo's, Mudge stood waiting for her by the frog pond. Yes, he would be happy for Lydia to drive him to the auto-parts store and the bank, as well as pay for their drinks afterward, in exchange for helping her with moving and groceries.

Almost, she thought as they carried bags into the cottage from the car. Almost, this amazing little house is worth losing my home and my lover and friends and the Fix-It Chix and Caffe Firenze.

Yeah. Right.

Chapter Six

Officer Kevin Kelly stood with his feet planted apart, his hands folded over his crotch, and listened with a frown to Wallace Hicks. Blabbity-blabbity pixels, blabbity-blabbity ethernet . . . Jesum crow! Trained though he was for police work, experienced though he was at disentangling the confused and often aimless narratives of local citizens, Kevin Kelly's ears refused to focus. *Shut up!* he wanted to shout. *I'm here to speak with Roosevelt Sherman! who turned the New England Patriots from a joke into Superbowl champions! Not you, you stoned freak.*

His eyes behind their sunglasses, resolutely aimed at the tires he had been called here to examine, kept straying to the sneakered feet nearby. The legendary feet of Rosey Sherman. Size twelve at least. The very same feet that ran 68 yards two years ago for a last-minute touchdown against the Rams. Funny squiggles on the ankles . . . like his shoes came with a logo and he'd cut it off. But who'd do a weird thing like that? Had he endorsed some brand of shoe? Kevin couldn't recall. A deal that went south when he quit the Pats, maybe? No way. They'd have to be loco. Corporate suicide, to diss such a hero.

On droned Wally Hicks, oblivious. Kevin's gaze inched up the blue-jeaned legs above the sneakers. Rosey Sherman's legs. Right here in Quansett! Unbelievable!

If motor-mouth here ever stopped yapping, he'd ask the man for an autograph. Get him to sign a parking ticket–wouldn't that flip 'em out back at the station!

"Thank you," said Roosevelt Sherman, in a warm baritone with just a trace of Southern lilt.

Shit, thought Kevin. *Is he thanking him or me?*

"Um," he responded ambiguously. "Mr. Sherman, is there anything you'd care to, um, add?"

The handsome dark head moved back and forth. "Wally's covered it just fine. His idea sounds good to me, but you folks live here, you'd know better than me."

"His idea." Kevin shifted to his detective voice, implying professional discretion.

"I mean, of course it's your call. If we can do that kind of follow-up."

"Uh-huh." What the hell was he talking about? This was vandalism, not rocket science. Some dumb shit with Mercedes envy or racial prejudice had slashed his tires. Inconvenient, sure, but only for the next hour. Fill out the insurance report, call Triple A, and by 4 PM you're driving home on a brand-new pair of radials. What's to follow up?

"Last thing I'd want to do, as a newcomer in town, is rock anybody's boat."

"Very gracious of you, sir." God, what huge arms the man had! Rock any boat in Hyannis harbor if he wanted to, including the Nantucket ferry. Bulging out of his polo shirt like a pair of Mounds bars. Those arms had caught the most passes in Pats' history. And could easily (Kevin couldn't help noticing) twist any cop from Bourne to P'town into a pretzel. He heard himself add, almost defensively, "The law is the law."

"Well now, Kevin," said Wally Hicks, "I don't guess you'll get any argument there. The question is, talking about justice and mercy and so forth, can the law kind of lean in the direction of Mr. Sherman's interest, as a man who might think about doing business in Quansett, settle his family here, and so forth."

Do business? Settle his family? Jesum Crow, thought Kevin. Roosevelt Sherman is moving to Quansett? Won't Herb Fox at the Cape Cod Times shit a brick!

He glanced at Rosey Sherman for a cue and thought he discerned a nod. "Well, I don't see why not."

"From the practical side alone," Wally Hicks persisted. "Not to mention the ethics, which if you want me to go over, I sure don't mind–"

"No. No need for that. Mr. Sherman," Kevin spoke man-to-man. "What's your view?"

The football champion considered. "Well, like I said, I'd go along with Wally, if that works for you."

Kevin glowed. "If it works for you, sir," he said magnanimously, "it works for the police department."

"Thank you," said Rosey Sherman.

This time Officer Kevin Kelly had no doubt who the man was talking to.

Mudge chose their destination: the Rusty Umbrella, on a side street in downtown Hyannis. Dim ceiling lights revealed round fake-wood tables on steel stems, ringed by stackable chairs. Cheap paneling covered the walls. The only decorations were two neon beer signs in the front window and a row of large plastic fish mounted on wooden ovals on the long wall across from the bar. A dart board, unscarred by darts, hung at the back; in order to play you would have had to stand in the restroom doorway. If there ever had been a rusty umbrella, it was gone.

Two men sat at opposite ends of the bar. Mudge and the balding bartender exchanged a nod as he and Lydia chose a table.

"What is this place?" She felt as though she ought to whisper. "Cape Cod HQ for the French Foreign Legion?"

Mudge grinned.

Comprehension dawned. "Mudge, are you old enough to drink?"

"Not at the Whistling Pig." Her original suggestion. "I am here."

Could a person be arrested for conspiring with a minor to consume alcohol? Unlikely. Anyway, Lydia thought, who cares? If he can hold a job, join the military, own a truck, shlep luggage and groceries, and screw girls (just guessing), he can probably handle a drink.

"His specialty is daiquiris," Mudge tilted his head at the bartender. "Strawberry's good now, while they're in season, if you're not OD'd from Leo's."

They ordered a pitcher of strawberry daiquiris. Lydia tried to recall if she'd seen a blender in her new kitchen. Cocktail napkins appeared, and a bowl of pretzels. She tested one between thumb and fingers, half expecting it to bend, and was pleasantly surprised when it snapped.

Had she bought any snack food on her first grocery run? Cheese puffs. No microwave popcorn yet. Was there a microwave? Yes. And a TV, though she hadn't checked for cable . . .

Suddenly, music. *Da, dah . . . Da, dah . . .* The familiar notes hit Lydia like a kick in the stomach. Miles Davis, "Kind of Blue." The album she and Fletcher used to hear in so many Cambridge pubs and shops they agreed it must be a requirement for doing business.

Conversation was now possible–indeed, essential.

"So, Mudge, how long have you been at Leo's? How do you like it?"

Since last summer, and not too bad. "Better now you're there. Sue was kind of a downer."

"Do you think she'll come back?" For the first time, Lydia was able to ask this question without a twinge of fear. "She usually does, doesn't she?"

He nodded. "If she hears about you, maybe not, though. Leo don't want her back, that's for sure. Dinah either."

Their daiquiris arrived. "Dinah! Should we have asked her to come out with us? I didn't even think of it."

"Nah. She's got another job. Never goes anyplace."

"Another job? What kind?"

Mudge shrugged. "Donno. Lotta people do that around here, especially in summer. That's when you make your money–tourist season." He slurped an under-blended strawberry. "How about you? You like working at the Back End?"

"Yeah. I do."

"You gonna stay for the summer? Now you got your own cottage . . . "

"Don't see why not," Lydia agreed.

He lifted his glass. "To the future."

They toasted. Without a white apron over his black T-shirt, Mudge was a strikingly good-looking guy. Strong cheekbones, huge brown eyes, chiseled nose, wide full mouth. Lydia loved his laugh, which she'd begun to listen for at work, as cheering as the tip horn or that pink rhododendron bush at the Blue Moon. Lucky for her he was so young. The last thing she needed in her new life was any more complications.

Speaking of complications . . .

"Did you know my friend DeAnne? Who worked for Carlo and Caroline?"

"Oh, sure." He chased a chunk of ice with his straw. "She came in for lunch with them sometimes. Her and me were like the only ones under sixty. She introduced me to this place, in fact. Nice girl. Woman," he corrected.

Lydia too had thought of DeAnne as a girl. For her it was an age label. Apparently for Mudge–gazing into his drink–it meant something else.

"You knew her pretty well?"

"Nah. Not really. We hung out a little."

An affair, Lydia suspected, that didn't become a romance. "What'd you think when you heard–?"

"It sucked." At last he looked at her. "It didn't make sense. You know? Not just falling off the ladder. Working overtime when she could've been partying?"

Lydia agreed. "Not the DeAnne I knew."

Mudge asked how she knew DeAnne. Lydia explained: Cambridge house, art classes, working together . . .

"What, at Legal Seafood?"

Whoops! "We had a side business called the Fix-It Chix."

"The Fix-It Chix," he repeated, charmed. "What'd you fix?"

"Anything. Plumbing, appliances, holes in the ceiling. You name it, we fixed it."

His eyebrows went up hopefully. "Cars?"

"Sometimes. Mostly houses. But I'll try and help with your truck if you want."

Mudge pressed his lips together and frowned into his daiquiri. After a moment he said, "You remember this morning? You said I look like I slept under a bridge?"

Lydia nodded.

"Well, I sort of did. With the truck not running, the last couple days? I slept under the Elephant Tree."

"Mudge! My god! It's been so cold at night! What about your family?"

"They don't care. I got a down sleeping bag, I'm fine. You know I'm Wampanoag, right? No problem. Only I can't take a shower in the men's room. Just wash in the sink. I was kinda hoping nobody would notice."

"Oh, I'm sure they didn't. I didn't, really. I was just being a bitch. But–shouldn't we go work on the truck? Like, right now? And then you can clean up at my place."

He was unconcerned. "It stays light a long time. We're OK." He topped up their glasses. "There's something I wanted to talk to you about, anyways."

Finally! thought Lydia. "What?"

"Well, you know, the food at the Back End, it's like, basic cafeteria, right? Burgers, sandwiches– I mean, Dinah's great, and better her than me, feeding that many people on Leo's budget. But I been thinking. Last summer, when Edgar Rowdey sent over his berries and I made that pie?"

"The famous Rowdeyberry Tarte."

"Right. That was totally cool. To do something that was mine, that I invented. And people loved it! And now you're making these incredible soups, and the veggie chili, and they're all hoping you'll stay, like even giving you a house! and I was thinking: We could do dinners."

An inquiring look: Did she get it? Not yet.

"I mean, these old folks who come to Leo's for breakfast, lunch– What do they do at night? Hot dogs? Pizza? What if they want to eat with their friends? What if they can't drive out of town in the dark? Well, so, what if they had a team of chefs to cook them a real dinner?"

Lydia was doubtful. "You mean, like, catering?"

"Maybe. That's one way. Say they want orange-glazed pork roast? or salmon poached in white wine? No problem! Or, the other way, get Leo to stay open one night. Like, Saturday night dinner party! We could experiment–chicken enchiladas with green chilis one week, then roast beef with Yorkshire pudding. The main thing," he refilled their glasses, "would be learning new stuff. And build a reputation. You already did that up in Boston, I guess."

"No. Not really." In fact not at all, Lydia thought, and felt her cheeks flushing. Because if there's one thing I've never been good at, it's commitment. "Is that what you want to do, Mudge? Be a chef?"

He swirled pink slush around in his glass. "Maybe. I never thought about it much before. Me and my buddies, it's like, make a few bucks and then party. Construction, lawn care, whatever. Leo's is the first job I ever stayed at. Even Dinah and Sue–get done and go home. But you– I mean, you can really cook, like spices and that, plus your Fix-It Chix? You can go anyplace! And I'm thinking, well, shit! I invented the coffee jello and the Moose Cake besides the Rowdeyberry Tarte. Why couldn't I be a chef? At least a dessert chef. Like how about mocha meringue pie? Ginger-peach cobbler?"

"Sounds good to me." Lydia grinned at him. "I haven't even been here a week yet, so who knows, as far as Leo handing over his kitchen and his customers and all." She raised her glass to his. "But hey, why not?"

"To the big time!"

For now, they agreed, the big time would remain a goal. Turning it into a plan would need a lot more thought, and more meetings like this one. Step One: reconvene on Monday for daiquiris and discussion. Step Two: build visibility, adding more inspired soups and brilliant desserts to the Back End menu. Step Three (which could follow as soon as they got bored with Step Two): decide whether to launch catering or weekly dinners.

Mudge had already named their hypothetical partnership: The Flying Wedge.

Giddy as they were from daiquiris and creativity, he and Lydia both found it tremendously encouraging that, working together, they had no trouble fixing his truck.

Chapter Seven

Twenty-Seven Merrie Lane, around the corner from a golf course in the leafy heart of Dennis, looked much as Lydia expected. She pulled into the asphalt driveway. *To boldly go,* she thought, *where no Morris has gone before.* The Ropeses' Ford sedan–a gleam of chrome, a whiff of Turtle Wax–filled half of a two-car garage. This was linked by a breezeway to a small split-level house with pale green siding, a scalloped aluminum storm door, and a white shingled roof. A red wooden bird on a stick whirred pinwheel wings beside the front walk.

On the phone yesterday Mrs. Ropes was shyly charming. How nice to hear from someone who knew DeAnne. Yes, terrible news, just terrible. The family was still in shock. As her friend–Lydia, was it?–must be, too, if she'd only just found out.

They agreed she would come by tomorrow around noon. "After church," amplified Mrs. Ropes. She offered lunch; Lydia politely declined. Already she had qualms about this visit.

A garden plot beside the driveway looked freshly plowed. Dug? Harrowed? Whatever they did to gardens on Cape Cod. Sacks of composted cow manure at regular intervals suggested they planned to go on doing it after she left.

Good. We'll make this quick.

Lydia smoothed down her most presentable T-shirt over her best cotton pants. Back in Cambridge, she and DeAnne and their housemates had woven their own family. No roots, no history, no expectations. Anyone who got on anyone's nerves–or fell in love–could move out. The group chose replacements; the web hardly quivered. Quansett families were obviously more tenacious. Each individual, it seemed, made one strand in a net which tightly held even strugglers like DeAnne.

What kind of hole must her death have left?

The woman who answered the door looked stronger than her phone voice. Short and stocky, in her late forties, Mrs. Ropes ("call me Cynthia") shared DeAnne's bronze complexion and flattish face. Lydia followed her out of the sunshine into a dim living room with half-drawn drapes.

Her husband, rising from his recliner, was taller and presumably the source of his daughter's deep-set brown eyes. Where DeAnne's thick black curls had come from was an open question, as neither of her parents had enough hair for comparison. For an instant Lydia wondered if their oddly similar navy-blue suits and white shirts were some kind of restaurant uniform, until she remembered church.

And of course, she realized sinkingly, they're in mourning.

"Pleased to meet you." Raymond Ropes's hand was muscular and callused–a working man's grip. What kind of work? Lydia couldn't recall. DeAnne hadn't talked much about her parents.

"We're so glad you could make it," Mrs. Ropes repeated. "The boys always come over for Sunday supper, so it's a nice family kind of a day. Four grandkids, we've got now, and one on the way. You're welcome to join us."

"Thanks, but I really can't."

"Whereabouts is your family, dear?"

"We're pretty scattered." In every sense: death, divorce, alienation. "My mother's in New Mexico. She married a realtor there after my father died."

"Oh, I'm so sorry." They had reached the central feature of the living room: a glass-fronted entertainment center with a full shelf of framed snapshots. "We've all stayed close to home, as you can see." Lydia looked obediently at assorted Ropeses at the beach, barbecuing on the deck, decorating a Christmas tree. "That's Charlie . . . and Jimmy . . . "

A curl of black ribbon draped a tall studio portrait of DeAnne. Her high-school photo, most likely, faded out below the V-neck of her dress. Lydia had never seen her hair so smooth–as if she'd sculpted it.

A flash of orange at her feet startled her backwards. Cynthia

Ropes tittered. "Ooh, Mr. Gordo! Scare the daylights out of us!"

Of course: DeAnne's ginger cat. The one family member she had frankly missed and often mentioned. I can't sleep without Mr. Gordo curled up on my leg, she'd complained, until Karin lent her a teddy bear. When she announced she was leaving after one semester, they'd half-jokingly blamed the cat.

Now he was staring at Lydia from halfway down the hall. He was bigger than she'd imagined, with a swinging belly and a tail that twisted at the tip.

If you hadn't lured her back here, Mr. Gordo, would DeAnne still be alive?

Mr. Ropes was asking his wife something about dinner. Lydia sat in a stiffly upholstered gold armchair and hoped they wouldn't give her the grand tour. DeAnne's room in Cambridge was Spartan: a futon, a computer desk and chair, a dresser. No pictures, no plants, not even a rug. I'd only get clay on stuff, she'd asserted, spreading newspapers. To Lydia, who cherished the clean-slate anonymity of this house, that sounded perfectly reasonable. Not to Fletcher, aspiring psychologist and fifth-generation Harvard grad. Covering up more than the floor, DeAnne! I see classic backlash here–excess simplicity as a rebellion against excess clutter in your past.

Lydia didn't want to know if he was right. Now that she thought about it, she didn't want to know anything at all about DeAnne's family or taste or childhood history. In fact she totally didn't want to be here.

"Can I get you some coffee?" offered Mr. Ropes.

"No thanks. I can't stay too long."

"Tea? Pepsi? Orange juice?" asked his wife.

Lydia shook her head. "I just– Since we never got a chance to meet while DeAnne was in Cambridge–"

"Raymond, bring out some of those cookies with the chocolate stripes. Now, Lydia. You said you found a job in Quansett? Does that mean you've moved down here for good?"

"Well." I have no clue how to have this conversation, Lydia thought. "For good, I don't know . . . "

"Of course. No need to decide that yet. But you like Cape

Cod, do you?"

"What's not to like?" came Mr. Ropes's gruff tenor from the kitchen.

"I've only been here four days," said Lydia.

"Cyn? Cyn-thia!"

"What is it, Raymond?"

"Where do you keep those cookies?"

"In the fridge. DeAnne," she turned back to Lydia, "I'll tell you, was happy as a clam to be back home again. Not that she didn't enjoy her time in the city–"

Happy as a clam. Why did people say that? How did clams have dibs on happiness?

"–the dirt and the noise," Mrs. Ropes concluded. "And the heat! Too much for us. But then we're spoiled."

"We have central air. Don't even need it." Lydia heard the vigorous ripping of cellophane. "Best climate anywhere."

"And of course the beaches. DeAnne just loved the beach. Swam as soon as she could walk. Didn't she, Raymond?"

"You bet." Mr. Ropes appeared with the cookies. "Spent her whole life here. Happy as a clam at high tide."

Ah.

"We understood her wanting to stretch her wings," said his wife. "Cross the bridge, have a little adventure. But to miss Indian Summer? The fall leaves and the Harvest Festival? Naturally by Christmas she couldn't wait to come home. Back with her friends and family. And her kitty! Gordo?" she called. "Kitty-kitty-kitty! Raymond, where's Mr. Gordo?"

"He took off," said Lydia. Birds to stalk, sunbeams to nap in, drapes to claw. We should all be so resilient.

"Poor baby, his little heart is broken." Mrs. Ropes's voice quavered. *Don't,* begged Lydia silently, clutching the arms of her chair. Of all the things to cry over, not the *cat*, for god's sake!

"Those people." Mr. Ropes thrust his plate of cookies at her. "Those *artists*."

Mrs. Ropes shook her head. "She was young, she wanted to stretch her wings. Of course she did! You just don't ever think–you don't imagine . . . "

"How do you ever know?" Mr. Ropes demanded rhetorically. With a protective hand on his wife's shoulder, he faced Lydia. "You met those folks she worked for? What's their names?–Song and Penn?"

Lydia nodded. "Really nice people."

"Couple of who-knows-what from New York! What business did they have with a girl like DeAnne? who's never been outside of Massachusetts?"

"Who else could have given her that kind of a job?" Lydia returned. "She sent me a postcard–she sounded so happy–"

"She could've got any kind of job she wanted. With her office skills?"

"She was a happy girl," said her mother.

"Secretary, receptionist, you name it."

"This was the kind of job she wanted, though. Did she show you the sculptures she did in Cambridge? Those beautiful blue urns? or the mother and daughter?"

His grunt was dismissive.

"She aced her classes. Her adviser said if she stuck with it–"

"But of course that was a hobby," said Mrs. Ropes. "Nowadays a young woman has to be practical."

"Can't count on finding a husband who'll support her," Mr. Ropes seconded. "Not these days."

"Did she tell you about the Fix-It Chix? Her job with me? Doing home repairs and carpentry?"

"Carpentry?" His eyebrow went up.

Lydia hadn't meant to get into this; now she couldn't stop. "She had a real talent for it. An artist's eye, plus the practical skills and coordination to back it up."

"I'm sure she must have mentioned . . . " DeAnne's mother frowned.

"Carpentry?" Mr. Ropes repeated.

"Bookshelves, closets, kitchen remodeling–she could have supported herself, no problem."

"Not our daughter." He slammed the cookie plate down on the coffee table. "Carpentry? No sirree Bob."

"Better than most men I've worked with."

"Well of course she always was a good seamstress," said Mrs. Ropes placatingly. "Liked to make her own clothes. That beautiful prom dress–remember, Raymond? Yards and yards of pink, all over the living room."

"Oh, yes," said Mr. Ropes. "I remember."

For a moment they were silent, picturing DeAnne like an angel in her pink prom dress. Time to go, Lydia thought. Say something pleasant and get out of here before I put my foot in it again.

DeAnne's father spoke first. "She had talent, I don't argue with that. And what did you say? Skills and coordination?"

Lydia nodded.

"I'm glad to hear it from one who knows. So now tell me this: How does a girl like that, who can handle bookshelves and closets and whatnot, fall off an ordinary ten-foot aluminum stepladder?"

"Good question." One point at least we can agree on. "What did the police say, if you don't mind my asking?"

He waved a hand dismissively. "Accident. Naturally! What else are they gonna say? She overbalanced. She shouldn't have been climbing a ladder alone, in those shoes. Pure bad luck she landed on her head. Hah! Close the case, that's all they care about. Check it off the list."

"They didn't know her," offered DeAnne's mother. "They looked at the place where she fell and so forth, but I don't see how that's going to tell them what happened."

"So you don't think–" Lydia picked her words. "I mean, was it a thorough investigation? Did they send detectives, take fingerprints and all that?"

"I don't know what they did," Raymond Ropes retorted. "They came up empty, is all I know. My daughter is dead, and those responsible get off scott free?"

"Responsible, how?"

"Criminal negligence!" His voice shook. "Who sent DeAnne up that ladder? Who was out boozing it up, for christ's sake, when they should have been there watching her?"

Not the accusation she'd expected. "Oh, no. You can't–"

"Oh, yes!" Raymond Ropes cut her off. "I've done some

looking into Mr. Carlo Song and Miss Caroline Penn. That's right: Miss, not Mrs. Living together for God knows how long, those two, without the benefit of wedlock. Maybe that kind of bohemian crap flies in New York, but not here on the Cape. Around here we still have morals."

Lydia glanced at DeAnne's mother. She had twisted half off her chair and was wiggling her fingers just above the carpet, cajoling the still-invisible cat.

"Mr. Ropes, have you met them? Have you talked to them? They're the kindest, most supportive–"

"Yes, I met them, and I don't care if they're Mother Teresa and the Pope. They killed my little girl." His jaw was rigid. "And you can tell them from me. If there's one sure thing besides death and taxes? They are going to pay."

Driving down Route 6A, Lydia seethed. Parents! Two more minutes in that suffocating room and she'd have lost it. *They're going to pay? What about you? Who yanked DeAnne out of art school? Who dragged her back here to be a secretary? Who's going to make you pay?*

Fortunately she'd fled before that happened. Raymond and Cynthia Ropes were bereaved, for god's sake! They loved DeAnne, and she loved them. What's your problem, Lydia? You came to offer them sympathy, not a fight. I mean look at him, poor bastard, rigid as a Marine in his La-Z-Boy, with his instant coffee and supermarket cookies. What was Raymond Ropes but a pawn in the hand of Fate? His daughter had been struck down, and as a man and a father it was his job to do something. Question: What? Answer: Blame somebody! Strike back!

Still, what excuse was that for attacking Caroline and Carlo?

Bohemian? Immoral? Hey, who strong-armed DeAnne into giving up her dreams? If you'd left her alone, she'd still be alive and doing very damn well in Cambridge, thank you. And so would I–minding my own business, in fact running my own business–

No, that didn't hold up. Even if DeAnne hadn't shafted her and the Fix-It Chix, Mr. Dickhead Rat Bastard would have.

A tree loomed into the road as she rounded a curve and nearly hit the Morris. Get a grip, Lydia! Straightening out the wheel, she forced her fingers to unclench. There ought to be a law. People shouldn't drive when they're too . . .

Too what?

Hungry! Who could stay focused on the road with her stomach churning?

She pulled into Cap'n Chilly's and joined the line at the take-out window. Not an ideal choice. Compared with the Cap'n's menu, Leo's was a gourmet paradise. Chilly Dogs, Chilly-n-Chips, Extra Hot Chilly . . .

The truth was, she hardly knew Caroline Penn and Carlo Song. How could she vouch for their characters? OK, DeAnne had liked them, and they'd complimented her cooking. Did that make them trustworthy human beings? Couldn't an axe murderer smile, say thanks, and leave a tip?

As far as that went, how well did she know DeAnne? Enough to recognize her talents and encourage her to use them. Not enough to judge her choices. If DeAnne had truly wanted to be a sculptor and/or carpenter, she'd have stayed in Cambridge.

Lydia ordered a mocha frappe; carried it around the little building to the patio in back. Half screened from the parking lot by a low hedge, she sat on a concrete bench and pondered.

What's this about, Lydia? Why the big agitation? So it wasn't exactly a day at the beach–what did you expect? These people just lost their only daughter. They're devastated. Bitter. Upset. So, good: you did the condolence dance. As Fletcher would say, you validated their grief and gave them a chance to vent. Very important, venting. Old Raymond's probably already sorry he said that revenge crap.

But what if he isn't?

What's my procedure here? Do I warn Carlo and Caroline? *Hey, sorry to interrupt your lunch, but you better hire yourselves a lawyer. And maybe a bodyguard.*

Oh, hell!

Talk to the cops? They must have spent enough time with DeAnne's father to know if he was a serious threat.

On the other hand, wasn't it the cops' handling of her case that had left him so angry?

Assuming he really was angry . . .

"It's not about money," he'd insisted when Lydia launched her hasty good-bys. "Anything this family ever needed, I provided. Nobody could ever say Raymond Ropes took a handout, not from the government, not from anybody. And if those two think they can buy me off?–you tell them, they've got another think coming."

He sounded like he meant it. But then you'd have to, wouldn't you? At least to your chosen messenger. And to the cops, when they'd interviewed him last month.

What kind of police force did a place like Quansett have? Capable of investigating a fatal fall off a ladder? There couldn't be many such deaths in a town this size. Maybe the cops' expertise didn't stretch past burglaries and bar fights.

But then how much expertise did you need to recognize an accident?

Because what else could it possibly be but an accident?–no matter how agile DeAnne was, and no matter how passionately you wanted to blame somebody for her death?

Oh, hell! thought Lydia again. That's what this is about. She slurped up the chocolatey dregs of her frappe. Not Carlo and Caroline. It's about me not wanting to agree with Raymond Ropes that there's something wrong with this picture.

Noise erupted behind the hedge. Over the engine-rumble of cars pulling in and out, a hubbub rose of excited voices.

Lydia carried her cup to the trash can, glad to be distracted.

A parade? Free Chilly Dogs?

Hands pointed. She could see him from here: Roosevelt Sherman, looming head and shoulders above the other customers in Cap'n Chilly's crowded little lobby.

That must be his wife, that slim silhouette nudging two small children ahead of her. When she stepped into sunlight she became 3-D striking: short springy black hair, sculptured cheekbones, and a movie-star figure even in shorts and a T-shirt. Rosey himself, also in shorts and a T-shirt but three times her size, carried a sleeping baby on his shoulder.

The line melted into chaos. Older customers stepped back, nudging each other. Younger ones pressed forward, begging for autographs, thrusting a napkin, a paper bag, a road map, a bare arm at the football hero. Clearly he was used to this. He managed to sign everything one-handed, nod and smile, without losing his grip on the baby.

Lydia headed for her car. The ideal moment to get out of this circus.

At the far end, partly hidden by a tree, she spotted a familiar blue Honda sedan. Behind the wheel she made out another massive figure, or rather the upper right half of one: the crown of a head, a shoulder, a bent arm, a hand to an ear.

What was Dinah doing here, talking on a cell phone in Cap'n Chilly's parking lot?

Wallace Hicks maneuvered his car through the gap in the yew hedge and into the parking lot at the Blue Moon Motel.

This being the brief doldrums between Memorial Day and summer, he found a space right in front of his target. A minute later his crystal-headed cane tapped on the door of Room 8.

Just to be standing here was half the battle won already. If Officer Kevin Kelly hadn't been so goggle-eyed over Roosevelt Sherman, he surely would have vetoed this plan. Kevin never could stand anyone else running things, even as a kid. Wally recalled Mrs. Kelly beating her fists on a tree in frustration at the flat-out impossibility of walking Kevin, his baby sister, and the dog to the store all at the same time. Wally's mother had assured her that her boy must be destined for authority–a doctor or teacher maybe. Personally, Wally wouldn't have bet on it. He gave Mrs. Kelly a world of credit that Kevin had succeeded as a cop–had mastered (or at least accepted) the helpful side of police work as well as the dictatorial side.

After a short nod of recognition, Officer Kelly had treated Wally as invisible. Another small but key victory. When the time came to launch his mission, the last thing Wally wanted was a cop breathing down his neck.

He tapped again on the door. Roosevelt Sherman–now, there was a man destined for authority! His quick ability to size up a situation and play it to win boded well, in Wally's view, for the Frigate, Quansett, and CodCast.net.

You could almost hear gears creaking as the cosmic machinery swung into motion.

The door to Room 8 opened a crack, and would have shut just as fast if Wally's cane hadn't blocked it.

"Rudy," said Wallace Hicks cheerfully. "How you doin' this fine afternoon?"

A young face appeared: glum chocolate-smeared mouth, wary eyes. He answered over intermittent blasts of machine-gun fire and screeching tires: "Good."

"I'm here to speak with you and your brother."

"You can't come in. My mom ain't home."

"Why don't you fellas come out, then? Turn off the TV, and we can talk in the fresh air."

More gunfire, and the thud of the door banging against the cane in another futile attempt to slam.

"I don't believe," Wally raised his voice, "you'd want your mom to be part of this conversation."

"Go away!" came a shout from inside the room.

"Go away," Rudy echoed, less certainly.

"But hey, it's your call. I'm happy to go on over to the Par-Tee Cone right now and talk to her."

Over the violent clamor inside he heard the older boy ask the younger: "What's he want?"

"Louis?" Wally called. "You're a football fan, right? You know who Roosevelt Sherman is?"

Rudy answered for him. "Sure. Rosey Sherman? The Patriots?"

"Louis?" Wally called again.

"Yeah! What?" came a muffled shout.

"Did you know that Mr. Sherman is in Quansett right now?"

That brought Louis to the door. He was two years taller, more truculent, more used to not being sure where or with whom he was living, and more steeled against disruptions than his brother.

"No way," he said scornfully.

"I kid you not." He looks half starved, thought Wally. They both do. He made a slight alteration to the plan. "And not only here, but he wants to meet you guys. Tomorrow after school. Take you out for pizza, I believe he said."

"Yeah, right." Louis's sarcasm was withering; but he remained in the doorway.

"No way," Rudy echoed. "Why would Rosey Sherman want to meet us?"

"Well, I reckon because he was young once, too," said Wally, "and you fellas slashed his tires."

Chapter Eight

Another cold morning. Warming up the Morris, Lydia realized she was four minutes early. Just enough time to go find Carlo and Caroline's studio.

From the tidbits she'd collected at the Back End, she knew where to look. Carlo and Caroline had bought the original Quansett Town Hall years ago, out from under a wrecking ball. Over time, they'd transformed an eighteenth-century shell into a designer showcase.

What was Raymond Ropes's phrase? "Bohemian crap"?

Lydia had resolved last night not to trip over her personal feelings while she followed the directions on DeAnne's postcard. That's all this was, right? Granting a friend's last request. Not opening any can of worms.

She took a right up Main Street, away from Leo's, toward the library and fire station. That must be it, behind that tall boxwood hedge. She peered down a gravel driveway. No car in sight . . . but a carved wooden sign confirmed in gilt letters: TOWN HALL. The building was plainer than she'd expected, like a New England church: a white clapboard shoebox with tall multi-paned windows along each side and dark-green double doors at this end. Above them, topping the roof peak over the sign, sat a white cupola.

Too puritanical for the Broadway-musical team of Song and Penn.

Then she started seeing ornamental touches. A painted weathervane flying from the cupola, pink and gold and green–a winged mermaid? Two big skylights in the roof. The white paneled side door had a brass lion's-head knocker, a wooden screen door with curlicued inner corners, and a wrought-iron shoe-scraper on the stoop. Long curved beds of chocolate-brown dirt lined the clipped lawn, edged with scallop shells, crowded with hopeful green leaves.

Inside that building, DeAnne had died.

Every morning she'd driven up this driveway, parked on that gravel, walked past those flowerbeds, opened that screen door.

Lydia thought: I have to get in there.

At the Back End she asked Dinah when Caroline and Carlo would be back from New York. Tonight, most likely. They generally waited until Monday to drive home, after the weekend traffic.

Lydia took the opportunity to ask her how the Back End's chili compared with Cap'n Chilly's. Dinah shrugged and said she never ate out anyplace but here. True or not, it was such a staggering statement that Lydia understood why Mudge hadn't tapped her for the Flying Wedge.

Had Dinah known DeAnne Ropes? Another shrug. Saw her in here a few times. Never talked to her.

On Saturday Lydia had requested the ingredients for curried cauliflower soup, and here they were. She pushed DeAnne out of her mind and whipped through breakfast. By the time Leo came down to harass the help, she'd already sauteed her onions and celery and was running carrots and potatoes through his ancient hand-cranked grinder. Build visibility! Also leverage: if she dazzled the customers today, she could lobby to start Wednesday's or Thursday's soup a night early.

As of 1:30, reviews were mixed. Edgar Rowdey, bless his heart, had tried it, liked it, and urged several friends to order a cup. (Short-list that man for the Flying Wedge!) A booth of ladies from Osterville enthused over the yummy new soup and vowed to return soon. A table of carpenters from Yarmouth groused about stinking up a good American restaurant with foreign smells.

Lydia had just stirred the pots and was back in the kitchen scraping the grill when a familiar voice called her name.

Alistair Pope waved across the counter like someone greeting an arriving passenger. His salt-and-pepper hair was wind-tousled, locks snaking over both eyes and the collar of his army jacket. "Sanctuary!" He slid dramatically onto a stool. "You have no idear what dragons I've had to slay to reach this refuge!"

"Oh, dry up, Al, will ya?" Dinah groaned. "There's folks here tryin' to eat."

"Not many," he retorted. "Maybe business would pick up if you'd remembah the customah's always right."

Lydia had forgotten how strange his accent sounded when she first heard it. Funny how fast she'd stopped noticing.

"Well then I guess if you ever want to be right," Dinah retorted, "you better place an order."

"How about if I awdah you to butt out so I can talk to ya sous-chef?"

Funny how a guy who couldn't keep his hands off her when they first met had vanished so completely that now she was struck all over again by his accent.

"You tell her, Al," said a red-flannel-shirted man two stools away.

"Come on, Dinah!" urged his plaid-flannel-shirted companion. "You gonna take that?"

Dinah swiveled. "You want to see your lunch any time soon, fellas, you better butt out yourself."

"Greek salad?" said Lydia.

"Here." A hand went up near the door.

She set down the plate without a glance at Alistair Pope. "I'll get you a fork."

He followed her, brushing his hair back ineffectually. "Lydia. I swear to god, I've been trying for days–"

"I'm working." She elbowed past him. "You want to try something? Try my new soup."

He caught her arm. "Yes! Put me down for a bowl."

"Put yourself down." She shook him off. "Pad and pen right there."

His wail trailed her back to the grill. "This blasted pen doesn't work!"

Dinah pointed her cleaver at him. "You're the movie mogul. Make it work!"

Mudge and Leo were catching all this in glimpses from the sandwich bar and the cash register respectively, both grinning. The customers at the counter munched and watched as attentively as if the Red Sox were playing. An incoming couple paused inside the doorway, trying to make out what was going on.

"A man could starve in this place!" howled Alistair.

Leo spoke up: "Lucky for you, Al, you got enough extra there to hold you over quite a while."

"If you can't give me a pen, give me a sword," Alistair demanded. "I'll open a vein and write my order in blood."

"Here you go." Leo held out his butcher knife. "You want my advice, stick to soup. That's the shortest word we got on the menu. You don't have to put down the curried cauliflower part. Being not much of a speller."

"Someday," Alistair muttered darkly. Dodging the knife, he stalked over to the crockery shelf for a bowl. "When I film my documentary on Crockett's Wild Animal Farm, I promise to bring the entire cast here for lunch."

He slapped his order slip on the counter. Leo picked it up. "Sorry, Al. Can't read this. But whatever it is, we're out of it."

What an excellent place this is to work! thought Lydia.

Alistair resumed his stool with a slump of resignation. His hair was in his eyes again. She did feel just a tiny bit sorry for him. Maybe, if he liked her soup . . .

He ate the whole bowlful without speaking. Finally he looked up. "Leo, this is the best curried cauliflower soup I ever tasted. Please convey my profound admiration to your chef."

Leo looked from Alistair to Lydia, ten feet away at the refrigerator, and back. "Not a chance," he drawled. "She'd only use it against me. They're all alike, these creative types. Give 'em an inch, they want a yard. Three weeks' vacation, overtime pay, dental plan . . . "

"Ignore him," Alistair told Lydia. "You're a genius, and he's a very lucky old man."

"Thank you," said Lydia, conceding a smile.

"Lazy, obnoxious, and mean as a troll, but lucky." He addressed the man nearest to him. "You! Have you tried this extraordinary soup? And you? Yes, you!"

Heads shook. "I don't like cauliflower," said one.

"You're another lucky man, then, because it doesn't taste like cauliflower. What it tastes like– Well, it's too subtle and rich to describe. Lydia! Bring everybody here a half a cup of your soup. On me."

"Are you serious?"

"And I need a piece of poster paper, this big, and a Magic Marker."

"Over there," she nodded at the patchwork wall that served as a menu.

By the time Lydia set out the cups and spoons, Alistair was tacking up a new sign: TRY QUANSETT'S NEW GOURMET SPECIALTY! STAR OF INDIA SOUP.

"This *is* good," said the man who didn't like cauliflower. "Spicy, but . . . good."

There were murmurs of agreement up and down the counter.

Leo walked over to the menu wall and picked up the Magic Marker. With a haughty glare at Alistair, he changed SOUP to SOOP.

"Star of India?" he asked Lydia. "When was I gonna hear about it?"

"Hey. I'm not the movie mogul."

She could feel Alistair waiting for his payoff. So, in the Back End spirit, she switched places with Mudge, filling orders in the kitchen instead of delivering them. That kept her out of Alistair's range until he came to the cash register.

"Lydia?" he called past Leo. "I need to talk to you."

"That'll be twelve dollars and eight-five cents."

"Lydia? Hello?"

"She's ignoring you. Fifteen cents change. And don't insult this establishment by dropping it in the bucket."

"Get out of the way, you doddering Cerebrus. Lydia!"

He loomed beside her. "What?" she said without looking up. Leo clanged the tip bell.

"If I've done anything that's offended you, I apologize. And I invite you–no, I insist that you come to tea this afternoon. Please."

Leo winked at her. "He must really like you," he stage-whispered. "I never heard him talk so nice to anybody before."

"Oh, do shut up."

"See? This is what the rest of us get. Abuse."

"Yeah," said Dinah. "Even his mother, if you can believe it."

"I can't," said Lydia to both of them.

Alistair glanced balefully from Leo to Dinah to her. "At least do me the favor of stepping outside for two minutes so we can finish this doomed attempt at a conversation in private."

Again Lydia felt a twinge of pity. "OK." And to Leo: "I'll be right back."

He didn't argue, but called after them: "One minute fifty-nine seconds!"

The sun was so bright she shielded her eyes. "Over here," said Alistair. "Under the tree."

Lydia stayed where she was. "You were heroic about the soup, but I really am working and I really did mean it about the two minutes."

He moved closer. "I really did mean it about coming for tea. I'm going to walk over to the Whistling Pig right now while you finish up in there, and pick out an irresistible selection of scones or cupcakes or whatever's currently on the cutting edge, tea-wise. I'll drive you over–"

"That's very sweet, Alistair, but I can't. I have a previous engagement."

"Cancel it. Have I told you about my house? Pre-Civil War. Five fireplaces, hidden staircase, more built-in bookshelves than the Quansett Public Library. You'll love it. According to legend, President Wilson dined there shortly after launching the League of Nations. I'll meet you back here in half an hour."

"Like I said: Not today."

"Lydia. I'm swamped with work. I may have to leave for the Coast on Wednesday. I put off a dozen urgent phone calls to come here for lunch; and it would be an honor and a pleasure to set all this aside for one more hour to enjoy a pot of Harrod's Afternoon Blend with you."

His hand cupped her cheek. Lydia felt a delicious electrical current run from his fingers through every nerve of her body.

"Only an hour?" she asked wanly.

He slid his hand down her neck, inside the back of her T-shirt.

"It's just tea."

She expected (hoped?) he would pull her close. She could almost feel his chest against hers, the muscular warmth of him, the tingle of skin on skin. But–owing perhaps to their audience–he only squeezed her shoulder. "Right here. Soon as you're through."

Mudge assured her he didn't care. In fact he'd have offered to postpone their Flying Wedge meeting, seeing as they didn't have anything to meet about, except he couldn't tell which way she was leaning.

Lydia kept the conversation on food while they closed up. Did the Back End always offer daily clam chowder plus a new soup du jour whenever the last one ran out? Yup, far as Dinah recalled. What were the biggest hits? Anything they know from a can, said Mudge. Tomato, split pea, chicken rice. Mushroom, said Dinah. Cream of anything.

"What about ethnic? Like, avgolemono, or borscht, or Turkish red lentil?"

"Not from Sue," said Dinah.

"She didn't like making soup," said Mudge. "You do, right?"

"You bet," said Lydia. "My strongest suit."

"How come?" said Dinah.

"That's how I learned to cook." Lydia handed her the plastic wrap. "There was this guy I wanted to impress–a gourmet. I bought a cookbook at a yard sale and started at Page One. Worked my way through the first section, which was soups. We broke up between . . . let's see . . . tomato bisque and vichyssoise."

Mudge was alarmed. "Can you do main courses?"

"No problem." She patted his shoulder. "Up in Cambridge I cooked for my housemates, dinner for seven, twice a week."

"Prodigious! How'd you fit that in with Legal Seafood and the Fix-It Chix?"

Dinah saved her from having to come up with an explanation. "Go turn over the chairs," she told him. "Lydia and I can wrap this up."

Mudge and Lydia groaned obligingly at the pun.

"Mudge, how'd you get into cooking?" Lydia called as he flipped chairs onto tables.

"Feeding my brothers and sisters. My dad was out a lot, and you can only eat so much pizza. But the Rowdeyberry Tarte, that's what got me into desserts. Dinah, how about you?"

"Air Force. Long story. Some other time, seeing's we're near done here. Now don't mix up that tuna salad with the chicken. And Lydia? Watch out for Al. He ain't as harmless as he looks."

Yeah, well, neither am I, she thought as she stood waiting by the frog pond. (Still not a frog in sight. Maybe they were out of season.) Do I need harmless? No. All I'm asking for is a break. If I were ready to hop off the griddle onto the grill, which I'm definitely not, it wouldn't be for a beefy combed-over forty-something Cape Cod filmmaker who talks like a parody of JFK.

No, not a break. What I most want from Alistair Pope is information. What can he remember about DeAnne? Especially her last day. Especially in relation to Caroline and Carlo.

Damn! Will you listen to yourself, Lydia? What are you now, a TV cop? Like the man said: It's just tea. Not Robert Johnson at the crossroads.

Here he came, speak of the devil, walking across the parking lot all pleased with himself and his pink cardboard box of pastries tied up with string.

Alistair's ancient Mercedes stood ten yards from Lydia's Morris, the last vehicles remaining. "We don't need two cars," he said. "It's just up the road. I'll bring you back whenever you say," he added, as Lydia frowned. "No worries."

Dinah's warning crossed her mind as she followed him toward the Mercedes. Should she trust him? It seemed silly not to. This was the man who'd fixed her flat tire and delivered her to Leo's. Did she trust Dinah more than Alistair?

"Can I ask you something?"

"Anything."

"You know DeAnne Ropes was a friend of mine. I can't help wondering– What happened that last day? I know you were busy, but you did talk to her, right? How did she seem to you?"

He had set his pastry box on the car roof and was rummaging for his keys. "What happened? We were filming. Have you ever been around a shoot?"

"Not really."

"It's a three-ring circus. People swarming all over the place. I was keeping tabs on the ones who worked for me, and of course the subjects–Song and Penn." He found the keys; unlocked his door. "In retrospect, DeAnne's become the most important person there. But at the time, she was just one more worker bee."

Lydia wished she could see his face. "Didn't you interview her?"

"I pointed a camera at her and asked her a few questions." Alistair turned. "She struck me as what my parents would call a nice girl." His expression told her nothing. "Young, sweet, not a go-getter, but excited about the filming. Eager to help out."

"So she didn't seem–"

"Troubled? Upset? No. Just the opposite." He climbed inside; reached across to open her door. "More like a kid when the circus comes to town."

The passenger seat was old leather, with the soft patina of a saddle or a baseball glove. "How did she get along with Carlo and Caroline?"

"That," Alistair turned the key, "you'd have to ask them."

On Main Street he forestalled further questions by pointing out landmarks: the best place to buy kitchen supplies, the town landing, an organic nursery, the county courthouse. The old cemetery stood across from a roadside stand that sold ice cream and gravestones.

After several miles they turned left onto a narrow street lined with ancient oaks. Over the railroad tracks . . . and there was Alistair Pope's house, a stone's throw back from the road. It had been neither strikingly restored, like Carlo and Caroline's, nor shockingly neglected, like Edgar Rowdey's. Lydia guessed that Alistair's approach to homeownership was to fix what broke, replace what fell apart, and ignore the rest.

His driveway (like mine! she noted with an inner purr) was a short stretch of flattened grass. Apparently from here you walked across the lawn to the back door. The front door was hidden behind enormous laurels and lilacs, marked only by a stone path that led straight to the street. A relic from horse-and-carriage days? Here and there around Alistair's spacious grounds stood half-grown trees, not clustered but individually placed, like statuary: several fruit trees, a possible walnut, and a feathery Japanese maple.

As for the house, she suspected from the outside that a stranger might get lost in it: low ceilings, half a dozen chimneys, and more dormers, gables, alcoves, and wings than she could count.

She girded herself. Time for the other conversation they'd been needing to have.

"You live here alone?"

"Aside from stray cats." He shot her a charming disarming smile. "And people. Now that you have a cottage on the Cape, you'll find everyone you ever met showing up on your doorstep."

It was enough of a dodge that she persisted. "So there's no Mrs. Pope chained in the attic?"

"I seem to be an incurable bachelor." The smile had faded to something more reflective. "Not on purpose, believe me. And you?"

"Recently sprung."

"Is that what brought you down here?"

"Partly." Lydia followed him across the lawn. "Mostly."

"Maybe someday when we're better acquainted, late at night, bottle of wine, you can tell me about it."

The grass was recently mown and dry. "On your right, the summer kitchen," he pointed at a small outbuilding. "Originally that's where they did the cooking in hot weather. The main house had a huge brick fireplace, and later a wood-burning stove, which doubled as a furnace. So, come spring, they'd move the fire out here."

"What is it now?" Lydia cautiously tried the handle of an iron pump.

"A quiet place to work when I don't want to answer the phone. Or put up friends, if they're small." He moved toward the house. "My nephews call it their playhouse."

It was half the size of Lydia's cottage. She couldn't resist turning the doorknob. Locked.

Before she could peek in a window, Alistair exploded behind her. "Damn and blast!"

He stood facing the back door with a piece of paper in his hand. As she started toward him, he crumpled it and turned. "Lydia, I am so sorry." He didn't look sorry, though. He looked furious, and perhaps alarmed. "There's a crisis. My neighbor." He flourished the note in his fist. "Will you be terribly kind and give me a raincheck for tea? Tomorrow?"

She was too stunned to be tactful. "What kind of crisis?"

"I'm not sure." Even to himself he must have sounded evasive, because he added, "It's a difficult situation. I can't say more without betraying a trust. But please believe me," his voice softened as he came closer, "this is the last thing on earth I want to do right now."

His hand rested on her shoulder. He looked so grim that she let herself believe him. "No problem."

"You're an angel." He drew her into a quick hug, and kissed her lightly on the mouth. "I'll take you back to Leo's."

They hardly spoke on the way. Alistair pulled his Mercedes up beside her solitary Morris. "Lydia, dear girl, forgive me."

Spotting a longer kiss coming, she had her door open before it could land. Alistair came out and around to meet her. For another try? No. From his outstretched fingers hung the pink pastry box.

"Till tomorrow, OK?"

He turned his car with a screech of tires, and left her standing alone with an assortment of tea-cakes in the Back End parking lot.

Chapter Nine

Damn and blast! Lydia echoed as she climbed into her own car. Too late now to revive her and Mudge's meeting plan, since she had no way to reach him outside work.

Too bad she hadn't seen that note. Then she'd know for sure if Alistair Pope truly did have to go battle a crisis, or if he'd just gotten cold feet.

Or didn't want to hear any more questions about DeAnne.

What was his problem with that? The little he did tell her had sounded . . . not false, exactly, but rehearsed. Maybe he'd been asked the same things so many times that his answers were automatic. Or maybe he was miffed. Maybe he'd latched onto her as an outsider–one woman (finally!) he could dazzle with his pre-Civil War house, his filmmaking, and his sexy male self. And when she let him down, turned a note into a crisis.

Too bad she hadn't looked at the door sooner, to see if there even was a note. Alistair Pope, she suspected, would not be above dramatizing a grocery list if it served his purposes.

Still, if that was a performance, he was some actor.

And why would he drive her all the way there, show her his summer kitchen, and then do a 180?

Surely not because she'd asked if he had a wife or girlfriend. In such a crowded frog pond as Leo's, whatever he told her would be easy enough to check.

One could go back to his house and investigate. See if his car's still there. Look in his windows.

Right, Lydia. And then cruise up and down the street searching for a neighbor in crisis?

One could say Screw it! Go home to the blissful tranquility of one's cottage–

Or one could recall one's priorities and get back on track. Drive over to Caroline and Carlo's studio . . . where lo and behold, there they were, unloading luggage from their silver Mustang convertible.

Carlo spotted her and waved. Lydia took this as permission to pull in behind them.

"Welcome home! Can I help carry things?"

"You're so sweet to offer." Up close, Carlo looked tired. He glanced at Caroline, burrowing in the trunk. "I don't imagine . . . "

Lydia picked up a shopping bag. "How was New York?"

A wan smile. "Grand!" Carlo went up the path; propped the screen door open with a suitcase. "Splendid as ever!"

"Over, thank heaven." Caroline emerged with a trailing pink geranium in a white wicker birdcage, which she handed to Lydia.

"Carlo, happy birthday," Lydia called after him.

"Thank you, dear. We heard you've got a place to live."

"Yes! It's a miracle!" The three of them entered a small foyer with a black-and-white tile floor. "I keep thinking I must be dreaming. Or I've walked into 'Goldilocks and the Three Bears.'"

"We're pleased to have you in the neighborhood," said Caroline.

"Wilkommen, bienvenue, welcome!" Carlo seconded.

He led the way through an arch into the main hall. The rich aromatic air told Lydia even before she saw it that she was stepping out of the ordinary world into an indoor garden. The floor was paved with multicolored flagstones: slate, ochre, terra cotta. Lollipop trees in Grecian urns flanked the doorway. Carved marble sarcophagi filled with shrubbery stood between the tall side windows. Overhead, white baskets of hanging vines caught sun from the skylights. In the center of this large open area, where two centuries ago starchy men in knee breeches had debated bylaws, bronze frogs spat shining arcs of water into a miniature Spanish fountain.

"This is . . . so . . . " Lydia stood gaping in all directions.

A balcony ran around three-quarters of the hall, screened from view behind the railing by rice-paper blinds. To the left, a pair of grand pianos (covered) sat behind a shimmery transparent curtain on a shallow stage. Discreetly arranged among the vegetation were assorted chairs and occasional tables, and two sofas upholstered in a large flower print of the same pastel earth hues as the flagstone floor.

Carlo's smile was sympathetic. "You haven't been in here before."

She could only shake her head.

"Our studio. Up above, our living quarters. Caroline has stage right, I have stage left. Kitchen and so forth in the middle."

Realizations were shooting through Lydia's dazzled brain like firecrackers. *The studio of the famous duo Song and Penn.* And, *These aren't flagstones, they're painted on. What's it called?– trompe l'oeil.* And, *Separate living quarters?*

And the biggest jolt: *This is where DeAnne died.*

Carlo was saying something about picking up Arson from the dog-sitter, but Lydia caught only fragments. She was looking for the most likely spot to set a ten-foot stepladder where falling off it would kill you.

"Tea?"

Caroline's voice floated down from the balcony. She stood in the center of the right end of the building, in an open square framed by rice-paper blinds, wearing (this must be a dream!) a frilled apron.

After several seconds' silence Carlo translated: "Lydia, won't you join us for tea?"

She shook herself. Then smiled back. "As a matter of fact, I would be happy to make a large and I hope delicious contribution."

Why she happened to have a box of pastries in her car Lydia did not explain and her hosts did not inquire. Macaroons, chocolate eclairs, poppyseed cake– Ten points to Alistair.

She had followed Carlo up a white wrought-iron spiral staircase into the room, or foyer, where Caroline had stood. Swinging doors on the left apparently led to the kitchen; through an archway on the right she could see a library. They sat in chintz-cushioned wicker chairs around a glass-topped coffee table and sipped from eggshell cups. Lydia half expected a flock of canaries to flutter through the treetops at her feet.

"Lovely tea."

"Ceylon," said Caroline. "A friend sends it from the Sri Lankan embassy in London. This is Dimbula."

Probably everything in this house, Lydia reflected, has a story. Carlo was already telling her about the old Town Hall: built in 1736, when Quansett was an independent village. He and Caroline bought it after the town fathers condemned it forty years ago. All public functions had long since moved to a modern complex on the south side, with plenty of parking and electric heat. ("And haven't they regretted *that!*" said Caroline.) For years the two of them came up from New York whenever they could, sleeping on the floor at first, drafting artist friends to help with their massive remodeling job. Ten years ago they formally retired and moved here full-time. Their favorite set designer painted the faux-flagstone floor; the urns and sarcophagi were props from *The Merry Minotaur*, the fountain from *Daisy of Spain*, pieced back together by Carlo with help from a local plumber. Caroline did most of the planting and pruning. ("Future topiary," said Carlo, "if Edgar gets his way.")

"And your friend DeAnne made our wonderful stage curtain."

"We'd been concerned about the pianos," Carlo explained. "Even up high and under covers, whether the dampness would bother them."

"DeAnne, half joking, suggested a giant shower curtain."

"Which we recognized immediately was a brilliant idea."

It's as if they're handing me an opening, Lydia thought. "She was amazing at that kind of thing. Did she ever tell you about our business in Cambridge, the Fix-It Chix?"

"Oh, yes," said Carlo. "With the greatest of pride."

"Your business?" Caroline arched an eyebrow. "Were you . . . ?"

"Under a different name."

She braced for questions; but Carlo spoke cheerily to Caroline. "Rather like our opera." And to Lydia: "We can't refer to it by title until it's finished. We call it the opera, or the project."

"A silly theater superstition," added Caroline. "Like calling

Macbeth the Scottish play."

"But not a problem unless we're working on more than one. Which is always a mistake anyhow. So it does serve a purpose."

"More tea?" Caroline lifted the pot: white porcelain, like the cups and saucers, delicately garlanded with flowers.

"Did you like DeAnne?" Lydia asked her.

The question hung in the air, while the teapot descended over her cup, pouring out a fragrant steaming arc the color of maple syrup.

"Yes," Caroline said. "We chose her out of a dozen or so applicants. Carlo?"

He nodded, and answered as she refilled his cup. "She had a flair we hoped to encourage. It's difficult for young people here. They can spend their whole lives on Cape Cod and never find out what possibilities the larger world has to offer."

"DeAnne had crossed the bridge and liked it, so we were hopeful she'd persist."

"And did she?"

"Alas, not quite as one could wish," Carlo said.

"She fell back in with local friends. And of course, living at home . . . " Caroline sat back in her chair and gazed into her tea-cup. The sculptural smoothness of her platinum hair reminded Lydia of DeAnne's high-school portrait.

"I went to see her parents yesterday," she said. "I'd never met them. It seemed like the thing to do."

"They blame us." Caroline's head came up. "Did they tell you?"

"Yes. Her father did. Emphatically, I'm afraid."

"Not surprising, really." Carlo poked at the remains of an eclair with his fork. "She should have died hereafter. Speaking of the Scottish play."

"I hope it's just sound and fury, signifying nothing," Lydia replied.

"What I saw was not so much Macbeth as Lear with the dead Cordelia." A note of severity had come into Caroline's voice. "There's the tragedy! Bullying the poor child while she lived, and then raging at the heavens for the consequences."

Carlo concurred. "I don't imagine he'd be so angry if he didn't in his heart feel responsible."

"Honestly, I despair of this culture of ours." Caroline sat forward. "Responding to death not by asking 'Who can I grieve with?' or 'How can we help each other?' but 'Who can I be angry at? Who can I hurt in return for my pain?'"

"We were devastated," Carlo told Lydia. "In our home! A girl we worked with every day and cared for!" He set down his fork. "I'll never forget. Coming in afterwards. Seeing her poor little clogs beside the ladder. Like slippers beside the bed, waiting."

Caroline poured him more tea, as if this were a gesture of comfort she had performed many times in the past month. "He got no joy from the police," she stated. "With that attitude. Insisting it must be our fault. When we weren't there, and hadn't sent her up the ladder, and in fact had told her to stop working and join us. Helen Wills I understand was quite sharp with him."

Lydia took a macaroon. "Do you have any idea why DeAnne fell off that ladder?"

"No," said Caroline. "In a word."

"Strictly speaking," said Carlo, "she and the ladder apparently fell together. But no. Why did she even tackle the wretched curtain? Alistair was the last one to come over, and he said she was just tidying up, on her way to join us. His crew would have done it the next day."

"It wasn't like her," Caroline concluded.

"That's what I'd say," nodded Lydia. "She did carpentry with me for almost three months, and I never saw her do a job she didn't have to, or take a chance she didn't have to."

She bit off a chunk of macaroon. Carlo and Caroline sipped their tea.

"If Alistair was the last one to come over, do you think– Could he have asked her to do it?"

A quick glance passed between them. "I doubt that," said Caroline. "But it is possible she was trying to impress him."

"We were awfully dull for her. You see," Carlo gestured, "how quiet it is here."

"Alistair may be three thousand miles from Hollywood, but at least he's a filmmaker. DeAnne would have left us for him in a minute, and who could blame her?"

"You mean, she might have been angling for a job?" Lydia's cheeks reddened. "I didn't think Alistair had any employees."

"He doesn't," said Caroline.

"He might not have mentioned that to DeAnne," said Carlo.

For a moment no one spoke.

"Well," said Caroline at last, "there's no point going on about it. Everything we can say we've said many times over. It's a sad, sad thing, that's all."

She carried the teapot out through the swinging doors. I should follow her, thought Lydia. Help with the dishes, tour the kitchen . . .

"Do you want to see where it happened?" Carlo asked.

"Oh. Well, yes. Actually I do."

So instead of Caroline in her ruffled apron she followed Carlo, whose salt-and-pepper hair, green pullover sweater, khaki pants, and loafers gave him the air of an ecologically conscious golfer.

"Does Caroline mind?" she asked when they reached the ground floor.

"Oh, no. She's just a bit more squeamish than I am. Or you are, I think."

He led her diagonally past the fountain to the a spot under the edge of the balcony. "Here," he said. "The film crew hung up a reflecting curtain along this side, so they could shoot toward the fountain. Movie lights over there," he pointed across the room. "After they wrapped, as they say, we all went over to the Whistling Pig to celebrate. DeAnne stayed behind to put things back in order. Apparently she decided to take down the curtain."

"And she set up the ladder for that?"

"The crew had left it up, but pushed it back out of the shot, so she'd have had to drag it over here."

"Not easy, but not that hard." Lydia walked under the balcony, picturing the scene from both sides. "How was the curtain held up?"

"That was quite clever really. Naturally we wouldn't let them nail it into the wood. So they screwed eyes–you know, steel loops?–into a two-by-four, which they laid behind the railing. Then fastened the curtain onto the eyes with hooks through grommets along the top, like a sail."

"But then couldn't she have unhooked it from the balcony?"

"You would think so, wouldn't you? Much safer. Unwieldy, though. The angle, and the runners for our shades, plus the weight of the curtain– Fastening or unfastening, they found it was easier to manage from below, from a ladder, than from above, reaching through the railing."

The bottom of the balcony, Lydia estimated, was twelve feet up, and the railing three feet higher. To unhook the curtain from eyes between the newel posts, DeAnne must have stood precariously near the top of her ten-foot stepladder. "She'd have set the ladder parallel to the curtain, right?–or she couldn't have reached the hooks. But if she tried to brace it against one of the balcony pillars, for stability, that would pin the curtain in place. So it must have stood out here on the floor, with no other support. "

Carlo was picking fuzz-balls off his sleeve. "When the crew hung the curtain up, someone on the ground held onto the ladder."

"As they damn well should have to take it down. Something that massive, that heavy–" Lydia shook her head. "Oh, DeAnne! What were you thinking?"

For a long moment her gaze moved from the ceiling to the balcony and along the railing, as if searching for some trace of what had happened. "Was that the police verdict? The weight of the curtain coming down knocked over the ladder?"

"Oh, they didn't confide in us. But what else could it be?"

"With her up so high and leaning out so far . . . " Lydia sighed, imagining DeAnne's alarm, then horror, at the instant she realized she was falling. "And she landed . . . where?"

Carlo about-faced and took three giant steps. "Here."

Standing beside the fountain, he pointed at a frog. "Oh, hell," said Lydia.

"Well, exactly. This is a prop, you know, so none of the stone parts are real; but the frogs are bronze on a steel frame to hold the plumbing. Poor DeAnne hit her head at just the wrong spot."

"Did you find her?"

"No, mercifully. Helen Wills happened to come by, from the state police–she wanted to watch the filming; we'd had a steady stream of onlookers–and she saw the door open, so she took a look inside. She called Kevin Kelly, that's our local policeman, and he came and found us. They had taken her away by the time we got here."

For a long moment they stood without speaking. The chuckling murmur of the fountain, the flicker of light in the moving water, seemed bent on erasing any trace of that horrific evening.

"You were Liz?" Carlo inquired.

"Yeah."

"DeAnne admired you enormously. She spoke of the Fix-It Chix as a turning point. When she realized for the first time that she had abilities she could use to shape her future." He paused. "She felt that she had treated you badly, and she regretted that. She wanted to make amends."

Lydia looked at him: not his kind earnest face, but his fingers picking lint off his sweater.

"Only she didn't know how. She'd made too big a mess to fix, she said–like putting Humpty Dumpty back together again."

"Oh, my god, Carlo . . . "

"I know, I am sorry, it's a dreadful image in retrospect, isn't it? But the point is, Lydia, DeAnne truly wanted to apologize, to try and repair your broken friendship."

Lydia let out a long sigh. "She did try. She sent me a postcard. Two days before . . . My life was so screwed up then, I hardly even read it. Not an apology–at least I didn't take it as one–more like, hey, no hard feelings, come visit. She sounded so cheery I wanted to punch her. And then I e-mailed her and it bounced back, and everything kept getting worse, and finally I threw my stuff in the car and ran. I guess I hoped, or thought, if I just showed up here . . . "

"Yes! Absolutely right!" Carlo patted her shoulder, gingerly, as if she might shatter.

"She wanted me to meet you. And see your studio." Suddenly Lydia's eyes were swimming. "I had no idea . . . "

"Of course not," he soothed.

"I should have done something! What if I'd come sooner? Or called her house? Anything! If I'd done anything at all, things might have shifted just enough, a fraction of an inch, for that moment not to happen."

"Lydia, my dear. We all think that. Everyone who knew her. It's impossibly arrogant, but who can help it?"

And he was here, she realized. He and Caroline were half a mile down the street. Celebrating with the movie people, while DeAnne stayed behind to clean up their studio.

They have to go on living where she died. While her father sics the cops on them, and no doubt any neighbors and media he can persuade, too.

"Oh, Carlo."

He patted her shoulder with more assurance. "Shall we rejoin Caroline?"

"Yes." She gave him a quick hug. "Thanks."

Chapter Ten

Evening was Wallace Hicks's favorite time to walk in the woods behind the post office. As long as he kept tossing the frisbee, Gromit would stay close and not run after skunks, leaving Wally free to reflect on karma.

Just when you'd had enough of hanging around here with one foot on the platform and one foot on the train. Just when you'd vowed to fish or cut bait. Kaboom! In walks a retired (or, you might say, re-tired) sports hero and kicks off a whole new ballgame.

Surprises had been dropping out of the sky lately faster than bird poop onto customers' cars. Just an hour ago, Rosey Sherman had flung open the door with a big grin on his face. Those two DePina boys were something else! Strong as a bulldog, that Rudy, with a wicked sense of humor; and Louis had the smarts and size to grow into a basketball player. Two large pizzas with everything they'd put away, the four of them. Oh, right, had he mentioned? He'd stopped by the Par-Tee Cone to meet their mother. Indira. Real nice girl. Turned out her boss was a Pats fan and let her off work early. Would you believe, with that mocha skin and black hair, she grew up on a Norwegian fiord! Heck of a story, couldn't follow it all–her mom was the sister of a Cape Verde tuna fisherman rescued at sea by her dad? who'd sailed down from Norway to negotiate with the Moroccans (or Angolans)? Anyhow, here Indira was, stuck on Cape Cod with two sons by a Portuguese captain who'd gone down with his trawler (the Indira, naturally) in Hurricane Bob. Now how was a girl like that supposed to manage? Scooping ice cream and handing out mini-golf shoes–was that any way to support two kids? Living on Section 8 in a fleabag motel! Well, we'd just see about that, the minute– Oh, right, had he mentioned? Ken Boose was going to sell him the Frigate. They'd just done the inspections this morning.

There wasn't much Wally could say but congratulations. When would the deal close? Wednesday. Then spruce up for a grand reopening Fourth of July weekend. Pretty quick, with so much to do. Rosey sure hoped Wally would stay on, seeing as he'd be the resident expert on just about everything once Ken left. Could they work out details later? Over dinner, say, at some water-front seafood place? Right now Rosey had to get back to Boston. Being with Indira and her boys reminded him how much he'd dumped on poor Thea lately. With more to come, she being the decorator in the family. She sure had enjoyed meeting Wally yes-terday. And the kids–Mike, Serena, even baby Shawn–had to be dragged away from playing with Gromit.

A cloud of dust, thought Wally as the SUV patched out of the parking lot, and a hearty hi-yo Silver! Away!

He'd felt dizzy, like anyone who'd just been unexpectedly sandbagged, and elated, like anyone who'd just been unexpectedly rescued. Both sensations bubbled inside him now as he scuffed along the path. Throwing the frisbee, wiping dog slime off his hand onto his jeans, Wallace Hicks hardly noticed the brilliant rhododendron blossoms, the new-leafed trees, root-ribbed path, or mud-rimmed pond. This was the future he was walking into!

As the resident expert on just about everything, couldn't he just about write his own ticket?

Was this the reward at last for his months of patience? For his faith that eventually the great wheel would turn from scarcity to abundance? With money, CodCast.net could rise to the next level. And with the dawn of a glorious new era for the cyber-conscience of Cape Cod, Wallace Bartholomew Hicks, AKA Pirandello, could finally launch his mission.

Funny, when you recalled that CodCast.net didn't even exist a year ago. He hadn't even been sure until the Airstream reached the Sagamore rotary that he was ready to cross that bridge. Trundling along Old King's Highway, admiring the fall foliage, he'd figured what the heck, might as well go on to Quansett. Say hi to Ken Boose, see how he was doing with his bookstore. Did he want a hand with those boxes in the parking lot? Next thing Wally knew it was two weeks later and he was still there. Helping out every afternoon, at a desk upstairs with such a fine view of the Frigate's front door and porte-cochere that, what the heck, why not set up a webcam? Now what was missing was a blog, to explain what his eye in the sky saw. Not enough, until he added a second, mobile webcam which panned from the mulberry tree over the parking lot, across Route 6A to Leo's driveway and the shops along the street, down toward the bank, back across to the Whistling Pig, and home again to the Frigate. Now, that was something! Each camera recorded the equivalent of a still photo every two minutes–enabling Wally to catch the DePina kids sneaking around Rosey Sherman's SUV with a knife. He doubted they had set out after this particular target. More likely they'd found the knife someplace and it burned a hole in Louis's pocket till he spotted that big old Mercedes. (And if the man believed those stories of their mom's, well, he and Gromit ought to get along like a house afire.)

The two-cam set-up had cost him a bundle, or would by the time he eventually paid it off. But suppose you could add a third camera, scanning all of Quansett from atop the Frigate's brick chimney. Who on the whole Cape, from Bourne to P'town, could remain ignorant of Pirandello then? Not Rosey Sherman nor Kevin Kelly nor any other person whose name Wally Hicks didn't choose to mention, even to himself, until the mission was ready for launch.

Step One: funding.

Over their seafood dinner he'd give the man a taste of what CodCast.net could do for his bookstore. Wally already had some waterfront restaurants in mind, that a guy like him couldn't set foot in unless a guy like Roosevelt Sherman was paying.

For now, he would listen to the siren song of half a Reuben sandwich, left over from lunch, calling to him from the Airstream's pint-sized icebox.

In the post-office lot a single car was parked. Gromit trotted over to investigate: an ancient Toyota, rusted and dented, blue-green paint faded to patchy aquamarine. Nobody in it apparently. Wally was pretty sure he'd seen it before–you'd notice that color, like a kids' wading pool–but he couldn't recall whose it was.

If Lydia had glanced in her rear-view mirror the next morning when she got to work, she'd have seen the same car parked behind the jewelry store that shared the Back End's lot. Instead she watched Mudge emerging from the Elephant Tree. He carried a rolled-up sleeping bag which he tossed into his truck. She waited for him at the front walk.

"What is it with the crows?"

A pair of the big black birds had swooped across the Morris's hood as she pulled in. Several more were cawing loudly between the Back End's roof and the tree.

"Donno, but they woke me up." Mudge was buttoning a blue cotton work shirt over the white T-shirt he'd presumably slept in. "My mom always thought they were a bad omen. My dad never believed in that stuff. He says they like the Cape for the road kill."

She held the door for him. "I thought your truck was fixed."

"Yeah, she's doing OK. I was just out so late last night– Oh, shit."

Lydia didn't grasp that he'd changed the subject until she saw an unfamiliar woman standing in the kitchen. Short and stocky, around her own age, with tousled red hair, ragged jeans and sweat-shirt, and a familiar-looking chef's apron.

"So call him then!" she flung at Dinah. "Ask him whose kit-chen it is!"

Dinah–arms folded, scowling fiercely–swiveled as Lydia and Mudge came in. The newcomer followed her gaze and broke into a smile.

"Hey, Mudge!"

"Sue." He didn't sound enthusiastic.

"Good news! I'm back."

Lydia's stomach clenched like a fist.

"Sue," said Dinah emphatically, "meet Lydia. Our new assist-ant chef."

"Ha!" Her giggle lasted a little too long. "Yeah. Right."

Lydia hung her jacket on its usual peg by the restroom alcove. Just act normal, she told herself. Like she said–it's not up to us, it's up to Leo.

With clumsy fingers she tied her apron strings around her

waist. Remarkable how fast you can get used to a job. Even if you grabbed it on the rebound. Even when you knew about Sue's famous boomerang routine. Even though this was only your sixth day of the week's trial you'd agreed to with Leo. Who then handed you the cottage of your dreams, and if that wasn't a seal on the deal, what was it?

Sue had vanished. Fled? No such luck. There was her elbow behind the refrigerator.

Half an hour till Leo's grand entrance. Like Caesar: thumbs up or down?

The Fix-It Chix in smithereens. Her bank account empty. The Caffe Firenze turned into a Starbucks. And Mr. Dickhead Rat Bastard–

Mudge slithered into his apron beside her. "Don't get into it with her," he murmured.

"Tell her that!"

Lydia strode across the kitchen like Clint Eastwood. "So what have we got?" she asked Dinah.

"Three toast for the yellow booth. One white, two brown. Mudge, coffee for you me and Lydia."

Sue reappeared with a bowl of strawberries. "Brown and white! Old Leo still won't branch out, huh? None of that ooh, weird crap, like Portuguese sweetbread." She set the strawberries on the sandwich counter, across from the grill, and grabbed a cleaver. "Dinah, you want these sliced?"

"Not by you."

Sue poured strawberries across the cutting board and flourished the cleaver like a TV cowboy's revolver.

"Stop that!"

Mudge stepped between them. "Coffee," he handed a mug to Dinah. "Sue, why don't you go sit down and I'll fix you some eggs."

"I'm fine." Chop-chop-chop.

"The heck you are," said Dinah. "I'm not gonna keep saying it. No unauthorized personnel this side of the register."

Chop-chop-chop-chop-chop.

Lydia, standing by the tall revolving toaster on the other side of the kitchen, spread butter on two slices of white toast and four of whole wheat. She stacked the plates along her arm, as Mudge shot an inquiring look at Dinah.

Before she'd taken three steps, a bowl of strawberries was twirling through the air in Mudge's hand.

"Put that back." Sue raised her cleaver at him. "Now!"

Lydia flipped toast onto toast and whizzed the empty plate like a Frisbee straight at Sue.

"Ow! Goddammit!"

The cleaver clattered to the floor in a crash of crockery. Mudge scooped it up by the handle without dropping a strawberry.

A cheer rose from the regulars at the counter.

Sue was hopping and clutching her wrist in pain, shouting pungent epithets at Lydia.

"Come on," Mudge murmured, and steered her, hobbling and cursing, toward the door.

"All right, all right." Dinah moved along the counter with the coffee pot. "Show's over, folks. Eat up or get out."

She turned to Lydia. "And *you*! Some arm you got there. Now that toast's worthless, probably full of slivers. Go make some fresh."

As Lydia placed a new row of brown and white slices on the rack, she could still hear Sue in the parking lot, yelling over the crows.

Although part of Lydia felt sorry for Sue, kicked out of a job she took for granted, a larger part vacillated between anger, worry, and relief. Anger: Who did she think she was, tritzing in after six days' absence like she owned the place? Worry: What if her retreat wasn't a surrender but only a strategic withdrawal? Relief: Bless Dinah and Mudge for standing fast!

She left it to them (and the customers) to brief Leo. Her function here was soup, not entertainment.

Not that the Back End's breathless pace gave her much choice. When Leo arrived, Lydia was pouring waffles. She did see Dinah take him aside near the cash register, but she couldn't hear them.

Edgar Rowdey came in then, and Leo went off to trade insults with him. The rest of the morning whizzed by so fast that she almost forgot about Sue.

She also forgot about yesterday's round with Alistair Pope until, as lunch was ending, she heard a familar ring. There he was, checking his cell phone, stowing it inside his jacket, sitting down to face her across the counter.

"You're looking well, Ms. Vivaldi."

"Thanks." You too, she didn't say, with a clean shirt and your hair combed back instead of straggling all over. "Did you solve your crisis?"

"What? Oh. Yes, I did. And two or three more since then. No rest for the wicked, which I'm sure you know includes all of us in the film business. How were the pastries?"

"Outstanding. How's that soup holding up?"

"Superb. Even better than yesterday. Are you ready for Tea, Take Two?"

She stabbed toothpicks into a BLT. "Sure, why not."

"Meet you outside when you're through."

Leo was approaching, so she nodded and moved down the counter to add a pickle slice and potato chips. Sue never was this conscientious, was she? So don't tell me I have to give her job back. And while we're at it?–don't twit me about Alistair Pope.

"He must really like you," Leo murmured, loud enough for Alistair to hear. "This is twice now he shut off his cell phone. Never seen that before."

"Excuse me, I've got work to do." Lydia stepped around him with her BLT in the air.

Leo sidestepped to block her. "Hey, slugger, I hear you got a heck of an arm there."

"You want to see it in action, keep standing between me and the guy who ordered this sandwich."

"Ooh!" He backed away in mock alarm. "I don't know if we've got enough plates for another catfight in the kitchen. One a day's about all we can handle."

When she glared at him, he added, "Don't point that thing at me! I'm an old man. I wouldn't have a chance against a rising young champ like you. You just keep up the good work and I'll get out of your way."

He scuttled toward the toaster. Lydia's mood rose like a helium balloon. Coming from Leo, that was high praise.

So all was well! She still had her job, Sue hadn't returned, Alistair was about to serve her tea and show her his house–

She set down the BLT with a smile, and glanced up to see an FBI agent standing in the doorway.

No. This was Quansett. And that was a woman. Charcoal pantsuit, pin-striped blue shirt, black pumps and shoulderbag. Dark hair pulled back from a face masked by aviator sunglasses.

Is she staring at me? Lydia wondered in panic. Every questionable act she had recently committed raced through her mind. Did I break Sue's arm? Has DeAnne's father gone on the warpath? Am I parked wrong?

The silhouette in the doorway removed her glasses. "Hey, Leo." A flat husky contralto. "Fried any stray cats lately?"

"Well now we're fresh out. But for you, Detective Wills?–I'll just go on out back and check my traps."

"Hey! Hell On Wheels!" As she came inside, the recipient of the BLT grabbed her hand. "What's new in the world of crime?"

"Not much at my end, Rick. How about yours?"

"Still on the loose, as you see. Old Chill back from spring training yet?"

"Not yet. Four more days."

"What's taking him so long?" Dinah threw in from the kitchen. "Havin' too much fun down there at Disney World?"

"Most likely. Chill sure does enjoy wrestling those alligators. Hey, Al."

Another handshake. "Hello, Helen. What brings you to this neck of the woods?"

She slid onto the stool next to him. "What's this I hear about a Mercedes slasher in the neighborhood?"

"Oh, that wasn't *here.*" Leo's skinny frame bent toward her, his voice and bushy white eyebrows bristling theatrically. "That was across the street. We don't encourage that element in our parking lot. You ask Istair here."

"I just did."

Alistair shrugged. "First I've heard of it."

Even to Lydia he sounded almost too nonchalant. The newcomer said, "You would tell me, right? If you got hit, or if you had any knowledge or information?"

"Certainly."

"Maybe your perp only goes for those new fancy SUV kind of vehicle," Leo suggested. "Not the old broken-down beat-up kind like Istair's got."

"No tire problems around here at all?" She slid her shoulderbag onto the counter. "Or suspicious activity?" Her hair was clipped back in a tortoiseshell barrette. Her face was broad and square, her olive-green eyes slightly almond-shaped, with thick black lashes. She exuded a female strength that reminded Lydia of DeAnne. "Well, that's good news."

"Makes your job easier," seconded Rick through a mouthful of bacon, lettuce, and tomato.

"Let's hope," she returned.

"You think it's like a grudge thing?" Dinah asked. "Against the Pats? Or him personally? Racism, maybe?"

"Could be. Or just like a general message: 'Stranger go home.' This town isn't always the most . . . "

"Hospitable?" Leo set a cup of soup in front of her. "Hah! You want hospitable, try this. Today's special: Star of India soup. Created by my brilliant new sous-chef."

She looked at him, then at Lydia, fixing her again with a you-must-be-guilty-of-something stare. "And your name is?"

"Oh, heavens to Betsy! This is Lydia Vivaldi. Helen Wills, state police detective and ace crime fighter."

The one who found DeAnne's body. "I'm glad to meet you," Lydia said.

"Yeah." Helen Wills stuck out a muscular hand. "Welcome to Quansett."

There it was, that same car. A beat-up turquoise Camry. Wallace Hicks rose from his computer, where he had just watched it crunch into the Frigate parking lot, and craned out the window. Yup, thar she blows! A real antique–one of the old 5-doors with the hatchback, before they flush-mounted the headlights. 1986? Whoever was driving it must thank his lucky stars that baby still ran.

Not a he but a she. Hair like an osprey nest, at least from up here. Built like a fireplug. Still, a customer's a customer. Wally swung his chair around and reached for his crystal-headed cane.

From the greetings Ken Boose was exchanging with the newcomer, he guessed she must be local. Ken didn't rouse himself these days for washashores. Gromit was sashaying around the two of them, tail wagging frantically, nose poking into the girl's blue-jeaned legs. She scratched his head with the hand that wasn't shaking Ken's.

I know her, Wally realized. That's Sue, from Leo's.

"Hey, Wally!" She half-turned. "How you been?"

"Can't complain. You?"

She looked almost as badly in need of an overhaul as her car. Besides her scrambled hair, both knees of her jeans and one elbow of her rumpled sweatshirt were frayed to fringe; and none too clean, either.

"I was just telling Ken, I feel like I been gone a month. What was it, like a week? Time sure flies when you're having fun!"

"Sue's been on vacation," Ken informed him. "Up in P-town."

"Early bird." Wally shook her hand. "Still kinda chilly on those beaches, eh?"

"Yeah, well, got to get in before the tourists."

"Right. Almost summer. Hard to believe."

"I'll be in the office," said Ken Boose. "You need a book, Sue, just ask Wally." He shambled between stacks and disappeared behind the door.

"Hey, Ken, nice to see you," Sue called after him.

There was a game Wally slipped into when customers came in: What book will they buy? After almost a year he was pretty good at matching folks with a genre, although he hadn't yet guessed a specific title. Sue was easy: None. If this girl ever picked up a heavier volume than *TV Guide*, Wallace Hicks would be very surprised indeed. He doubted she would even read a cookbook unless

Dinah flattened it on the counter in front of her.

So he skipped over his professional duties and asked: "Did he tell you the big news?"

Sue's blank look was such an obvious No that Wally wondered if he'd put his foot in it. Ken Boose had yet to say a word to him about selling the Frigate. Maybe Rosey Sherman's announcement was meant to be confidential. Better not take chances.

"We had a tire-slashing here a couple days ago. Mercedes SUV. Belonged to the football star Roosevelt Sherman."

"Huh! I heard of him. Who did it? Do you know?"

"As a matter of fact, since you ask, I was the one who solved the case."

"You? You're shittin' me."

"Nope. Swear to God. But–" He mimed buttoning his lips.

"Oh, so, what, you're the FBI now?" She sounded skeptical. Hell with it, thought Wally. Some chances a man just has to take.

"Does the name Pirandello ring a bell?"

"You mean, like, CodCast-dot-net? Sure. Best blog on the Net. Why?"

It was a moment so sweet that Wally stretched it out to a full half minute before he told her.

Chapter Eleven

Helen Wills didn't try the Star of India soup. She was gone when Lydia returned from serving the last orders in the back room. So was Alistair. Buying more pastries, Lydia hoped, especially that poppyseed cake.

Again she took her time cleaning up, waiting for the others to leave before she went out to meet him. Mudge had asked her while they shared leftovers if she and Alistair Pope were . . . you know. She'd retorted that no, she didn't know, but no, they weren't. He'd invited her to tea, that's all. To see his historic house. Why? Did the entire staff of Leo's Back End think she should watch out for Alistair Pope?

Mudge shrugged: No opinion. Just asking.

They agreed to have another Flying Wedge meeting soon, and exchanged phone numbers. Lydia told Mudge she'd be home in an hour and a half if he wanted to use her shower.

Now the yellow Morris and Alistair's blue Mercedes were the only cars in the lot. He'd probably offer to drive again. So she didn't need her fleece jacket . . .

Walking around to toss it on the passenger seat, Lydia saw that both tires on this side were flat.

Not just deflated. The wheel rims rested on asphalt.

"Fuck!" she shouted to the crows. "Double triple quadruple fuck!"

What with her new job, new cottage, and new life, she'd never taken her old tire to a garage. And that was for patching; even if you could afford it, you couldn't just stop in anyplace and buy a new Morris tire. Like the gearshift, which resembled an insect's antenna, they were toylike compared to American cars. Whoever had done this had immobilized her for a good while.

She crouched to look closer. Multiple stab wounds, apparently, although it was hard to tell from the crumpled rubber.

This couldn't be a coincidence. Not right after a warning from a state police detective.

Was there a mad slasher on the loose? Or was someone sending her a message? "Stranger go home"?

Who'd want to get rid of her, though, after just six days? Helen Wills? That made no sense. A copycat, then? One of the customers who'd overheard her questions, or heard through the grapevine about the incident across the street?

Not Alistair, surely.

"Fuck," Lydia repeated, as the obvious answer caught up with her.

When he crossed the parking lot with yet another pink cardboard box of pastries, Alistair was shocked and sympathetic. "What a terrible thing to do to you!"

He crouched to inspect the damage. "Mm. Definitely a knife. I don't know what to say, Lydia. Except please don't think this reflects anyone's opinion but one disturbed and jealous individual."

Straightening up, he gathered her into a hug. Lydia burrowed gratefully against his shoulder. "My poor car!" she lamented into his army jacket.

"And your impossible fourteen-inch tires!" Alistair rubbed her back. "Well, we'll just have to call Triple A and twist some arms."

"First," she untwisted herself from his arms, "I need a sugar fix."

They opened the pastry box on the Morris's hood. Alistair snapped the string with a single yank. Lydia skipped the poppyseed cake for a brownie.

"I have to say, though, this is not like Sue. She's normally an easygoing person." He bit into an eclair.

"What, so it's my fault? I unhinged her?"

"No, no! It's strange, that's all. Not a reaction I'd have predicted."

"I guess the job thing must have hit her harder than we realized." Lydia licked chocolate off her fingers. "I'm not sure what I should tell that detective."

"Tell what detective?"

"What's her name, Helen Wills? You remember, she said to let her know if anything like this happened. Weird, huh?"

"Mm! Well, all of it, don't you think? You and me meeting over your flat tire last week, right after Sue took off, and then somebody slashing Rosey Sherman's tires at the bookstore, and Sue showing up this morning and Helen this afternoon, and now here we are, our second attempt to have tea, and we're back at Square One. Do you have a napkin in this car? Or a paper towel?"

I know some other ways to remove that blob of custard from your chin, Lydia thought. But not here. Not now.

"Let's go inside," she proposed instead. "There's a whole sink. Plus a phone."

"I'd offer you mine, but the reception here is a joke."

"No problem. I'll use the land line."

Finding Leo's hidden key, unlocking his empty restaurant, she felt more like a criminal than ever, never mind the afternoon sun lighting their way. Leo himself had gone out as usual after they closed. Still, she stifled an urge to tiptoe.

"Triple A says maybe an hour," she told Alistair when he emerged from the men's room. "I left a message for Detective Wills. What do you think? Should we have tea here?"

"Not a chance! You've been chained to this galley all day. Come on."

He led her across the parking lot to the street. "I hope you're not one of those people who doesn't like bookstores. And mulberries."

"Mulberries?" Her brain did a quick search. "Like silkworms eat?"

"Close, but no gold star. Silkworms eat the leaves." They poised on the verge, waiting for a break between passing cars. "Have you been in the Frigate?"

"Not yet."

"You must. It's extraordinary. Like a gigantic yard sale. Organized on the same principle as Boston street signs: if you don't know where you are, you shouldn't be here."

"Is that where we're going?"

"For tea? No."

They dashed across Route 6A. "This tree," said Alistair as they came under it, "is one of the best-kept secrets in town. Every June, about two weeks from now, a rich crop of mulberries will start dropping in a purple mess onto the sidewalk, onto boxes of books, unwary tourists, and passing cars. Every year Ken Boose threatens to cut down the tree, and the usual suspects including myself talk him out of it. But the one thing nobody does, aside from me and several hundred birds, is pick the berries."

The tree was magnificent: not as massive as the Elephant Tree, but vast and venerable, its arching, angled branches drooping with small green leaves.

"We'll come back in two weeks for you to try them."

Ahead and to their right, opposite the Frigate's porte-cochere, a swathe of unmown grass separated the parking lot from a long driveway next door. Alistair led Lydia across this plush green carpet to a trio of boulders. He wriggled a tall bottle of iced tea out of his pocket. On the tallest rock he set his pink cardboard box and the tea. On the shortest one he spread his army jacket.

"Madame, your table is ready."

"What about my car?"

"No worries. We'll see the truck from here."

They sat basking in the sunshine. Lydia let Alistair talk while she ate poppyseed cake. She expected more about his house, or maybe his films. Instead, prompted perhaps by the setting, he launched a friendly lecture on the books of Edgar Rowdey. What? She hadn't read one since childhood? Sacrilege! Any librarian should be strung up by her thumbs who'd give *Hidden Turnips* or *Havoc at Happenstance Hall* to children. She must try again! "Get past the plot, that's the first thing. Like Nabokov. It's just a vehicle for the writing, and in Rowdey's case, the drawings. Stunning per se, but absolutely riveting in counterpoint: simple and subtle, straightforward and secretive. What child can appreciate that? I ask you! Pearls before swine."

She let his voice flow over her. When he finally paused for a swig of tea, she stepped in.

"Alistair, there's something I–"

"The man's a genius," he added. "People use that word lightly, even about me on occasion, but in his case it's the plain truth. Photographic memory. He's read everything, and remembers all of it."

"Yes, well. There's something I need your help with."

He made an encouraging sound.

"I'm not doing so great with losing my friend DeAnne. I really want to know what happened that last day. Anything you can tell me. Like, why'd she stay at the studio instead of join the party at the Pig? Taking down that heavy curtain. Wasn't that your crew's job?"

"Mm." He considered; handed her the bottle. "It's a mystery to me. You should ask Carlo and Caroline."

"I did. It's a mystery to them, too."

"Well, there you go." He brushed crumbs off his jacket.

"But you were the last one who saw her, weren't you? They said you came over after the crew. You said she was tidying up and she'd be there any minute."

"Did I?" He frowned. "You see, this is the drawback to being asked the same questions over and over. It fuzzes the original memory. I can vividly picture twiddling my thumbs for hours on end at police headquarters, but as far as that night . . . "

"Alistair, come on! What's the point of having a sharp mind if you don't use it? Focus! You're in the studio. Filming's over. Everybody's gone down to the Pig to celebrate, except you and DeAnne. Why? What's she doing?"

Alistair cocked his head at the mulberry tree. "Straightening cushions? Collecting coffee mugs, rinsing them out in the sink. I'm coiling cords and whatnot, waiting for her to finish. Nothing personal, but I don't like to leave that many thousand dollars' worth of equipment alone with someone who doesn't work for me and who may or may not remember to lock the door."

"Did you try to hurry her up?"

"Probably. She must have balked, since I did eventually go on without her."

"What changed your mind? Can you remember what you said to her? or she said to you?"

He was still considering when a tow truck turned into Leo's driveway. Lydia ran after it, wiping her hands on her jeans. Alistair gathered up their picnic and followed her.

The truck driver listened to Lydia, but when he finally spoke, he addressed Alistair. Part of her was annoyed–hadn't she just told him the Morris was hers? Another part was glad Alistair was here, since this young man–"Buddy," according to his shirt pocket–apparently had a problem with female car owners. When he left them to hook the chain onto the disabled Morris, Alistair assured her that Buddy was only a pumper of gas, and she could expect better from the mechanics at his shop. Which was not to say they'd necessarily stock her tires.

A flash of blue lights, a crunch of gravel, and an unmarked cruiser swept into the parking lot.

"Lydia, right? I got your message," said Helen Wills. "So what's the story here?"

She too spoke to Alistair. Lydia felt him weigh whether to make an issue of this and decide not to.

"Look for yourself." He led her around the truck.

Lydia stayed where she was. Obviously they know each other, she reasoned. As a woman you couldn't possibly climb to the position of detective if you were as sexist as a twenty-year-old grease monkey. But then what woman would become a state cop in the first place unless she liked dealing mostly with men?

She could hear their voices sporadically under the clank and clatter of Buddy hauling the Morris onto his flatbed. It's my car, she thought, but this sure is not my territory.

She retreated into the Back End to wash her hands and retousle her hair. Six days . . . After Sue worked here for how long? Six months? Six years? Was she a hometown girl, like DeAnne?

Just as well it's Alistair and not me accusing her of slashing tires.

Did he stonewall the cops about DeAnne, too, or just me?

Why? After the big seduction ritual, why blow his best chance to score? One tear-jerker reminiscence and I could be sobbing on his shoulder. Instead, I get this crap that he forgot he was the last person who saw her alive?

Stop! Lydia ordered her reflection in the ladies' room mirror. This is not the time! You have a wounded car to deal with. And not just Alistair but a state police detective waiting for you in the parking lot.

Buddy had the truck loaded and ready to pull out. Alistair and Helen Wills stood beside his window, talking. Alistair's face looked strained.

"Lydia." The detective stepped toward her. "You need to go to the garage with Buddy and your car. You can call your insurance company from there; tell them I've got the report. That'll save you a trip to the station."

"Thanks."

"You want to talk to Jim," Alistair advised tersely. "Owner and head mechanic. He's expecting you."

"He'll get you a ride home," added Helen Wills.

"Thanks," Lydia said again, feeling more than ever like a foreigner. "And Alistair, you're an angel. You're an archangel."

That made him smile. "Not at all."

She climbed into the cab beside Buddy, kicking aside two Pepsi cans, a half-flattened Burger King bag, and a clump of stiffened rags. Alistair had not, she noted, proposed a third time to have her over for tea.

Nor did he reissue his invitation the next day. Lydia had called Mudge from the service station and hit the jackpot: a ride home in his sputtering truck after the Morris was disposed of, followed by a ride to Hyannis for groceries, then company for a spaghetti dinner, and–the grand prize–a ride to work the following morning. Jim the mechanic had promised to move mountains to have her new tires by this afternoon.

Lydia half expected Alistair to appear at breakfast, impatient to hear the latest about her automotive adventures. Apparently he found the suspense more bearable than she did. Not until the Back End's clock (set five minutes fast) was striking two did he fling himself, gasping, through the door.

Mudge was at the cash register. Leo had already called it a day and taken off with some friends from Waltham. Lydia, having delivered the last lunches, was combining clean-up with her daily chat with Edgar Rowdey. Per Leo, she'd been careful not to treat him like a landlord; still, between her gratitude for the cottage and his appreciation for her soups, they were cautiously becoming friends. He'd taken to lingering later and later over his lunch, while she'd shifted her share of closing chores from the kitchen to the back room.

Dinah told her afterwards what she'd missed.

"Al comes busting in here like Rocky Raccoon, hollering he's so famished he could eat a stega-saw-wus, and Mudge says Sorry, we're closed. Well, you know Al, or maybe you don't, but anyhow, he never was one to take no for an answer. Awright then, just a bowl a chili, he tells Mudge. Who says again: Sorry, but we're closed. No yaw not, says Al. Didn't you see me just come through that daw? Now me, I'm over scraping down the grill, grease up to my elbows, keeping my mouth shut so's not to jump in and stir things up worse. Mudge being a more agreeable kind of person, as I'm the first to admit. And he tells Al, nice as pie, That door's only open for folks to go out. And Al says, I didn't see any sign to that effect. Waya's Lydia?"

"Oh, god," said Lydia. "Where was I?"

"Out back dumping the steam tables," Dinah replied with relish. "Which Mudge so informs him. And Al, being way up on his high horse by now, tells Mudge to go get you. 'She'll make shaw I don't stahv.' Well, Mudge is up to here. I mean, checks to ring up, and the bell and the horn– So he tells Al it's his choice, go try the Pig or come back tomorrow, but the Back End is flat closed! And Al busts a gasket. Who the hell do you think you ah, snotty kid, wait till Leo heahs about this– So that's when I come round and open the door and say Al, you heard the man, get your butt on outta here NOW."

Lydia stood mesmerized with a jar lid in her hand. "And he went?"

"Damn right he went! I could whup him when we were kids

and I can whup him now. As well he knows."

That Lydia doubted; but Dinah's round face was so ruddy with pride that she just shook her head in admiration.

"Not right off, o' course. Can't back down from a woman right in front o' people. So he mutters something about gonna find Lydia, and glares at me. Tail between his legs."

"He didn't, though. Find me."

"No. Lucky for him, and you, Edgar Rowdey comes up to the register right then. 'Shall we go check on the frogs?' If you ask me, he heard every word. Figured he'd give Al a way to save face."

"What a sweetheart! Isn't he?" Lydia screwed the lid onto the jar and carried it to the refrigerator.

Dinah nodded. "Nicest famous person I ever met. So that was that." She resumed wrapping leftovers. "Off they go into the sunset."

"What about Mudge? Where is he?"

"Most likely out back doin' a Wampanoag victory dance." She grinned. "Some day, huh? Start off with Sue goin' wacko and end up with Al. Must be a full moon!"

And that's that for the tea plan, said Lydia to herself. Throw a tantrum over a bowl of chili? Threaten Mudge in front of the customers? Screw you, Alistair Pope! You've just blown a whole week's worth of flirting. No amount of charm, skin contact, or roadside rescues would make me go home with you now.

She stared into the refrigerator and couldn't remember why she'd opened it. Surprise, dismay– Anger rising, the hot flush of betrayal she'd stifled all week. Men! Back-stabbing bastards! How could Dinah laugh about it? Nonchalantly unrolling plastic wrap–

Because she knows him. She's seen this before. Didn't she just warn me yesterday?

OK. Got it. Screw Alistair Pope. No–don't screw Alistair Pope. Cross him off the list and move on. Think about the cottage, the Flying Wedge–

Crash! The front door flew open. "Dinah!" Mudge shouted. "Lydia!"

The panic in his voice made them both drop what they were doing and hurry toward him. "What? What is it?"

Without answering he ran back out. Lydia followed him. Halfway down the path he halted and turned to face her and Dinah, lumbering behind her. He looked so shaken that Lydia stopped. Whatever had just happened, she knew she was going to regret finding out.

Dinah pulled up alongside, wiping her hands on a dishtowel. "What?" she barked at him again.

Mudge pointed to the frog pond. Curling into the water was a thin ribbon of crimson.

Its source lay at the other end: Alistair Pope, staring sightlessly into an overhanging branch of the Elephant Tree.

Chapter Twelve

"You didn't–?" Dinah's voice was horrified.

"Me? No!" Mudge sounded too distraught to say more. "No!"

Lydia didn't see their expressions. She couldn't look at anything except the still shape splayed under the tree. Time and her brain both froze. Only her heart pounded in her ears like a kettledrum, and her feet started toward the pond.

A hand caught her arm. "Don't." A hoarse whisper.

Her eyes met Mudge's. "I have to! Help him, or find out–"

"I already did."

"Oh, Mudge. Oh my god." Lydia's arm went around him.

"Is he–?" came Dinah's voice behind them, smaller than Lydia had ever heard it. "Mudge! Is he dead?"

He reached out an arm for her, too. "Yeah. I'm sorry."

The three of them huddled together on the path. "I had to turn him over," Mudge explained. "His face was in the water. I thought . . . if I could . . . "

Lydia thought she might vomit. Her stomach was heaving ominously. But to be sick would require detaching from this three-way embrace, which at the moment was all that was holding her upright. Not an option.

"We gotta call the cops." Dinah stirred, but didn't pull away. "I should call Kevin."

"Right," Mudge conceded.

"Not a doctor?" Lydia asked faintly, hoping against hope. "Shouldn't we call a doctor first? Just in case? I mean, of course I believe you, but if there's any chance . . . "

"I will go call 911." Dinah staggered, collected herself, and made her way slowly back up the path.

Impossible. The thought buzzed around them like a cloud of gnats. Half an hour ago that was a man. Three-dimensional, endowed with motion and voice and the full range of human idiosyncrasies. Who lost his temper when thwarted; offered help in crises; spoke with a quaint accent; was vain about his thinning hair; gave a glamorous new name to curried cauliflower soup. Alistair Pope. Who now lay lifeless beside an ornamental pond. *Impossible.*

Lydia found herself crossing the short distance toward him as if in slow motion. As if sheer force of wishing could revive him where Mudge had failed, and when she reached him, he would sit up–

She pushed back the tree branch; and Alistair's head moved.

Lydia stumbled backward. What–?

Two bead-like eyes stared into hers. Then something shot through the air and splashed into the water.

It took her several seconds to grasp what she'd seen. Not Alistair's soul leaving his body. Not a killer demon fleeing the sacrificial site. A frog, Lydia. Just a frog, OK? See, there it goes, that bump surging across the water's surface, sending a V of ripples behind it.

With a shudder she turned back to Alistair.

His head, half turned away, rested on wet stones. Pond water had twined his hair into black strands which clung to his neck and cheek, like a garter-snake Medusa. The shoulders of his army jacket were soaked to dark olive, flecked with bits of dead leaves. The rest of him was dry–ordinary, really, except for one sneakered foot crooked over the other knee.

She moved closer. No question from here of his reviving. His face might have been a wax model's; it certainly wasn't a man's. He looked emptied of life, as if all his blood had drained away into the little pond. Against that white skin the slack lips were bruise-blue. You'd never guess from his stark, grim face that Alistair Pope had ever laughed, flirted, or enjoyed himself. His eyes, mercifully, were closed.

What must have happened in his final seconds to change him like that?

Part of her wanted to kneel beside him, as if to comfort what was left of him. Another part could only stand frozen. *Too late. Anyway, you're not supposed to tamper with the scene of . . .*

What? An accident? A crime?

She stepped back, and bumped into Mudge.

"Did you see the frog?" she blurted.

He took her arm, as if she too might fall.

"What happened to him? Do you know?"

"There's a banged place on the other side," Mudge's finger ran back from his temple, "like he hit his head on the rocks. Maybe he tripped? or had a heart attack?"

She followed him back to the path. "What did you do? To find out–if he was–"

"Well, first I called to him. Like, 'Hey, are you OK?' But he didn't move, and I saw the blood in the water, and I thought, for sure something's wrong. I didn't want him to drown, you know?–so I grabbed his shoulder and pulled him up. But his head just kind of flopped." Mudge swallowed. "That's when I saw the banged-up place. And his face–well. I couldn't find a pulse, so I did CPR, in case he had water in his lungs, but . . . " He took a long breath. "I could tell. I mean I could tell as soon as I touched him, but you don't . . . you can't, you know . . . "

Lydia squeezed his hand. "You're amazing. I can't believe you had it together enough to do all that."

"I was so mad at him!" Mudge said sorrowfully.

"Yeah, me too. But you understand, right?–this is totally not your fault."

"When he was yelling at me, in front of all those people? I thought I could kill him."

"But you couldn't."

"No. I couldn't."

We have to say this now, thought Lydia, because very soon the cops will be asking him and me and everyone who was in the restaurant a thousand questions, and everything will start to feel so bizarre that they, and even we, may wonder if what we know is true.

"The banged-up place on his head," she said. "Could you

tell–?"

A siren interrupted her, wailing up the road.

"You mean, like, did somebody hit him?" Mudge spoke over it. "I donno. I wondered that too."

In seconds, blue lights were flashing in the driveway. She let go of Mudge's hand. Not Helen Wills about tires this time.

A burly young man in a dark blue police uniform, with a freckled face and carrot-colored hair bristling under the rim of his hat, climbed out of the patrol car.

"Hey, Kev," said Mudge.

"Hey, Kev. That him over there?"

"Yup."

The cop pulled a walkie-talkie off his belt and spoke into it, too low for Lydia to hear.

"Kev?" she asked Mudge.

"Our local cop, Kevin Kelly. Oh, you mean me? That's my first name, is Kevin."

Officer Kelly hung up his walkie-talkie and strode toward the frog pond.

"Your name is Kevin?"

"Yeah. I don't use it. There's so many Kevins around here–"

He stopped, as the other Kevin knelt to inspect the supine figure half under the tree. How can he do that? thought Lydia, cringing as the stranger turned Alistair's head, pressed a finger against his neck, lifted his wrist. He's so young!–hardly older than Mudge.

"Aw, man." Sounding aggrieved, Kevin Kelly rose.

"What, is he still dead?"

"Yeah." He walked over to Mudge and Lydia. "I gotta call my sergeant. Get the big guns over here."

"Kev, did you meet Lydia Vivaldi? She works with us at Leo's."

"Hey." He held out the same hand that had just checked Alistair. After an instant's pause, she shook it. "Good to meet you. Scuse me for one second."

He returned to his squad car. Lydia called after him: "Is an ambulance coming?"

"Any minute."

"Don't forget, Kev," Mudge added, "I already moved him."

All Lydia could see of Kevin was his blue-trousered knees and shiny black shoes. "Yeah, well, you shouldn't of."

"I had to, man. His head was in the water."

Should I tell him about the frog? she wondered. And answered herself: Only if you want to sound like a flaming idiot.

Kevin Kelly pulled his legs into the car and closed the door.

"So how'd you turn from Kevin into Mudge?" she asked instead.

"Well, it's kind of a long story, but basically, my dad picked my first name and my mom picked my middle name, which is Mudjekeewis. And like I said, half the guys on the Cape are named Kevin."

"Mudjekeewis? Is that an Indian name?"

"Kind of." His mouth twisted in a reluctant grin. "My mom was a little fuzzy on the Native American thing. It's actually a title of the Ojibway chiefs, but she got it from 'Hiawatha.' You know the poem? Mudjekeewis was Hiawatha's father, the brave warrior who killed the great bear and became the West Wind, like the ruler of the winds."

"Wow." Lydia felt as though she'd walked into a dream, or kaleidoscope, whose fragments kept shifting too fast for her to grab hold of an image.

And here came Kevin Kelly again.

"They're on their way," he told Mudge. Lydia wondered if anyone on Cape Cod would ever speak to her if there was a man available to talk to instead. "I'm gonna need statements, so don't go anyplace. You want to help me tape off the scene?"

"Sure."

"Hold it!" Lydia insisted. "What if he's still alive? I mean, I know he looks– But shouldn't you at least try to resuscitate him?"

Kevin gave her a grim smile. "He's not alive."

She was considering a crack about crows and road kill when she heard the welcome double-note crescendo of a siren. Kevin returned to his car, presumably for a roll of yellow tape. Meanwhile, up the driveway came a blocky red-and-white truck. Parking near the pond, it spilled out–

Firemen?

Lydia had expected white-coated medics bearing stethoscopes and IV tubes. Still, a pair of firemen in dark-blue T-shirts, suspendered pants, and rubber boots seemed no more unreal than the rest of this dreadful afternoon.

Behind the ambulance chugged a full-fledged fire engine, wooden ladders along both sides, hoses coiled on top. More firemen jumped out, and firewomen, till six of them were coming toward the trio under the tree. Two wore raincoats and helmets. Two others carried a stretcher.

"You guys better go," Kevin told Mudge and Lydia.

They walked toward the restaurant and watched from there. When the front firefighter, crouched beside Alistair, stood up and shook her head, Lydia did an abrupt about-face. Until now, she couldn't stop hoping . . . But if he was beyond hope, she didn't want to see the rest.

Inside, she found Dinah slumped at a back table. Her head was buried in her arms. When she glanced up, her plump cheeks were streaked with tears. She had tracked Leo down by phone, she told Lydia; he was on his way back. "Are they gone yet?"

"The fire truck's leaving. But they didn't take . . . " Alistair? The body? "I think more cops are coming."

"Hah. Don't expect we'll see the back of them anytime soon."

"Can I get you anything? A glass of water? Coffee?"

"Oh, don't make coffee or they'll all want it." A volcanic sigh heaved through Dinah's great bulk. "I knew Al since we were kids. Wasn't crazy about him, but still."

"Yeah." Lydia slid into a chair opposite. "It sucks."

"And this is only the beginning."

They sat in silence for a minute, each reviewing what had happened and what might happen next.

"Hell On Wheels was just a couple years behind us," said Dinah. "Man, is she gonna be bullshit! And Chill off in Florida?"

Lydia grasped at the last straw. "Chill off in Florida?"

"Her husband," Dinah translated. "Chill Wills? Short for I don't know what, aside from being a computer geek. Al's sister Maria was in their wedding."

That was a scene Lydia couldn't picture: Detective Helen Wills marching down the aisle in a white dress and veil.

"One of those opposites-attract things nobody thought would last. They started out rivals at the academy. Got married the same day they graduated."

Whether or not this had anything to do with Alistair's death, at least Dinah was regaining her assurance. "She's a detective, right?" Lydia asked. "How come she's not here?"

"Helen's state, Kevin's local. He's always first on the scene. She don't come in till later. Once the regular detectives check it out. And then it might not be Helen. Whoever's on duty down there."

There was a pause. "Later? You mean . . . if the local cops think it was a crime?"

"Oh, no. Pretty much anybody that didn't die in bed, you're gonna get the state cops. I guess they got a better lab." Dinah was mopping her face with a paper towel. "But what do I know? This is the first time we ever lost a customer right on the premises."

"Oh, cripes." Lydia slid back her chair. "My tires!"

As heartless as it seemed to worry about her car when the man who had helped her get it towed was lying dead beside the frog pond, dealing with mechanics had to be a better way to use up this doomed afternoon than hanging around the Back End. The tires were in, Jim reported; the Morris was ready to go.

Could Dinah drive her over? No. Not now. Somebody had to tell the neighbors. Somebody had to stick around, mind the shop, until Leo arrived.

"Hey, you guys." Mudge's head poked around the corner. "We got the perimeter secured. Kev wants to take your statements. And Pete Altman's on his way over. I gotta wait for him, seeing as I was the one who found him."

"Jesus, Mudge! You under arrest?" Dinah hauled herself to her feet.

"Nah." He was unperturbed. "Just, like, assisting the police with their investigation."

"Yeah, right. And I'm Britney Spears. Mudge, you gotta call a lawyer. Now, before you say one more word to these guys."

"Oh, come on, Dinah!" He leaned in the doorway, youthful and graceful. "This is Kev and Pete."

"They're cops," she said forcefully.

"So, what do you think? They're gonna string me up?"

"How do I know what they're gonna do? I just know anybody who trusts a cop is a fool."

"Well now, Dinah," put in Lydia, "it's not like he has a choice."

"All they want is me saying on tape what I saw. It's standard procedure. For the record."

"Yeah. And hey, let's get your fingerprints while we're at it, and how 'bout your DNA?" She faced him. "We could call Fred Jones. He's right up the street, be here in two minutes."

"Forget it, Dinah."

She scowled and carried her paper towel over to the trash can.

"How about your folks?" asked Lydia.

"No way."

"Now, that is just plain dumb!" called Dinah.

"Lydia," Mudge gripped the back of a chair, "can I ask you something?"

He stood there without speaking until Dinah reached the front room, rolling up the sleeves of his blue work shirt. In the dim interior light, that shirt was the clearest part of him Lydia could see. Strong brown arms . . . that had lifted Alistair Pope's inert body and tried to save his life.

Which meant those stains were probably not barbecue sauce.

With Dinah out of sight, Mudge lowered himself into the chair. "I need you to do something for me."

"Sure."

"Have you told anybody about me sleeping under the Elephant Tree?"

"No."

"Well, don't, OK?"

Lydia had the unpleasant sensation that she was glimpsing the future, and it looked as repellent as today. "You mean, like the cops?"

"Yeah."

"I won't if they don't ask me. But, Mudge, if they do? I have to tell them. Why? Did they ask you?"

"No, but Kev was snooping around there." His mouth twisted. "It's got nothing to do with what happened! You know that."

"Yeah, but it's kind of out of my hands." She sighed. "I hate to say this, but Dinah might be right about calling a lawyer."

"No way!" Roosevelt Sherman guffawed. "Are you kidding me?"

"Swear to god," said Helen Wills.

They were leaning against his sun-warmed SUV in the parking lot behind the Frigate. Her cruiser stood angled a few feet away. Rosey had just driven down from Boston, forty-five minutes early for his closing in Barnstable with Ken Boose and their lawyers. Helen, spotting the arriving Mercedes, had pulled a high-speed U-turn and fishtailed in after him.

"Mike Maloney's sister. I'll be damned."

"You know he was just here, too. Couple of weeks ago. Came up for Mom's birthday."

"Well, you tell him I'm sorry I missed him. Heck, it's been so long– He still got that rat-tail mustache? Snidely Whiplash, we called him."

"Oh, sure. Everybody still hassles him about it. Except my mom–she says at least it's not a tattoo! I should carry a picture. I've got a whole scrapbook someplace. The two of you in your JV jerseys? Cute as puppies."

"Unbelievable. Mike's little sister. A Cape Cod cop."

"Hey. State police detective, please."

As if to emphasize her point, Helen polished the top of her black pump on the back of her well-cut trouser leg. Rosey wondered if she knew how macho-feminine she looked. And if she was toting a shoulder holster under that Wall Street jacket.

"Mike wasn't real happy about it. With his reputation?–you

can imagine."

"Oh, yeah." He was still grinning. "Don't even open that can of worms!"

"Hey, it surprised me as much as him. I was pretty wild myself back then."

"I'll bet you were." The loud approach of a siren out on Main Street kept him from saying more. He ran his eyes over her again: a five-foot-nine-inch bundle of contrasts. Hair like a nun, pulled back smoothly from her face, versus shiny coral lips and thick-lashed olive-green eyes. The rumpled pin-striped suit versus the come-hither curves underneath. She was built big, like her brothers. Her fidgeting fingers–cleaning a nail, straightening her cuff–suggested she still had more energy than she knew what to do with.

"Wasn't your dad in law enforcement?" he asked when the noise stopped.

She nodded. "On the Exmouth force for twenty years, taught at Four C's for eight. He wanted his sons to follow in his footsteps. Instead he gets a linebacker for the Dolphins, a tax accountant, a general contractor, a bartender, and his only daughter a state cop who was supposed to have a houseful of kids by now."

Rosey wasn't fool enough to ask her why she didn't have children. He did take the opportunity to pull out his wallet and show off his own trio. Their mother, too. He told her about wanting to spend more time with his family, in a place where they could put up a rope swing, build a tree fort, and Thea could grow all the flowers she wanted. Any time a woman suddenly got friendly, even a cop, he liked to make it clear he was spoken for.

"They're so adorable. I'm wicked jealous. Chill and me are still hoping, but no luck so far." She brushed a leaf off the hood of his SUV. "You must really like kids, huh?"

"Sure do."

"Taking on those two DePina boys who slashed your tires? What a story! Can you imagine if Parade magazine got hold of it? Rosey Sherman's retirement: running a small-town bookstore and reforming juvenile delinquents."

"Now don't you forget, Helen, that's confidential."

"Don't worry, my lips are sealed." She ran a finger across her moist pink mouth, making Rosey glad they'd both declared where they stood. "I mean, seeing as I shouldn't have even stuck my nose in this case, except how else could I track you down?"

"Well, now you've got my card, let's not wait for another crime to keep in touch."

"For sure. As a matter of fact, I've got a favor to ask you, if you don't mind."

Here it came. No matter how casual or cordial the encounter, there almost always was a catch. An autographed photo, a donation to the Benevolent Fund, an appearance at some worthy charity's awards banquet . . .

But she didn't get to tell him what she wanted. Someone was hurtling slowly toward them, waving both hands: a huge, frantic white-aproned figure like a human avalanche erupting into the Frigate's parking lot.

Chapter Thirteen

The shadow that fell across Lydia and Mudge's table was Kevin Kelly's. This time he was followed by a taller, older, slower man in civilian clothes.

"Hey, Pete," said Mudge.

"Hey, Kev."

As they both rose, Lydia wondered if Mudge felt as edgy as she did. What right did these invaders have to walk into Leo's restaurant after hours without permission? Didn't they have enough to keep them busy outside? What did they want in here?

"You got any coffee?" Kevin Kelly asked Mudge.

"I'll make some." But first he introduced the newcomer to Lydia: Detective Pete Altman.

Nothing about him matched her idea of a detective. Denim sport jacket, khaki slacks, tattersall plaid shirt . . . Manager of a used-car dealership, maybe, or a teacher at the community college. Thick salt-and-pepper hair, parted on the side, fell over his left eyebrow. Next to Kevin Kelly's terrier energy, Pete Altman had the baggy jowls, big bones, and good-natured eyes of a bloodhound.

His handshake wasn't as crushing as Officer Kelly's. Nor did he bristle with authority. Still, Lydia guessed this was the cop to watch out for.

"Make it a big pot," he advised Mudge. "We've got the rescue squad going and forensics coming. The more caffeine you give us, the sooner we'll be out of your way."

Good! thought Lydia.

"Forensics?" she asked him. "Does that mean you know what happened?"

"Not yet."

Kevin Kelly stepped in as if he couldn't stand not to run the show. The department's forensics experts–also known as CSS, or Crime Scene Services–were called for any unattended death. Until they examined the evidence at the scene, no one could say if a crime had been committed. If foul play appeared likely, CSS would then hand off to CPAC–the state police Crime Prevention and Control unit. For now, he and Detective Altman would continue to conduct interviews with Mudge, Lydia, and anyone else who'd been present at the time of the incident. After that they were free to resume their normal movements.

Does someone give them a script, Lydia wondered, like flight attendants, that makes them sound like robots?

Mudge, at the coffee machine, asked: "Did the rescue squad take him away?"

Pete Altman shook his head. "That's up to the medical examiner."

Oh, one more thing, added Kevin, sidling toward the sandwich bar. Please refrain from leaving the premises until authorized by the police. Lydia asked what exactly he wanted in the kitchen. Kevin said nothing. Lydia asked if he would please refrain himself out of there, then, until authorized by Leo.

"Where's Dinah?" he asked her, sidling back out.

"Wasn't she out front?"

No, she wasn't, and he sure hoped she wasn't dumb enough to take off with an investigation in progress, because any attempt to obstruct–

"Hey. Kev." Mudge handed him a mug of coffee. "Chill."

He set another mug and a cream pitcher on the counter. "So, you guys think it was an accident?"

"Can't say," Pete Altman returned. "Cause of death will be determined by the M.E. What might have taken place at the scene, that'll come from CSS, like Kev just said. Until we get their reports, and pending notification of the family, we'd appreciate your help keeping rumors to a minimum."

Had to be a script.

"Mind if I take this outside?" he asked Lydia.

If you say no to a cop, does he put you on the suspect list? "Long as you bring it back."

Mugs in hand, Kev and Pete headed for the frog pond.

Mudge poured coffee for him and Lydia. She asked if he thought those two poker faces really didn't know yet how Alistair had died. He shrugged: hard to tell. But it made sense they'd stonewall until they broke the news to his family.

Which consisted of . . . ?

Mudge didn't know. He was more worried about breaking the news to Leo.

Lydia told him what Dinah had said. But now where was Dinah?

"And as far as that goes," said Mudge, "where's Sue?"

Lydia cupped her hands around her mug. "Do you think she had something to do with this?"

"You got me. I wouldn't've thought so. She's a little crazy but not, like, violent. But then I wouldn't've thought . . . " He let it trail off.

Lydia swiveled her stool to face the windows. There they were, Kevin the cop and Pete the detective, plus a bunch of other officials, swarming between the parking lot and the Elephant Tree. It looked like an Easter egg hunt for grown-ups. Only instead of colored eggs, every minute or two a latex-gloved hand would hold up a pair of tweezers and drop something (invisible from here) into a plastic bag.

Pete stooped over the silver-blanketed form beside the pond. That she didn't want to watch. What she wanted was for Alistair Pope to be somewhere else, the interviews done, the parking lot empty as it should be at quarter to four in the afternoon. She wanted this creepy ritual to be over. She wanted to pick up her car and go home.

"Yeah, well, fuck protocol," Dinah panted, "and the D.A.'s office too. You don't want to take my word? Cross the street! See for yourself. Al Pope laying by the frog pond, dead as a doornail."

Rosey Sherman folded his arms. "Are you saying . . .?"

"She's not saying anything," Helen Wills intervened. "Excuse me, folks." She walked toward her car, pulling out a cell phone.

"This is that big fellow, that filmmaker?"

Dinah nodded. Now there's generosity, she thought, a man the size of Roosevelt Sherman calling Al a big fellow. "Walked out of Leo's not an hour ago, and next thing you know . . ."

Helen Wills rejoined them. "Gotta go. One request: Don't spread this around yet, OK?"

"You gonna call Maria?" Dinah followed her toward her car.

"Yeah. Soon as I can." She climbed in. "Not looking forward to that, I'll tell you."

"Give me a ride back."

"Can't. Protocol." Helen was already starting the engine.

"I can, though," said Rosey. "Let's go."

He helped Dinah into the passenger seat. Ahead of them, Helen's cruiser swiveled out the driveway in a cloud of clamshell dust. As the Mercedes followed, its rear bumper scraped asphalt.

Wally Hicks watched from the doorway. Somebody had to stay behind and man the Frigate. At least, that was what he'd told his soon-to-be-boss. (His present boss hadn't stirred from his arm-chair siesta.) Wally had come galumphing down the stairs when he recognized that what looked like a giant snowball rolling across Route 6A was more likely a messenger. Dinah's news blew today's sales clean out of his head.

Al Pope was dead. Drowned in Leo's frog pond.

Damn! When the great wheel finally creaked into motion, didn't it just turn into a karmic steamroller!

Wally managed to keep his face blank and goggle-eyed until both vehicles left the parking lot. Then he scrambled back up the stairs.

One more month–one more week even–and CodCast.net might have caught the whole thing!

Count your lucky stars, Hicks. What chance of any hot shots in the stills? Three percent? Five? Still, the job had to be done.

Feeling half like a man whose lottery ticket is one digit off the winning number, and half like a man who's just hit the jackpot, Wallace Hicks settled in at his computer, exited the Frigate's daily spreadsheet, and opened Pirandello.

Across Route 6A, Helen Wills's cruiser squealed into the Back End parking lot.

Leo stood in the doorway, wiping his hands on a dishtowel which he waved in greeting. "What are you, the Lone Ranger?"

"What are you," Helen retorted, "Davy Crockett at the Alamo?"

"Too late. Your troops over there," he flapped his towel at the pond, where police officers heavily outnumbered frogs, "already charged in and took over the place. Formerly known as the Back End Gourmet Restaurant. Now HQ for the police interrogation squad. Oh, excuse me. Did I say interrogation? I meant investigation."

Helen strode off to join her colleagues. Leo strolled over to join Rosey and Dinah, who had parked across from the squad cars, between Mudge's battered pickup truck and Dinah's dark blue Honda.

"Good afternoon, Mr. Sherman. And Ms. Rowan! So nice that you could join us!"

"Back off, Leo." She pulled her blouse into order. "Who d'you think held the fort while you went off gallivanting?"

"Gallivanting! I leave here for one hour, to just once in my life take a break like a normal person instead of slaving from dawn to dusk–"

"Is there any news?" Rosey interjected. "Have they got any theories?"

"Don't look at me. I'm just the owner. Ask Paul Revere here," he nodded at Dinah.

The last thing I need right now, thought Dinah, is to be standing smack out here in the open like a fox between two packs of hounds. And next to last is listening to Leo run off his mouth, when he should be in there with a broom or a cleaver or a shotgun or whatever it takes to shoo the cops out of his restaurant and my kitchen.

"Coffee," she declared.

"Oh, step right inside. Help yourself. I'm sure the law enforcement personnel running the kitchen would be happy–"

"Shut up, Leo. Mr. Sherman?"

"Rosey."

"Rosey. Give me a lift to the Whistling Pig?"

Sitting across from him in a booth, Lydia still couldn't quite believe Pete Altman was a detective. Unlike everyone else at the Back End, he seemed unruffled by the death of Alistair Pope. Maybe he was nearing retirement after a long, uneventful career on the force. Or maybe he'd seen too many corpses to mind one more.

He had interviewed Mudge first, then gone outside to check with the group searching the cordoned area. When he came back, he asked her to choose a booth where she'd be comfortable. She picked one in a back corner, with a yellow-topped table.

He set up his tape recorder between them. "I know you already gave Kev a statement. Officer Kelly. Since you were one of the first witnesses on the scene, I'd like to ask you a few more questions. I'll be recording this conversation, if that's OK?"

His smile was fatherly, disarming. "Sure," said Lydia.

He pressed a button and spoke at the tape recorder, as if he didn't entirely trust it. She liked his voice: the husky baritone of an ex-smoker. "June 6, 3:55 PM. Detective Pete Altman interviewing"–he checked his notes–"Lydia Vivaldi. Right? Is that Ms.?"

She nodded, wondering how serious a crime it was to give the police a name you'd only been using for a week.

"Since we don't know yet if this was an accidental death, I need to read you the Miranda warning."

He recited the words Lydia had heard so many times on TV that they sounded as meaningless as a commercial.

If you tell a cop No, I don't understand, or Yes, I do want a lawyer, does he put you on the suspect list?

"OK. Ms. Vivaldi, would you please tell me what happened this afternoon? Starting with when you first knew something was wrong."

He's gone off the script, she thought as she answered. Because Kevin's not here? Because he can tell I hate that kind of BS? Because he wants to put me at ease, because that's his job, because if he pretends to be a regular person I'll let down my guard and tell him incriminating things I don't even realize?

Don't start liking this guy, Lydia!

What did Dinah say? Anybody who trusts a cop is a fool.

She tightened up her own script. "I interpreted this as meaning that some kind of emergency was taking place." Not bad, Lydia. "After exiting the restaurant I proceeded rapidly in the indicated direction." Good–keep the spotlight on you, not Mudge.

"Excuse me." Pete Altman's mouth was twitching as if he were either annoyed or trying not to laugh. "Are you saying, you heard Mudge call your name, you ran toward him, and followed him out toward the pond?"

Lydia gave him a fishy stare. "Yeah."

"Did you touch the body?"

"No." She shuddered.

"How close did you get?"

"A couple feet? He was mostly under that branch, so I moved it back. Up till then I hoped– I thought maybe there was still a chance we could help him."

"When did you recognize who it was?"

"Soon as I saw him. When we first came out of the restaurant. His face was kind of turned to the side, but I could see it was Alistair."

He leaned over the tape recorder. "Note: Alistair Pope is the deceased." To Lydia: "What else did you see?"

She shut her eyes for an instant, recalling. "His hair was wet, and part of his clothes. That army jacket he always wears. One leg was bent." She opened her eyes. "And there was a frog on him. Sitting on his head? When it saw me it jumped in the water."

The detective's mouth twitched again. "A frog."

"Yes."

He wrote something in his notebook; Lydia couldn't see what.

"Any wounds or signs of violence? Any sign of how Mr. Pope got in the pond?"

"No. But–" Stop, Lydia. Don't speak for Mudge.

"But what?"

"Well, I could see he was dead, so I didn't want to, you know, mess up the scene."

"Did Mudge tell you he'd moved the body?"

"Yes. Pulled his head out of the water and gave him CPR. But it was too late."

He asked what happened after that, and she told him. So much to cover; so much to leave out! He hadn't asked how, or how well, she knew Alistair–or Mudge either, for that matter. He probably didn't know that Alistair had yelled at Mudge for refusing to serve him lunch, or anything about Sue, or slashed tires–

"Tires!" she interrupted herself. "When we get through with this, would you remind me I have a question for you?"

He leaned back, arms stretched out along the bench top, Mr. Informality. "I won't remember. You better ask me now."

OK, she thought; how deep do we go here? "Somebody slashed two of my tires yesterday. Can you find out if there's been an investigation? So I know if I have to put in an alarm or jack up my car insurance or whatever?"

"Sure." Fingers interlaced behind his head. "What made you suddenly think of that?"

"I guess . . . Alistair stayed with me to wait for Triple A. In that same parking lot. The day before."

"I'm sorry." He sounded as if he meant it. "Were you guys friends?"

Part of her yearned to tell this sympathetic man everything that had happened between her and Alistair Pope, from his original roadside rescue up through the horror of seeing his wet dead body lying by the frog pond. Under the Elephant Tree, where just a few days earlier–

Anybody who trusts a cop is a fool.

"Well, I've only been here a week. I must have met two hundred people working at Leo's, and most of them I like, but *friends* is probably too strong."

"What about Mudge?"

"What about Mudge?" she returned.

"Is friends too strong for him, too?"

She almost smiled. "Mudge and Dinah and I are teammates. Think Celtics front line."

"OK then." Pete Altman's arms lowered; he sat forward.

"This is only a preliminary inquiry, you know, to get your memories down while they're fresh. One last question: Did you see anything unusual around the Back End recently? Any strangers, or fights, or anything at all involving Alistair Pope, that might be relevant?"

"Like I said, I've only been here a week. For me, it's all unusual." She hoped he would take that as an answer. When he kept on staring at her, she amplified: "I see lots of strangers, and everybody at the Back End fights with everybody else, that's the dynamic, and I don't know Alistair Pope well enough to know what's unusual for him. Or relevant for you."

"Aha. Well then, is there anything else you'd like to add? That you think we should look into, or that might help us along here?"

Lydia shook her head.

"Thanks for your help, then, Ms. Vivaldi. We may call you if further questions come up. And if you need to go off Cape for any reason, please call this number." He handed her a business card.

"Hold on a second." That halted him with one finger on the Stop button. "What about my tires?"

"Wait right here."

He returned a few minutes later, clipping his cell phone back onto his belt. "Who took the call? You did report it, right?"

"Yeah. Officer Wills. Helen Wills."

"Huh." Detective Altman nodded. "Nothing yet. Try back tomorrow."

He didn't explain. After a moment Lydia understood: slashed tires in a Quansett parking lot was a problem for the local cops, not the state police. Helen Wills's report could take days to wend its way through the system. With a murder on Kevin Kelly's desk, she'd be lucky if he even gave it a second look, never mind investigating if Sue was the culprit.

Thanks anyway, Alistair.

Chapter Fourteen

It would have satisfied Dinah Rowan just to sit beside Roosevelt Sherman in regal silence as they drove up Main Street. If she spotted a few friends to wave at from his Mercedes SUV, she'd reach the Pig a happy woman. But–frosting on her cake!–Rosey wanted to talk.

"This fella Pope, what do you think? He slipped on the rocks, knocked himself out?"

"Could be. Kinda hope so. Better he slipped than somebody pushed him." Was that Berry and Joe Morton? She waved just in case. "Then again, kinda hope not. If Leo gets hit with a lawsuit, we can kiss off the Back End."

"Does he leave a family?"

"No wife, if that's what you're asking. Or kids. God forbid," she added under her breath. "His mom, though, and a bunch of sisters and brothers."

Fred Jones' red convertible pulled out of the bank drive-in, but Fred was busy watching the road.

"He have any medical problems? Heart condition, anything like that?"

Dinah shifted her gaze from the window to Rosey's wide brown face. Below his aviator shades, mouth-watering curves of cheek and jaw shifted as he spoke, like ice cream melting under hot fudge. She had to look away again to keep her mind on their conversation.

"None I ever heard of. Aside from being a pissant, but that was more of a problem for everybody else than him."

"Enough of a problem for somebody to shove him into that frog pond?"

"Damned if I know," Dinah replied to a passing bicyclist.

"Don't seem likely, but I wouldn't rule it out. Al was always tromping on somebody's corns."

They had arrived at the Whistling Pig. Rosey offered to go in and buy the coffee. Such gallantry! But Dinah wasn't about to pass up the chance to be seen with Quansett's biggest celebrity. She allowed him to hold the door for her. When their bare arms brushed, heat whooshed through her like lighting a match in Leo's gas oven.

Fortunately Connie McNally herself was at the register. Although she was too much the lady to comment, Dinah knew she'd be on the phone the minute they left. Rosey made it perfect by greeting Connie by name. And, to top it off, he knew Dinah took her coffee white.

"You been watching me?" she asked him as they walked back to the car.

He grinned. "You're hard to miss. Like me."

Well, not exactly. That too, she reflected, would feed the grapevine tonight: "Two Americanos, Connie, one black one white."

He couldn't stay long, Rosey explained on the way back. He had a closing to get to. Before he sank his fortune and his future into Quansett, though, he'd like to believe . . .

After several seconds Dinah asked: "What?"

"Well, let's say, there's nothing funny in the water."

"How do you mean?"

He stopped the car halfway across the parking lot. "Two people dead in a month who fell on their head? In my old line of work you might let that pass. Around here, I'd hate to see it get to be a trend."

She was about to object that there was no connection at all between DeAnne Ropes falling off a ladder and Al Pope pitching into Leo's frog pond when she realized she couldn't be sure of that.

On the Back End's small patch of lawn, nothing had visibly changed since they left. Leo stood on the front walk hollering at Helen Wills, twisting a dishtowel in his hands, popping it at her occasionally for emphasis.

"Some kind of detective you are! What the heck good are

you? Get on your Nextel, why don't you, and find out! Go to the top! Ask questions!"

Trooper Wills remained calm. "You want questions? Here's one for you. Where were you when this happened? Out having a real meal at a real restaurant?"

"Now, now. No need to get nasty."

"How much nastier can it get?" Rosey murmured to Dinah.

"All I'm asking, as a citizen and a taxpayer–"

"Leo, I'm a detective, OK? Not a magician. These things take time. When the guys tell me they're through, we'll go. When the M.E. says remove the body, I'll call Nickerson. As far as the D.A.'s office–"

"As far as the D.A.'s office, you tell Denny from me," Leo loomed over her. "If he ever wants to eat lunch here again, he better damn well get off his butt, send whoever he needs to send or call whoever he needs to call, and find out who killed Al Pope in my frog pond!"

"Hold on," Rosey Sherman stepped in. "He was killed?"

"We have no evidence of that!" Exasperation had begun to creep into Helen Wills's voice.

"What do you think it does to my business, losing a customer right on the premises?" Leo continued undeterred. "Next thing you know, some durn fool's gonna blame the food, and then how'm I supposed to support my staff?"

"Hey," Dinah joined the scrimmage. "Who supports who around here?"

"How's a newcomer like Mr. Sherman here supposed to know this kind of thing don't happen every day?"

Out of courtesy Rosey protested, though privately he thought it was a fair question.

"Are you through?" Helen Wills demanded. She folded her arms and glared at Leo. "First of all, the investigation's barely started, so don't get so het up. Second of all: What do you think, this is only about you? Jesus Christ, Leo! I've known Al–how long, Dinah?"

"Junior high at least."

"We're talking about losing a friend here! Somebody we

played baseball with. Went swimming with. So don't talk to me like I'm just some bureaucrat, OK? I've got feelings, too."

Dinah lifted an eyebrow at Leo. She still didn't dare look at Rosey Sherman, although she'd have liked to see his reaction to Helen's unprofessional outburst.

"You want to move this thing along? How about you quit griping and give me some help. Where were you when Al died?"

"Where was I?" Leo frowned threateningly. "Funny, but I would've sworn I just heard you say I was someplace else."

"I'm not telling you, I'm asking."

"For what, Detective Wills? An alibi?"

"You got a problem with that?"

"Maybe I oughta call my lawyer. Maybe you oughta read me my rights."

"Maybe you oughta put up or shut up."

"Shit or get off the pot," Dinah seconded.

"Fish or cut bait."

"Hey!" Leo shrank back in mock fear. "Gang up on me, why don't you? Brutes! Fine. I was lunching up the street with some friends of mine. Off-Cape types–can't enjoy their meal without a cocktail."

Helen Wills had pulled out a pad and pencil. "Where was this?"

"Where do you think?"

"Leo–"

"How many places are there up the street where a person can have lunch and a drink?"

"The Pig?" Dinah interceded.

He nodded, smugly.

"What time did you leave here," asked Helen, "and how long did you stay?"

Leo shrugged.

"You don't know?"

"I wasn't expecting the Spanish Inquisition."

"No one expects the Spanish Inquisition," said Helen. "Did you meet your friends here or at the Pig? What time was your lunch date for? Did they show up early, late, or right on the dot?"

Inch by inch, they established that Leo's friends had called him at the Back End shortly after one, and met him at the Whistling Pig at one-thirty. They had planned to drive to Provincetown together after lunch, but Leo stopped at home to pick up a jacket.

Where were his friends now? Bar-hopping their way up Commercial Street. Enjoying a weekend off, unlike some people.

Helen refused to be drawn. If Leo hadn't personally seen the body, nor spoken with the police, why did he assume Al's death wasn't an accident?

Well, the big fuss. Flashing lights and sirens, yellow tape, cops squashing his new grass, scaring off his frogs, wanting free coffee and doughnuts. And what Mudge said about the banged spot on Al's head.

"Dinah," she turned. "You saw him after Mudge found him, right? Did you see this banged spot?"

"Nope."

"Did you get the idea from Mudge, or from anything else, that somebody killed him?"

"You're the detective. Did they?" Dinah countered.

"I told you, I don't know yet. I'm asking you. Did you get the idea–"

"Nope. I can tell you, though, if somebody did kill him, it sure as hell wasn't Mudge."

There was a pause, as if Helen was considering how hard to push this line of inquiry.

"OK," she said finally. "Well, OK then." She slid her pad and pencil into her jacket pocket.

"That's it?" Leo challenged her. "You're leaving?"

"Yup. Gotta get back to work."

"Well, you have a nice day, Detective Wills. That sure did get us exactly nowhere, thank you very much."

She flashed him a grin. "Welcome to the glamorous world of law enforcement."

It was a mystery to Lydia how the Cape Cod police functioned. In her opinion, all the cops and all the civilians ought to gather in one place. The chief detective should interview the civilians one by one, while the lesser cops fanned out to search the area. When a clue was found, it should be brought in to HQ, where the chief detective would assess its importance. Instead, everybody seemed here to be milling around at random. Who was in charge? What sense did it make for Pete Altman to sit inside the restaurant taping sessions with her and Mudge, whose statements Kevin Kelly had already taken, while Helen Wills questioned Leo and Dinah and Rosey Sherman (Rosey Sherman?) out on the front lawn?

As for the body, the rescue squad should have taken it away an hour ago, not left it lying beside the pond under an aluminum-foil blanket. How did they expect to find out how Alistair died when the medical examiner hadn't seen him yet? Wouldn't his wounds congeal, his hair and clothes dry, rigor mortis set in? What if somebody tampered with him? And how could the searchers know what to look for until they learned what killed him?

After Detective Altman turned off his tape recorder, Lydia asked if this was when she got to resume her normal movements. She was prepared for him to scold her for being flippant, or warn her again not to go anywhere without permission. Instead he merely said yes and walked away.

Some of her complaints she aired to Mudge on their way to pick up her car. Leo and Dinah refused to leave the Back End. Mudge guessed they wanted to keep an eye on the silver. Lydia guessed they wanted to erase all signs of enemy occupation.

She told him about the frog. He agreed that was creepy.

"What bothers me the most, though," he said, "is not knowing anything."

"You mean, like, if the cops have a theory?"

Mudge nodded. "On TV you see the case from the inside. But here we are smack in the middle of it, and we don't have a clue. Like, what if I'm lying in bed tonight and the door crashes open and they haul me off to jail?"

"How they can possibly arrest anybody when they haven't talked to anybody but us?" Lydia replied heatedly. "What about the other, like, hundred people who ate lunch at Leo's? While we were in the kitchen working our butts off, anybody could have seen

Alistair, or been with him."

Mudge said what was in both their minds: "Like for instance, Edgar Rowdey."

He slowed as they neared the mechanic's. "Do you think the cops'll find out about their thing of looking for frogs? Or care?"

"No idea." She scanned for the sign: appliance outlet, sporting goods, lawn furniture, pet supplies. "On TV, they find out everything."

"But on TV it's always a crime, and everything's important. You know?"

Lydia agreed. "Whereas here, like you said, we have no clue. Maybe Alistair walked out the door, went on a frog hunt all by himself, and one hopped in his face and knocked him in the pond. So it wouldn't matter what they find out–his frog thing with Edgar Rowdey, or yelling at you about the Back End being closed, or me going to his house for tea– Oh, there it is!"

Mudge pulled into the lot. Lydia jumped down from the truck.

"You want me to wait?"

"No need." The yellow Morris was parked out front. She half expected it to run up and welcome her, like a pet left at the kennel. "Thanks!" she called to Mudge.

He took off in the direction of Hyannis–for the Rusty Umbrella, she guessed. She walked around her car. "Hey, you." She patted its fender. "Nice tires!"

Jim had gone out on a call. The woman at the desk reluctantly set aside her crossword puzzle to write up the bill. There goes my first paycheck, Lydia reflected with an inward sigh as she signed the receipt. Now, how do I keep this from happening again? Park right next to Leo's? or over by the shops?

If Sue did slash her tires, she must be congratulating herself on her timing. Lydia couldn't see the cops ever getting around to busting her unless she was dumb enough to try it again while they were still swarming around the Back End.

On the other hand, if you had to be the target of a vengeful ex-sous-chef, you'd want one who liked to disappear. Leo, Dinah, and Mudge all evidently took it for granted that, tire-slasher or not, Sue wouldn't be back to cause any more trouble.

Chapter Fifteen

Wallace Hicks pushed back from his keyboard. Nothing. Nada. Niente. His legs were stiff, his butt was sore, his neck hurt, and he still had the Frigate's daily sales to record. Two hours of combing through stills had yielded a detailed account of cars passing up and down Route 6A, tourists walking in and out of the shops across the street, dog-walkers disrespecting the geraniums around Louise French's realty office, and birds squawking and flapping at each other in the mulberry tree.

Only three shots he judged to be worth keeping. The first one showed a fire engine turning into Leo's driveway–an unusually artistic composition for a webcam, the long ladders angled just right to balance Louise's porch railing, the big tires echoing the round jewelry displays in the window next door. Wally thought he might e-mail it to the Cape Cod Times. The other two were a pair. In one, Roosevelt Sherman was helping Dinah Rowan into his SUV at the Frigate; in the other, he was helping her out again at the Whistling Pig. Coincidence, Wally had no doubt. A man who'd married a stunner like Thea surely wouldn't fool around with a behemoth like Dinah. Still, you never could tell. Wally took his motto from the Coast Guard: Semper paratus.

"Hello?" Someone down below was knocking on the open door by the stairs. "Wally? You up there?"

"Be right down."

He could have asked her up. But more than an appreciative fan, he needed a stretch, and she might bring news.

She stood framed in the doorway, not as aesthetically pleasing as that fire truck but close enough. She'd managed to wash her face and impose order on her bird's-nest hair. Even her jeans looked cleaner.

"Hey there, Sue."

"Hey, Wally. How's it going?"

"Not bad. You?"

A sigh escaped from her. "Well, not great, actually."

He ushered her into Ken's office–or, rather, Rosey Sherman's office, since the closing ought to be done by now–and sat her in the guest chair. Gromit stuck his head in her lap. Sue scratched his ears. Wally took the owner's chair. "Want to tell me about it?"

"Oh, gosh." He could see she did want to, but wasn't sure how. "You got anything to drink around here?"

"Instant coffee, Diet Pepsi, or H2O."

"Can I have a glass of water?"

He brought one for each of them. "OK, Sue. Spill it."

"Well, I sort of need a favor. I need a place to sleep tonight." Wally waited, and in a moment she added, "I thought I was all set, but . . . It's kind of a long story."

"I'm not exactly running ragged here keeping up with the customers."

That made her smile. She rubbed her knuckles on Gromit's head and began again. "Last week, you probably know, I quit Leo's. I mean, not like resigned, but Dinah was hassling me?–and it was like too much and I split. This place where I was living, in Hyannis?–my roommate ran off with her boyfriend like the day before. So I'm like, what about the rent? And I'm freaking, and Dinah's hammering on me, and I'm like, That's it. I'm outta here! Get a job in P-town, make some serious bucks for a change, or Orleans where I know this bartender, but–nada. So I came back. I thought I'd sleep in my car, like out behind the P.O.?–but sometimes they tow there, so I went over to a friend's. Who's got this huge place, plenty of room . . ."

She stopped. Wally could see she was weighing how much to tell him. Like I care where you spent the night? he thought. Kind of sweet, though, how she was pussyfooting around it. Maybe he did care just a little.

"This is just between you and me, right?"

"Don't see why not." He lifted his glass to hers.

"Well, this person wasn't home. And I let myself in." Sue's

tone was defensive. "I mean, no big thing, OK? All his friends know where the key is." She sipped water. "So, fine. I go in to work the next morning, he's still not home, no problem. Only this new girl shows up that Leo found like five seconds after I split. Huge hassle! You might've heard? Anyways, Leo's not there, so I go back to my friend's. I'm like, you're buddies with Leo–talk to him! Help me get my job back! Plus he's got this teeny little cottage where I can stay while things work out. Now, he thinks I should look other places besides Leo's. Summer's starting, tons of jobs– So, fine. I run into somebody who knows somebody up in Bourne who's looking for somebody– And I come back here, I mean across the street?–and fuck! There's cops crawling all over the place."

Sue leaned back and stuck her legs out straight. Gromit, wagging his tail uncertainly, wriggled under her knees.

"So I ask this cop what's going on, and he says there's been an accident. And I'm like, Is it serious? And he's, no comment. Which is like, Yeah it's fucking serious!"

She shifted forward, bringing a yelp from Gromit. "What happened? Do you know?"

Wally had no reason to suppose Sue had shared a deep personal bond with Alistair Pope. Still, he answered with care. Aside from softening the blow, he wanted a clear reaction from her.

He got what he expected: shock mixed with a dash of horror, a sprinkling of grief, and a pinch of relish. What he didn't get was any certainty as to whether Sue had told him the truth, the whole truth, and nothing but the truth.

She asked the obvious questions. He gave her what few answers he could. "Of course, if they do figure it was murder," he concluded, "I'm about the last person in this town who's gonna hear about it." And added, as a safety precaution: "Being as I barely knew him–"

"Me either!" Sue interrupted. "I mean, he ate at Leo's, so, sure, I knew like where he lived. But as far as *know* him . . ." She grimaced and shrugged.

"I'd recognize him if he came in here for a book, but that's about it."

"Yeah. I hope . . ." She frowned. "With all the people in Quansett who had some grudge against him, I hope the cops appreciate. I mean, what I'm saying is, I guess I wouldn't be totally surprised if somebody, you know."

"You mean, he had enemies?"

"Oh, well, *enemies*, I don't know. He pissed people off, that's for sure. You'd hear shit at Leo's, like, 'that Alistair Pope, who the hell does he think he is?' But you couldn't prove it by me. I got along with him fine."

"Me too."

"I mean, not like I knew him that well, which I didn't, but I never had any problem at all."

"Me neither. Now, Ken Boose–"

"Oh, Ken! He hated Alistair! I heard him tell Leo once, he tried to steal a book from here. Pretended he just forgot to pay for it."

"Ken said he had to run right out the door after him," Wally nodded. "Course, he's an old skinflint anyways."

"Like Dinah. Chop off your hand if you eat a leftover doughnut. She used to jump all over Alistair every time he'd come in just before closing. Never made a damn bit of difference. Course, Dinah yells at everybody. Me the most."

"You know," said Wally, "if it's just for a night or two, you could crash on the couch in my Airstream."

"Cool!" Sue shifted forward as if she might jump up and hug him, but Gromit's bulk stopped her, still sleeping under her legs. "Wally, you just saved my life!"

"No problem. Seeing as it's you," he added, aiming for a lighter note, "and not for instance Dinah."

"Yeah." She giggled again. "Man! If I ever got that fat I'd shoot myself!"

"You should have seen her this afternoon. Riding with Rosey Sherman?"

"Omigod! What were they in, a Hummer? No–a Sherman tank!"

Wally took this opportunity to tell Sue about the Frigate's change of ownership. Her eyebrows went up; she wondered if he'd remodel the place or what. Then she veered back to Rosey and Dinah.

"But isn't he married?"

"Sure is. Gorgeous girl, and three beautiful kids."

"Then why . . .?" She giggled. "Men! Honest to god!"

"Well now, I don't imagine this was, you know."

"Are you kidding me? Dinah?" Sue grabbed the lead, happy to be the informer for a change instead of a listener. "You haven't heard about her other job?"

"No."

"You'll never guess. Not in a million years."

"You're right about that," Wally agreed.

She leaned forward and told him in a stage whisper: "Phone sex!"

In his mind's eye, Wally slipped a pair of photographs into an envelope which he locked in the secret compartment of his desk. "Well, I'll be damned," he said. Which at that moment struck him as a real possibility.

When Lydia made the hairpin turn around Quansett's town green, she faced a sight she'd never seen before. Edgar Rowdey stood on his porch steps holding a potted plant.

She drove through the gap in the hedge. He waved.

She parked the Morris under the magnolia tree and walked over to see what he was up to.

"Hul-lo." He wore a khaki canvas hat and gloves. A dark wisp–a leaf?–had caught in his white beard.

"Hey. Are you gardening?"

"Oh, after a fashion." He held up the pot. "I found black pansies. Who could resist?"

They weren't true black, but close: a deep velvety purple, like the night sky.

"You heard the news?" she asked.

He nodded. "Leo phoned." With a muddy gloved finger he pushed up his glasses, leaving a smudge on the side of his nose. "You were there? When he was discovered? The police and so forth?"

"Yeah." Suddenly Lydia felt exhausted. I need to sit down, she thought. Now.

"Dear, are you all right?"

After three hours of answering questions, grieving, worrying, and second-guessing, the simple concern in his voice made her eyes water.

"Come in for a cup of tea."

She followed him across the porch. The famous author's sanctuary she hadn't dared hope she'd ever be asked inside. This was not how her wish should have come true.

Edgar Rowdey set his flowerpot down on a bench near the front door, and his hat and gloves with it. Around the other side of the house he opened a side door and gestured for her to go in.

The room they entered smelled of cat. There was an ancient porcelain toilet to the right, but this clearly was an objet d'art, like the stained-glass window propped on a table behind it and the row of rusted brass tools on the mantelpiece straight ahead. Scuttling sounds in the next room suggested that the resident cat (at least, Lydia hoped it was a cat) had run for cover.

She followed him past a pair of short Ionic columns, a pyramid of cardboard book cartons, a stand-up plywood Cheshire cat, a dozen framed oil paintings hung on the walls and stacked against the fireplace, a wrought-iron floor lamp, a carved wooden coatrack with brass hooks, a once-fat armchair whose stuffing had apparently been clawed away some time ago, and a shearling jacket draped over a tea table which looked as though its owner had dropped it there one day after winter ended and forgotten it. Altogether the room reminded Lydia of a small museum she'd visited once in England.

They passed through a hall where a staircase met three doors, into a large country kitchen. More scuttling, and a flash of tabby tail. Ahead of her, Edgar Rowdey circled a long oak table to inspect a row of small dishes on the stone hearth of yet another fireplace. Along the mantelpiece ran a parade of vaguely creature-shaped rocks, like inflated animal crackers. Inside the fireplace sat a gigantic ball of brown rope.

"What kind of tea will you have?"

Lydia itched to grab a soapy handful of paper towels and scrub down the table. Her host dusted it off with a crumpled linen napkin instead. From a cabinet he lifted an angular willow-pattern teapot which she suspected had come from China centuries ago.

"Anything. Black, if you've got it."

"Keemun? Earl Grey?"

"Earl Grey. Please, let me help."

"Oh, no, no." Most of the wall between the doorway and the stove was drawers and cupboards. Edgar Rowdey opened one after another, pulling out clean napkins, flowered plates, a box of tea, a perforated ball, a jar of honey. Silver knives and spoons, slightly tarnished, came from a rack beside the sink. Lydia thought of the elaborate sanitation rituals at the Back End: no smoking or animals, all dishes washed in scalding water, tables and floors scrubbed daily, food preparation surfaces rigorously disinfected.

"There are crumpets," he told her happily. "A friend brought them from Cornwall. Do you prefer elderberry jam or currant?"

They cleared off chairs by moving stacks of mail to the metal chaise-longue frame at the end of the room, under the windows looking into the magnolia tree. Why a frame without cushions? It was painted the same vivid yellow as Lydia's Morris, which she glimpsed through the branches. She wondered if this had factored in Edgar Rowdey's decision to lend her the cottage.

Over tea (which was excellent) she asked him how many cats he had. With a grimace he confessed: "Seven." And added, "Not deliberately, I assure you! People are forever telling me about kittens that no one wants, that will be destroyed unless they find a home. And I always say No, *don't* bring it over, I have more than enough cats, I *can't* take another one; and they bring it over anyway, and I'm helpless."

Lydia spooned elderberry jam onto her plate. "Have the police talked to you about Alistair Pope?"

It came out sounding more like a change of subject than she meant it. She'd been thinking that no cop would be mulish enough to suspect a man who couldn't turn away a stray kitten of shoving his friend into a pond.

"Kevin Kelly phoned. He said he's making a list of everyone who was at Leo's when it happened, or shortly before. So that, once they know, the detectives can go right out and ask their questions."

Mild as his manner was, his phrasing surprised her. "Once they know . . .?"

"That it wasn't an accident."

Not *if* it wasn't an accident.. "You mean . . . Do you think someone killed him?"

"Oh, heavens, yes. I'm afraid so. As many times as we've walked around that pond together?" He paused, as if for Lydia to catch up. "Did you see his shoes?"

"Not really." Suddenly she couldn't imagine why she hadn't looked. "There was a frog on his head."

He nodded sympathetically.

"Couldn't it have– I don't know. Spooked him? and he tripped?"

"Mm. I suppose." His rings clinked against his teacup.

"But you don't think so?" When he didn't reply, she continued: "Too big a man, too small a frog?" Silence again. "Well, and he had leaf litter on his clothes. So he must have been under the tree, not just by the pond."

"Mm."

How can an author of gruesome little books, Lydia wondered, be so disengaged? "What about his shoes?"

"Oh, well, he swore by them. Leather sneakers, some well-known brand if you follow that sort of thing. Versatile and flexible, he said. Good for everything–jogging, driving, filmmaking– He could have crossed a chasm on a rope bridge. He could have walked up a playground slide."

Lydia gazed into her teacup; inhaled the fragrant bergamot, watched the black flecks settling at the bottom. "What about medical problems?" she asked against hope. "Like a heart condition?"

Edgar Rowdey shook his head. His face was thoughtful, but there was sadness in his voice. "One can only wish. So to say." After a moment he continued: "Dear soul though he was in many ways, Alistair was not one to suffer in silence. If he had troubles, he shared them. Or triumphs. He came in crowing from his last doctor's visit–lungs of an athlete, body of a twenty-year-old, and so forth."

He bit into a crumpet. Lydia set down her cup, which was trembling in her hands. She took deep breaths. Follow the White Rabbit down that hole, drink that tea, eat those crumpets, and how can you be surprised when your surroundings start to quiver and quake?

In the few days she'd known Alistair Pope, she'd found him charming, elusive, contradictory–in short, a typical guy. Maddening at times, but knowable. Not, as her host had observed, a man to keep secrets. Today he'd become a mystery. If Edgar Rowdey was right, some aspect or action of this man had turned another human being into a murderer.

"Do you have any idea why somebody would kill him?" she asked.

With crumbs cascading down his beard, he answered, "Oh, who knows?" He brushed at his sweatshirt. "Who knows why anyone ever does anything?"

The phone rang: an old-fashioned bell sound from a wall unit near the sink. Edgar Rowdey ignored it. After four rings Lydia said, "You might want to get that. Under the circumstances."

She could tell from his end of the conversation that it was a friend calling, with news about Alistair's death. There was no question of eavesdropping; all she could hear was an occasional murmur of surprise or concern. Finally he said, "Let me check," and put his hand over the mouthpiece.

"Carlo," he told her. "Wondering about dinner. Caroline thinks Leo shouldn't be left alone. Will you join us?"

"Yes." She guessed they had agreed that she shouldn't be left alone, either. "I'd be honored. What kind of dinner?"

His eyebrows rose above the wire rims of his glasses. "Isn't that always the question!" He consulted the phone and relayed the answer: "Caroline says pizza would be simplest, but Leo may insist on fixing spaghetti."

"I propose," said Lydia, "that Mudge and I will cook. "

Chapter Sixteen

Would it jinx the Flying Wedge to be launched by Alistair Pope's death? If so, too bad. Lydia reached Mudge by cell phone at the auto parts store. He told her she was prodigious and of course he'd rather come back and cook dinner for six than go out drinking. They agreed she would buy fresh bread at the Whistling Pig while he swung by the Barnstable Harbor fish market to check out the day's catch. She would meet him at Village Deli and Produce in half an hour.

Lydia brought notes on the diners' preferences ("Like we don't know by now?" said Mudge) and a handful of $20 bills pressed upon her by Edgar Rowdey as a condition of accepting her offer.

Still in the state of unreality that had descended over them at the frog pond, the partners rolled their shopping cart through canyons of fruits and vegetables. With less than two hours until dinner, the Flying Wedge's debut would feature maximum elegance with minimum time, labor, and travel.

Since Leo insisted on making spaghetti, their main course would be fresh flounder drizzled with black butter on a bed of pasta tossed with garlic, lemon zest, peas, and parmesan cheese. For appetizers Lydia would roll cherry tomatoes in strips of spiced ham and sun-dried tomato tortillas spread with cream cheese. On vegetables they punted: a salad of mixed greens with more cherry tomatoes and a lemon-garlic-parmesan dressing.

Mudge assured Lydia he could pull off a mango-blackberry custard tart for dessert, if she didn't mind homemade jam instead of actual berries.

"How about champagne?" he asked as they steered toward the checkout line. "To celebrate your one-week anniversary?"

"I wish! But . . . celebrate? No way."

"Goes great with flounder."

"Still. Anyhow, Edgar says Carlo's supplying wine."

Mudge asked Lydia when she'd started calling him Edgar. She said she hadn't yet, but since she'd have to call him something soon–like, tonight–now was a good time to warm up.

In the parking lot she added, "He's pretty sure Alistair was murdered."

"How come? Does he know who?" Mudge tucked their groceries into the Morris's footwell. "He wasn't even there, was he?"

"No." Lydia outlined Edgar's reasoning. "I have to say, after seeing his house? plus his books? This is a man with a–well, let's say, a unique mind."

Turning into the Back End's driveway, Lydia was relieved to find the parking lot and yard empty. The lawn still looked trampled, but except for a cordon of yellow crime-scene tape, there was no sign of what had happened here three hours ago. She forced herself not to think about where Alistair's mortal remains were right now.

Just as well the Flying Wedge would have the home court advantage for its first game. In Leo's kitchen she could find a cleaver or a salt shaker, a baking dish or a basting brush, with her eyes shut.

Eyes shut. Clammy skin, pale and opaque like a mannequin's. Blue lips that just this morning had been warm, mobile, pink with life.

She sliced ham with unnecessary vehemence. That's what you get, Lydia! You run away and think you're shedding your problems like a snakeskin. Instead, out of the frying pan into the fire.

"Mudge!"

"I'm right here."

"It is good we're doing this, right?"

He twirled a giant colander on his fingertips. Warm brown eyes and lips smiled at her. Life goes on, they assured her, and feeding your friends is a fine way to help it along.

Edgar (as they both were now calling him) had astutely offered to drive Leo over to Carlo and Caroline's for a glass of wine. When the hors d'oeuvres were ready, Lydia would deliver them there, while Mudge made piecrust. After appetizers, the four other diners would join the chefs at the Back End. That way most of the work should be done before Leo invaded the kitchen.

"OK." She untied her apron. "I'm off with the munchies."

Mudge held out the toothpick-bristling platter. "Lydia?"

"Yeah?"

"You don't think– None of them could have killed him, did they?"

"No." She spoke more positively than she felt. "Come on, Mudge! They're like twice his age and half his size. And old friends. You know?"

"Yeah." But she could tell he wasn't totally convinced, either.

We have to find out for sure, she realized in the car. After DeAnne, nobody can stand another month of wondering.

No convivial laughter or conversation greeted her at the studio. Hearing nothing but the crunch of her own feet on the gravel driveway, Lydia wondered if the group inside had just asked each other the same question about her and Mudge.

"How's it going?" she asked Carlo, who met her at the door.

"Oh, look at these lovely treats!" He managed a gallant smile. "We're a bit subdued, I'm afraid. Better now, with something to chew on. Besides the events of the day."

"Is there any news?"

"Not yet. Leo's chafing at the bit. Caroline's persuaded him not to go pestering the police till after he cooks the pasta."

They agreed to convene at the Back End in twenty minutes. And yes, he and Caroline had a lemon zester she and Mudge could borrow.

Some weird pair of couples we are, she thought in the car. The Ropeses would choke on their Nescafe.

Mudge's piecrust was browning in the oven, and he'd assembled the salad. Had he ever met DeAnne's parents? Lydia asked, chopping garlic. No; why? Oh, no particular reason. At least, she added to herself, not until we find out if Alistair was murdered.

They found out during the lull between dinner and dessert.

So far, the Flying Wedge's debut was a grand success. Mudge, buoyed by praise and wine, had made a short promotional speech. Carlo, Caroline, and Edgar promised to become regular clients. Leo brushed off the idea of in-home catering and grandly volunteered the Back End for any future gourmet adventures. Then he headed for the phone.

Lydia, carrying dishes from their back-room table to the kitchen, didn't try to stop him. Only extreme good manners had kept Alistair Pope from dominating the conversation all evening.

"Get me Pete Altman, will ya?"

She decided she might as well stick around and load the dishwasher. Leo's side of the conversation alternated between silence and bluster. She took her time hand-washing the knives. She measured out coffee. Mudge came in to get the pie. Lydia lifted a finger to her lips.

"You want to put that in English for me?" Leo asked in a grim voice.

He wouldn't tell them anything until the whole group was together in the back room. Then he announced: "I just talked to Pete Altman over at the police station."

"What did he say?" asked Carlo.

Leo's frown deepened until his bushy white eyebrows almost met above his nose. "He said the medical examiner says somebody whacked Al Pope on the head."

Mudge set down his pie on the next table.

"Of course they don't just come out and tell you straight–lot of Latin words, abrasions and contusions–but that's what they mean. Somebody whacked him, and then shoved him in the frog pond. Or he fell." Leo's voice caught; he cleared his throat. "More likely fell; there was leaves in his hand, like he grabbed onto the tree. Anyhow, he drowned. Dammit."

The silence that followed grew louder the longer it went on. Caroline broke it by raising her glass. "To poor Alistair. Nobody deserves that."

Carlo poured wine into every glass, and they all joined in the somber toast.

After a moment Lydia asked, "Did he say anything else?"

"Like pulling teeth. What the heck does he think I'm gonna

do, go on Oprah? They're investigating, end of story. Not like I need him to tell me, every one of us at this table, you can bet we're right on top of the suspect list."

"They're investigating it as a murder?" asked Carlo. And answered his own question: "Well, I suppose they would, wouldn't they? Whether he fell or was pushed. If someone attacked him, he's a victim."

Mudge, still standing beside the table, arched an eyebrow at Lydia. She shook her head. This was no moment for pie.

"We're all victims!" Leo slammed both hands on the table. "Why don't they just bring in a wrecking ball? You think they even care what a murder investigation's gonna do to my restaurant? Like I got insurance for this kind of thing? Yellow tape all over the place, cops giving my customers the third degree, and don't even start with the gossip. Who's gonna want to eat lunch at a crime scene?"

"Half the Cape, I dare say," Caroline replied drily.

"Present company, needless to remark," Edgar observed. "Count your blessings."

"It could have been me, is that what you're saying? It could have been any of us! We don't know, do we! The killer could be lurking out there right now. I live here! On the premises! What about that? I could be next!"

"Oh, stop hogging the limelight," Edgar told him. "Not that anyone who knows you doesn't want to kill you; but whoever killed Alistair must have been after him in particular."

"Why do you say that?" asked Carlo.

Edgar didn't answer immediately. Lydia suspected they were all entertaining the same thought: *Who–including me–had no motive at all to kill Alistair Pope?*

Caroline stepped in. "He enjoyed upsetting people." Her voice was calm, her demeanor as unruffled as her sculpted platinum hair. "It was almost a reflex."

"The imp of the perverse," said Carlo.

She nodded. "An irresistible urge, once he'd brought something to the brink of success, to ruin it."

"Along with whoever else was involved." Carlo sounded

uncharacteristically bitter. "Is that what you mean, Edgar?"

"Oh, well, yes, from the motive side. I was thinking of the other side. Opportunity. The person in question must have either lured him under the tree or planned to meet him there after I left, wouldn't you say? For this to happen without witnesses, in such a public place?"

"That's right," Mudge spoke up. "If they got together here, or the parking lot, I would've seen them, or you could," he nodded at Leo and Lydia, "or anybody who came out of lunch late."

"Planned or not," said Caroline, "this person–shall we call him X?–took a great risk."

"So did Alistair," Carlo observed. "Stepping out of sight with someone who meant to kill him?"

"Premeditated murder!" Leo exploded. "Call a spade a spade! Lurking! Stalking! Attacking! We've got a homicidal maniac on the loose!"

"Oh, I don't know." Lydia had been fighting back a shudder, recalling her own rendezvous with Alistair Pope in that leafy sanctuary. "Maybe they were just talking or something, and it got out of hand. Couldn't it?"

"Absolutely," said Carlo. "Surely that's more likely than . . ." He let it trail off.

"Unless," said Edgar, "X knew the back way."

"Aha," Caroline said softly.

"What back way?" asked Lydia.

Everyone began to explain. Leo, being loudest, prevailed. "Through the far side of the tree. Historical Society headquarters, the old Captain Josiah Richards House. Captain Shipcrash he was known, on account of he couldn't navigate a dinghy into the harbor without running it on the rocks. Left his homestead to the town, in gratitude for a lifetime of rescues. Big old mansion full of antiques. Fancy garden, nature paths, picnic tables and so on."

"If you walk under the tree and up the hill behind it," said Caroline, "you'll come to their parking area."

"Cars in and out all the time," said Carlo. "No one the wiser."

There was a short silence as they considered this new factor.

"Excuse me." Mudge leaned over the table as if he couldn't

wait another minute. "Are you all ready for dessert? Can I serve the pie?"

Seeing how urgently it mattered to him, they assured him they were and he could. Mudge presented his piece de resistance: a gorgeous layer of dotted purple fanned across a creamy yellow striped surface, framed in a perfect fluted crust. Everyone oohed and aahed. Mudge cut slices to order, then passed around a bowl of whipped cream flecked with lemon zest. Lydia slipped back into the kitchen for the coffee.

Again conversation ceased. People who had sworn half an hour ago they would never eat again requested just one more tiny sliver. Mudge beamed as his pie disappeared. Lydia wondered how soon the cops would find out he'd been sleeping under the Elephant Tree, and how long it would be before she saw that smile again.

"Are we assuming, then," asked Caroline, "this X is someone Alistair knew?"

"Can't be," said Leo around a mouthful of pie. "A tramp. Take my word for it. Nobody from around here."

"How could a total stranger have caught him at just that spot, at just that moment?" Carlo countered.

"Accident. Bad luck."

Murmurs of disagreement. Caroline's eyebrow arched. "A homicidal hobo?"

"Well, maybe not a total stranger to *him*," Leo said crossly. "Somebody he ticked off in New York. Working on a movie or whatnot. One of those theatrical types."

"Alistair didn't work with theatrical types. He made documentaries."

"What about those kids in black he brought up here? Come in asking for chai or chewbotty or whatever the heck it was. Girls with tattoos, boys with earrings–don't tell me that bunch wasn't theatrical, plus a few sandwiches short of a picnic. One of them, you can bet on it. Some crewman."

"Or woman," said Carlo.

"Ha! She'd have to be a body-builder, to knock down a fella the size of Al."

"Oh, they were," said Carlo. "Mostly. Hoisting lights and so forth?"

"Some kind of lady wrestler. Like those gals on the WWF. You seen them on TV?"

"You know, the thing about Alistair's crew," Caroline said, and stopped.

"Fists like sledge hammers!"

Edgar Rowdey made a noise in his throat. "Do you mind?" A limp chunk of mango, speared on his dessert fork, hovered above a leftover puff of whipped cream. "Can we not go on about this? I for one am still trying to enjoy the fine work of our two brilliant chefs."

Carlo raised his coffee mug immediately. "Hear hear!"

"To Lydia and Mudge!" Caroline seconded.

"Two?" Leo demanded. "Two brilliant chefs? What, you think perfect spaghetti al dente grows on trees?"

It worked! Lydia thought happily. We did it! Just like in Cambridge: feed people a really good meal, and watch their spirits rise like a souffle.

Not until she was pouring coffee refills did she register that Edgar's change of subject also had worked.

Was it simply from squeamishness, or good manners, or both, that he'd steered the conversation away from Alistair Pope? Or had he spotted a land mine he didn't want his friends to set off?

They'd settled into normal after-dinner chitchat: summer plans, gardening, Carlo and Caroline's opera, a play they'd seen in New York. No clues there.

Well, fine! thought Lydia. Gather ye rosebuds while ye may. Plenty of time tomorrow to dodge bullets.

Chapter Seventeen

When the bullets started flying, they came from an unexpected direction.

Charmed by his own eloquence, Leo made an earlier-than-usual entrance Thursday morning and summoned his staff to the kitchen. The people of Quansett, he declared, depend on the Back End. Like the Washington Monument, or Yellowstone Park. The Back End depends on its crew. Therefore, he, on behalf of Quansett, was counting on Dinah, Mudge, Lydia, and Bruno to keep things going exactly the same as usual. If customers want to talk about the tragedy, don't get sucked in. Tell them we share their grief and move on. They got a problem with that, let 'em go harass the cops. This is a restaurant, not an information booth. And if some nosy parker pulls out a camera, well, do what you gotta do.

Leo retired upstairs. The kitchen crew returned to work. Seemingly every soul who'd ever eaten at the Back End, or heard about it on the news, or read about it in the paper, showed up for breakfast. Leo's instructions were ignored. Service slowed to a crawl. Leo reappeared, combed and shaved and dressed for work, and hollered at both staff and customers. Mudge told Lydia he'd never seen the place so full.

Around ten, the crowd began to thin. Lydia was serving two orders of Egz Bennie to a booth in the back room when she glanced out the window and spotted a man shooting photos of the frog pond.

Leo had gone to the basement for supplies. Dinah stood by the grill fiercely whipping something in a bowl. Mudge, at the cash register, was ringing up a large family.

Lydia stepped outside to investigate.

The intruder must have climbed over the yellow crime-scene

tape. Judging from his camera, his clothes, and his concentration, this was no garden-variety nosy parker. Not only his long lens but the padded camera bag over his shoulder suggested a professional. He looked her age or a little older, with wavy dark-blond hair curling over the collar of his Red Sox windbreaker. His jeans were rolled up over brown leather boots with waterproof bottoms, as if he'd come prepared for wading.

"Hey," she called.

The camera lowered. "Hey," he grinned back. Then, taking in her apron: "You work here?"

"Yes. What are you doing?"

He held out his hand. "Dave Wheeler, Cape Cod Times." His grip was strong, like the detective's. "Pete Altman–Detective Altman?–wanted some follow-up shots."

Half of Lydia was intrigued. The other half, mindful of her responsibilities, asked: "So you're also a police photographer?"

"Not really," he answered cheerfully. "We just ran into each other at another scene up the road. Figured, while we're in the neighborhood, might as well–"

"Another scene?" she interrupted. "Was somebody else–?"

"Oh, no, no. Just a burglary." He was still unobtrusively looking her over, a reaction Lydia was used to from Leo's customers, who evidently didn't run across many women with green-streaked hair and multiple earrings. "Who are you, if you don't mind my asking?"

"Is this for publication?"

"Not unless you sneak into a photo."

"OK then. Lydia Vivaldi." By now she could say it almost automatically.

"Lydia Vivaldi," he repeated, with evident approval. Of her or the name? "You been here long?"

"A week. Where's Detective Altman?"

"Under the tree." Dave Wheeler turned to look. Lydia, following his glance, couldn't see anyone. She wondered if this was a devious papparazzi trick. She wished Leo or somebody would come out and take over as watchdog.

"Why would he bring you instead of his own guy?"

His grin reappeared. "I'm a better photographer." As if he appreciated her dilemma, he added, "I used to work for the department. Now I just help out sometimes. How about you?"

"What?"

"Did Sue take off for good this time, or are you just helping out?"

The overhanging branch rustled. A shoulder appeared through the leaves, in the same denim sport jacket Pete Altman had worn yesterday.

"I gotta go," said Lydia. "You guys about through here?"

"I am," said Dave Wheeler. "Hey, look at that."

Perched on the layered rocks along the pond's back rim sat two frogs, goggling as if they didn't want to miss a word of this awkward conversation.

Already the restaurant had filled up again. Lydia didn't get a chance to tell Leo what was going on outside. Dinah had half a dozen orders waiting on the sandwich bar. She'd just loaded a tray when a ruddy, well-fed man slammed through the front door.

"God damn it, I've been robbed!"

Immediately an electric buzz ran through the restaurant. Leo rushed toward him.

Lydia heard the story in pieces as it, and she, circulated.

Ed Roberts had arrived home an hour ago on the red-eye from Los Angeles to find his expensively furnished house stripped of valuables. Rugs, silver, state-of-the-art entertainment center, golf clubs, jewelry, even his antique model-train collection, gone! The police, the security company, his insurance agent, and the Cape Cod Times had just finished swarming through the place like ants at a picnic. Yes, of course he had a list, and some of the pieces were marked, but what the hell! Where was the alarm system? How did the crooks get away with that much loot–a brand-new 48-inch plasma TV, for christ's sake!–and nobody saw a damn thing?

Another scene up the road. Well, Mr. Wheeler, mused Lydia, haven't you had yourself a busy morning!

Edgar Rowdey had sauntered in during the hubbub. He sat

with his nose in a paperback book at his usual table, behind the banquette opposite the steam tables in the back room. Lydia had wondered why he hadn't come in earlier, and guessed the crowd had put him off. She found his mug on the mug shelf and brought him coffee.

"Thank you, dear." He set down the book. "And again, for that splendid dinner."

"My pleasure, I assure you."

"I take it we've had another burglary?"

She nodded. "What is this, a hotbed of crime I've landed in?"

One white eyebrow lifted above the rim of his glasses. "One does wonder, doesn't one?"

"How many is this? Carlo and Caroline's neighbors . . . "

"Cathy and Eric Stevens. Last week. Were you here then? Before them, the Vincents, on Shore Road."

"Shore Road. Isn't that where Ed Roberts lives?"

"It attracts the kind of people with the kind of belongings that attract thieves," he nodded. "Poor Pete Altman must wish he'd stayed in traffic control."

She got the impression Edgar knew, or suspected, more than he was saying. "Do you, or he, or anybody have an idea who's behind this?"

"Me? Mercy no. As for the rest, I daresay you'll hear a theory at every table."

He reopened his book: *God's Bits of Wood* by Sembene Ousmane. Happy as a clam at high tide, thought Lydia. "I'll be back," she stated.

On her way to the kitchen for his Scram Egz and Ing Muff, she eavesdropped for theories. The only ones she heard were vague and predictable: "Some kind of criminal gang," and "Nobody from around here." It surprised her that the Back End customers had shifted their focus so quickly from Alistair Pope's murder to Ed Roberts's plasma TV.

Dinah flipped a griddle cake and caught it. "Saw you talking to Dave Wheeler outside." With the other hand she scrambled eggs. "Was he over at Ed's? Put on two brown toast and a muff, will you?"

Forking bread onto the revolving toaster, Lydia repeated what little she'd learned from the photographer.

In Dinah's opinion, those thieves were either mighty smart or mighty lucky. The local police force only had two detectives. This being normally a slow time of year, between Memorial Day and tourist season, the other one–Bob Scanlan–was away on vacation. "Pete's OK, but he ain't the fastest gun in town. Not the guy you'd want juggling two jobs at once."

Lydia delivered Edgar Rowdey's breakfast. He murmured thanks without looking up from his book.

Back in the kitchen, she resumed: "What about Helen Wills? Isn't she a detective?"

"Helen's state, not local. They're floaters. Go anyplace there's a homicide, drug bust, big stuff like that. Hey. And speak of the devil."

Not Detective Wills, but Detective Altman. His eyes looked tired, and his thick salt-and-pepper hair was tousled. From poking around under the Elephant Tree? He stood just inside the door, as if reluctant to plunge any deeper into the hubbub of gossip. Lydia resumed chopping, after a quick glance confirmed that Dave Wheeler wasn't with him.

Leo, who'd been condoling with Ed Roberts in the back room, hurried past the kitchen.

He and Detective Altman met by the cash register and raised their hands for quiet. "Ladies and gentlemen, may I please have your attention!" Leo bellowed. "Hey! Shut up, will ya?"

A ripple spread outward of customers tapping spoons on glasses. Slowly the hubbub faded.

"Good morning," said Pete Altman. "Thanks, Leo. For anybody who doesn't know, I'm Detective Altman of the Exmouth police force. You probably all heard we're investigating an incident that occurred out by the pond here yesterday. Me and State Police Detective Wills, we're working together on this, and they've brought over their mobile crime lab to help us out. Now, I'm going to ask all of you that were on the premises yesterday between one and three PM to give us a hand. I mean that literally. What we want is your fingerprints, plus a strand of hair. Strictly voluntary, no pressure. And no rush–you go right on and finish up your lunch. If you're eating something messy, or greasy, like a sandwich or french fries, please wash your hands. Then the troopers outside in the mobile command center will take your name and contact information, and process you through."

"What if we weren't here yesterday?" someone called.

"Then if you'll just check in with Officer Kelly, and you're free to go."

Another shout: "What if we ain't got a hair to spare?"

That drew chuckles. "Hey there, Jack," Detective Altman quipped back, "nobody says it's gotta come off your head."

Through the screen door behind him, Lydia glimpsed a large white RV. She wondered if the cops were going to run DNA tests on everyone who'd been at Leo's yesterday afternoon, or if they'd found a hair (on Alistair? under the Elephant Tree?) that they were trying to match. Again she was struck by the irony she and Mudge had noted yesterday: how fascinating police procedure was to watch on TV, and how disturbing when you were in the middle of it and could only guess what they were after.

Leo went first. Lydia thought he was grandstanding, until Pete Altman came back a few minutes later and murmured to Dinah, who handed her spatula to Lydia and followed him outside. By then the customers were getting restless, so half a dozen of them went next. Then it was her turn.

If not for Kevin Kelly standing by the door, arms folded and feet planted firmly apart, leather-holstered pistol and baton hanging from his belt, eyes hidden by his visored hat, she might have felt like a movie star walking up the trailer steps. No champagne or make-up team inside, though. More like election day: a thirtyish woman in a blue blazer smiling at her from behind a table; a slightly younger man in a green golf shirt, not smiling, handing her a clipboard. Lydia wondered if they were really state police until she spotted the woman's rubber gloves and the man's semiautomatic pistol.

She filled out the form; allowed the female cop to press her fingers onto a stamp pad and roll her prints onto a sheet of paper; asked the male cop for a mirror so she could pick out a hair that wasn't green.

"Where's Detective Wills?"

"Oh, she's busy with the case." The female cop tweezed Lydia's hair into a tiny plastic bag. "She's over there leading a search right now."

"Of what? His house?"

"Thank you, Miss Vivaldi," the male cop intervened. "Can I see your I.D., please?"

She froze. "What?"

"Some form of identification, such as a driver's license?"

Stupid! Why didn't I see this coming? What imp of the perverse made me write my brave new name on the form? Now they'll arrest me, and Leo will fire me, and Sue will take over my job–

"Miss Vivaldi?"

"Right." She reached into her jeans pocket. "Only . . . I need to explain."

As she spoke, she could feel both cops' eyes on her, like the frogs on the pond ledge. The man took her license without a word and handed it to his partner. She examined it–no hurry–and handed it back.

"How do you get paid?"

"Excuse me?"

The female cop repeated her question. "You work here, right? Does Leo write you checks?"

"Oh. Yes. Well, only one so far, for the first three days. But I told him. I mean, of course, I had to. He said he didn't care. He said, or somebody said, Cape Cod's like the French Foreign Legion anyway."

"Which name goes on your paychecks?" put in the male cop.

"My old one. The one on my license."

"OK." He made a note.

From his partner came a sound of disagreement. "We'll look into it," he assured her.

"Don't leave the Cape," he told Lydia.

Chapter Eighteen

On the other side of Route 6A, AKA Main Street, AKA Old King's Highway, Wallace Hicks asked himself what in holy jehosophat he'd gone and done.

This wasn't the first time he'd confronted that question. Early this morning, as his brain staggered into consciousness, Wally had realized his left arm was still asleep. Crushed under the weight of a warm body. The same body that was pressing against his chest and leg. Furless. Not Gromit, who wasn't allowed in his bunk anyhow.

Last night came back in fragments. Him and Sue eating pizza at the picnic table behind the Frigate. Her chugging her Rolling Rock and magically producing an almost-full fifth of Wild Turkey. Him matching her with a joint the size of a Tiparillo. Stars tilting crazily through the branches of the mulberry tree as the two of them staggered, giggling like loonies, into the Airstream. Him pawing through cupboards, searching in vain for his spare sheets.

As daylight washed over him, Wally gingerly pulled away the strand of curly hair stuck to the corner of his mouth. Like the possibility never crossed your mind, Hicks? Like you didn't manage to find the condoms while you couldn't find sheets for the couch?

The tsunami that at midnight had swept him up like a giddy surfer now felt like a tide that had gone out and left him beached. Hell's bells! Letting karma guide the mission was one thing. Waking all tangled up with a girl you hardly knew was a whole nother kettle of fish.

Why was she here, of all places? What was she up to?

What would she want (expect? demand?) from him when her eyes opened?

His foot groped for the floor and landed in slime. Another memory dropped into place: Gromit sneaking off into the bushes with the pizza box.

Cleaning up the mess sent prickles rushing up and down his arm. Suddenly he felt fingertips dancing on his bare shoulder. Sue lay grinning at him, all pink skin and breasts and bird's-nest hair. She murmured something he couldn't quite catch. When he leaned closer, she pounced. For two seconds Wally resisted. Boxes to open. Books to shelve. Clarity to regain. Then the tsunami rolled over him again, and he forgot everything except why he'd let this happen in the first place.

Fortunately the Frigate didn't open until half past ten. At 9:55, Wally unlocked the back door. Sue refused to wash up in the Airstream. If they took a quick shower together in the shop's bathroom upstairs, that left just barely enough time to eat breakfast, walk Gromit . . .

At quarter past ten, panting on a towel in the geography section–the one clear patch of floor big enough for two adults to get horizontal–the same question whisked through Wally's mind again: What the jumpin' jiminy are you doing, Hicks? Have you gone loco?

Only by persuading Sue to walk Gromit over to the Pig for take-out coffee and pastries did he manage to spruce up himself and the shop before the boss arrived. Luck was on his side: Roosevelt Sherman was too full of the latest news to ask why there were wet footprints alongside the World Atlases.

"Five-thousand square-foot house, cleaned out. Electronics, valuables, everything!"

Wally made suitable noises of sympathetic astonishment.

"Second one this month, according to Connie. Which our realtor sure as heck didn't mention, when Thea and I looked at that Colonial two doors down. Safe and private, she told us. Most people don't even lock their doors. Ha!"

They moved into the office. Rosey Sherman's first act of ownership had been to clear enough space for two brand-new upholstered rolling chairs, privately christened Papa Bear and Mama Bear by Wally. Day by day, the Frigate team was inching through Ken Boose's erratic records.

As his brain engaged, Wally discovered that his head

throbbed. His stomach felt queasy. God willing, Sue would come back any minute with coffee. No. God willing, given the necessity for explanation, Sue would take her time. Hang around the Pig for a while. Long enough to wear off her attitude of having a right to be here. The last thing he needed–

"Some quiet little town, huh?" Rosey rolled himself up to the desk. "Yesterday a murder, today a heist. I ran into Ken Boose at the Whistling Pig–man, is he glad to be getting out! Just in time, he said, what with chain stores, coyotes, and now this crime wave."

"Murder?" Wally had to clear his throat. "You mean, Alistair Pope . . .?"

"That's what they say."

The throbbing in his temples became a pounding like kettle-drums. Wally strained through the din to hear more.

"Somebody knocked him out and pushed him in the pond."

"Who? Do they know?"

"They'd sure like to find out. They're asking questions all over town. Who had it in for him? Or, if it was just some tramp under a tree, wrong place at the wrong time kind of thing, why jump him like that?"

Wally's stomach was churning dangerously. "Mm," was all he could say.

"One thing I'm kind of concerned about . . ." Rosey shook his head. "The last person to see him alive was Edgar Rowdey. There was some buzz at the Whistling Pig about them going at it out there. Which, I have to tell you–"

The door rattled. Hinges creaked. Rosey Sherman stopped talking and swiveled his chair. The familiar clickety-clack of Gromit's eager paws was followed by flip-flop female footsteps.

"Hey there." Sue held out a brown paper bag.

"What?" Wally persisted, though he could see this chat was over.

"Coffee, Mr. Sherman?"

"Well, good morning. Thank you very much."

She winked at Wally, who couldn't help smiling back.

"I'm Sue," she told Rosey, handing out cups. "Used to work in the neighborhood. Came by to say hi to my old friends." She ticked her cup against Wally's. "Sure was a surprise to find out Ken Boose sold the Frigate."

"Kinda surprised him, too," said Rosey.

Wally took a long grateful swig of life-saving white coffee, no sugar, and hoped she wouldn't be shy about producing the pastries he'd given her ten bucks to buy.

"Any news on the crime wave?" Rosey inquired.

"Yeah, well, blah-blah-blah." She perched on a filing cabinet. "That's all they were talking about at the Pig. I guess the cops are over at Leo's now, with the van?"

"The van?" asked Wally.

"RV they've got that's like a crime lab? Jim Byrne said forget about taking suspects down to HQ–now they take the van to the suspects. You know, fingerprints and shit?" She reached into her brown bag.

Rosey was intrigued. "The cops here have a mobile crime lab?"

Wally stepped in, so as to prevent Sue from being distracted. "Not the Exmouth cops. This'd be either the county sheriff's department or the state troopers."

Sue fished out a smaller bag and ripped it open: cinnamon buns, cheese Danish, muffins.

"State troopers? Aren't they for, like, speeding?"

Wally grabbed a blueberry muffin as the quickest and neatest to wolf down at a crowded desk. (Later, with luck, he and Sue could share the sticky buns, and lick the sugar off each other's mouths and fingers.) "These are detectives."

Rosey took a Danish. "Were they after anybody particular at the Back End?"

Sue shrugged. "Whoever killed Alistair. I guess they don't have much of a clue. Jim Byrne said they're getting everybody's fingerprints who was around there yesterday, so they can match them up."

Wally nodded. "Create a database."

"Did they find prints at the scene?" Rosey asked Sue.

"I don't know."

"Won't get 'em very far if they didn't," Wally observed.

"Or if they did." Rosey was frowning.

"Why not?" Sue asked him.

"If you committed a murder, would you go back the next day to the scene of the crime for lunch? And voluntarily hand over your fingerprints to the cops?"

"Huh," said Wally. "When you put it like that . . . "

"Voluntarily?" asked Sue.

"I'm no lawyer, but I doubt they can force anybody. Not without a warrant."

"Oh, I get it. So then, whoever says no, they're a suspect!"

"Yup," said Rosey grimly.

For a few moments no one spoke. Wally wondered how it would affect Leo's business, and Quansett's morale, to have a mobile crime lab identifying potential murderers in the Back End parking lot, and whether Pirandello's readers would expect him to go over and investigate, or if that would be the height of stupidity, given that you could hardly reach manhood in the United States of America without being picked up by the cops for something, which they might very well keep buried in their secret files, like a cocked pistol, in case you ever pulled a threatening move such as exposing their shenanigans online.

"Well." Sue stretched. "Gotta get my buns on the road. Ha ha."

"Thanks for the refreshments," said Rosey.

"Yeah," Wally seconded quickly, in case she felt tempted to explain. "Thanks for all of this. It's been great to see you," he added.

"Back atcha," she patted his arm.

"Where you heading?" Rosey asked her.

"Up to Bourne. I heard about a job. Guy's supposed to be back today."

"What kind of a job?"

Oh, no, thought Wally. Don't go there.

"Whatever. Cooking? I don't care. Anything pays more'n eight bucks an hour."

But Rosey had that familiar speculative look. "You ever done inventory?"

Sue shrugged. "I done everything one time or another."

"We sure could use some help around here. Nine bucks, twenty hours a week to start?"

Sue held out her hand. Rosey's large brown fingers gripped her slender pink ones. Wally battled to keep his expression cheerful as he silently asked himself again: Dammit, Hicks, what the H-E-double-toothpick have you gone and done?

Chapter Nineteen

Curiosity might have kept Lydia watching the cops move people through their mobile crime lab, if work hadn't called her inside. She did wait to make sure Edgar Rowdey got out OK. She hadn't liked the aggressive way Kevin Kelly hustled him up the steps.

Besides, business was slowing. Most cars that nosed into the driveway paused, turned around, and sped off.

Here he came: lanky, nonchalant, a distinctive figure with his almost-bald head, Santa Claus beard, and bright yellow sweater.

"You look like Jonah escaping from the whale."

"Moby Dick," he agreed, examining his fingers.

"Where's Ahab when we need him?" Lydia walked with him toward his black VW wagon. "Assuming you've still got both legs?"

"Oh, yes." Edgar rubbed a smudge off the paperback book he'd been reading at breakfast. "This is only a fishing expedition. Not likely to catch anything, I imagine."

A TV truck was pulling in behind the big white RV. "Why's that?" asked Lydia.

"Hm. Well, you know, for the police, this is a nightmare. Not one but two serious crimes dropped in their laps, with no solid leads on either one. Poor bunnies! The press already nipping at their heels, and here comes television. What can they do but buzz about like a swarm of busy bees? They can't have had time yet to process anything from either site–hairs, fingerprints, and so forth. Or, for that matter, decide who's in charge of what. Still, where there are news media, wheels must visibly turn."

"Decide who's in charge of what? Isn't that automatic?"

"You may well ask! Who knew what a labyrinthine law-enforcement structure we have on Cape Cod? I certainly didn't, until I asked those two officers inside. Moby Dick belongs to them–that is, the state police. They're called in by the district attorney to help local departments on big cases, such as murder, which the D.A.'s office expects to prosecute later on. I suppose that's only common sense–while they're assisting, they can make sure to collect all the right evidence for court. However! For crimes other than murder, it's the Barnstable County Sheriff's Department that backs up the local police. What do they call it? BCI? Something like that. Anyhoo. Besides their own acronym, they also have their own white whale, and their own criminal investigation officers. CIOs."

"Wow," said Lydia. "Why is that? Duplicate systems?"

"I have no idea. This being New England, they may have just grown that way, like the streets of Boston, or crabgrass." His eyebrows bobbed expressively. "In any event. Here we have our own dear Kevin Kelly, who'd rather be scouring the Roberts place with a fine-tooth comb, out in the parking lot cooling his heels on guard duty. Because a few hours ago, his two unrelated break-ins turned into a string or a spree or whatever the term is, and hopped into the detectives' bailiwick. Meaning Pete Altman's bailiwick, since Bob is on vacation; plus whatever CIO the sheriff sends him for forensic purposes. Not to be confused with his partner on the murder case, state police detective Helen Wills, and *her* forensic team, who have an acronym as well, but don't ask me what it is."

This, thought Lydia, is why he writes books about bizarre crimes and I cook soup. "You found out all that while they were taking your fingerprints?"

"I was curious."

"Well, can the burglaries hop back to Kevin Kelly, then? or the whatsit, the CIO? Somebody besides Pete Altman? Since the murder's more important."

"Important." He dug his keys out of his pocket. "To whom? Ed Roberts might argue that Alistair Pope can't return from the dead, but his stolen goods are out there waiting to be recovered. His neighbors might argue that until the burglars are caught, no home in Quansett is safe. Whereas there's no indication that whoever killed Alistair will go after someone else."

He opened the car door. "Do you believe that?" she asked him. "That whoever killed Alistair won't go after anyone else?"

"Oh, who's to say?"

He spoke lightly, flippantly, in the tone Lydia was coming to recognize as ducking the issue.

"Don't you think," she persisted, "that's a more urgent question than whether Ed Roberts gets his TV back?"

"It is to us. Needless to remark."

Lydia's heart was pounding. "And what about the possibility Alistair isn't the first victim? What if–"

An emphatic baritone voice cut her off. "Miss Valentine?"

Detective Altman was approaching across the parking lot.

Edgar's eyebrows rose above the rims of his glasses. Lydia shuddered.

Pete Altman's shoes crunched on the gravel. She felt like a rabbit frozen in a field, hoping against all probability that something will distract the diving hawk.

"Can I have a minute?"

Inside, the detective had looked tired; here, he radiated exhaustion. His work day must have started as early as mine, she realized. And mine at least is almost done.

"Sure."

Edgar shut his door and leaned against the car.

"Mr. Rowdey, you don't need to stay."

"Oh, no bother at all."

Lydia drew in a deep breath and let it out. Bless Edgar! What could the cops do to her with Quansett's top luminary watching?

Pete Altman flipped open a notebook. "I understand from Trooper Brustein that since you arrived here last week you've been using the name Lydia Vivaldi. The one you gave me. But your real name is"–he checked his notes–"Liz Valentine?"

Here we go, thought Lydia. "Yeah. Well, sort of. I haven't tried to deceive anybody, if that's what you mean. I told Leo–"

"Hold on. Let's stick to basics, OK? Your name is not Lydia Vivaldi. Right?"

"No. Yes. It is now."

"Legally?"

"Well, legally; I'm not sure how that works. I haven't, you know, gone to court to change it. But this is the–"

"Then legally," he interrupted, "your name is Liz Valentine? Or Elizabeth?"

"That was my name when I got my license."

"Is that the name on your Social Security card?"

"I don't have a card. I have a number, but . . . "

"In which name?"

"Don't take this wrong. Lynn Vail."

He stared at her. Then he took out a pen. "Spell that for me."

Lydia glanced at Edgar. If these revelations shocked him, he didn't show it. His expression remained mildly curious but placid.

"What are your parents' names?"

"William and Charlotte Vail. They were then. When I was born."

"Oh. Have they changed their names, too?"

"My father's dead. My mother's remarried. Mrs. Richard Leidesdorff."

"Phone number?"

"I'd have to look it up."

"You do that, Miss Vail." Detective Altman folded his arms, a caricature of patience. "And I'll need your social security number, and your previous address and employer."

Not the right time to explain about the Cambridge house and the Fix-It Chix. "All that's back at the cottage. I can call you when I get off work."

She could see *No* on his face before it came out of his mouth. So, evidently, could Edgar. "If I may," he interjected. "Leo needs Lydia back in there for lunch. Poor man."

"Maybe Leo needs to know that *Lydia* has been working for him under false pretenses."

"Now, Pete," said Edgar. "She's already said she told him. And look at Alistair Pope: he was Al until he went into films. These things happen. It appears to me a more pressing question might be–" He stopped. "But it's not my business. Sorry. You go right ahead."

"No," said Pete Altman. "You go ahead. What's your question?"

"Have you found his cell phone?"

Pete Altman's sagging eyes opened a little wider. "Excuse me?"

"Alistair's cell phone? He took it everywhere. Like a pet Chihuahua. Was it with his body?"

There was a pause. "What kind of cell phone?"

"Oh, dear, I wish I could tell you. Not my field, I'm afraid."

Lydia said, "Not a smartphone. The long thin fold-up kind. Silver and blue. I don't know what brand, or what service. It had a ring tone like a doorbell."

"There you are," said Edgar, as if handing him a gift-wrapped package.

"Mm." Pete's upper lip twitched, as if he'd just opened a gift-wrapped box of nightcrawlers. "OK. And he generally carried this phone where? Do you know?"

"Left inside pocket of his army jacket," said Lydia.

"Aha. Well, suppose the deceased didn't have a phone like that on him." He was still addressing Edgar. "Where else would you look for it?"

"Oh, heavens, I'm not a detective. I have no idea." Modestly he pushed his glasses up his nose. "You didn't find it, then?"

"Affirmative," said Pete. "We didn't. What about you, Miss Vail-Valentine-Vivaldi? Do you know of any other place Alistair Pope might have left his cell phone?"

"No. Unless– In his car? I mean, I didn't know him that well, but– Like Edgar said: he took it everywhere."

"Well." He made notes. "OK then. Thanks for your assistance." He held out a card to Lydia. "Miss–"

"Vivaldi," she inserted.

"Call me at this number. Soon as you're done here, understand?"

"Affirmative," said Lydia.

She yearned to speak to Edgar alone, but Detective Altman appeared in no hurry to leave, and she really was overdue back at work.

The hubbub inside the Back End confirmed Edgar's theory about importance. Here, the priority was food. A few people griped about ink on their hands, or invasion of privacy, or what the world was coming to. First and foremost, though, they wanted to eat.

The Star of India Soop (Lydia noticed with a pang) was almost gone. Before she rushed home to call Detective Altman, she'd have to make a new batch. Not curried cauliflower, though. Not today. Maybe not ever.

Dinah looked ready to explode. As Lydia delivered orders, Mudge came in the front door and replaced Leo at the cash register. Leo roved from table to table, making jokes, slinging insults. Distracting the customers from Moby Dick, thought Lydia, as if his life depends on it.

Why was Edgar so curious about Alistair's phone? Was it just a quick way to get Pete Altman off her back, or a crucial clue to his murder?

Altman seemed like a reasonable guy, for a cop. Surely she could make him understand that sometimes a person got so fed up with herself that she needed a fresh start. In which case it wasn't just her hair color she had to change, or her job, or where she lived, but her identity. Common sense, right?

Unless you were a cop, and common sense was the least likely explanation for anything.

The breakfast crowd was drifting toward the cash register. Time to start the soup, before the lunch crowd arrived.

That raised another question: Had Sue disappeared for good? Could anything be that simple? Vanquished in one skirmish?

In the kitchen, Dinah was stowing eggs and setting out onions.

"Hey," Lydia caught an onion rolling off the counter, "you heard any news from Sue?"

"Hah! Don't ask me. I'd be the last to know. Mudge! Any news from Sue?"

He shook his head; handed change to a customer. "Ask Leo." He honked the tip horn.

"She mighta hoist the white flag," said Dinah, flaking the outer skin off an onion. "Being more of a runner than a fighter, and a lousy cook besides."

"That's what Alistair said." Only a week ago: unbelievable. "Do we have enough of these babies for French onion soup?"

Dinah decimated her onion. "A whole crate. Go for it."

A regular called from the counter: "Hey, you shoulda seen her whipping that knife around ten minutes ago! Just like what's-his-name. Errol Flynn."

"Dinah!" Lydia was reloading her tray. "What'd I miss?"

"Nothing. Those need a garnish."

"Two jackasses come in from the van bitching about ink on their fingers," said the woman next to him. "You tell it, Dinah."

"Bunch a crap." Dinah attacked another onion. "One of 'em goes: 'They want to stop crime?–why don't they cut to the chase and arrest that big'–" She looked up from the butcher block with tears in her eyes. "Well, I'm not gonna say the word. 'Drivin' a big-ass Benz like he's the King of Africa,' he says. 'You let them in, and there goes the Cape.'"

"In fucking credible," nodded the T-shirted man at the counter.

"Now, I'm at the stove flippin' eggs." Dinah laid down her knife to wipe her eyes. "And I come over: 'What did you say?' And the two of 'em stare at me, dumb fucks, no clue. Then the other one: 'Oh. Well, just nobody was getting robbed and murdered around here until this affirmative action shit, you know?' And I went nuts. You know how they say, I saw red? I never knew what that meant before. But I was so mad, it was like my eyes filled up with blood. All I could see is red."

"You shoulda seen her," seconded the other man at the counter. "Like *Jaws*."

"No idea what I said, but next thing I know I'm wavin' this around"–Dinah picked up the knife–"and the two o' them's scrambling their ass outta here like their pants was on fire."

"*Attack of the 50-Foot Woman*," grinned the T-shirted man.

"Now I gotta go blow my nose and wash my hands." Dinah set down the knife again. "Friggin' onions! Start that order, will you?"

She sailed off to the ladies' room. Lydia picked up the slip.

"Can you believe it?" said the woman. "Jerks don't know

Roosevelt Sherman?"

Two BLTs. "Do you get much of that around here?"

"What?" returned the man in the T-shirt. "Crime? Racism? Football ignorance?"

"I'd like to say no, but I'd be lyin' to ya," the other man answered Lydia. "We got our share of bigots. Criminals, too. Drugs, that's the most of it. Behind the other crap. Not just the Cape–anyplace where you got fishing boats, seaplanes. Tourists walkin' around with big wads of cash, while the locals are workin' three four jobs to make ends meet. Some folks get pissed off."

"Those two weren't working any three four jobs," said the woman. "That kind, the whale belts and red pants?–they just don't want anybody rocking their boat."

"Hey, even some of the guys I grew up with," the T-shirt said. "Carpenters, plumbers–salt of the earth, but they won't work on a crew with outsiders. Blacks, Brazilians, whatever."

"Wampanoags." His friend glanced at Mudge, who'd gone to remove "Chix Pot Pi" from the menu board.

Lydia put bread on the toaster. My peaceful new home! she thought venomously. How does that go? "Et in arcadia ego."

"Lydia, right?" the T-shirt called after her.

"Yes!" She ripped lettuce.

"You got any coffee jello today, Lydia?"

"Let me check with Mudge. He invented it, did you know that?"

"Huh."

"And the Rowdeyberry Tarte. And the Choklit Moose cake." Slicing a tomato.

"How about that."

"He's a very gifted chef. We're lucky to have him." Shut up, Lydia! "He and I are starting a catering service. The Flying Wedge. Gourmet dinners at budget prices."

"You got a brochure?" inquired the woman.

"Not yet." Here came Dinah from the ladies' room. "Soon."

"Sounds good," said the sport jacket.

"What's that?" asked Dinah.

"Two BLTs, one brown, one white, coming up," said Lydia.

Chapter Twenty

One hundred eighty-four books had been dusted off and recorded in the Frigate's database. Two rolls of paper towels, filthy and crumpled, overflowed the Frigate's wastebasket. Only crumbs remained of the morning's pastries. Coffee had been fetched (again); Gromit had been walked (twice). The webcams had been checked, admired, adjusted. Fourteen customers had been helped; six books and five postcards had been sold. Now, at last, Sue and Wally sat at the picnic table behind the shop eating sandwiches, while Rosey (who'd provided them) manned the front desk.

"I'm not saying she did it," said Sue. "All I'm saying is, is nobody ever got murdered around here before she showed up."

Three hours ago, Wally reflected, I couldn't keep my hands off her. Now I'm hoping her filthy fingers won't touch my avocado-and-sprouts on the way to her ham-and-cheese.

"Or their house robbed, either. You know?"

"Summer's starting," said Wally. "Weekenders, tourists, college kids, all kinds of people back and forth over the bridge."

"What, are you making excuses for her?"

"Excuses?"

"For stealing my job? Throwing dishes at me? Trying to break my arm?"

"No," said Wally. "But how do you figure she'd know it was your job?"

"Sue-chef? Please!" She sucked mayonnaise off her thumb. "Whose side are you on, Hicks?"

She reached toward the sandwiches. Wally pounced on his remaining half. "Hey. I said I'll check her out. Just don't hold your breath."

They chewed in silence. Even on a wooden picnic bench it

felt good to sit down. Stretch those cramped legs. Like Gromit, lolling nearby on a sunny patch of grass. This was one heck of a busy morning, Wally reflected. Back in the olden days, i.e., last week, you might not get fourteen customers in a whole day. Could the man have already launched his publicity blitz?

You'd think, though, if people had heard about the Frigate's change of ownership, they'd have said something. Wanted to meet the legendary Roosevelt Sherman; get his autograph. Or at least looked for the sports section, instead of heading straight to fiction.

Wally's mind meandered back over the books he'd sold today. A new Carl Hiaasen, a used John Grisham, two hardcover Ed McBain, a beat-up P.D. James . . .

Jehosophat!

Was that why the sudden boom in business? "Welcome to Quansett, Crime Capital of Cape Cod!"

What a crazy idea! This sleepy little village, where dogs had been known to snooze in the middle of Main Street? Where the most illegal act ever caught by the webcams was Louise French dumping her ashtray behind a bush?

On the other hand.. . .

If karma was catapulting Quansett into fame, who had more right–indeed, responsibility–to report this news than Pirandello?

First chance he got, update the blog. Post that "Crime Capital" headline, with a flashy photo. (The fire engine–perfect!) Describe the murder, including eyewitness quotes from Leo's customers. Track down some neighbors and/or family members for background. And for color, stroll over to Shore Road after work tonight with Gromit and a camera.

What about the long range?

Suppose the Frigate's resident expert on just about everything were to advise his new boss to order more crime novels. Suppose sales soared. Suppose Grisham, McBain, et al. could be lured here for book signings. (Some of those guys must be football fans.) Suppose the Frigate became known all over southeastern New England as the premiere spot for beach-blanket thrillers and fireside chillers. Wouldn't that call for a hefty bonus?

We've already got a date for a fancy dinner at a waterfront restaurant, Wally reflected. I just need to remind him.

And make sure (he noted, watching Sue's pink tongue run across her grime-streaked upper lip) we don't include her.

After his late breakfast, Edgar Rowdey didn't return to the Back End for lunch. Carlo and Caroline showed up a little after twelve, apparently in fine spirits, though Caroline beelined for the ladies' room to wash the ink off her elegant fingers. Dinah remarked to Lydia that those two deserved a medal in her book, seeing as they could have split when they spotted the cop van, and instead there was Carlo badgering Leo to sit down and join them, and was that a true friend or what?

Traffic had picked up again in spite of, or because of, Moby Dick. Mudge overheard a table of tourists congratulate each other on the most thrilling meal they'd ever enjoyed on Cape Cod. Lydia asked a couple of regulars why they'd braved the cops, and they told her they didn't want to be left out. The grapevine was buzzing–why be the loser who missed the big event?

By closing time, Lydia was exhausted. Moby Dick had left the parking lot. Only a few customers lingered over coffee in the back room. There were so few leftovers that she and Mudge and Dinah had the kitchen cleared up by two-twenty. She was glad she'd made French onion soup while she had the chance. After such a wild day, even phoning Detective Altman seemed restful by comparison.

Edgar's car wasn't parked in its usual spot by the magnolia tree. When Lydia called the number on Pete Altman's card, she got his answering machine.

She flopped on the sofa in relief, propped up her tired feet, shut the past two days' events out of her mind, and focused on what she wanted to do with the rest of this afternoon.

(1) Nap. (2) Trader Joe's.

In Cambridge, her addiction to Trader Joe's had been a household joke. Here in Quansett she'd kept it quiet, to protect her new identity: Lydia Vivaldi, gourmet chef! Who'd believe that if they saw her loading up a shopping cart with frozen risotto and bottled bearnaise sauce? Now that Pete Altman had semi-blown her cover, she didn't care. If the customers did, let them eat cake.

Today's trip would be more leisurely than her quick stop with Mudge on moving day. First, because she had a kitchen to stock. Second, because every minute she spent debating between lavash and pita bread, burritos or tamales, was a minute of not thinking about Alistair Pope.

Finding the Hyannis store was like hunting through a maze. When at last Lydia parked in front of her faux-Victorian target, stepped through a sliding door, and spotted a familiar wall mural of curling sheet-metal ocean waves, she felt as spent and triumphant as a spawning salmon.

Inside, however, lay a minefield. Fletcher tossing TJ's truffles into her mouth. Curling up to watch the news with Fletcher and a plate of TJ's pot-stickers. Fixing dinner for the house: sauté garlic in TJ's olive oil; add a bag of TJ's fresh spinach, slices of TJ's chicken-pesto sausage, a jar of TJ's marinara . . .

She was resolutely steering through frozen foods when a woman's voice said, "Lydia?"

In the seconds before she recognized Cynthia Ropes, Lydia glimpsed what DeAnne would have looked like if she'd lived twenty more years.

"Hey," she stammered. "Hi. How's it going?"

"Cynthia Ropes." She held out her hand, icy from the bag of french fries she'd just dropped into her cart.

"Sure."

Cynthia's flattish face was more animated here than in her own living room. Even her silver-streaked dark hair looked livelier. Maybe it was her clothes: a butter-yellow golf sweater over a fuschia polo shirt and matching shorts.

"I've never been here before," she confessed; and Lydia recognized the same Dorothy-in-Oz amazement she used to see on newcomers at the Cambridge Trader Joe's. "Do you shop here?"

"Not on the Cape. I did up in Boston."

Lydia watched Cynthia scan her cart and change her mind about asking for recommendations. Lydia's choices tended to come in plastic tubs: tzatziki, salsa, two kinds of hummus. Cynthia's were mostly boxes (cereal, pancake mix) and cans.

"Is your job going OK? Cooking at that restaurant?"

"Yeah. It's great. Except yesterday," she added. "That was awful. You might have heard."

"You don't mean– Alistair Pope? That's the place where you work?"

Lydia nodded. Cynthia's mouth shut and her eyes widened. Why? Had she known Alistair? Or did she think his death had some connection to DeAnne's?

At last her head moved slowly back and forth. "Horrible. Such a lovely kind man."

This was so unlike anything she'd ever heard anyone say about Alistair that for an instant Lydia wondered if Cynthia meant somebody else. "I just pray the killer won't get away with it," she went on. "Won't shut him up!"

"How do you mean?"

"His movie! That's why he was murdered. To stop him showing it." She rubbed her cold hands together, reminding Lydia creepily of Lady Macbeth. "Oh, you won't hear that from the police. When did they ever listen to the likes of us? Don't waste your time barking up the wrong tree, that's what Raymond says. I'm more of an optimist. He sees the glass half empty, I see it half full. I said to him, now, Raymond, they've got their procedure. If they just do their job, they'll find out we were right! Even if they never admit it."

"Right about what?"

Cynthia's eyebrows went up. "DeAnne," she replied, as if that should be obvious. "Our little girl. Who did *not* just accidentally for no reason fall off a ladder!"

"Are you saying–"

"He knew that! Alistair Pope. He was on our side! The nicest note he sent us, with such a great big floral arrangement, we had to put the leaf in the dining room table. Raymond said then: He knows! I said, Now, let's not jump to conclusions. Maybe he just wants to cheer us up. DeAnne, you know, thought so highly of him. But then, when the police wouldn't help, Raymond called him. Left a message on his machine. And then a few days ago, his assistant called us back. She said Alistair wanted us to know the movie was almost done, and he was sure we'd be pleased, since he changed it around to put DeAnne in it."

Her mouth quivered. "Wow," said Lydia. "You mean, he'd shot footage of her while he was following Caroline and Carlo?"

"Well, he must have," said Cynthia. "She'd be so happy!"

True, thought Lydia, although not as happy as if she'd lived to see it. "What does he say about her in the film? Do you know? Is it about how she died?"

"This girl didn't go into that. She said Alistair would call us when it was done. He's been rushing back and forth to New York to finish it up. That's why we didn't hear from him."

A dozen questions were bouncing around in Lydia's brain. "So she called you a day or two before–?"

Cynthia nodded. "Monday. Or maybe Tuesday. We were just crushed when we heard."

"Did you tell the police?"

"The police!" Cynthia sniffed.

Lydia, sensing a long detour ahead, interrupted. "I mean, about this call? That Alistair's film might shed some light on DeAnne's death?"

"Raymond says why should we keep telling them things, when they never listen?"

"Except how could it?" Lydia answered herself. "He hardly knew her. Right? And he sure didn't know when he was shooting that she was going to fall off a ladder."

"Well, don't you think he must have put that together afterwards? They can do all kinds of things nowadays."

"She didn't tell you what was in the footage at all? The assistant."

"No. Just, he wanted us to know."

"Where did she call from? New York?" Lydia was picturing that wide empty lawn outside Alistair's house-cum-office on Monday afternoon, with no other car in the dirt driveway.

"She didn't say. I thought here, but now that you ask– Well, she'd met DeAnne, so she must have worked on the film here. But then she apologized for missing the funeral, being too far away."

Cynthia paused, considering. "We lost the call part way through and she had to call back. Bad reception, she said. Which sounds more like the Cape than New York, doesn't it?"

"Sure does." An assistant of Alistair's visiting his Cape house on Monday? He could have picked her up from the airport or bus station in his car. Except why then invite Lydia for tea? Had he thought the assistant was leaving before he showed up late at the Back End for lunch? Could she have missed her plane, or bus, and come back, leaving that note on his door? A neighbor with a crisis . . . Why not just say his assistant was unexpectedly in town? No, it didn't add up.

"Do you remember her name?"

"I should, shouldn't I?" Cynthia sighed. "We were trying to think, just this morning over breakfast–the end of the bran flakes, that's really why I came here, a neighbor of mine said these are excellent–anyway, all we could remember was that her first name was kind of unusual. Starting with D. Not Debbie. Darcy? Something like that."

She turned her grocery cart, ready to resume shopping. Lydia scrambled to recall the other question she wanted to ask. "So this call was just FYI?" she hazarded. "No clue who wanted to stop the film?"

"No," Cynthia's head shook vigorously. "I can't even stand to think about it. I just hope and pray the police will do their job. Raymond– Well, it's very upsetting for both of us."

They agreed it was nice to run into each other, and a shame about Alistair. Cynthia headed for the pizza section. Lydia stared at her grocery list without seeing it. Not until she reached the check-out line did she remember her last-but-not-least question: What did Alistair write in his condolence note that convinced Raymond he knew DeAnne didn't just accidentally fall off a ladder?

Roosevelt Sherman surveyed his domain and was pleased.

Now that Wally and Sue had cleared out those front stacks, Rosey could walk right into the store. All the way to the office, without sidling or stepping over books. Not bad for Day One.

Tomorrow: the stairs.

He'd gone upstairs during the inspection, of course. Ken and Wally must have cleared a temporary path. A more suspicious man than Rosey might think Wally hoped to keep the boss out of his computer room. That day when he'd produced the stills of Louis and Rudy DePina stalking through the parking lot with a knife, he'd been vague about how CodCast.net worked. Not that it was hard to figure out. You had to know the basics just to function nowadays, much less run a business.

A less easy-going man might have pulled the plug. Can't let an employee run amok. Spy on the neighbors? Post whatever he wants under the Frigate's banner? But when Rosey checked out the website, he was impressed. This was a guy who knew books. Loved books, in fact, with a passion Rosey was pleased to have representing his shop. As for the webcams broadcasting Quansett's sleepy main street to the world–aw, heck! How could any chain store beat that?

The more time he spent around Wallace Hicks, the more optimistic Rosey grew about their prospects together. Dovetailing talents: just what you looked for on a team.

Sue, now, was another story. He'd hired her as a kind of homeopathic remedy for Wally's infatuation. Not that he had anything against her. Stick a full-grown man in a trailer on the outskirts of nowhere with only his dog for company, and he could do worse. No, Sue's problem was timing. Rosey recognized when a woman like that was flapping her wings. Wally and the Frigate, he guessed, were her last perch in Quansett. She'd fly as soon as a door opened; which on Cape Cod in June could happen tomorrow. What he feared was Wally swallowing the hook, so that when she took off, she'd rip his guts out.

Plus Rosey already had two stockers lined up. The DePina boys. He'd promised them part-time jobs as soon as school let out.

The goal was to get his ducks in a row for the Frigate's grand reopening on July Fourth. Too perfect a shot to miss: parades, fireworks, families, cookouts, and a giant wave of tourists eager to dip their toes in old-fashioned small-town America. Rosey had already reviewed his plans with the Cape Cod Times and Quansett Beacon.

And with Helen Wills, who'd offered her youngest brother's band to play at the Frigate's gala post-parade barbecue, and promised to speak to a cousin at Town Hall about permits.

On the office wall Rosey had hung a grid outlining the path to Independence Day. A journey of a thousand miles starts with a single step, as Thea liked to say. Tomorrow she'd be down with the kids for another weekend of house-hunting, while Rosey focused on the Frigate.

Next step: line up the keynote event.

He'd known for weeks what he wanted. How do you launch a revitalized bookstore? With a celebrity book signing. Like a christening bottle of champagne smashed across the Frigate's bow. And who was Quansett's celebrity author? Edgar Rowdey.

Two problems. One, according to everyone he'd asked, Edgar Rowdey didn't do book signings. Dinah said she could count his public appearances on the thumbs of one hand, and that must be six or eight years ago.

Two, according to Helen, there was no guarantee he'd be free on July 4. Unless Rosey had misunderstood her, Edgar Rowdey was on the cops' short list of suspects in Alistair Pope's murder.

They'd run into each other in the take-out line at the Whistling Pig. Helen's face looked raddled with exhaustion. Rosey insisted she join him in the Mercedes–sit back in a cushy leather seat for five minutes and enjoy her coffee. "You won't be much good searching Pope's house if you can't keep your eyes open."

"Or arresting his friends," she agreed drily.

"His friends?"

"I mean– Nothing. Forget it."

"You mean–?"

"Nothing," she cut him off.

"Helen!" He twisted around to face her. "Who are you talking about? Not . . . Edgar Rowdey?"

She pressed her lips together and shook her head. He could see from her stricken expression that he'd hit it. She wouldn't answer, though, no matter how he posed the question. All he could get from her was that this was a criminal investigation and she ought to know by now to keep her mouth shut.

"Why? Because he was the last person to see him alive?"

"Everybody is a suspect, Rosey. You included."

"Well, sure! Me, I can see. But a frail old fella who writes books? How's that even possible?"

"Have you seen his books?"

"C'mon, Helen. Talk is cheap. How many sports columnists can throw a touchdown pass?"

"Compared to a touchdown pass?–hitting a man with a rock is child's play."

"There'd have to be a motive, though. Those two guys were old friends."

"I can't discuss it, OK? Give me a break!"

"Sure." He patted her knee. She was chugging her coffee, preparing to go back to work. "If you'll give me a break."

Helen lowered her cup to frown at him. "What?"

"Solve this thing before my grand opening."

That brought a thin smile. "For you? No problem."

Now the only impossible task he had to accomplish was persuading Edgar Rowdey (who Rosey was sure had *not* killed Alistair Pope) to sign books at the Frigate's Fourth of July barbecue.

Tomorrow.

Chapter Twenty-One

For Lydia, Friday morning was when things escalated from weird to scary.

It started with a drizzle that darkened the sky, as if the sun had decided not to rise all the way. The trees around her cottage hunched over, heavy and wet. As she started through the hedge toward the street, one of the Morris's wheels spun on the mud-slick grass. Low-hanging branches whipped her windshield and sprayed it with raindrops.

Already Lydia had come to count on Mudge to cheer her up on difficult days. But by 7:30, Mudge hadn't appeared.

"Oh, now, calm down," Dinah scoffed. "He's done this plenty of times."

"Not since I've been here."

"And how long's that?" She handed Lydia an empty coffee pot. "You'll see. His truck broke down, or he stayed out late with his buddies and overslept, or some kinda family problem– He'll come running in here any minute, full of excuses. Leo'll blow off steam, end of story."

Whether or not Dinah believed this, Lydia didn't. Her head turned every time the screen door banged. Edgar Rowdey arrived as usual, in a bright yellow slicker and hat. Umbrellas began to fill the tin pail by the door. Even Roosevelt Sherman showed up, for the first time this week, brushing water off his Pats jacket, and sat at the table next to Edgar's.

Leo, descending from his upstairs apartment, demanded accusingly: "Where's Mudge?"

Dinah said, "Don't ask me."

Lydia said, simultaneously, "That's what I'd like to know."

"Hmf." Leo grabbed an apron. "Well, I guess I'll just have to take care of the customers myself, if the rest of the staff don't bother coming in to work."

He stepped behind the cash register. Immediately all three regulars drinking coffee at the counter, who Lydia wouldn't have sworn were awake, stood up and sauntered over to pay.

After insults had been exchanged, money collected, and the horn tooted, Lydia asked, "Leo, aren't you worried?"

"Worried? What, about Mudge? Now why the heck would I worry about him? He's the one oughta worry about me! Who's the healthy young fella here, and who's the old man with a dicky ticker who shouldn't be running himself into the ground like a galley slave?"

Dinah shoved two plates of eggs at her, and Lydia hustled them off to the back room. She didn't think she could stand listening to Leo complain just now. Not when Mudge might be lying unconscious somewhere, or worse.

On her way back to the kitchen she stopped at the windows. No bodies by the pond.

The drizzle had stopped, anyhow. She was considering whether to sneak outside and look under the Elephant Tree when the door banged again, and Dave Wheeler walked in.

"Hey, Dinah." He sat on a stool at the empty counter. "Hey, Lydia."

"Hey," said Dinah. "Coffee?"

"Thanks."

He was wearing the same waterproof boots and Red Sox windbreaker over jeans as the last time she'd seen him. "Hey, Dave. Any news?"

"As a matter of fact," he confirmed. "I was just down at the police station, and I heard they've got Mudge in there."

Lydia's eyes fixed on his hands, cupped around his coffee mug. Don't tell me, she thought. If they found him someplace, skidded off the road . . .

"Pete Altman took him in an hour ago for questioning."

She breathed again. The huge sigh that came from Dinah showed that, bravado notwithstanding, she too was relieved.

Only for a few seconds. "Has he got a lawyer?" Dinah

demanded. "Pete's not gonna do anything stupid, now, like lock him up, is he?"

"That I don't know."

"Does he think Mudge was involved with the murder?" Lydia asked.

"I imagine that's what they're talking about."

Leo chimed in from the cash register. "Why the hell didn't he call us? Isn't he entitled to a phone call? Two minutes to inform his employer what's going on?"

"Is he, though?" Lydia countered. "They don't have to give him a phone call if he's not under arrest, do they? If he's not, you know, suspected of anything?"

"I think you're right," said Dave.

"Then that's good," said Dinah. "That's OK, then."

"Right," Leo seconded. "Come on, folks. Show's over! Back to work!"

Lydia ignored him. "What else do you know? Did you see him?"

Dave leaned back on his stool. "What I told you is pretty much all I can say."

He glanced at Leo, ringing up an order, and Dinah, sliding her spatula under a pile of grated potatoes. Lydia thought she saw one eyebrow twitch.

"Let's go out for a cigarette," she proposed.

Both of Dave's eyebrows went up. "You smoke?"

"No."

He grinned and swung his feet to the floor. "Well then let's go."

They walked through wet grass around the opposite side of the building from the pond, past the stockade fence that enclosed the garbage cans. As soon as they weren't visible from the restaurant, Lydia faced Dave and asked again: "What else?"

"Not much." He pushed his hair back behind his ear. Intent though she was, a corner of Lydia's mind envied him those tawny waves. He probably never has to do anything with that hair but wash it. Forget about salons, never mind streaks or spikes. "I had some photos for Pete, and when he came out I could see he had somebody in there, so I asked him how it was going, and he said not bad, early days yet, but we found out who was sleeping under the tree."

"Mudge." Lydia bit her lip.

"You knew that."

"Not on the record I didn't."

"On the record, we're not having this conversation." Dave was half smiling, but his voice was dead serious. "Does that work for you?"

"Yes." For two seconds their eyes met. "I don't need to tell anybody. I just need to know if there's anything I should do." In case he mistook that as a request for advice, she added, "So . . . ?"

"They found a bunch of stuff under the tree. What you'd expect–gum wrappers, beer cans, cigarette butts. Also, the remains of a campfire. And near the fish pond, some rocks with traces of wood ash and blood."

"What does that mean?"

"I don't know. Maybe somebody took them from around the pond to make the campfire and then put them back."

"Mudge?"

Dave shrugged.

"Alistair's blood?"

"Looks like. And before you ask?–no, Pete wouldn't say if that means they've got the murder weapon."

"Any fingerprints?"

"He wouldn't say that, either. They might not even know yet," Dave added. "They're still just collecting the pieces. They've got a ways to go before they can put the puzzle together."

"Well, but Pete Altman must think Mudge sleeping under the tree, the campfire, all that, is related to the murder, right?"

"I can't speak for Pete. But that's generally why they bring somebody in. Is to find out."

They had reached the end of the fence. "This whole thing is getting . . . " Lydia shook her head.

"Creepy?"

"I was thinking more crappy. But–yeah."

She turned and led the way back, more quickly than they'd walked out. Neither of them spoke.

At the corner of the fence, Lydia stopped Dave with a hand on his arm. "Oh. Did he say if they found Alistair's cell phone?"

He was looking at her fingers on his sleeve. "His cell phone?"

She removed her hand and explained. Since Edgar Rowdey had posed the question to Detective Altman in the parking lot yesterday, she reasoned, it couldn't be confidential.

No, said Dave, Pete Altman hadn't mentioned Alistair's phone.

"But I tell you what." He fished in his jeans pocket. "Take my cell number. Just in case– Well, you never know."

Lydia thanked him and slid his bent card into her own jeans pocket.

He held the door for her. Leo, behind the cash register, shot her a withering look. Lydia smiled at him, and asked Dave if he'd like more coffee.

She'd half expected to be mobbed with questions; but only Leo asked her what the heck she thought she was doing, taking off without a word in the middle of the morning, sticking him with a restaurant full of hungry customers. Dave said that would be the day, when the Back End was full at ten-thirty on a Friday. During the repartee that followed, Lydia caught up with Dinah.

Several people on their way out, however, had questions for Dave Wheeler. What progress were the police making on the burglaries? Had they tracked down any of the stolen goods yet? Did Pete Altman have any clues to who'd done it? Oh, yes, and what news on the murder?

Lydia wondered if Edgar Rowdey was hearing this from the back room.

She followed Dave outside again after he finished his coffee and Chix Pot Pi, to ask him one last question.

"Jurisdiction. Is Pete Altman really going to stay in charge of both investigations?"

"Hm. Well, technically he might. He may have to."

Huddled under Leo's little portico, they inched aside to let a customer pass. Lydia shivered. "Off the record?"

"OK, now, I'm no cop. I can only give you my personal opinion."

"That's all I want."

"My crystal ball tells me you're gonna see Pete step back from the murder. On that case he's got Helen Wills behind him, who, A, is a pit bull, and B, has all the resources of the state police and the D.A. behind her. On the burglaries he's got a county CIO, who's a real nice guy with not much experience. You've probably noticed, it's the burglaries that've got half of Quansett breathing down his neck."

He zipped his windbreaker. Long hands with strong thin fingers. The hands of a pianist. Or (duh!) a photographer.

"So then why is he grilling Mudge?"

They both turned as a large noisy vehicle clattered into the parking lot.

Dave tilted his head: "Ask Mudge."

But all Mudge would tell her–slamming the truck door, hurrying into the restaurant–was that he was OK, everything was OK, and Leo must be ready to kill him.

They segued separately into the late-morning routine. Edgar Rowdey had left; so had Rosey Sherman. Carlo and Caroline sat in the back room, in nonmatching London Fogs (olive for her, khaki for him), with a man and a woman Lydia didn't recognize. Leo grumbled loudly that it was high time some folks remembered their responsibilities, confounded younger generation, on their cell phones every damn minute except when they really need to make a call; and patted Mudge's arm as he turned over the cash register.

It wasn't only the rising tide of lunch that kept Lydia (and, she guessed, Dinah and Leo) from grilling Mudge. It was his face. The cheerfulness had gone out of it. His mouth continued to smile, but his eyes seemed to tremble, as if one wrong word might bring tears.

Which naturally made Lydia all the more anxious to know what had happened at police headquarters.

Finally he spoke to her, behind the big refrigerator–the one spot in the kitchen where you couldn't be seen from the restaurant.

"I got a message for you." He glanced at her across a large bowl of potato salad.

"What?"

"You know Hell on Wheels? The state trooper?"

"Yeah. I mean I know who she is. Did you–"

He interrupted: "She wants you to come in at three. Police HQ, South Exmouth."

"Mudge!" A chill ran through Lydia that had nothing to do with the bacon she was stowing. "Did she say why?"

"Nope. Well, the murder. She was nice about it, though."

"What do you mean?" Aside from her own concerns, she hoped to hold him long enough to find out what had upset him.

He didn't look at her as he reached in for ketchup and mustard. "Like saying come in after work, instead of drop everything right now and if you lose your job, tough shit."

She squelched an impulse to hug him. If you want to comfort a man who's been disrespected, don't treat him like a little kid. "That sucks."

"Yeah." He turned to go.

"Did she say anything else?"

"Nope."

Lydia threw her last lasso: "Phone number? Directions?"

"I'll tell you later."

Later. OK. The cops are pouncing on the Back End's employees one by one. Meanwhile, we've got customers to feed. Tables to clear. Coffee to refill.

She thought "later" had come at quarter to one, with a brief lull in the lunchtime rush. Dinah stood by the sink eating a sandwich; Leo was hobnobbing in the back room. Mudge, at the register, rang up one last party. Before Lydia could go talk to him, though, a familiar voice called her name.

Alistair?

The jolt ebbed. No; Alistair was dead. That wasn't his thickly accented bark, anyway, but the sardonic drawl of Edgar Rowdey.

"Yoo-hoo! Waitress!"

He fluttered his fingers at her from the doorway to the back room. The other hand pushed his glasses up on his nose. No slicker now, just a frayed yellow sweater. Like a ray of sunshine in the middle of the Back End. Lydia couldn't help smiling as she went to see what he wanted.

Not food. He had an invitation for her.

Every Friday at five-thirty, he explained, he and Caroline and Carlo met for drinks at the Whistling Pig. Could she join them this afternoon?

Lydia replied truthfully that she'd love to, if Detective Wills let her out in time.

"Mercy! Are you under arrest, dear?"

"Oh, no. Just called in for questioning."

"Didn't we do that yesterday? And the day before?"

"Yes, we did. But apparently that was just the beginning." The friendly concern in his eyes moved her to add, "Detective Altman had Mudge in for questioning all morning."

"Oh, dear." Edgar frowned. "I wondered where he'd got to. Poor bunny. Leo must have been unbearable. Did he say," he shot a glance at Mudge, "how it went? If they're anywhere near solving this awful business?"

"No. He didn't, yet, and it doesn't sound like they are."

"Hm." His gaze drifted to the menu board. She waited for him to speak–ideally, to utter the one brilliant insight that would pop this awful business like a balloon, and flip everything back to normal–but he just went on peering at lunch selections.

After half a minute, Lydia stirred, to let him know she couldn't keep standing here while customers edged past and Dinah stacked up orders on the sandwich bar.

His eyes swung back to her. "If you can," he continued as if there had been no interruption, "stop by the Pig when you're through, and have a drink, and let us know you're all right, will you?"

"Sure."

Just the idea that friends would be waiting for her, that someone would notice if she vanished into the legal system and never came out, buoyed Lydia through the next two hours.

Wallace Hicks tilted back his chair and stared at the ceiling. Life, he reflected, is a long and rocky uphill climb. Sometimes there are flowers along the path, like in the woods behind the post office. Sometimes you find the pond hopping with frogs, and sometimes it's iced over. But every once in awhile, you catch a break.

Sue had taken off after their semi-picnic lunch. Wally hoped she'd gone to Bourne to check out that restaurant job. He also hoped she would come back tonight. He was aware that his hopes regarding Sue didn't match up. They splayed out in different directions, looking a little silly, like Gromit's legs when he snoozed on his back. That was OK, though. For one thing, after ten months of waiting for karma to kick him through the goalposts of a game he refused to play, he was used to feeling divided. For another, his wishes were only a minor factor here.

What Rosey Sherman wanted, now, that was a major factor. Not an easy man to read. Under his outer layer of bonhomie, Wally sensed other strata not yet uncovered. Take last night's events, for instance. For all their tiptoeing around–or, Wally's tiptoeing around and Sue's tromping across the landscape in Army boots–they hadn't fooled Rosey for a minute.

Well, Hicks, what do you expect? A man spends his career in professional football, he's bound to learn more about women than most guys pick up in a whole lifetime.

Really it was a shame they didn't know each other better. Wally would have given the left front wheel off his Airstream to ask Rosey Sherman straight out for advice.

Not that you could ever solve women problems that easy. An experienced friend might help you, but in the end, women were unpredictable. All you could do was look at things their way, as best you could, and guess which way they'd jump.

In Sue's case, Wally was banking on her realizing that it was in her best interest to come back tonight. First of all, for a free place to sleep, plus good company to share it with. And second of all, because Wally now had the power to grant her wish from last night.

He pictured the scene: her stomping in all grumpy because

she didn't get the Bourne job, or bouncing in all happy because she did. Talking a blue streak as she came up the steps. Stopping cold when she saw him standing in the Airstream's tiny living room, no T-shirt, his lean but well-muscled body radiating sensuality.

She strips off her clothes and steps into his arms. His tongue flickers over her earlobe. "You were right," he murmurs. "Legal Seafood has no record of ever employing a Lydia Vivaldi."

Mudge finally opened up (a little) when they were closing down the soup section.

Through lunchtime he'd dodged well-meaning questions, and slowly–by working hard to make up for the lost morning–recovered his balance. Lydia had forced herself not to push him. She wasn't exactly in top form either, with part of her still reflexively checking the door, as if Alistair was bound to barge in any minute and whisk her off for tea.

Now, she thought, hauling the chowder pot out of its hole, I'll never see that Civil War house of his. Or what's inside the summer kitchen.

"Let me take that," said Mudge's voice behind her.

"Hey," said Lydia, and gave it to him.

"Sorry about this morning."

"Not your fault."

They lifted the French onion soup together (half gone, Lydia was pleased to see). "I was just glad you made it back in one piece," she added.

"Yeah, well."

He carried the chowder and she carried the onion soup to the kitchen.

"I wrote down directions for you."

"Thanks. What should I be ready for? Thumbscrews? The rack?"

A small grin spread across Mudge's face, like sun seeping through clouds. "The Spanish Inquisition."

"Oh, great!"

"You're getting her, though, so who knows. I got him. Altman. His thing was, I was the one who found the body, and they figured out it was me who slept under the tree, so why wouldn't I be the killer? Which is, like . . ."

"Nuts," supplied Lydia. "Grasping at straws."

Soups covered and refrigerated, they returned to empty the steam tables. "He eased up some after the first hour. Said they have to rule people out. Anybody who was here that day."

"So are you ruled out now?"

"I donno. I kind of doubt it. Shit, I hope so! Except . . . "

He was opening the side door. After a few seconds Lydia asked, "What?"

"I might have screwed up."

His somber expression as he faced her sent another chill running through her innards. "What do you mean?"

"When I first got there, it was weird–we're talking, he's asking me questions, and all of a sudden he's like accusing me. 'You were the last one to see Alistair Pope, we have witnesses who'll testify you two had a fight–' And I'm like, 'So? Everybody had fights with him.' And he's like, 'Oh yeah? Name one other person besides you!' And I said, 'Edgar Rowdey.' And then I'm like, Oh shit. And he's asking me what kind of fight did they have, and when, and what can I say? I told him it was nothing. Just this routine they do: Pope wants to make a film about Rowdey. Rowdey says no, only not straight out, since he can't say no to anybody. Pope grabs on like a bulldog. Rowdey tries to shake him off. Pope says I can do it with your help or without it. Rowdey changes the subject. You know?"

While he spoke, they carried the full aluminum bins to the side door. Thoughts splashed through Lydia's mind as she and Mudge dumped water onto the laurel bushes under the windows. "Wow," she said at last.

"They can't be thinking he'd kill him. Would they? Over that?"

"Are you kidding me? OK, I know–his books. But how could anybody who's ever spent five seconds with Edgar Rowdey think he'd kill anybody, over anything?"

"Well, yeah!" Mudge was relieved.

"Of course, I'm not a cop." Lydia paused outside the door. "And he just invited me to meet him and Carlo and Caroline for a drink tonight. So I'm not unbiased, either."

"Nobody's unbiased," said Mudge. "That doesn't mean you're wrong." He fitted the bins together. "I was gonna ask if you want to go for strawberry daiquiris, but that's a better offer."

"Not better. Just . . . different."

"Better for the Flying Wedge," he grinned. "Our future."

He looked so much more like himself than he had all day that Lydia resolved to reach that future as soon as as humanly possible. "I'll do what I can," she promised. "As soon as I get out of the–" What?

"Frying pan?" Mudge suggested.

"Clutches? Talons?"

"Mousetrap."

"Thanks a lot, pardner."

He hefted the steam trays onto one shoulder. "Don't forget the directions."

"From what you're saying," she followed him inside, "it sounds like the cops are doing procedure as much as investigation at this point. Right? Ruling things out?"

"Right."

"OK. So Helen Wills wants to talk to me, and Pete Altman just spent half the day talking to you. Doesn't that sound like what Leo said the other night? We're on a suspect list?"

"Yup." He set down the trays with a metallic clatter. "Right up at the top."

Chapter Twenty-Two

Driving toward police headquarters, Lydia reviewed what else Mudge had given her along with directions.

Although Quansett had its own fire station, post office, and public library, it shared a police force with the Town of Exmouth's other three villages. Being the smallest and quietest beat, it generally drew the cop with least seniority (right now, Kevin Kelly).

Go south from Quansett and you'd come to West Exmouth, the biggest village, where the police station was. To its west was South Exmouth, to its east was North Exmouth. There was no East Exmouth.

Although its other cops rotated among the four villages, Exmouth had only two detectives, Pete Altman and Bob Scanlan, who took turns wherever a crime happened.

Helen Wills and her fellow state troopers–officially dispatched by the Barnstable County district attorney in Barnstable Village–had their HQ in Bourne, up near the Cape Cod Canal, and their barracks in South Yarmouth. Detective Wills herself was working out of the Exmouth police station for now so as to stay close to her local partner, Detective Altman.

In her head Lydia heard Edgar Rowdey's airy remark yesterday in the parking lot: "Who knew what a labyrinthine law-enforcement structure we have on Cape Cod?"

She parked in front of a sprawling, anonymous two-story brick structure which Mudge had accurately described as looking like an old high school. Bring the umbrella? No. After a few fits and starts, the rain had stopped. The police shared this building with the town's other functionaries: animal control officer, tax assessor, shellfish warden. Lydia walked up concrete stairs, down a hospital-green hall under fluorescent lights in acoustical-tile ceilings. So this was what the postwar town fathers chose over Carlo and Caroline's 18th-century shoebox.

Like every police station she'd ever seen, Exmouth's stopped you in the foyer. First you stood at a high counter and spoke through a grille in a plexiglass panel to a uniformed, armed, suspicious officer. Then you sat a few feet away in the waiting area until someone came out to escort you into the inner sanctum. Much like her gynecologist's office.

Instead of a chirpy medical aide in scrubs, however, her escort was a chubby female cop in a too-tight uniform, pinched at the waist by her utility belt like a balloon animal. The expression on her face fell somewhere between grumpy and grim, possibly from discomfort. She avoided meeting Lydia's eyes as she ran a wand over her for weapons.

Helen Wills sat at a gray formica-topped desk in a small windowed room, holding a cell phone to her ear. She gave Lydia a brief nod, waved her to a chair, and went on listening intently. The wall by the door was glass, opaque behind venetian blinds. Nothing on the desk but a short stack of manila folders, a styrofoam cup, a few pens, and a tape recorder. Impersonal but private.

The phone snapped shut. "Hey, Lydia." Detective Wills rose and reached across the desk to shake her hand. "Sorry about that."

Up close she looked even more intimidating than at the Back End: taller than Lydia and ten years older, no apparent makeup, dark hair pulled back from her face. Built like an Amazon and dressed like an FBI agent, with a grip strong enough for a Fix-It Chick.

"No problem."

"I appreciate your coming in after a full day's work. I'll try not to keep you too long. I already apologized to Mudge, but I'll apologize to you, too, for my partner throwing a monkey wrench in Leo's machinery this morning."

"Thanks." That was a surprise.

"You want coffee? Water? Juice?"

"I'm fine." So far, this wasn't as bad as Lydia expected.

"It's not really Pete's fault. He's under the gun–well, you can imagine. Most of the time we go weeks without a serious crime, aside from summer. Now all of a sudden he's got a murder plus a string of burglaries dropped on his plate."

She paused. "Yeah," said Lydia, to keep up her end of the bonhomie. "That's gotta be tough."

"I'm hoping to lighten the load. This'll be just you and me, if you're OK with that?"

"Sure." Lydia glanced at the blind-shuttered glass wall. "And the tape recorder?"

"Right. Good you reminded me." Helen Wills pressed buttons. "My husband's coming home tomorrow, so I'm a little distracted." She shot Lydia a smile. "He's been away since Memorial Day. Too long! OK. Let's just . . ." She handed Lydia a clip-on microphone. "Can you pin that someplace, like on your sweatshirt? Good. And I'll do mine; and we're all set." She pushed another button. "Friday, June 9. State trooper detective Helen Wills interviewing Lydia Vivaldi. AKA Liz Valentine, AKA Lynn Vail."

Shit! thought Lydia. Dinah was right: Only a fool trusts a cop.

And here came the Miranda warning, in case anybody was under any illusions about this interview.

"OK. That's the boilerplate out of the way." Detective Wills flashed her another smile. "Don't worry. It sounds worse than it is."

Easy for you to say, Lydia retorted silently.

"Now I just need to go over the stuff we already know. Recap your statements and so on."

She opened the top manila folder and read from a computer printout. If those are her notes, Lydia realized, no wonder she got to be a state police detective. In Helen Wills's brisk summary, the afternoon of Alistair Pope's death morphed from a horrifying tumult into a logical sequence of events. You began to sense a purpose to this investigation. Not just to collect fingerprints, statements, and blood-stained rocks, but to uncover missing facts which would fill in the gaps and complete the emerging narrative.

She looked at Lydia over the folder. "Is that an accurate version of what you reported?"

"Yes. In fact– You really nailed it."

"Next step, nail the perp." She replaced the folder; pulled out another one. "So let's do it! What else can you tell me? Anything you saw or heard that day? or before? or after?"

The folder contained a blank pad. Detective Wills uncapped a ballpoint pen and looked inquiringly at Lydia.

Lydia shook her head. "Sorry. You've got it all right there."

"Hmm." The pen tapped the pad. "OK. Let's go outside the box. Maybe find something, you know, hiding in the shadows. Like, what about the people who came by Leo's that afternoon? I'm not asking for a list of names. But did anybody unusual show up? What kind of conversations were floating around? Any theories about how the victim died?"

Again Lydia shook her head. "I can't remember anything like that. Unusual people–just you and the other police officers. And theories–basically, he tripped and fell."

"Is that what Mudge said when he told you he'd found the body? He tripped and fell?"

"He said he didn't know what happened. Only that he pulled Alistair out of the water, and tried to resuscitate him and couldn't, and there was a banged spot on his head."

"You didn't see this banged spot yourself."

"No. Like I said in your report. He was half turned over. I just went close enough to make sure there wasn't any chance we could save him."

"And you knew that how?"

"From looking at him." She swallowed. "He looked–well, definitely not alive."

"I'm sorry," Helen Wills said gently. "I know this is hard. Losing a friend, and then all these questions dredging it up again. But these are things I have to know. You'd spent enough time with him when he was alive so the difference was clear? No doubt in your mind?"

"No," said Lydia. "I hadn't spent that much time with him. I knew he was dead because his face looked like something out of Madame Tussaud's, and there was a frog sitting on his head."

Would she take the detour? No. "You had lunch with him, though. Right? The first day you met."

"With him and Leo. Who offered me a job."

"And you went to his house."

That was new. Lydia's almost-visit to Alistair's house was something she hadn't mentioned to either detective. Questions raced through her mind: Did somebody (Mudge?) tell them? When they searched Alistair's grounds, did they find a clue? A green hair? Fingerprints on the summer kitchen doorknob?

"Not exactly." How much to say? "He invited me over for tea, but we had to cancel."

"Why?"

"He got a message from a neighbor. He said. Who urgently needed his help."

"Aha." Helen Wills's nod was sympathetic. "So, walk me through this, Lydia, OK? He invited you, when?"

"At Leo's. I was working. He came in for lunch."

Lydia gave the most stripped-down account she could manage. As with Pete Altman, she was determined not to lie, not to raise any red flags, and not to cast suspicion on anyone else. This time it wasn't so easy. Detective Wills didn't share her partner's willingness to listen without comment. She sat relaxed but upright, jotting notes on her pad, her eyes on Lydia like a hawk watching a mouse. As soon as she got the answer to one question, she fired off another one, drawing out details that Lydia would rather not have given.

Finally she rebelled.

"You know, I appreciate you need to be thorough and all, but this is a waste of time."

Helen Wills leaned back a fraction of an inch. "How do you figure?"

"Like I said: nothing happened! I didn't go in, I didn't see anybody, I didn't look at the note, he didn't read it to me–"

"Then why do you have a problem talking about it?"

"I don't–" She stopped. "OK. You know what the problem is? Talking about it puts weight on it. Makes it seem important. Which it wasn't."

"And you know that how?"

"Because I was there!"

"Well, I wasn't." Helen Wills placed her hands flat on the desk. "That's the problem with a murder investigation. I'm groping in the dark. All I know is what people like you tell me. And, sorry, but 'It wasn't important' gets me totally nowhere."

For a moment they looked at each other. Then the detective sat back in her chair. "So he's driving you back to Leo's. What did he say? What did you say?"

On the interrogation went–getting totally nowhere, in Lydia's opinion–for another half hour. By the time Detective Wills proposed a break, she knew most of what had ever passed between Lydia and Alistair Pope, from his original roadside rescue to their ad-hoc tea on the rocks beside the Frigate, up through discovering the Morris's slashed tires and turning the case over to–ta da!–Detective Wills.

When she probed into the nature of their relationship, Lydia said it was still in the exploratory stage. Physically? asked Helen Wills. He seemed like a touchy-feely kind of guy, Lydia said, typical movie biz, not in a pushy way.

"How did you react to that?"

"I was kind of flattered. Kind of wary. I just broke up with somebody, so I wasn't ready to get into anything. But it was nice to be treated like an attractive woman."

"Were you attracted to him?"

"He's not my type. And a lot older than me." I don't have to tell her everything, Lydia rationalized. Just no lies.

"So you didn't have a sexual relationship with him?"

"You mean, did I sleep with him? No. Like I said: I never went inside his house, and aside from that and having tea across the road, the only place I ever saw him was the Back End."

To her relief, Detective Wills left it at that. Lydia really, really didn't want to mention their make-out session under the Elephant Tree.

"OK. Let's take five."

They stood up; stretched. "By the way," Lydia reached toward the ceiling, "did you find out who slashed my tires?"

"Yeah. As a matter of fact I did." Helen Wills was swiveling from side to side, standing beside her chair, hands on her hips. "Sorry, it slipped my mind. So much going on–"

"Was it Sue?"

"Who used to have your job? Nope! Turns out, a couple of

kids found a knife and went on a preteen crime spree. Kevin Kelly tracked them down. The first car they hit was Rosey Sherman's, and he's such a sweetheart, he didn't want to bust them. Made Kevin tear up the report."

She paused, as the door opened and a young man in civilian clothes delivered two bottles of water.

"Thanks," said Helen.

"You know Rosey Sherman?" asked Lydia when he had gone.

"Old friend of my brother's," Helen nodded, twisting off her lid. "That's why I got into it. Which of course Kevin didn't know. So he didn't tell me, and I didn't tell you."

Lydia held out her bottle for a friendly click: no harm done. Then she took a chance. "What else aren't you telling me?"

"What else do you want to know?" Helen returned. "How many crimes have you managed to get involved in in one week, Lydia Vivaldi?"

"Is that a crime? My name?"

"Not unless there was intent to deceive."

"Then I'm fine." She raised her bottle and drank a toast to herself. "Have you found the murder weapon?"

"I can't discuss that." Her face revealed nothing.

"How about Alistair's cell phone?"

"His cell phone?"

"Yeah. Detective Altman said it wasn't on his body. You know how strange that is, right?"

"That's right," she mused. "No, it hasn't turned up yet."

"Do you think whoever killed him stole it?"

Helen laughed. "Listen to you! Miss Third Degree! I don't think anything. Part of my job description–no making up theories without evidence." She sat on the edge of the desk. "A lot of things can happen to a cell phone. I did keep an eye out for it when we searched his house this morning. But I'd have to say, that's the least of my worries."

Picking her words, Lydia asked, "Did you find new worries in the search?"

"Get real, girl! No way am I answering that."

"Well, OK then, what about the blood?" Until she heard herself say it, Lydia hadn't realized the question was still troubling her. "Why was there blood in the pond? Did it all come from the wound on his head? Or were there other injuries?"

Helen Wills thought it over for half a minute, drinking water. Calculating what? Lydia wondered. How much she can tell me within the bounds of her job description? How to keep this going so I'll feel like I owe her whatever else she wants from me?

"I don't have an answer to that," she said finally. "I haven't gotten the M.E.'s report yet. Why? You got a theory?"

"Not a theory. I was just curious about his earring."

"Don't stop." Helen set down her water bottle.

"Was he wearing it when you all picked him up? You know he had a gold earring."

"Yeah."

"Don't ears bleed a lot? I thought, maybe if it got pulled out during the struggle– Was there a struggle? Or did he just, like, topple over?"

"Lydia," said Helen Wills, folding her arms. "Why are you so curious?"

"Why am I curious?" To Lydia this was a question so bizarre as to verge on insulting. "Why wouldn't I be? I mean, damn! This guy helped me fix my tire, and get a job; he was friends with the people I work with, and he's murdered a few feet away? And now here you are, grilling me about every teeny little thing that had anything to do with him– How could I possibly not be curious?"

Detective Wills considered that in silence. After a moment she said, "What's the buzz at the Back End?"

She sure is doing a good job of keeping me off balance, Lydia thought. Because she's a skilled detective or because she's a prick?

"Everybody's curious," she returned. "About the murder, and also about the burglaries."

"Huh. What do they say about the burglaries?"

"They're worried they could be next."

"That's it? No pet theories?"

"Tons of pet theories. The favorite is a gang from off Cape, probably drug dealers. Or transient construction workers. The other view is, the pinpoint strikes suggest they're local. Garbage men? The kids who deliver papers? Landscape gardeners? Mail carriers? The cable guys?" Lydia looked straight across the desk. "What do you think?"

Detective Wills looked back at her. "Whoever they are, we will catch them. No question about that."

"Are you working on that case, too?"

"No, I'm not." Helen Wills picked up her water bottle again. "That's an Exmouth case. Pete Altman's other top priority."

Meaning, thought Lydia, the cops subscribe to the local theory. "So you've only got the murder?"

"Only! In my dreams."

As Helen drank, Lydia presented her biggest question. "Are you two the same team who investigated DeAnne Ropes's death?"

The detective made a negative sound and shook her head. "I did, with Bob Scanlan," she said after she'd swallowed. "The other Exmouth detective. Why?"

It occurred to Lydia belatedly that if she claimed DeAnne as a friend, someone she'd lived and worked with, she'd be giving herself a motive for Alistair's murder. "I knew her up in Cambridge," she compromised. "I had the idea of calling her when I came down here, but then I found out."

"I'm sorry."

"Were you– Well, you must have been."

"Must have been what?"

"Totally sure it was an accident?"

Helen gave a sardonic sniff. "Yeah. That's my job, is to make sure. Why? Do you have some other theory?"

Don't antagonize her, thought Lydia. "I went to see her parents," she said carefully. "They aren't convinced. Her father's pretty distraught. He thinks there's more to it, and he thinks Alistair agreed with him. His wife said that's why Alistair was killed."

A nod and a raised eyebrow told her Helen Wills had heard this before. "You're saying this is their opinion, or yours?"

"Theirs. Except I'd agree DeAnne wasn't the kind of person who'd fool around on a ladder."

"Did anyone say she was fooling around? According to the evidence, she made a few small misjudgments that unfortunately added up to one big mistake." Helen tapped her water bottle on her desk. "Nobody ever wants to accept that. A young life, somebody you love? It shouldn't happen! But it does. All the time."

She knew Alistair, Lydia reminded herself. She's probably just given his sister–her friend and bridesmaid–a similar unwelcome explanation.

"And as far as a link?–that's inevitable. Two deaths so close together, two victims whose paths had just crossed, you're going to get people swearing they're connected. Well, our forensic team went over that studio with a fine-tooth comb. Bob and I interviewed Song and Penn, the Ropeses, Alistair Pope and his crew–everybody who was there that day. Hours of testimony. In the end, all we can go on is the facts. Whether that satisfies anybody or not."

Detective Wills shook out her arms. "Back to the case at hand." She picked up her notepad. "Just a few more questions. One: What do you think the chances are Mudge had anything to do with the attack on Pope?"

"Zero."

Her eyebrow went up. "They were at each other's throats fifteen minutes earlier."

Lydia, feeling jet-lagged by the speed with which they'd changed subjects, was emphatic. "Mudge doesn't go ballistic just because somebody harasses him. He can't. He wouldn't have lasted this long. I mean, look at Leo!"

"OK," said Helen Wills. "Let's look at Leo. Likes to pick fights, loyal but tough with his employees–"

"Can we cut to the chase?" Having finished her water, Lydia wondered where the restrooms were. "Nobody at the Back End killed Alistair. Not Mudge, not Leo, not me, not Dinah, and I don't see how it could have been Bruno, although I've never had a conversation with him."

"And you know that how?"

"They aren't like that! *We* aren't. We're all difficult, OK, a little weird in our different ways, but we get along, because that's how adult-land works. You know? You get mad at a customer, you get over it."

"Somebody killed him, Lydia. Right after he walked out of your restaurant."

"Not us. We were inside closing up."

"You weren't."

"I went out back to dump the steam tables. Five, ten minutes max."

Helen was making notes. "And then there's Edgar Rowdey. He personally escorted the victim out the door, right? To the pond. Where they had some kind of bust-up. Did you catch any of that?"

"No, I didn't." She hoped the detective couldn't read in her face that she was recalling what Mudge had told her: Alistair badgering Edgar to make a film that Edgar wanted no part of. "But, come on! A famous artist, the nicest old man on the planet, hits his friend with a rock and drowns him, because they can't agree how many frogs there are in the pond?"

"Is that what they argued about? Frogs?"

Anything else, Lydia assured herself, was hearsay and not her job to report. "That's what they always argued about."

"OK." Helen Wills stood up. "I'd say we're through here for now. When the interview rolls back around to frogs again, it's done." She pulled a card out of her breast pocket. "I appreciate your help. Anything else you think of?–call me. Day or night. That's my cell number on the back."

It was such an abrupt end that Lydia had to struggle to lower her defenses. Helen Wills continued talking–may need in future, don't leave the area without, please don't discuss–but Lydia's brain was still processing their last round. Had she called a halt because she knew she wasn't getting the whole truth? Did she really think Edgar Rowdey might have killed Alistair? Did she suspect Lydia herself? Was this just another fishing expedition, or would the hooks buried in her questions snag on some innocent remark–if not today, then tomorrow, or next week–and reel Lydia (or another poor fish) back into this small gray room?

Chapter Twenty-Three

On the other side of Exmouth, Edgar Rowdey hung up his damp slicker. Water! Anything so copious ought to supply a book idea; but what new could one say? Seventy percent of the earth's surface. Half to three-fourths of the human body. Essential in all its forms–solid, liquid, gas–to life of every kind. Polar bears and seals. Squid, whales, goldfish. Bacteria and planaria, cephalopods and arthropods. Algae, kelp, lichens, grass, rhododendrons.

The rhododendrons around the post office had hit their splashy peak. Far too splashy for his taste. They reminded him of over-designed ballets, all bright frilly skirts and legs scissoring flamboyantly in the air, till you might as well be watching the Rockettes. He preferred the simplicity of the myrtle that appeared every spring beside his front steps, flat purple blossoms poking through green ivy, or the diffident exoticism of the white-blooming clematis that twined up his porch columns and draped itself from his roof.

Respiration; photosynthesis. From gas it comes (hydrogen and oxygen) and to gas it evaporates. Magical properties: The universal solvent. Surface tension. Osmosis. Turgor.

"Hello, Connie," called Caroline Penn. "Hello, Edgar!"

He re-entered his surroundings. Raised his eyes from the page they had rested on without reading. Took in the glass-topped table beneath his book and the flowered chintz tablecloth under that; white bent-wire chairs, ruffled chintz curtains, the long ornate wooden bar behind which Connie McNally stood shelving teapots. And Caroline and Carlo approaching from the light-filled doorway.

"Hul-lo." He flipped over his book.

"What are you reading?" Carlo pulled out a chair for Caroline.

"Oh, nothing."

"Nothing?" Carlo peered. "*The Aspern Papers*?"

"I thought you didn't like Henry James," said Caroline.

"I don't," said Edgar. "I pick one up every couple of years to remind myself how deeply I loathe him."

"You haven't gotten very far," said Carlo.

"I wasn't reading. Didn't I just say? I was thinking."

"Not about current events, I hope." Caroline flapped open her napkin.

"Too depressing." Carlo wiggled his chair closer to the table. "Worse than slouching around Venice buttering up old ladies."

Connie McNally came over to take their order. They'd known her as the bartender here for twenty years, the loud proprietor's quiet wife. Since his death, Connie had expanded her flair for mixed drinks to coffees and teas. In her work clothes–a black dress with a white collar and apron, a snood over her auburn-and-silver hair–she looked like a turn-of-the-century Irish maid.

Yes, that was her niece Lucy helping out last week. Trying out the job before she started full-time for the summer. A lucky break, finding good help this early in the season. Which Leo had done at long last, Connie had heard, with his new sous-chef? Such a shame about Alistair Pope– But now they'd better not start on that, or they'd never get their drinks.

"Lydia may join us later," Edgar said as Connie departed. "She's being interrogated by Helen Wills, poor bunny."

"Heavens!" said Caroline. "They can't suspect Lydia of killing Alistair, do they?"

"Who's to say?" Edgar shrugged.

"I daresay they suspect all of us," said Carlo. "I can't speak for Lydia, but we three have more reason than most to want him out of the way."

"But how would the police know that?" asked Caroline. "I can't imagine Pete Altman has the staff to go chasing down every Pandora's Box that wretched man opened, do you?"

"If he can't find any real leads," said Carlo.

"Edgar?"

"It isn't Pete Altman who's asking the questions at this point." He closed his book and moved it aside. "Helen Wills I think will call up whatever resources she needs."

"Oh, my," said Carlo. "Best wishes to her, then, to close the lid as soon as possible."

"They've set the funeral for Monday, at Pius the Tenth." Caroline unbuttoned her quilted silk jacket. "Assuming they release the body. Should we go, do you think?"

"I wouldn't be caught dead," Edgar stated.

"You forgot, he doesn't do weddings or funerals," Carlo reminded Caroline.

"Well, the wake tomorrow will be plenty. Oh! And didn't we have a surprise this morning! Did you know Sue's working at the Frigate now?"

"Sue?" Edgar's eyebrows went up. "Leo's Sue?"

Carlo nodded. "We walked in the door and there she was, sprawled on the floor, rummaging among the books–"

"Heaven help them," murmured Edgar.

"–Filthy as a street urchin, and pleased with herself as the cat that ate the canary."

"As well she might be," Caroline observed. "The stacks have gone down by half at least."

"I don't think we'll want to mention this to Lydia," said Carlo. "From what I hear, it wouldn't be welcome news."

"She's bound to find out."

"Perhaps not right after her session with Hell on Wheels, though."

Their drinks arrived: gin-and-tonics for Carlo and Edgar, a Merlot for Caroline. Connie set out napkins, then their glasses, and a plate of mixed biscuits in the center.

"Where was Wally Hicks?" Edgar inquired.

"Upstairs, I would imagine," said Carlo. "Hiding."

"We did have a nice chat with the new proprietor," said Caroline.

"Offered our congratulations. Have you met Mr. Sherman?"

"Yesterday," Edgar confirmed. "A welcome addition, don't you think?"

"I was quite impressed with him," Caroline agreed. "Aside from Sue. But then I don't suppose . . . How could he know?"

"What havoc she wreaked on Leo?" asked Carlo. "Or her affair with Kevin Kelly?"

Conversation stopped when Lydia walked in. She radiated shell-shock, as Mudge had when he'd arrived at work. Edgar and Carlo both rose in sympathy to welcome her. Even Caroline greeted her with a hearty smile.

To Lydia it felt weird to sit down with three people she normally waited on. Part of her yearned to sink silently into their familiar company, as into a hot bath. Another part, recognizing this trio was more of a jacuzzi, went with her need to talk.

First: rituals. Lydia was introduced to Connie McNally by Caroline, with flattering biographical tidbits supplied by Carlo. They shook hands and assured each other it was a pleasure. Lydia ordered a margarita, on the rocks, with salt. More biscuits? Oh, by all means, said Edgar.

That done, Carlo requested a full report on her interview with Detective Wills.

This felt weird, too: flipping sides, answering the civilians' questions about the cops. No, it didn't sound like they had any solid leads. Or suspects, beyond anyone with opportunity or motive. Mostly Lydia had been asked to expand on what they already knew. Her relationship with Alistair Pope–"especially if we were having an affair, which we weren't." Gossip among the Back End's customers. Alistair's squabbles on that fatal afternoon with Mudge and Edgar.

Edgar's eyebrows went up, but he didn't sound concerned. "She got that from Mudge, I take it?"

"I guess. Apparently they kind of tricked him into mentioning it. Mudge felt bad–"

"Oh, heavens. No need."

"Anyhow, since I wasn't there, I said it must be the frogs you argued about."

General approval. Caroline wanted to know what else she'd learned.

Not much. They hadn't found Alistair's cell phone, wouldn't

commit about the murder weapon, and weren't sure if the blood in the pond might have come from his head wound, his earring, or some other source.

The earring interested Edgar. "Did she say if he was still wearing it?"

"No," Lydia realized. "I asked her, but she never told me."

"Do you think she believed you about not having an affair with him?" asked Caroline.

"Why wouldn't she?"

"Well," said Carlo, as if it were obvious. "She's the police!"

"I think we can safely infer," said Edgar, and paused as Connie delivered the biscuits and Lydia's margarita.

"Infer what?" Lydia stabbed a lime wedge with her straw.

Caroline's eyes met Edgar's, then shifted to Lydia. "That he was sleeping with somebody. Is that what you meant?"

Edgar nodded.

"From the questions, or from the attack?" Carlo inquired.

"Oh. Well, both and neither. The police searched his house yesterday. Thursday morning. He died on Wednesday afternoon. His housecleaners don't come in till Friday."

Exactly the right amount of salt slid into Lydia's mouth on a sip of exactly the right sweet, tangy blend of citrus and tequila. Impossible to fully savor this moment and take in Alistair Pope's duplicity at the same time. She chose the margarita.

"Ah," said Carlo. "Dirty laundry."

"It's an ill wind that blows nobody good," said Caroline. "Alistair's habit of leaving his messes for other people to clean up works in someone's favor for a change."

"Who was it, do you think?" Carlo asked Edgar.

"Oh, who knows?"

"That soubrette he was fondling in New York?" Caroline guessed.

"Who brought us coffee? With the Louise Brooks haircut?"

"No, the small mousy one. What did he call her? Daisy? In the leggings and smock, like a French schoolgirl."

"Delsey," said Carlo.

"Omigod," said Lydia.

The others stared at her.

"That's the assistant who called the Ropeses. DeAnne's parents." Reluctantly she unwrapped herself from golden tequila cobwebs, a caterpillar writhing too soon out of her cocoon. "I ran into DeAnne's mother at the store yesterday. She said Alistair's assistant had called to say his film was almost done. He wanted them to know he'd put DeAnne in it. She couldn't remember the name, but it was something unusual, like Darcy."

"Almost done," murmured Caroline.

Sleeping with somebody, thought Lydia. Wouldn't you just fucking know it! After he told me he'd given that up, with those lost-dog eyes. Kissing me, inviting me for tea–

"When was this?" Carlo inquired.

"What? Oh. The phone call? Early this week. Monday, maybe Tuesday." She looked from Carlo to Caroline and back. I'm not the only casualty here, she realized. And asked, "Did you know? Did he call you, too?"

"Oh, yes." Carlo slowly revolved his glass, lime wedges tumbling over ice cubes. "That he'd put DeAnne in the film? Yes, we knew."

"We saw it," Caroline amplified. "He screened it for us in New York last weekend."

"We decided to let it sit for a few days," said Carlo.

"Before calling a lawyer," Caroline completed, "or other people who might help us stop him releasing it."

They spoke in the same matter-of-fact, slightly off-key tone Lydia remembered from the day she'd helped them unpack from their trip. How could she have missed it?–the earthquake shuddering under the landscape?

Edgar told her, "Needless to remark, this creates a certain awkwardness with respect to the police investigation."

Lydia looked around the table, from one calm, pain-stricken face to another. "If you don't mind my asking, what exactly did he do?"

Caroline answered. "The film we'd agreed to was a documentary about our work in musical theater, up to the opera which is still in progress. However, when DeAnne died . . . "

She paused; Carlo continued. "Alistair blustered a good deal, but we didn't realize how affected he was."

"If he was," said Caroline tartly. "We tried to believe that. But it was hard not to suspect he'd simply recognized a hook. Even PBS can't resist scandals."

"You see, way back in the early years– When was that, Caroline?"

"After *Daisy of Spain*. Before we bought Town Hall."

"Our first flush of fame, two hits in a row on Broadway. We threw a celebration party at a friend's Long Island beach house. It ran all weekend, and in the wee hours of Sunday morning, there was a drunken fight. We weren't even aware of it. One of the stagehands and his girlfriend. She ran off, he thought back to the city, but apparently she went up to the widow's walk on the roof. No one missed her until brunch. She'd fallen through the railing onto a flagstone patio. Broke her neck."

"It was dreadful." Caroline shook her head sadly. "A day none of us will ever forget. Certainly not that poor young man."

"Alistair tracked him down," said Carlo. "Working as a janitor now, I believe. After DeAnne died, he–that is, Alistair–decided to bookend his film with the two deaths. Or, as he called them, tragedies."

"Misnomer," Edgar agreed. "Still, there goes the story." His fingers flickered like a departing butterfly.

Caroline nodded. "In the version he showed us last weekend, our whole lifetime's work–the songs we wrote, the shows we created, the wonderful people we worked with, the great ebb and flow of twentieth-century theater–all comes off as incidental."

"A mere interlude between disasters," said Carlo.

"Did he–" Lydia started, and stopped.

"Go on," said Caroline. "It's all right."

"What was Alistair's take on DeAnne's death? Did he treat it as an accident?"

"Hm." Caroline pursed her lips.

"He took care not to say," said Carlo. "So as to crank up, you know, the–"

"Titillation. That was the point. Hinting the parallel was too strong to be a coincidence, when he damn well knew better."

A silence followed. After a minute Connie came over to ask if they needed anything.

"Another round," Edgar confirmed.

No one spoke as their empty glasses were cleared away. Lydia clung to hers, still half full, and shook her head at Connie.

"Well," said Caroline eventually. "Back to the present. Where were we?"

Carlo addressed Lydia. "When this Delsey called DeAnne's parents, was she phoning from here or New York?"

"Mrs. Ropes wasn't sure. I wondered that too, since she said it was either Monday or Tuesday, and Alistair came in for lunch both days. Alone but late, which would be kind of strange if he had company."

"Mm," Caroline concurred.

Edgar asked, "Did your chat with Mrs. Ropes come up in your chat with Helen Wills?"

Lydia summarized what they'd said and what she'd withheld. "I didn't want her jumping to conclusions. Like that's why I came to the Cape, to do a nemesis on Alistair."

"Nimbly reasoned," Carlo patted her hand.

"I remember that investigation," said Caroline. "They were very thorough, she and Bob."

"Drove us round the bend," Carlo recalled. "You expect them to appreciate how upset you are, and of course they're thinking, if you're this upset, you must be guilty."

"So that when they finally decide no crime was committed," Edgar observed, "you're relieved to be off the hook."

"Well, yes. Naturally!"

"Why do you say that?" Caroline wanted to know.

Edgar pushed his glasses up his nose. "Lydia is thankful her session with the authorities is over. You and I and Carlo wonder who Alistair was having an affair with, but Lydia is content to enjoy her margarita."

"It's an outstanding margarita." Lydia swirled the dregs.

"I don't follow you," said Carlo.

"Not important," Edgar shrugged. "My jumping-bean mind."

"We were wondering if Delsey came down from New York with Alistair," Carlo answered Caroline's original question, "and if he left her at his house in postcoital bliss to dash over late to Leo's."

"Whereupon she picked up the phone and called DeAnne's parents?"

"If she did, it was a cell phone," Lydia interposed. "Mrs. Ropes said she had bad reception." Her tongue lifted a clump of salt off the rim of her glass.

"Alistair's cell phone is still missing," added Carlo.

"Curiouser and curiouser!" Caroline arched her elegant eye-brows.

"It doesn't track," Edgar objected.

"No," Lydia concurred. "Both of those days, he invited me over for tea. It didn't work out; but why would he even ask, if his girlfriend-assistant was here?"

"Would he have brought her to Leo's?" Carlo asked Edgar. "Shown her off?"

"Oh, I should think so."

Connie, delivering their drinks, gave them time to reshuffle this motley deck. Lydia surrendered her empty glass. Question to self: Are you OK to drive? Answer: Who cares? Even in her golden haze, this was a reply Lydia recognized as a red flag. She took two biscuits and asked for a tall glass of water.

The talk drifted to other subjects: how the opera was coming along, whether Edgar intended to finish *The Aspern Papers*, when the Flying Wedge might stage its next feast. Lydia's mind wandered away and back again. When a break opened up in the conversation, she said, "I do wonder who Alistair was having an affair with. Did you get the idea in New York it was Delsey?"

"I didn't," said Caroline. "Oh, they flirted. He was addicted to it, as you know. But always–"

"Noncommittal," supplied Carlo.

"What about DeAnne?"

Caroline set down her drink. "Alistair and DeAnne? Now that's a troubling thought."

"Actually I meant did DeAnne have a boyfriend," said Lydia.

"Like on the crew, maybe. But–is that possible? Her and Alistair?"

"Surely not." Carlo shuddered.

"What made you ask?" Edgar inquired.

"She sounded so happy in the postcard she sent me. Looking forward to something. The film, I thought, but then I remembered . . ." How much she envied me and Fletcher? Hah! Don't go there, Lydia. "How much she wanted to be in love."

"What do you think?" Edgar asked Caroline and Carlo.

"Well, of course, she was young, female, and in good health, which would have been enough for Alistair. On the other hand, I didn't see any sign of a full-blown romance." Caroline looked at Carlo, who shook his head. "With him or anyone else. Not that we'd necessarily have known."

"But he did flirt with her?"

"Oh, yes," said Carlo. "And she with him. When he sat her on the sofa to shoot, I thought he'd never let go of her shoulders. What do they call them–chemises? Bustiers? Those little tops, you know, like French underwear."

Lydia's brain was reeling all over again. Off his radar, was she? Just one more worker bee? Had Alistair Pope ever told her the truth about anything?

Edgar, perhaps reading her mind, passed the biscuits.

Get a grip, Lydia.

"What happens to the film now?" she asked.

A wry chuckle came from Caroline.

"Ah, yes," said Carlo. "Inquiring minds want to know! In fact are on tenterhooks."

"Whatever tenterhooks may be. Edgar, there's a book for you." Caroline turned to Lydia. "We're waiting for the lawyers to resolve certain contract issues. Who owns what, how finished it truly is, who's to make the final touches, that kind of thing."

"From our viewpoint," said Carlo, "there's a nice documentary in there, if you cut away the sensationalism."

"From the Ropeses' viewpoint as well," said Caroline. "Whatever they may wish or believe, I can't imagine they'd care for how ruthlessly Alistair Pope has exploited their daughter."

Chapter Twenty-Four

When they all trailed out of the Whistling Pig, the afternoon's first belated sunbeams were sparkling in the surrounding treetops like a canopy of emeralds. Caroline and Carlo waved as they drove off. Edgar and Lydia, parked next to each other, lingered to shake off rain gear and stow it in their respective back seats.

Lydia suspected that Edgar also wanted to make sure she was sober enough to drive. He seemed untouched by his two gin-and-tonics, which struck her as grossly unfair. But then (she recalled) he'd eaten his usual three-course lunch, whereas she'd gulped down a scoop of leftover potato salad before heading for police headquarters.

As soon as she got home, microwave a burrito and heap it with salsa. Cut up that avocado–was there cheese?

Or grab some fresh air first. Several customers had mentioned a path through the woods behind the post office, where enormous multicolored rhododendrons were in bloom. A little muddy, maybe, but you couldn't beat sunshine on new leaves and wet flowers.

"Do you ever walk behind the P.O.?" she asked Edgar.

His eyebrows went up. "Mercy no."

"You're not a walker?"

"For recreation? No. Only from the house to the car."

"I thought I'd go check out that path people keep talking about. It's a nature preserve, right? Flowers and a pond?"

The eyebrows narrowed. "Are you sure that's a good idea?"

"Why?" She bristled. "Do I look too drunk to walk a straight line?"

"Oh, heavens no. Not in the least." He paused; she could see him weighing his words. "Under the circumstances . . . Well. Never mind. If you do go, would you knock on my door when you come back?"

It was his labored nonchalance that gave Lydia chills. "Edgar, what is this? Do you think I'm in danger?"

"Oh, surely not. Better to be safe than sorry, that's all."

The cliche sounded so evasive that she almost snapped: "Safe from what?"

For a moment he looked panicky, poised to retreat into his car. "Hummy hummy hoo. How to put it?" Elbows braced against metal, he gazed at the trees. "No one would have dreamed of warning Alistair off a stroll around the frog pond. What could possibly happen? And yet. Here we are. Now, suppose someone's hackles are up. The police are asking you questions. You knew Alistair; you knew DeAnne. Is this cause for concern? Most likely not, but who can say? Therefore, caution. Carry on, by all means! But when you're at home, lock your doors. Will you? Don't go for long walks alone in strange places. Tell the Girl Scouts to peddle their cookies elsewhere. That sort of thing."

Given his expertise with that sort of thing, Lydia found it slightly reassuring that he seemed more afraid of scaring her than of her being ambushed by Alistair Pope's killer. "No problem."

A sigh of relief.

"I won't order any pizzas, and I'll wait to walk in the woods till I have company."

"Good. Good." He disentangled himself from the car.

"But you said I knew Alistair and DeAnne. Does that mean you think they're connected?"

Edgar looked surprised. "Well, we know that. The film and whatnot."

"I mean, you think their deaths are connected?"

"Oh. Well, yes. I'm afraid so."

The chills were stronger this time. "Edgar, are you saying– Do you think DeAnne was murdered?"

His glasses slid down his nose. "Don't you?"

Instead of strolling around the nature preserve, Lydia power-walked from the Whistling Pig to the Christmas Tree Shop on the corner of Willow Street. This was where you went for anything you ran out of: candy, shampoo, towels, stationery, a flashlight, patio furniture, pie tins, pancake mix. Lydia had been wanting sunblock. Now she wanted motion.

Wondering how a skilled carpenter could fall off a ladder, she'd discovered, was nothing compared to hearing Edgar Rowdey agree DeAnne hadn't died by accident.

Not that he had evidence. Like everyone at Leo's, he'd picked up his facts second-hand. At first he'd merely been startled by the implausibility of DeAnne's fatal choices. Staying behind to take down the film crew's curtain? Climbing an unbraced ladder alone? Toppling at just the angle where her head would hit a bronze frog? All of which, he hastened to add, evidently had happened just as reported. Still, the mind boggled.

What changed boggling to suspicion was the eerie similarity between DeAnne's death and Alistair Pope's.

Lydia replayed the next part of their conversation as she strode past the thrift shop, past the bank.

She'd been leaning back against the Morris, staring up into flickering green maple leaves. "What eerie similarity?" she asked the tree. "A big heavy curtain knocking over a ladder, versus somebody whacking somebody with a rock?"

"Two people in the middle of life's journey, minding their business, both felled by bumps on the head?" Edgar's voice was mild. "And what about the frogs?"

"OK, the frogs." She straightened up to look at him. "But nobody ever thought Alistair's death was an accident. At least, not for long. I mean, X might have sneaked up behind him, or they ran into each other and got in a fight, but he wasn't just, la-dee-da, minding his own business and, *bam!* Was he?"

"I doubt X sneaked up," Edgar returned. "Unless this was a left-handed assailant, they'd have to be standing face to face. Given the blow was on the left side of his head, near the ear."

"Well, then why didn't he run? Or fight back? If he's facing some wacko who picks up a rock? Or did he hear footsteps behind him, and turn around, and surprise!"

"Not a complete surprise, surely. Alistair chose to join X

under the tree. And X evidently chose to park at the Richards House, walk down to the tree, and wait for him."

"But it can't have been a planned rendezvous." Lydia folded her arms. "Or he wouldn't have bullied Mudge about lunch five minutes earlier."

"No. Too true."

"What, then? Do you mean– X was somebody he knew, who lured him under the Elephant Tree to kill him?"

"Mmm . . . "

Edgar was gazing across the parking lot as if that wasn't quite what he meant. "What?" she persisted.

"Well, that's the eerie similarity. Somebody he knew, yes, I imagine so, who lured him under the tree. But . . . to kill him? In point of fact, X didn't kill Alistair. Nor DeAnne, either."

Was he offering a reprieve? Some miraculous non-fatal path out of this labyrinth? "Edgar, what are you saying?"

"Alistair was hit on the head with a rock, but he died by drowning. DeAnne fell off a ladder, but she died by striking her head on a bronze frog. Two inches one way or the other . . ." He let it trail off.

Lydia felt as if she'd been hit on the head herself. "How's that? X attacks both of them, and they both die, but X isn't a murderer?"

"Oh, I wouldn't let him off the hook so lightly. Or her," he amended. "There's no virtue in committing an almost-murder and leaving Fate to drop the last feather on the scale." He stretched out his arms and interlaced his long fingers. "On the face of it, one might suppose X wanted the satisfaction of destroying his or her victims, without the responsibility."

Another silence followed. After a moment Lydia asked, "What if they'd survived?"

"Well, exactly," said Edgar.

"They'd have gone to the cops. Wouldn't they? Shot X down in flames. Why risk it?"

"Would they?"

A surge of irritation: why couldn't he give her a straight answer? Then she saw the absurdity of expecting one: a double murder diagnosed and solved, tied up and gift-wrapped, in the parking lot of the Whistling Pig?

"Maybe Detective Wills can enlighten us." His knuckles cracked. "I'm stopping by for a chat tomorrow morning."

Lydia gaped at him. Edgar answered her unasked question: "I didn't want to upset Carlo and Caroline. They're already on tenter-hooks, waiting to be called in at any moment–and then they've had such a wretched week, and Carlo's birthday and all–why drop the other shoe?"

"Will you–"

He interrupted before she could ask if he meant to share his ideas with Helen Wills. "I'll be in for breakfast as usual. Lunch as well, I should think; Mrs. Wills claims to have other plans. See you then."

Now Lydia stood in front of a display rack and asked herself if 30 or 15 was what she needed for a Cape Cod summer. With no beach time but Sundays and afternoons . . .

Why would anybody commit an almost-murder?

To her–not that she was any expert–it made no sense. If you were crazy or angry enough to strike someone down, why not finish the job? Why go through stalking, hiding, luring, attacking, the whole nine yards, and then leave the tenth yard up to Fate?

And on top of that, why did Edgar believe X would trust the victims not to go to the cops if Fate blew it?

The only reason Lydia could think of was if X had something on each of them–some blackmail-worthy secret DeAnne and Alistair didn't dare bring to the cops' attention.

That didn't make sense, either. Alistair, OK, maybe; but DeAnne? You'd just about have to believe she took up drug-dealing or prostitution the minute she hit Cape Cod.

Oh, fuck. Was it possible Alistair had gotten her pregnant? Or hooked on something?

No way. They'd known each other how long? Four or five days?

Unless they'd crossed paths earlier, before her semester in Cambridge.

Yeah, right. There's DeAnne living with her parents, slipping the leash to screw around with Alistair, and instead of locking her in her room and kicking his ass halfway to the bridge, Raymond and Cynthia send her off to the city alone to study art.

"So are you gonna buy anything, or just stand here till the store closes?"

Lydia jumped. Dinah stood beside her, filling the aisle in an aqua T-shirt and khaki shorts big enough for an Army tent.

"Sunblock," she managed.

"Yup, that's what that is." Dinah's shopping basket contained double-A batteries, a bottle of skin lotion, and a khaki baseball cap. "I'm heading out for a walk down back of the P.O., to check out those rhododendrons. You want to come?"

They parked behind a row of mail trucks. "Can't do this in the daytime," said Dinah. "There's a little lot down that drive, but they only got a couple of spaces. I figure, leave those for the folks with dogs and baby strollers."

Lydia followed her across a stretch of grass, dabbing #15 on her nose. Dinah positioned her new baseball cap. "Anyways, it's about exercise, right? People fork out a bundle to join the gym, and then get all bent outta shape if they can't park right in front. God forbid they should bruise their fancy sneakers walking thirty feet to the door! Me, I go the old-fashioned route. Summer on Cape Cod! All the exercise you want for free!"

They crossed a tiny asphalt parking area. Two paths diverged into the woods. Dinah veered left without hesitation.

"You come here much?"

"Nope. This is Day One of my new fitness plan. I got a friend, big guy like me?–but on him it's all muscle. He's looking for a house where he can put in a workout room. I'm thinking, goddammit, I lived here all my life! I know the places the tourists don't ever hear about. What am I doing, go home every day, veg out in front of the TV? I pay taxes for this!" She waved her arms at oaks and birch trees, raspberry bushes and poison ivy.

"So you've been here before? You know your way around?"

Dinah's hat bobbed vigorously. "Over there, picnic area. This way, path down to the pond. Rhododendrons."

She sounded short of breath already, though they were walking slowly, picking their way around puddles. Lydia wondered whether to throw in a remark about taking it easy on Day One. Considering how touchy Dinah could be about her cooking, better not.

They proceeded in silence, with Dinah in the lead on a one-lane dirt and gravel track. The woods were scrubbier than on the mainland, mostly oaks and pines, filled in with vines and underbrush, edged with bachelor buttons and Queen Anne's lace. I needed this, thought Lydia. Flowers! Trees! Grass! Fresh air!

Funny, in retrospect, that Edgar's logic centered on physics. *If a right-handed assailant swings a rock . . .* What about *who* and *why*? Who knew both Alistair and DeAnne? Did they have any other connection besides his film? Did anyone else have a reason to stop it besides Carlo and Caroline?

But killing DeAnne wouldn't–didn't–stop the film.

This is where I came in, Lydia thought in exasperation. Why would anybody go after DeAnne?

In front of her, Dinah pointed: the first rhododendron.

What Lydia had pictured was a row of neat round shrubs dotted with pom-poms. This was one green-leafed giant, taller and wider than Dinah, tapered like a Christmas tree, twinkling with raindrops. Some of its branches were tipped with pineapple-shaped buds; on others, these had opened into pink blossoms as bright as neon and as big as a baby's head.

"Holy cow!"

"Just wait," Dinah grinned.

Around the next bend was a whole cluster of the huge bushes, blooming in every shade of pink from seashell to lipstick. Since Dinah's chest was heaving, Lydia circled the little grove slowly, marveling at each flower. How could she have lived this long without noticing the paradox of rhododendrons?–the small delicate fluted cups that together became a vivid ball of color? It seemed miraculous to her that something so glorious could exist in the middle of Quansett, and only the two of them here to appreciate it.

Then she heard the sound.

At first she thought it must be Dinah, panting. No: Dinah was standing still on the path. The sound came from a different direction, somewhere behind her.

Human breathing? And a voice? More than one. Suppressed, urgent.

Hey, Lydia! Congratulations! You win the un-fucking-believably stupid prize! How long ago did Edgar warn you not to go off in strange places by yourself? Half an hour? And here you are, alone in the middle of fucking nowhere! Except for Dinah, who's too massive and slow to run, or put up a serious fight, or maybe even make it back to the car. Brilliant!

She crept toward the path. "Can you hear that?" she asked softly.

Dinah nodded. They stood frozen, listening, peering in every direction as if by staring hard enough they could see through bushes and trees.

After a moment Lydia pointed.

Dinah nodded again. She was grinning.

That took Lydia by surprise. "Do you know . . . ?"

"I sure's hell know *what*," Dinah whispered gleefully. "Just not *where*. Or *who*. Let's check it out."

She went first. Lydia tiptoed after her. When they find our bodies, will they shake their heads at what incredible morons we were?

The sounds grew louder: gasps, grunts, groans. Not because we're getting closer, Lydia realized in enlightenment and relief; because *they're* getting closer.

Dinah beckoned her to an eye-level gap in a thick screen of vines and leaves.

The pale pink buttocks pumping in the air she didn't recognize. The face on the ground she did, although the eyes were shut and the mouth open, by the bird's-nest tangle of auburn hair jerking back and forth on its pine-needle pillow.

Chapter Twenty-Five

Lydia backed off, quick and quiet. Not from Sue's sex life. She was retreating from the pop-up image of what might be happening right now, fifty miles away, in what used to be her and Fletcher's bed.

Concealed behind the rhododendrons, she turned to Dinah.

But Dinah hadn't followed. There was her broad back, still at the observation hole.

Fuck! thought Lydia. What does she think, I'm going to hang around here while she watches Adam and Eve get their rocks off?

Judging from the noise, that could be any second. He was groaning now; she was shouting. Ecstasy? Instructions? Lydia didn't want to know.

She was weighing whether to head back alone when she heard a pop.

"Shit!" came a shriek.

Lydia stepped out from behind the bush. Dinah swiveled and was beating the air with both fists. "Cut it out, asshole!" she bellowed into the woods. "There's *people* here!"

What was going on?

Another pop. This time Lydia thought she heard a short high whine, like a rocket-launched mosquito.

"Hey, motherfucker!" Dinah shouted. "It ain't deer season and we ain't deer!"

Lydia ran toward her.

"Did you hear that?" Dinah was quivering with rage. "Some fucking tourist–"

"Come on." Lydia grabbed her arm.

They trundled back up the path faster than she'd have believed possible. The trouble was, Lydia wasn't sure which direction the shots (if they were shots) had come from. Asking Dinah would mean stopping for her to catch her breath. Anyhow, did it matter? There was only one way back to the car, the post office, civilization.

The police.

Lydia patted her pockets, and remembered stowing her bag in Dinah's trunk.

"You got a cell phone?"

Dinah shook her head.

Past the first rhododendron. A loud crack: another shot or a stick breaking underfoot? Oh, please, let Dinah be right! Some moron tourist, who stopped when he realized. Friday afternoon; wasn't that most likely? End of the work week, new gun, traffic jam, pocket flask . . .

"We sh–" Dinah wheezed.

"You OK?"

She nodded. She was gasping for breath, her cheeks and neck flushed scarlet, but she kept on valiantly stumbling along the path.

"Talk at the car," Lydia advised.

Seconds later she understood. *We should have helped Sue and her boyfriend.*

Yeah. Maybe. Or maybe they were the ones with the gun.

In the parking lot, Dinah half-collapsed on the hood of a silver SUV. The driver–leaning into the back seat, clipping a leash onto her beagle–straightened up to protest.

"Don't go in there," panted Lydia. "Some jerk just shot at us."

The woman shut her mouth, shut her dog in the car, and pulled out a phone. "Call 911?"

Lydia nodded gratefully.

The beagle howled in disappointment.

The police dispatcher promised to send someone out. At Dinah's car, Lydia called Detective Wills. She said she'd come right over. Yes, they should wait there as the dispatcher had requested. No, they shouldn't try to rescue the pair in the bushes.

Within five minutes, Helen Wills's cruiser came barrelling down the drive and into the nature preserve's little parking area. Dinah and Lydia walked back from the post-office lot to meet her.

"That was quick," said Dinah.

"Yeah, well, possible gunfire in a public place does that to me. Hey, Lydia." They shook hands. "So," she turned back to Dinah, "what have we got?"

"I'd say some nimrod trying out his new pistol."

"A pistol, huh? Two shots?"

"Two before we hightailed it outta there. Maybe one, two more. Couldn't tell for sure. Or where from, either. Not close range, though."

Helen looked inquiringly at Lydia: Anything to add? Lydia shrugged: No.

"OK. There should be a local cop here any second. I'm gonna go on in and see what I can do about those lovers."

"Sue, who used to work at Leo's," said Dinah, "and Wally Hicks from the Frigate. So if it's Kevin Kelly coming, you better split 'em up before you bring 'em out."

"Oh, Jesus," said Helen.

"You know how guys get who been chuck-holed. Even cops. Especially cops."

Helen's hand went to the V of her jacket. "Wait in the car. And if anybody comes out, don't go after them. Call me. OK?"

"No problem," said Dinah. "Your show. Run it your way, fine with me."

They didn't go back to Dinah's car, though, but leaned against Helen's cruiser. The incongruity of watching a woman in gray slacks and blazer stepping cautiously into the woods, one hand under her lapel like Napoleon, made Lydia feel again as though she was dreaming.

"Chuck-holed?" she asked.

"Oh yeah." When Dinah shifted her weight, the whole cruiser bounced. "Sue had a thing last year with Kevin Kelly. I doubt either one of 'em took it too serious, but he didn't like her cutting him off. She's a loose cannon, that girl. I hope she don't mess up Rosey Sherman's business like she did Leo's. Mine either, far's that goes."

"Yours, how?"

"Not cooking. My other job." Dinah grinned. "Phone sex."

Lydia was staggered. "Phone sex?"

"Yup. Course most of my clients are off Cape. Too risky here. Yeah, that's how I pay my mortgage. Don't spread it around."

"How does it work?" Lydia couldn't resist asking.

"Well, it ain't exactly rocket science. The company sets up the appointment, tells me what the guy wants, and when we get on the phone, that's who I am." Her voice changed to a dewy soprano: "'Hi! I'm Bambi! I just turned seventeen!' Or, I got one guy, he likes Helga to suck his toes. I do a goot Cherman acc'nt."

Lydia's stunned expression made Dinah chuckle. "Tell you this, I picked up a tip or two from Sue back there."

Mercifully, in Lydia's opinion, she stopped talking as a car sped up the driveway.

Not the cops but a battered silver-blue Subaru wagon. It pulled up in front of them.

"Something I been wondering about, though," Dinah continued.

Dave Wheeler clambered out, bandoliered in cameras.

"Never mind. Later."

"Hey, Dave," said Lydia.

"Hey." He looked pleasantly surprised. "What're you guys doing here?"

Dinah informed him with pride: "We're the ones who got shot at."

He scanned the mail trucks, the woods, the parking area. "Is that Hell on Wheels?"

"She went in to nab the perp and rescue a pair of lovebirds."

"Catch you later, then." He took off down the path.

Lydia was considering whether to feel miffed until she heard the siren approaching from Main Street. Flashing lights, a screech of tires–

"Here comes Kevin," said Dinah.

They went to meet him. Officer Kelly frowned from the Subaru to them. "Is that the Cape Cod Times?"

"Hail, hail, the gang's all here." Dinah shook his hand. "Kevin, you remember Lydia?"

"Dammit," he shook Lydia's hand, "he's got no business interfering with a police investigation!"

"Helen'll shoo him out, then. She said you'd want our statements. If you don't, Kevin, just say so and we'll be happy to head on home."

That refocused his attention. "You wait here," he ordered, "while I go straighten this out."

Hand on his holster, Kevin Kelly marched across the asphalt.

He'd almost reached the path when four people emerged from the woods: Dave Wheeler, Wally Hicks, and two teenage girls with a cocker spaniel on a leash.

Lydia and Dinah were too far away to hear what they said to each other. Lydia hoped Dave would come over and fill her in. Or call her. Did he have her phone number? Maybe she'd call him. She distinctly recalled him giving her his card, if she could just remember where she put it.

Kevin and Dave appeared to be doing most of the talking. After two or three minutes, Dave led Wally to his Subaru and opened the passenger door. Kevin walked the girls and dog down the driveway alongside the post office.

"Well, damn!" said Dinah. "What about us?"

Now Lydia did feel miffed. "Yeah! What are we, chopped liver?"

"Hold on," said Dinah. "Here's the cavalry."

This time it was Helen Wills escorting Sue, who stopped when they hit a sunny spot to brush pine needles off her bare legs. Having checked that the men were out of the way, Helen let Sue into her cruiser.

"Hey," Dinah murmured. "Nice work."

"Thanks," said Helen. "No sign of your gunman."

Dave Wheeler had gotten out of his car and raised his camera. Speaking of gunmen, thought Lydia. He's done this so many times, like a TV western, you hardly see the moves.

"Hey, what is this? Open season?" Helen held up a hand in protest. "Put that thing away and get him out of here, will you, before Kevin comes back?"

Dave waved an OK, then waved to Lydia and Dinah before

driving off with Wally.

"I'll call Kevin on the Nextel," Helen resumed. "Make sure he does a full search of the area after he takes the Ward kids home. Will you tell him exactly where you were, what happened and so on?"

"No problem," said Dinah.

Alone again, she and Lydia moved to a picnic table near the mouth of the trail, where the sun was stronger. Neither one of them mentioned the possibility that they'd just come close to being killed. Lydia suspected that if she even thought about it, she'd start shivering uncontrollably, never mind the sun. Time for another dab of #15? More like time for dinner. That overdue burrito that was supposed to soak up her margarita. What a day!

When Kevin Kelly returned, he brought a tape recorder from his patrol car and peppered them with questions. Why did they think it was shots they heard and not a car backfiring, a door slamming, a kid setting off firecrackers? Dinah said she had her own pistol–yes, licensed, thank you–and spent enough time down at the Rod and Gun Club to know the difference. But she couldn't tell where they came from? Nope. Sorry.

She did most of the talking. Aside from having nothing to contribute, Lydia couldn't look at Officer Kelly without picturing his blue uniform strewn around the bushes as he flung his chunky freckled self on Sue.

Dinah stayed behind while Lydia led Kevin Kelly far enough into the woods to explain where they'd heard the pops. (He refused to call them shots.) Then, to her disappointment, he walked her back out again. They were free to go, he announced. In fact they were ordered to go. No, he had nothing to tell them at this time. He couldn't start searching the area until he cordoned off the path to prevent civilians from potentially contaminating the scene, as well as endangering their lives. The way he drew back his shoulders and puffed out his chest as he said this reminded Lydia of a courting pigeon.

Dinah dropped her off at the cottage. Out of courtesy Lydia invited her in, but Dinah said she'd take a raincheck. They were both ready to see the last of each other until tomorrow.

Talk about anticlimax! Wally Hicks muttered to himself. One minute you're Adam in the garden, climbing the pinnacle of bliss, and next minute you're in a fucking three-ring circus. Gunshots, yelling, cops– Scrambling for your clothes, no clue what all the commotion's about, if somebody's trying to whack you or somebody got whacked, and suddenly it's not funny, that line about Quansett being the crime capital of Cape Cod.

And do they even inform you what's going on? No. You step out of the bushes into the damn Cape Cod Times photographer. What's he here for? Tomorrow's front page? Or just to escort you out, like this is a bust, better throw your poncho over your face, hide from the media, except your poncho's wadded under your arm, prickly with pine needles, and he is the media. Not giving you one second to be the man and protect Sue, who, OK, is looking and acting even pricklier, but who wouldn't?–hustled off half-dressed by a female Jehovah's Witness.

Wally reviewed these exasperating events while he shelved books. On his to-do list, shelving fell near the bottom. He'd picked it so as to stay in the front of the shop, near the door, in case Sue came back. Recognizing that maybe she never would. Which gave special appeal to slamming each volume violently into its slot.

Damn! Had karma turned on him already? Had he shot himself in the foot, so to speak, by betraying his warrior purity?

That can wait, Hicks. Right now it's about damage control.

If Sue got dropped off at her car, she should've been back long ago. They'd parked at the package store–Wally's strategy for getting her away from the Frigate without Gromit. Then, brown paper bag of Wild Turkey in hand: Hey, how about a little walk? Stretch our legs after a long day's work. Look, here's a path into the nature preserve. Why the two of them had to be escorted out separately Wally didn't follow, but no problem; they'd meet up at the Frigate. So where was she? He'd made the Cape Cod Times guy drive past the package store: no rattletrap blue Toyota in the lot. Was she pissed at him because their private tryst turned public? Dammit, that wasn't his fault! If she wanted to blame somebody, blame Dinah, standing out there gawking. Blame that snake Lydia.

Just one bright spot in this wrecked afternoon. Thanks to–

what was his name?–Dave Wheeler. Toward the end, after they'd left the woods. Slow down the playback here. We're driving up Main Street toward the Frigate. I ask him the same questions again he wouldn't answer when we got in the car. What's your deal? How'd you show up so fast? You monitor the cops on that CB radio? He chuckles: You got it. Before the paper, I worked for the Exmouth P.D., he says. Deal is, if I shoot anything they need, I hand it over, and they give me a break on access. At which point I remark on Ms. Jehovah's Witness not showing a whole lot of sympathy on the access issue. And he says Well, she's out of that loop, being a state trooper. I mainly deal with Pete Altman, you know, the detective? I most certainly do know, having sold Pete a couple dozen crime novels these past two years. Which leads us into a vigorous discussion of Elmore Leonard versus Carl Hiaasen, and puts us on a comradely footing. So I can then ask, Who gets the photos you just shot, Pete or the paper? Meaning that I would be mighty relieved to know Sue's and my overexposed asses won't appear on the newsstand tomorrow. He says Don't worry, this was probably a washout. If I do have anything anybody wants, it won't be of you. And that's when I tell him I sure would appreciate a look at those pictures. In return for which favor, I have a little something upstairs to show him.

Giving silent thanks for Trader Joe's, Lydia slid her burrito into the microwave.

She'd vowed not to ask herself any more pointless questions on an empty stomach. Such as, Were those really pistol shots? Who would choose the woods behind the Quansett post office for target practice? What were the odds of a trigger-happy tourist turning up in the same place at the same time as all three female members, past and present, of Leo's kitchen staff?

Light-headed from tequila and adrenalin, you couldn't hope to solve such a riddle.

What it needs, Lydia thought, is the penetrating mind of Edgar Rowdey.

As soon as she'd finished eating, she walked under the magnolia tree to see if he was home.

Twilight had darkened to deep blue evening. A few last rain-drops fell from the heavy leaves onto her head. Lights glowed behind drawn curtains in the kitchen and the room above it. Lydia picked her way up the unlit porch steps and along the front of the house, past the front door, around to the side where they'd entered for tea. Found an antique doorbell. Pressed the button.

And waited.

After a minute she pressed again.

Broken? She knocked on the door.

Nothing.

Knocked again, harder

Leo's warning came back to her from the day she'd moved in: Any questions, don't ask the man in the big house. He's a recluse. Knock on his door, he won't answer.

But I'm not looking to borrow a cup of sugar! she protested silently. Come on, Edgar! We're talking life and death here!

No response.

Lydia retraced her steps back to the cottage. Edgar would be at Leo's for breakfast. What she ought to do now–really, all she could do–was shut off her brain, wash her dishes, and get some sleep.

Odd that Detective Wills had scheduled his interview for tomorrow, with her husband coming home. Then what? Would she take the rest of the weekend off? Turn over the case to Pete Altman? Or, if he still had his hands full with the burglaries, just let it sit until next week?

Unacceptable. No way, thought Lydia, scrubbing a plate, am I waiting three days to find out if some wacko who's already killed two people may be chasing me with a loaded gun.

She dried her hands and picked up the phone.

Three rings, then a click and a voice: "Detective Helen Wills."

"Hi. This is Lydia Vivaldi. I'm sorry to bother you so late, but– Have you guys found out anything about this afternoon?"

There was a pause, as if Helen Wills was changing gears. "Lydia, if we'd found out anything you should know, I'd have called you."

"Thanks. It's just– This is all really strange to me." I'm talking too much, thought Lydia. "You know? Going for a walk and having somebody maybe shooting at me?"

"Is there a reason why you think you were the target?"

The dryness of her tone hit a nerve. "What, you mean aside from I'm out in the middle of nowhere and bullets start whizzing around?" Lydia retorted. "I've only been on Cape Cod for like ten days. Maybe this happens all the time here, but where I come from, it's a big deal."

"Sorry. Of course." Lydia got the feeling Detective Wills was tearing herself away from a TV show she really wanted to watch. "We did find the weapon. No sign of the shooter. If it's what Dinah said–some idiot shooting at crows or whatever? who heard her yell, ditched the pistol and ran? That kind of thing does happen here. Tourists think they cross the bridge into a magic bubble. Vacation! Anything goes!"

"So, what? End of story? Case closed?"

"There's not much more we can do. Other than give you the obvious advice–exercise caution, and if you do have any enemies, you'd tell us, right?"

"I don't," said Lydia. "At least none you haven't heard about." Not strictly true; but the past is the past, and not Detective Wills's business. "Well, OK then."

"You don't sound OK."

"No. I am. It's just– I guess, coming on top of the two–" She stopped herself before *murders*. "I mean, coming right after Alistair, and DeAnne."

"Lydia," said Detective Wills, "what do you know that you're not telling me?"

"Excuse me?"

"I'll ask you again: is there a reason why you think you're in danger?"

Suddenly all the day's tensions came roiling up through Lydia like lava in a volcano. "What kind of a crazy question is that? What would you think if you were a stranger here and the first two people you knew both got hit on the head and died? And then you go for a walk in the woods, get away from it all, and somebody starts shooting, and you're running for your life? Hey, you think I might be in danger at all? Or is it just me? Just paranoia?"

"Hey. Take it easy."

"What do you think, I get my kicks out of making phone calls like this? Harassing cops? No. I want to know what threat level we're at here!"

Her voice was shaking. "Right. Sure," Helen Wills replied soothingly. And went on: Calm down, don't worry . . . Lydia tuned her out. Get a grip! she told herself. The last thing you need is to fall apart in a phone conversation (which may be monitored) with a state trooper.

She wedged herself among the sofa cushions. The metallic stream of sounds in her ear re-formed into words and phrases: any similarity between DeAnne's death and Alistair's was pure coincidence; so was the timing of the gunshots in the woods; if Lydia was concerned for her safety, the local officer on duty could stop by and check on her.

She caught at a stick bobbing in the flow. "Pure coincidence? How do you know?"

"Maybe not pure," Helen Wills conceded. She sounded glad to hear Lydia talking again. "At this point, you're right, we can't be sure. There's always the chance of a copycat factor."

"Copycat, like how?"

"Well, like if Alistair's killer knew about DeAnne, he might try and make his crime look like the same kind of accident. Set it up on rough ground, with rocks."

"You mean, so you'd think he tripped and hit his head?"

"Exactly."

"But you didn't."

"No, we didn't. Are you all right, then? or do you want me to–"

"So what you've got," Lydia interrupted, "or at least you might have, is a murderer disguising something as an accident that's actually an attack."

"It's possible. That's not to say it's likely."

"Couldn't the same thing have happened with this shooter in

the woods? He missed his target, so he dropped the gun and ran. Hoping you'd chalk it off to some looney-tune tourist."

"Don't do this, Lydia."

"And couldn't the same thing have happened with DeAnne?"

"Stop! I mean it. I know you're upset, but–let it go."

"I'm just saying."

"Well, don't. Leave the detective work to the professionals."

"Fine."

"Seriously. I don't want to hear tomorrow that you were broadcasting your theories around Leo's, or anyplace else. OK?"

In spite of herself, Lydia bristled. "Why's that?"

"Because this isn't a game, it's an unsolved murder case. Right now, you don't appear to be in danger. Let's keep it that way."

Chapter Twenty-Six

Mudge was satisfactorily shocked to hear about Dinah and Lydia's brush with death, as Dinah called it. So were the Back End's early-morning customers. Lydia, recalling Helen Wills's warning, wondered if Dinah was pushing her (or their) luck. Just when she hoped the story had finished its rounds, Leo came downstairs, and loudly threatened to fire them both for telling the whole restaurant before him.

A couple of regulars at the counter reported nothing in the Cape Cod Times about gunfire at the nature preserve. Dinah speculated, with relish, that the cops were keeping a lid on it.

"Is this for real?" Mudge murmured to Lydia as she passed the register.

"Oh, yeah. I mean–were they really gunshots? Who knows?"

"Who was doing it in the bushes?" On that point Dinah had stood mum.

"Tell you later." A party of three was arriving to pay their bill. "Hey, nice ring. Is that new?"

Mudge lifted his hand to show it off: a heavy gold band with a faceted black oval stone. "Early birthday present."

Edgar Rowdey arrived as usual for breakfast and immersed himself in his usual paperback. Lydia hurried over with his coffee. How would he react when he heard about the sniper? "I told you so" would be beneath him; what she wanted was to know why he'd told her so. But as soon as she started talking, he interrupted: barely time to eat, must dash off to meet Detective Wills, catch up later.

Saturday being the Back End's busiest morning, she didn't object. People were all but fighting each other for tables. Some of them, in crisply pressed jeans and windbreakers, looked like tourists; others had the sleepier, sloppier air of locals. When Dinah handed out midmorning bagels, Lydia asked her if weekend traffic was usually this heavy.

"Nah." Dinah's nose wrinkled. "We're still gettin' rubber-neckers. All the way from the lower Cape, to see the murder scene."

"Nothing to see," Lydia objected. "Mudge, when's your birth-day?"

"Week from tomorrow."

"I'll bake us a cake," said Dinah, "if the crowd thins out."

"They're sure making Leo happy," said Mudge. "Maybe he paid the Times to hush it up about you guys getting shot at."

"So's not to scare off business," Dinah agreed. "Except I bet you we'd get even more."

"Does the Cape Cod Times take bribes?" asked Lydia.

"Why else would they send out a photographer and not print anything?" countered Dinah.

It was a good enough question that Lydia resolved to ask Dave Wheeler the next time she saw him.

Meanwhile, she had customers to feed. Here came Carlo and Caroline, with two athletic-looking male friends. They wrote down an order for one Today's Speshul–spaghetti with meatballs–and three Keesh with Sallid, and sat in a green-tabled booth.

When Lydia passed Caroline filling cups at the soda machine, she asked if anyone knew the time of Alistair's wake tonight. Lydia said this was the first she'd heard of it. Was there a funeral this weekend, too? Monday, said Caroline, at St. Pius the Tenth. She and Carlo, not being Catholic, would pay their respects tonight and skip the mass. Too bad the family had to wait almost a week, but how could they plan anything until the police released his body?

Lydia walked away feeling stunned. Why hadn't it occurred to her Alistair would have a funeral? And a wake tonight! You'd think somebody would have mentioned it. What did you do at a wake? Wear dress-up clothes. Black? And real shoes. Stumble through an unfamiliar ritual. Murmur words of comfort to grieving family members. That was bound to be strange.

Still, she had to go. Bad enough to have missed DeAnne's–what did they call them? Ob- something. Obloquys? Obsequies?

By twelve-thirty, Edgar hadn't returned. The lunch rush was peaking when Roosevelt Sherman walked in with his family.

Leo hurried over from the kitchen to welcome them, followed by Dinah.

Up close, Rosey's wife looked even more stunning than at Cap'n Chilly's. She wore white–a tennis outfit?–and carried the baby on her shoulder. Brave, in Lydia's opinion. But then they probably didn't do their own laundry. Rosey held the hands of a small boy and smaller girl, both in bright-colored shorts and Cape Cod T-shirts. The little girl paused to inspect the painted iron cow in Leo's fireplace. Lydia hoped she was too young to read the sign on the mantelpiece: *Unaccompanied children will be sold as slaves.*

The Shermans took the booth that Carlo and Caroline's party had left. Mudge asked Lydia if she'd mind switching so he could deliver their orders. Having been on her feet for most of the past five hours, Lydia was happy to sit at the cash register.

Leo shooed her off ten minutes later, muttering about celebrities and groupies and the price of fame.

Business continued so brisk that when Dave Wheeler walked in the door, around one-thirty, it took Lydia a moment to remember what she'd meant to ask him.

He laughed. "Bribes? Ha! You should see my shots! Two girls walking their dog. Hell on Wheels poking into a bush. We're not exactly talking Pulitzer Prize here."

The Shermans had gone. Bruno was still cleaning up children's detritus–shredded napkins, spilled food–around their booth. Otherwise, the lunch rush was tapering off. Lydia had kept an eye out for Edgar Rowdey, but he hadn't returned. Only two booths and a table in the back room were waiting for their orders.

Dave sat at the half-empty counter, and said yes to Dinah's offer of coffee. He looks like he just got out of the shower, thought Lydia. Clean, combed hair, fresh shave, and a blue work shirt that smells like a sunny clothesline.

And me all stinky with sweat and grill grease. Dragon breath, food stains on my apron–

"Hey," Dave murmured as she turned to go. "Can I talk to you?"

Dinah had a round of orders ready for the back room. "Not right this second," said Lydia.

A man two stools away leaned over to ask Dave about the burglaries. The spaghetti-and-meatball special, served in shallow bowls, needed a slice of garlic bread added to each rim. Lydia did that and hoisted the tray.

He wants to talk to me. Maybe that's why he's here.

She felt irrationally cheerful. Her ambivalent curiosity of last week–would Alistair Pope show up for lunch?–seemed long ago and far away. This was more like when she'd joined the Cambridge household, and discovered both Cape Cod and Fletcher in one memorable weekend.

A slice of garlic bread dived off its bowl onto the tray. *Get a grip, Lydia!*

She retrieved the bread, and herded a restless clump of potato chips back to safety beside a club sandwich. Ten more minutes and everyone was served. As she'd anticipated, Dinah didn't mind covering while she took a break with Dave Wheeler.

They walked around the side of the building as they'd done yesterday morning. (Only 24 hours ago! Incredible!) This time the grass was dry. Dave wore running shoes instead of boots, and no Red Sox jacket.

"You asked about the gunshots in the woods," he said. "Did you hear anything afterwards from the cops?"

"As a matter of fact . . . " Lydia recounted her phone conversation with Helen Wills.

For at least twenty seconds, Dave didn't speak. "You sure?" he asked finally. "She said it looked like some nutball shooting at crows, who panicked and threw away his pistol?"

"Well, not for sure, but that sounded like their only theory. Why?"

Another pause. "Are you still OK with keeping this confidential?"

"Yes."

"Seriously. Cross your heart?"

Lydia's chipped green fingernail made an X over a smear of tomato sauce and two grease spots.

"There's something weird going on here."

"Duh!"

"No. I mean– The reason the Times didn't print anything about the shooting is because it's connected to the murder."

He stopped walking and looked at her. "The pistol Kevin Kelly found in that rhododendron bush? Was Alistair Pope's."

Lydia frowned. "But that's not what she told me at all."

"Yeah, I got that."

He watched her as if waiting for more. She shook her head. "Are you sure?"

"They found out last night. I thought they were going to tell you, to stop you going on any long moonlit walks. I thought, after that, you might . . . I don't know. Want a civilian to talk to."

Lydia gave her head another shake in hopes of clearing it. "I'm not understanding this."

"Yeah. Well." Dave kicked a pebble. "It sounds like Pete and Helen aren't on the same page, for starters."

"She said she'd have called me if they'd learned anything," Lydia repeated stubbornly. "Do you think– She must not have known yet. Right? I must have talked to her before they got the lab report."

"I guess."

"And then she didn't call me again because she'd already offered to send over a cop, and I said no? Or because she suspected I was holding something back?"

They'd reached the end of the stockade fence. Lydia faced him. "You don't sound convinced."

Dave replied with a half-shrug. "I get the feeling that for her this is kind of . . . personal."

"Meaning what exactly?"

"Alistair was an old friend of hers, so she's pissed? Nobody gets away with murder on her watch? Or she has some agenda of her own?" He stood silhouetted against the slatted wooden fence, almost as if he were posing for a mug shot. For the first time Lydia noticed he had no camera. "They always keep back some things." He started walking slowly back toward the restaurant. "Details only the perp would know. But I still don't . . ."

"Me neither." The implications were beginning to penetrate. "I mean, dammit! This is my life, my safety she's screwing around with! Lydia Vivaldi, walking target! Am I overreacting? No. How did somebody get Alistair Pope's pistol? They stole it, right? What did Pete Altman say about that? Do they have any suspects? Any clues? Fingerprints? Empty holster? Anything?"

"They're investigating."

"Great. That's it? Just, Alistair's dead and somebody took his pistol. Now, who do you suppose that might be? Maybe the same wacko who bashed him with a rock and shoved him in the frog pond? What do you think?"

If he'd advised her to calm down, she'd have hit him. "Don't ask me," he said mildly. "Whatever the cops know, I don't."

"They're investigating. And meanwhile, I should just go on with my life, and Dinah too, and Sue and Wally, and hey, let's just hope Mr. Trigger-Happy was shooting at crows?"

"You want to know what I think?"

"Yes!"

"I think this is why Helen Wills didn't call you. She didn't want you to go putting pieces together when they haven't found all the pieces yet."

"Easy for her! She wasn't bouncing through the woods like Bambi with a big red X on her back!"

"Lydia." Dave gripped her arm. "It's OK."

"It's OK she lied to me?" She resisted the warmth and strength she could feel pulsing from his hand through her cotton jersey. "How is that OK?"

"It's over. You're safe. Whoever took that pistol? doesn't have it now. He threw it in a bush."

"The cops have it." She was calmer now in spite of herself. "They're investigating."

"Corny but true."

He dropped her arm. She looked at him. "Sorry. I sounded like Leo, didn't I?"

He laughed. "You're entitled."

They pondered separately. Then Lydia asked, "How did you find all this out?"

Her eyes returned to his face. Not that she had any confidence she'd know if he was telling the truth (those long-lashed green eyes!); but she felt compelled to try.

"You remember I gave Wally Hicks a ride back yesterday. What Hell on Wheels told him in the woods was the tourist shooting crows theory. Then this morning I talked to Pete Altman, and he said they ID'd the weapon last night." He was speaking with such careful precision that Lydia couldn't doubt a word he said. "I asked him if he'd told you, and he said Helen would take care of that. Maybe I misunderstood," he added. "He was kidding around about her husband coming home, and how distracted she was."

"What about Dinah and Wally and Sue?" Lydia asked. "Did somebody tell them? And the two girls with the dog?"

"I don't know." They stepped onto the paved walk. Customers were approaching from both directions: full ones downhill from the Back End, empty ones uphill from the parking lot. "I only asked about you."

The next wave engulfed them before Lydia could find out whether that was because he regarded her as uniquely fascinating, or as the most likely to crumble after a conversation with Hell on Wheels.

Back inside, Dinah had spaghetti and a salad waiting for Dave, and a tray full of filled orders waiting for Lydia.

Confidential. She set bowls on tables; smiled at customers. That meant she couldn't tell Dinah the cops had ID'd the weapon–unfair, in her opinion, if not downright dangerous.

There was Ed Roberts, speaking of crimes, waiting in the register line. He looked recovered from last week's losses. Ready to tackle the sporting demands of this sunny spring afternoon with three golf buddies, a full stomach, new khakis, and an emerald-green polo shirt.

Would Helen have called Dinah? Old friends . . . Maybe that

was who Detective Wills told Pete Altman she'd call, and Dave (or Pete) had misunderstood.

Ed strolled over to the counter; clapped Dave on the back: Any news down at the Times? Why hadn't they caught the bastards yet who ripped him off?

At the cash register, a mother crumpled a paper napkin to wipe tomato sauce off her small son's face. Her husband handed Mudge a $20 bill. Mudge held it in his left hand as he rang up their meal with his right.

Ed Roberts screamed and leapt toward the register.

"That's mine! Goddammit! That's my ring!"

The little boy wailed in terror. His mother stumbled, knocked aside by Ed's bull-like charge. The father whirled around like a matador to defend his family. Mudge thrust the twenty into the cash drawer and slammed it shut.

Ed lunged across the counter, scattering salt and pepper shakers. Mudge backed into the kitchen.

Lydia flattened herself against the menu board.

"Give me that!" Ed shouted at Mudge.

Dinah hovered between the sandwich bar and the grill, trying to decipher what was going on. The father pulled his wife to her feet; she scooped up the little boy and hugged him close. From the back room Leo hustled toward the fray.

Mudge was twisting at his finger now. Ed, still hollering, had straightened up and veered toward the open gateway beside the register into the kitchen.

Dave Wheeler had magically pulled out a camera and braced himself against the wall to shoot.

"Here! Take it!"

Mudge held out his hand; but Ed tackled him and flung him to the kitchen floor. He would have jumped on top of him, but Dinah–in a grand homage to Rosey Sherman–blocked him, then forced him backward through the gateway.

Everyone was shouting now: Ed, Mudge, Dinah, Leo, the customers.

And there stood Edgar Rowdey at the front door, gaping.

Leo comforted the frightened family trio. Dinah helped

Mudge onto his feet. He looked stricken, baffled, horrified. One hand still was in a fist–clutching the ring, Lydia guessed. Some birthday present!

Ed Roberts slumped, panting, onto a stool at the counter, and took out an iPhone.

"What are you doing?" Lydia went to him.

"I'm calling 911!" His thumb punched the numbers.

"Don't do that," she beseeched; but he shouted over her, to the others: "Citizen's arrest! Hold that kid till the cops get here!"

She stopped herself from grabbing his phone. This was too large and public a mess for a small-scale solution.

Leo, evidently on a similar track, beelined for Dave Wheeler.

In the kitchen Dinah helped Mudge brush himself off. It looked as though he wanted to go talk to Ed Roberts, but Dinah was urging him against it. Ed had one hand to his ear, the other to his chest. The last thing we need, Lydia agreed silently, is a heart attack in the middle of rush hour.

She fetched Ed a precautionary glass of water.

Dave lowered his camera. Leo sidled over to placate Ed. Dinah and Mudge between them made change for the family trio, who hurried out the door. The other customers either lined up to pay or drifted back to their seats. Lydia spotted Edgar settling at his usual table in the back room.

It was Kevin Kelly who showed up, siren wailing, lights flashing, with a sidekick Lydia hadn't seen before. Ed Roberts brushed Leo aside and loudly accused Mudge of being part of the gang who'd robbed his house. Mudge–after a murmured "Hey, Kev"–handed Kevin the gold-and-black ring. His partner whipped out a Zip-Lok bag for it. Dinah returned to work, grimly slinging spaghetti into bowls, stabbing toothpicks into sandwiches. Lydia just as grimly delivered them. She didn't speak to Dave Wheeler, once again busy shooting, and glared coldly past Ed Roberts when he followed the two policemen and Mudge out to the parking lot.

"Well, good afternoon," Edgar greeted Lydia cheerfully.

She set down his spaghetti and meatballs so hard the garlic

bread rattled. “Not so much. Parmesan?”

“Oh, by all means.” He glanced around. “Have Carlo and Caroline been in?”

“Long ago,” said Lydia, and went to find the cheese.

Leo had taken over at the cash register. Now that the commotion had subsided, the Back End was emptying out. Dave Wheeler sat alone on his stool at the counter, finishing his salad, no camera in sight.

Edgar’s book lay unopened on the table. “What was all that hoo-hah?”

She handed him the glass shaker and explained: Mudge, ring, birthday, Ed, cops.

“Merciful heavens. I don’t suppose any clues emerged about the robbery?”

“Not that I could tell. But you know Mudge had nothing to do with it!”

“Of course not.” He sprinkled cheese. “Still.”

“What?”

“One can hope this is a wedge.”

Leo was waving at her. “I have to go,” said Lydia.

“Ta ta,” said Edgar.

Up front, a staff meeting was underway. Dinah–flourishing the house phone–insisted it was their duty to hire a lawyer for Mudge immediately, before the interrogation started. Leo maintained they couldn’t act without his permission, and maybe his father’s, too, and if they were serious about helping him they should track down his dad. Dinah said that would take too long, whereas Fred Jones’s office was right up the street. They’d already left a message on Mudge’s family’s answering machine, but what if Lincoln Miles was gone for the day? or the weekend? Leo said obviously they should call Wampanoag tribal headquarters. Dinah asked how the hell he expected Wampanoag tribal headquarters to find a man who wasn’t home. Leo said maybe they had a cell number. Dinah said they probably weren’t even open on Saturday.

“Excuse me,” said Dave Wheeler, and pointed. Four customers waited at the cash register, listening avidly.

“What are you gawking at?” Leo moved into place.

"Hey you," said Lydia to Dave. "With friends in high places. Make a phone call, will you?"

He nodded and took the phone she handed him. "I'll see what I can find out."

By the time Edgar Rowdey came up to pay for his lunch, Dave had found out that nobody, including Mudge, had reached Lincoln Miles. Pete Altman and his CIO partner had interviewed Ed Roberts, who conclusively identified the ring, and Mudge, who said he'd found it this morning in the Back End parking lot.

"Found it in the parking lot?" Lydia repeated.

Dave nodded. "That's what he told Pete. Under his truck."

She scanned the circle of faces. One of Edgar's eyebrows had popped up; otherwise, nobody looked surprised. She must be the only one who'd heard Mudge say the ring was a birthday present.

"The cops'll never go for that," Leo grumbled. "They'll squash him like a bug."

"They can't," said Dave. "Not without evidence."

"Ha! Mudge? You kidding me? Straight to the County Jail!"

"For finding a ring?" asked Lydia.

"For reasons I'm not at liberty to discuss," Leo said darkly.

"If you mean his record, say so," said Dinah. "We're all friends here. Except maybe the Cape Cod Times."

"Hey," Dave raised his hands. "I only shoot the news, I don't report it."

"Mudge has a record?" Lydia was astonished.

"Minor," stated Dinah.

"Drugs," Leo amplified.

"What kind of drugs?"

"Does it matter?" countered Leo.

"Yes!"

"You guys know about this?" Dinah asked Edgar and Dave. They both nodded. "Dealing cocaine," she told Lydia. "Not much. A stupid kid thing."

"They'll put him away," Leo insisted. "Lock him up till he's old and gray. Till I'm dead and in the ground."

"A matter of minutes," murmured Edgar.

"No," said Dinah. "What they'll do is bug him to death.

Track his every move. Harass all of us and everybody else who comes in contact with him, to make him crack under the pressure."

Oh, hell! thought Lydia. She slumped onto the stool next to Dave's. Dinah was still talking about the cops: whether they'd wait until they found his father to start searching Mudge's truck, his belongings, his family's home . . .

What was happening to her beautiful new life? So hopefully she'd launched it, like a paper airplane; and so fast it was spiraling out of the sky! First DeAnne dead, then Alistair murdered; yesterday a sniper stalking her and Dinah with Alistair's pistol; and now Mudge, her partner in the Flying Wedge, a suspect in a string of burglaries he didn't commit.

The worst thing, she reflected, is being helpless! If I could take arms against the slings and arrows of outrageous fortune, and by opposing, end them!–but instead here's Dave and Leo spreading doom, Edgar advising me to stay home with the door locked, Helen Wills keeping me in the dark, and Dinah predicting worse to come.

"Hey you." Dave spoke quietly. "You gonna just sit there till we all go home?"

"What?" she retorted. "You need more coffee? Pot's over there."

But she slid off her stool. If you can't fight, work. Serve spaghetti. Provide cheese. Maybe even refill a mug or two.

He stuck out his arm, gently blocking her way. "Are you OK?"

She almost pushed him aside (what a stupid question!), but a smear of tomato sauce on one stubble-darkened cheek stopped her. "No." She shook her arms, shoulders, head. "Now that you mention it, no, I'm not OK."

"How can I help?"

Touching him was not an option. That much she'd learned from her on-the-rebound flirtation with Alistair Pope. Rather than look at him, she scanned the Back End. Leo was ringing up the next-to-last customers. Dinah had begun scraping off the grill. Edgar Rowdey sauntered toward the back room where he'd left his coffee mug and his paperback book.

"Grab that man," she pointed. "Find a table. Have a seat. It's conference time."

Chapter Twenty-Seven

Somewhat to Lydia's amazement, Dave followed her instructions.

She informed Leo and Dinah she was taking a short break, and followed Dave and Edgar to the blue booth in the far corner. Good choice: the nearest customers were three tables away, deep in a discussion about bass fishing.

Edgar set down his mug and book and scooted in with his back toward the room. Dave slid in across from him, against the wall. Lydia sat a safe foot away from Dave. From here she could watch Edgar's face and still keep an eye on the restaurant.

"Thanks for doing this."

"Not at all." Edgar spoke with his customary graciousness, but his eyes were on the window. Already plotting his escape?

"Did you see Detective Wills? What did she say? Are they getting anywhere?"

One of Edgar's cumulus-cloud eyebrows rose above the rim of his glasses and sank again. The silence grew so loud that Lydia could hear Dave's stomach rumbling. Don't clam up, she pleaded silently. Don't walk out. Just tell me!

"Hummy hummy hoo." More seconds passed. "Where to begin?"

"The murder investigation?" Lydia suggested. "The gunshots in the woods?"

Into the ensuing pause Dave inserted: "Did she say if they're connected?"

Edgar sighed. "Oh, well, yes. One small thread in this mare's nest. Otherwise, nothing's connected to anything! The murders to the burglaries, the burglaries to Mudge–"

"Murders? Plural?" Dave interrupted.

Edgar glanced at Lydia. "I'm afraid so. Alistair, you know, and DeAnne Ropes. Not a point I broached to Detective Wills, needless to remark."

"Why do you– How do you know that?"

Lydia cut in, to keep things moving. "I worked with DeAnne in Cambridge. Home repairs. She was an expert at climbing ladders."

Dave still had an inquiring eye on Edgar.

"Shoes," he said. "But I believe Lydia's concern is larger. What's to be done? Mudge carried off by the police, Alistair's wake in a few hours– Leo's beside himself. I've never seen Quansett so agitated. One more week till the tourists arrive, and then what?"

Lydia nodded emphatically.

"Isn't that a problem more for the cops than us?" Dave put in.

"Well, exactly! What are they *for*?" The irritation in Edgar's voice made Lydia glad she'd called this meeting. "This shouldn't be up to us! Your friend Pete Altman; thirty-some years on the force. Normally he'd cut right through it, like Alexander and the Gordian Knot. Only he's exhausted, poor bunny! Limp as a grape, with Bob on vacation and a crime wave sweeping through town."

Edgar paused to sip coffee. Lydia wished she could see Dave's reaction.

"Up to us?" he returned.

"Mm. Well. Inquiring minds and so forth." The heavy rings on Edgar's fingers clinked against his mug. "It may be I've been watching too much TV."

"Why? Because you think we can do something about it?" asked Lydia. *"Can* we do something about it?"

"Oh, who knows? Naturally one wishes all the best to the police. Mudge's arrest might pop open the burglary case, and from that, the murders. We're perfectly free to go on waiting, hoping solutions will simply unfurl, like the flowers that bloom in the spring."

"But what if they don't?" she completed.

Lydia felt Dave shift beside her, gauging how to respond. Was he alarmed by the turn things were taking? She'd invited him on impulse, with an idea his connections might make him useful. Now that she and Edgar had apparently hopped aboard the same train of thought, would Dave join them or jump off?

Her instincts told her to jump first.

"Who besides me wants a glass of water?"

The soda machine was up front, but there was a water pitcher here in the back room. Only the bass-fishers still sat talking, and a couple finishing dessert. She took her time pouring. Let the guys do their guy thing. Give Dave time to digest, as a long-time resident of Quansett and recorder of local events, that two of his neighbors have been murdered.

When she came back to the booth, both men stopped talking. Lydia set down three glasses. "So what'd I miss?"

"Thank you, dear."

Edgar wasn't smiling. "Back to Square One?" she tried. "News from Hell on Wheels?"

After a few seconds Dave said, "She told him what I told you." He too sounded somber, and concerned. "That they ID'd Alistair's pistol."

Lydia perched on the end of his bench. "Did she say why she left me out of the loop?"

No answer. What is this, guys, Twenty Questions? Forget about it!

Dave prodded: "No?"

Edgar made a small uncomfortable sound and drank water. "Not in so many words."

"Edgar," said Lydia, "spill the beans, will you? Before Leo hauls me back up front?"

Eventually he spoke. "None but her nearest and dearest could call Mrs. Wills a forthcoming woman." Gazing into his glass. "Professional discretion and so forth. Just now she's running the murder investigation more or less on her own, holding various fates in her hand, and keeping her cards close to her chest." He tipped the glass as if to check that it still held water. "I became quite curious to know–well, what she's thinking."

"What is she thinking?" asked Lydia.

"Oh, dear." He sighed. "That you killed Alistair."

When she regained consciousness (as it seemed to her), Lydia was sitting in a wooden booth in the far corner of the Back End. Her forearms stretched out in front of her on the blue formica tabletop. Her fingers looked pink and wrinkled, like shrimp, extending from yellow cotton sleeves lightly spattered with the day's menu. Across from her, Edgar Rowdey watched her anxiously over his glasses. Beside her, Dave Wheeler still smelled freshly laundered in a work shirt the same sky-blue as Edgar's eyes. He was rubbing her right shoulder, kneading reassurance into tense muscles.

"How is that possible?" Lydia heard herself ask. "How can she possibly think that? How can she possibly not know that is totally fucking ridiculous?"

She would have gone on, but she realized that Edgar couldn't answer the question until she stopped asking it.

"I wouldn't call it a theory," he said with concern. "In the sense of handcuffs looming or anything. Really, at the most, a plausible scenario."

"A hypothesis," said Dave. "That's what they generally look for, to start. An idea they can test against the evidence they've collected."

Edgar nodded. "Not that she put it that way. I must admit, I was impressed with her style. Doling out bits of information between questions, to make the subject feel like part of the team."

Lydia wasn't interested in Detective Wills's style. "What did she say about me?"

"Hummy hummy hoo." Edgar pushed his glasses up his nose. "Well. Point One: Alistair was killed outside the Back End while you were working. He had asked for you, and might have gone out to look for you. Point Two: It was Alistair who first brought you here. At the time he showed a certain personal interest, and you've been seen together since then. Point Three: You knew DeAnne, who died working on his film; you might have blamed him for that. Point Four: You changed your identity when you came here. That always unsettles the police. Point Five: Alistair shared his bed with a woman the night before he died."

"Not me! God dammit, I told her!"

A thumb dug gently into her shoulder. "Plausible is the key

word," said Dave. "If all she wants is a viable candidate."

"One could add Point Six," Edgar continued. "Since you've only recently arrived on Cape, you lack the roots here that sometimes shield people from police interest."

"She told you this?" Lydia demanded. "Did she actually say all this crap? Here's why Lydia Vivaldi's a murderer?"

"Oh, no," Edgar assured her. "Name a suspect to me? Heavens no. It took a good deal of winnowing to glean as much as I did." He took another drink of water. "As for conclusions, those she let me draw for myself."

"Not much of a leap," Dave observed drily.

Lydia turned on him. "What, do you believe it?"

"Hell no." His eyes met hers. "I'm no detective, but I can tell facts from guesswork."

Not the full vindication she'd hoped for. He's media! she reminded herself. It's in their job description: Trust no one. Not even someone they know, and like, and should realize is innocent.

"Why did she tell you all this?" Dave was asking Edgar. "Or wasn't she aware of it? I mean, you eat here every day. Didn't she figure you'd tell Lydia? Or Leo?"

"You may well ask! I found the whole exchange extraordinary. Certainly she was aware of it. Was she out to put a cat among the pigeons? Stir up talk in the absence of solid leads? Send some kind of message?–but to whom, about what?"

"Stir up talk," mused Dave. "None of this was confidential?"

Edgar shook his head. "She took care to say nothing explicit. No accusations; not even a statement of fact. What's the expression? Maintain deniability?"

"What about the shots in the woods?" Lydia was still wrestling with being labeled a murder suspect, explicitly or not. "She can't think I stole Alistair's gun and shot at myself!"

A regretful sigh: "On the contrary, I fear."

"You could have staged it to throw her off the track," Dave suggested. "Win her sympathy."

"After, what? Carrying a pistol in my apron pocket all day?"

"Hiding it in your car?"

"This is totally fucking ridiculous!" Lydia's fists pounded the table in frustration. "It's–it's–"

"Circumstantial," supplied Edgar. "But plausible, from the police viewpoint. That's why I bring it up." Lydia clasped her hands, and his eyebrows lifted. "Given human nature, and the nature of her job, now that our detective friend has come up with this idea, she's liable to cling to it."

"Sounds to me like, bottom line, Hell on Wheels shouldn't be running this investigation alone," Dave said.

"That's for damn sure!"

"Because, Point One, whatever objectivity she came in with, she's losing it. And Point Two, between Chill coming home and too much work, she seems more focused on wrapping this up than who she pins it on."

"Indeed." Edgar sighed. "Normally, one could rely on someone in her position not to go careening about like a tailless kite. And if she did, her partner would reel her in."

"And now that's up to us?" asked Lydia bitterly.

"Well, it's not obligatory."

"Good idea, though, right? Before half of Leo's staff is behind bars. I mean, if you guys ever want to eat lunch in this town again."

"Should I speak to Pete?" asked Dave.

"Speak to him?" Edgar thought it over. "Listen to him, by all means. Ask him questions. I don't know that you need to say much. Busy elsewhere or not, he's well aware this is still his case."

"Especially for the next two days," Lydia put in.

"One assumes Detective Wills briefed him before taking off," Edgar nodded. "If she told him even as much as she told me, he's bound to be surprised, or concerned, or at any rate talkative. Which is where the robberies come in."

They both stared at him without comprehension.

"I admit, it's a bit more Rube Goldberg than one would wish."

"What is?" Lydia persisted.

"Sorry, dear. If one could help Pete Altman solve the robberies, that would catapult him back into the murder investigation. Useful, don't you think? Objectivity, fresh energy and so forth?"

"Aha," said Lydia, although privately it sounded to her more like a thumb in the dike than a practical plan for finding a murderer.

"One, meaning us?" asked Dave. "How? What have we got that the cops don't?"

"You have access, to both the police and the media. You," he turned to Lydia, " know everyone involved, without the local biases; and you're more motivated than most."

"Not just for myself." Lydia folded her arms. "What about Mudge?"

"Mudge," said Edgar, "is the fulcrum."

Heading toward the cash register, Lydia decided age hadn't withered Edgar's brain one bit. His problem was that he reasoned faster than anyone else on the planet. He leapfrogged over logical steps that a normal person like herself had to take one by one, and landed at a conclusion sooner (and often in a different place) than other people.

When Dave had asked him what he meant about Mudge being the fulcrum, Edgar looked surprised. To him it was obvious. Not for a minute would the police believe Mudge had found a valuable piece of jewelry in the Back End parking lot and worn it in to work. Presumably, as he'd told Lydia, he'd gotten it for his birthday. From whom? Someone close enough to him–family member? girl-friend?–that he hadn't questioned the gift. Someone he now must suspect of being involved, directly or indirectly, with the burglaries.

However he felt about that, Mudge wouldn't name this person to the police.

"But won't he have to?" asked Lydia. "I mean, won't they keep hammering on him until he talks?"

"They can't," said Dave. "If they don't have any evidence against him besides that ring, they have to let him go."

"You might," said Edgar, "give him a call."

"Me?" Lydia bridled. "Why?"

"Well, he knows you know he didn't find it under his truck."

"But, Edgar! Isn't that like–what? The pot calling the kettle?"

"Surely not. Helen Wills can't have started any wheels turning yet."

"You're losing me," said Dave.

"Even supposing she wanted to send a SWAT team after Lydia, what myrmidons could she muster in Quansett on a Saturday afternoon?"

"Kevin Kelly," Dave acknowledged with a trace of a grin. "Are you thinking, if Lydia talks to Mudge, he might tell her what he won't tell the cops?"

Lydia looked sharply from him to Edgar. "I hope you don't take me for some kind of stool pigeon."

"Heavens no." Edgar pushed up his glasses. "Look at it from Mudge's point of view. He's bound to have realized that Ed Roberts's ring is the best, if not the only, lead in this case. Where does that leave him? He's a responsible young man. I imagine he'd rather help the investigation than not, if he can do it without betraying anyone."

"Oh," said Dave. "You mean, he'll be so turned around by now, he'll want to talk things over with somebody he can trust."

He's not the only one! thought Lydia. I'm so turned around myself, I feel like that wooden bird out front of DeAnne's house with the pinwheel wings.

"You don't agree with Dinah, then?" she asked Edgar. "About the cops putting a tail on Mudge? Tapping his phone?"

"Not without a court order," said Dave. "Which on a Saturday afternoon–"

He didn't finish. Leo was stalking toward them, brandishing a broom in a menacing manner.

They slid out of their booth–Lydia first, to disarm Leo. She heard Dave say he'd buy Pete a beer later on. The rest was drowned out by Leo's loud complaints about lazy employees and inconsiderate customers.

Lydia persuaded Leo to give Bruno back his broom. Edgar and Dave exchanged phone numbers. Dave said good-by to Lydia with a pat on her shoulder. Edgar murmured that he'd wait for her in the parking lot.

Fifteen minutes later she found him leaning against his car, inking in a crossword puzzle.

She leaned against the Morris, parked one space away.

Edgar glanced up, then resumed writing. OK, thought Lydia. Right. Long deep breaths. Agitation out, tranquility in.

She focused on the hot metal under her back; felt the sun warming her hair and the tops of her ears. An unseen bird warbled giddily from the Elephant Tree. The faint aromas of grilled meat, garlic, cooking oil, and fresh-cut grass still hung in the air.

"Thirty-six hours, huh?" she asked his bent head. "That's our window of opportunity? Till Hell on Wheels wraps up her weekend of marital bliss?"

"Mm."

"She just, like, confided that in you? 'Now that I've found the killer, I'm taking two days off for hot sex?' What are you, Dr. Phil?"

"Oh, well, I asked. Not in so many words, needless to remark." Edgar looked up; capped his pen. "But that was on my list when I called her to arrange our meeting."

"You called her? Edgar! Are you serious? You invited yourself down to police HQ to be interrogated?"

"Why not?" He folded his magazine and tucked it under his arm. "As the last person who saw Alistair alive, aside from X, I was bound to be of interest. I preferred she get to me sooner than later. Having questions of my own."

"And she went for it. She answered your questions, told you her weekend plans– What else did you find out? Besides that I killed Alistair?"

"Oh, a few things. More interesting is what I didn't find out. They collected his computer, films, files, and so forth, to comb for enemies. Not his answering machine, however, which was blank. And not his cell phone. Remarkably, that doesn't concern her. She shrugs: He could have lost it–dropped it, left it somewhere. It could have been taken from his body by X, or from his car afterwards, or from his house, before the police search."

"X, meaning me." Lydia's nose wrinkled. "You think that's why she shrugs off the phone? She knows I don't have it? Whoops! Big hole in her nice little theory!"

"Now, now," said Edgar. "Step back. The point of interest, if any, was that the phone might have been stolen at the same time, by the same person, as the pistol."

His tone suggested there was more to this than met the ear. Lydia shook her head. "What? Guns count, cell phones don't?"

"Well, yes. But what struck me was her remark about the police search."

"That was the next day. One of the cops in Moby Dick told me. I asked where Detective Wills was, and the cop said, She's leading a search."

"Doesn't that strike you as odd?" Edgar returned.

"Odd, like how?"

"If you were a detective, when would you secure the victim's home and car and so forth?"

"Huh." She began to comprehend. "Right away! At least lock things down, even if you couldn't search till later. But you're saying, she told you the cell phone and pistol might have been stolen before the cops got over there."

"Needless to remark, it didn't occur to me to drive by Alistair's that first afternoon looking for yellow tape. Nor did Mrs. Wills choose to tell me just how they'd been negligent. Or just how negligent they'd been." He pushed up his glasses. "You were aware he kept a spare key hidden outside?"

"No," said Lydia. "I was not aware of that."

"For friends and emergencies, he said. There was a time," Edgar sighed, "when we never locked our doors at all. Most of us adapted grudgingly. Or halfway, like Alistair. Whether his list of friends included any officers of the law, I don't know."

"So even if the cops did secure the house, they could have missed the key. Is that what you're saying? Was it someplace hard to find?"

He nodded. "Hanging on a tiny hook halfway up the trunk of his peach tree."

"Then X could have just gone over anytime and let himself in."

"If X knew where it was."

"You mean," Lydia's mind was boggling again, "if X was on Alistair's list. Right? Edgar! You think Alistair was killed by somebody he thought was a really close friend?"

"One more riddle in the larger enigma," he replied noncommittally. He brushed a bug off his sleeve. "And then there's his earring."

"His earring! Did they find it?"

"Oh, no. Detective Wills suggested rather hopefully that he might not have worn it that day, owing to a torn earlobe. Hmph! I assured her he did. Add one more to the items X apparently made off with. Not just a killer, but a magpie."

"The torn earlobe, then– Do you think X just ripped it off?"

"If so . . . " For a long moment he didn't speak. Then he completed: "It's a puzzling sequence. X hits Alistair with a rock. Alistair falls down, unconscious. Onto the ground or into the water? X pulls off his earring. Never mind his wallet, which would have been simple. Does X remove the earring and then push Alistair's head into the pond? Or reach in after him, and get soaked up to the elbows? Isn't X concerned the pain or the water or both will revive him? We know he's still alive, because he drowned, and also because bleeding stops with death, and there was blood in the pond. Why take such a risk for an earring?"

"It was gold," said Lydia. "An antique."

"Then why not plunder his house? Alistair surrounded himself with antiques, rare books, works of art– Why break into such a treasure chest and come out with only a pistol?"

"Don't ask me. I never set foot in the place."

"One wonders," said Edgar, "how Detective Wills explains it."

In another parking lot a few blocks away, Rosey Sherman wondered when modern technology would invent a car seat that a man could lock down without risking a hernia.

He'd sent Thea and the kids on up the path into the woods. No fear they'd get too far ahead. Even with Shawn in the stroller, the Sherman family moved slower than a camel caravan. Plenty of time for Daddy to catch up before they reached the pond.

Rosey had been waiting for that moment. He pictured it as one of those childhood landmarks a boy never forgets. (Especially if Mom's caught it on video.) He and Mikey would sneak up slow and quiet like Indian scouts, scare all the frogs at once and watch them splash-plop-splash into the water. They'd practiced at the Back End after lunch. Not that you could get much of a dry run from two little peepers perched on lily pads. But, hey! Last time he'd eaten at Leo's there were no frogs at all. Anyhow, it didn't matter. After Foxborough and Boston, an after-lunch walk in Quansett's nature preserve was practically a jungle safari.

He yanked the car seat one last time. Good to go. They'd be driving around the rest of this afternoon, looking at houses. And stopping by the Frigate, since Wally was there alone. No sign of Sue by lunchtime, when Rosey left him. Excellent! Whether she'd overslept or taken off for good, Rosey had made it clear their waterfront business dinner would not happen while there was a chance of Sue's horning in.

Today he'd taken the next step and chatted with that kid at Leo's. Mudge. Fast and cheerful ringing up customers, and an efficient, good-humored waiter. Perfect! Keep Wally upstairs, inventory and orders and so forth, and Mudge on the floor. Books, authors, all that he could learn. Attitude was the main thing.

His grin when Rosey asked for his phone number suggested Mudge would be a willing recruit. Part time, to start, so as to keep peace with the Back End. Call him tonight, maybe, after they got home from the Willses'. First cookout of the summer! Come over around five, Helen had proposed. Kind of early to eat, but then outdoor barbecueing always took longer than you figured. She'd promised they'd be through by seven. She had a wake to go to.

Chapter Twenty-Eight

Back at the Frigate, Wally Hicks rang up his eighteenth sale.

Eighteen in one day! And not even summer yet!

His previous personal best was thirty, scored last Fourth of July. Quansett's annual parade had given the cause of literature a break by passing right by the store. Hundreds of clapping parents and tourists had nothing to do for the next hour but browse the shops on Main Street. Ken Boose stood out front beckoning them in, grinning like the Cheshire Cat, until the fire department opened its annual barbecue up the street. So many people crowded into the Frigate that Wally had to lock Gromit upstairs so as not to wear out his wagging tail.

Today was only June 10. Most of the kids were still in school. For these two weeks between the end of winter and the start of tourist season, a working man ought to be able to kick back a little. Stroll around in the sunshine. Take a frisbee break with his dog on the beach, before signs, ticket-sellers, and rent-a-cops showed up to spoil things. Hang out at the picnic table with his–well, whatever she was–enjoying a leisurely sandwich.

Instead, his fingers were going numb from ringing up customers; and he hadn't seen or heard from Sue since yesterday.

That was part of her appeal, Wally acknowledged. You never knew where you were with her. Like lottery tickets, which people kept squandering their money on because when you won, the thrill was worth it. Anyhow, he wasn't looking for a commitment. Not on top of the mission he'd handed over to karma when he first got here, now belatedly lurching into motion. Sex without obligations: who could beat it? Who made the rule that a warrior had to be pure, anyhow? Really, Sue's roller-coaster ride qualities suited his needs just fine.

Only . . .

A book slapped down on the wooden counter. Sale # 19! *Phineas the Feckless*, by Edgar Rowdey, with an empty hamster cage on the cover.

That was a surprise. This girl he'd noticed ten minutes ago in nonfiction and pegged for something more eco-political. Malcolm Gladwell, maybe, or Barbara Ehrenreich. She didn't look offbeat enough for Rowdey, in those striped leggings and sweater and a handful of dishwater-blonde hair pulled back in a scrunchy.

"You a fan of our famous local author?" Wally pressed buttons. "You know he lives right up the street here."

"Yeah." She adjusted hexagonal spectacles. "He was a friend of Alistair Pope's, wasn't he?"

"So they tell me." Oh, lordy, not another rubbernecker!

"Maybe I'll meet him tonight, then. At the wake."

Wally looked closer. "Are you . . . family?"

Her head gave a small abrupt shake. "Associate, friend, co-conspirator, comrade-in-arms, you name it."

"Aha. Well, sorry for your loss. That'll be $15.81 with tax."

"Thanks." She drew a platinum Visa card out of a minuscule handbag.

"You worked on his films? Here in Quansett?"

"Mostly New York. Sometimes here. Once in a while Boston, at GBH. Wherever he needed me."

He couldn't tell if it was her narrowed eyes or her eye make-up that made her appear to be peering down her nose at him, even though she was too short to have been able to see him if she did. Not snobby, he judged. More like the world jangles her nerves too much to face it straight.

"Did you know him? I heard the police still don't . . ."

A quaver in her question suggested a third explanation: she'd been crying.

Wally recalled Ken Boose's story of following Alistair Pope outside to point out that he'd forgotten to pay for that book in his pocket, whereupon Alistair huffed that Ken ought to pay him for bringing a stream of literate, solvent customers to this godforsaken backwater. He recalled how, when Alistair first came in after Wally himself started working here, he'd pretended not to recognize the man whose life he'd wrecked eighteen years ago.

"Only by sight and reputation," he replied evasively.

"He was the best," she asserted. "People throw around words like genius and tragedy, but I'll tell you–"

The door slammed. "Hey, Wally!" Sue's hair was a tousled haystack, her shorts and T-shirt rumpled, her feet bare, her grin inebriated. "Wassup?"

Wally Hicks had wondered occasionally how it would feel if your life passed before your eyes. His few near-fatalities–mostly back in his motorcycle days–had produced only adrenalin. Now he hoped it wouldn't feel like this: To look at a woman's face burning with grief for a dead man, then at the blank face of your recent sexual partner, and shiver from the cold breath of karma on the back of your neck.

"My name is Sue!" she caroled. "How do you do!"

"Hi, Sue." The other woman spoke it like an epithet.

"And who are *you*?"

"Delsey. A friend of Alistair Pope."

"Well hey me too!" Sue was dancing now, a parody of a tap routine. "He's fun to screw! Boop-boop-a-doo!"

"Sue," Wally stepped out from behind the counter, "why don't you go take a shower? Get some coffee?"

"I'm leaving." Delsey's eyes were slits.

"Don't go cause of me!" Stumbling into a bookshelf, Sue erupted in giggles.

"Sorry about this," said Wally. "Is there anything else I can find for you? We've got a film section–"

"I'm all set."

"Where's old fart-face?" Sue asked him. "Our store got bought," she explained to Delsey. "Did he tell you? The football star? Sherman Tank!"

"Sue, now, simmer down, OK?"

"Why should I? He hates me."

"Come on. He hired you when nobody else would."

"This is the bookstore Rosey Sherman bought?" Delsey interposed. "I just read about that in *The Atlantic*." She scanned the counter and surrounding shelves with new interest. "Amazing! Is he here?"

"Not just at the moment."

"Fart-face! I'm going up and take a shower. You wanna come?" Sue leered.

"No," said Wally. "I'm working."

She swung her hand at his head–caress or slap?–and missed. "Too bad for you!"

Halfway to the front door, Sue stopped again. *Go!* Wally willed her. *Go on! Get out!*

Instead, Carlo Song and Caroline Penn walked past her, out of bright sun into the Frigate's dim interior.

"Customers," trilled Sue.

Caroline arched an eyebrow. "Hello, Sue," said Carlo.

"Hello, Carlo." Delsey spoke from the counter, where she stood poised like an alert gazelle. "Hello, Caroline."

"Well, Delsey! Isn't it?" Blinking, Carlo held out a hand. "Welcome to Quansett."

"Sorry we meet again on such a sad occasion," said Caroline. "You're here for the wake, are you? Did you just get in?"

"Yesterday." She hesitated, as if weighing which way to jump. "Nicky and Jean'll be here this afternoon. Some of the GBH office, too. We're all just devastated," she added emphatically. "A tragic loss to the film world! Nobody can believe. Such a brilliant, vibrant man!"

Caroline and Carlo murmured sounds that could be taken for agreement.

"And they still don't know who killed him? They don't even have a suspect?"

"Not yet," said Carlo. "They're investigating."

"Have they decided what will happen to the film?" asked Caroline.

"Not yet," said Delsey.

"Well," said Caroline, "we'd better be going. Perhaps we'll see you later."

"Give our regards to your colleagues," said Carlo, following her out the door.

Too late it occurred to Wally that he should have asked them if they'd come in looking for anything particular.

"Bitch," muttered Sue. "I bet she did it."

Delsey's head swiveled. "You can bet she wanted to." She glanced from Sue to Wally and beyond as if checking for predators. "You should see the film. I mean, Alistair's work is always brutally honest, but this time he really took off the gloves."

Wally followed her gaze around the store. If the Frigate had other customers, they must be browsing safely out of earshot. "Now, I can't picture those two . . ."

"I can," said Sue. "I bet they killed him."

"Somebody killed him," Delsey said fiercely. "Who had more of a motive?"

"But they're a couple of harmless old–"

"–Artists!" she interrupted. "Where do you think that creative energy comes from? The dark side! Every artist has it. I mean, look at Alistair."

Well now, damn! thought Wally. That's some neat trick, to be a world-class shithead and convince women it just proved you were an artist.

"Look at Edgar Rowdey!" Delsey held up *Phineas the Feckless* in its blue-and-white Frigate bag. "Book after book about gruesome ways to die. Hel-*lo!* Harmless? I don't think so! What was he so afraid of, that he refused to let Alistair film him?"

Sue grabbed for the book. Delsey swung it out of reach. "They weren't born old. You think those two made it to the top on Broadway, and him on the best-seller list, without breaking a few kneecaps?"

Wally found himself drifting back into a suspicion he'd hoped he'd outgrown: that all women are natural-born idiots. He wished Delsey would stop, before she got Sue started again.

"And Rosey Sherman! I mean, not to tell tales out of school, but how many people know why he *really* quit football? That's what fascinated Alistair, is the stories that get buried. Not the road trips, the drugs, the girls–everybody's heard about that. He used to call us the Truth Squad, digging up the dirt behind the facade. The failed steroid tests. The hushed-up rape case. And you know what happened when Alistair approached Sherman about doing a film? He laughed! Pretended it was a big joke! What kind of balls does that take?"

"He could be the killer," Sue nodded. "Totally! With those giant hands? Grab a rock–"

"Don't," Wally interrupted. "Jesus H. Christ! What's got into you? Slandering the man in his own store?"

"Fuck him!" Sue flung her arms in the air. "And you know what? Fuck you too! I'm outta here!"

Wally and Delsey watched her stagger down the front step and around the corner into the parking lot.

"Is she OK?" asked Delsey.

He contemplated her pinched mouth, half-closed eyes, hair slicked back like some kind of New Age nun. "Well, she's drunk, she's broke, she's nuts, and I guess she just quit her job. But aside from that, yeah. She's OK."

"I'm sorry if I offended you."

"Don't worry about it."

"OK, well, see you at the wake?"

"Enjoy your book," said Wally.

Back in the sanctuary of their indoor garden, Caroline and Carlo settled onto a flowered sofa with tall glasses of fruit punch lightly spiked with rum.

"What did you think?" Carlo asked.

"Blinded by adoration?"

"Or protesting too much?" Ice cubes clinked gently against his glass. "Easy nowadays to zip up here from New York. Unlike our reckless youth."

"In that Barnum-and-Bailey office, they might not even notice."

"Nor object if they did."

Caroline slid a bowl of wasabi peanuts toward Carlo. "We could call what's-his-name at GBH."

Carlo munched reflectively. "I liked the green-shelled ones better. These are too greasy. But didn't Fred say not to talk to them while the case is pending?"

"We'd have to make it off the record." Caroline held up a peanut and examined it. "I find the flecks of seaweed unnerving." She popped it in her mouth. "He knew more about Alistair's affairs than Alistair did himself."

"He's bound to know if they've settled the rights."

"That's what we can't ask him, Carlo."

"He'd probably tell us, though. As a courtesy. Oh, well; too risky, I suppose."

"Still," said Caroline, "I dread facing the wake so uninformed. Trailing clouds of suspicion, no less."

"So soon after DeAnne," Carlo concurred. "Speaking of Fred."

"Really, you'd think the police would have at least produced a theory. It's not as if a man can be murdered in a vacuum! Right outside the Back End–didn't anyone see anything? As many corns as he trod on, they should have a dozen suspects!"

"Edgar's corns that last afternoon," Carlo pointed out. "And Mudge's."

"Hm. That's true."

"Delsey. What a jolt."

"Wasn't she? It hadn't crossed my mind that they might all come trooping up here. Mourning, do you think, or sleuthing?"

"Mourning, sleuthing, toasting, and mythologizing, I daresay." Carlo ate another peanut. "We don't have to stay long."

"I wonder if it will occur to Pete and Helen that X is likely to be at the wake."

"Should we mention it?"

"No!. Poke a stick in a wasps' nest?" Caroline swirled the ice around in her glass. "You know, though, I believe I'll call Edgar. He may want to ride over with us."

"Excellent idea," said Carlo. "Someone's got to do something!"

Chapter Twenty-Nine

Mudge didn't answer his cell phone. Shouldn't they have let him go by now? Lydia hung up and paced across the living room. Ed Roberts had jumped him shortly before closing, so the cops must have come around two o'clock. An hour and a half . . . how long did it take to interrogate somebody? Would they pull up his juvenile records? Wait for his father? Go back to Leo's and search his truck? She wished she'd asked Dave more questions about police procedure.

Well, Mudge would get her message when he turned his phone on. Meanwhile, with the wake looming, better grab a shower and a nap.

She was dreaming about the Fix-It Chix when her phone rang.

"Are you OK?" she blurted.

Not the first thing she'd meant to say. "Yeah." Mudge didn't sound OK. "I'm at the Back End. They're going through the truck. I should be out of here pretty soon."

"Can we get together?"

"I was going to ask you if I can clean up at your place."

Lydia had a pitcher of iced tea and a plate of sandwiches ready when he arrived. No, he assured her, no one had followed him. Yes, he'd stood by his story about finding the ring in the parking lot. No, the cops didn't believe him, and yes, they were pissed. Tough! Personally, he didn't care if they ever caught the gang who ripped off Ed Roberts. Guys like that always came out on top, one way or another. If Ed wanted sympathy, let him spend a couple hours being third-degreed by Pete Altman.

This didn't bode well for approaching Mudge as a responsible citizen eager to help the police.

He emerged from the shower somewhat calmer. Lydia led him

onto the little deck behind the cottage to brief him on her conference with Edgar and Dave.

For the past two days she hadn't come out here for fear of being shot at. Until then, she'd loved this spot: a small wooden island of peacefulness and privacy wrapped in trees, warmed with the aroma of sun-baked pine needles and a murmuring chorus of birds. Now, with Mudge for backup, she reclaimed it. If you're going to go after a gang of housebreakers, you can't let some gun-toting (or formerly gun-toting) wacko scare you off your own deck.

They sat in white wooden chairs, Mudge toweling his hair dry. He frowned as she explained Edgar's idea of solving the burglaries as a springboard to solving the murders. No one, she emphasized, wanted to twist Mudge's arm. She hadn't asked him who gave him the ring for his birthday and she wasn't asking now. "But what other clues have they got? According to Edgar, that makes you the fulcrum."

"Huh." He thought it over. "The fulcrum. That's like worse than a POI."

"A what?"

"Person of interest. One step away from a suspect. Cop talk for anybody they think might know something, who they haul in for questioning. Today, me. Tomorrow, could be you, Leo, Dinah, my family– So I don't want to tell you anything that puts you in that position, you know? Where you have to decide about keeping it secret or not."

"Sure."

"Still . . . "

Lydia waited.

"There's this situation. Somebody I need to see, who I can't just go and talk to, because who knows if they're watching my truck or tapping my phone?"

Lydia refilled their iced tea glasses. "Do you want me to make a call for you? Pass on a message?"

Mudge considered. "That wouldn't do it," he said finally. "What would be good is if you could call, or I could use your phone, and we could maybe drive there in your car?"

"No problem," said Lydia. "One thing, though. I'm already a

POI." She summarized what Edgar had said about Helen Wills's plausible scenario. "He thinks I'll be OK this weekend, while she's off duty. But after that . . . "

Mudge tossed his towel over the deck railing. "This is so fucked!"

"Yeah."

"He's right. Somebody's got to do something! If we don't, like, jump in, the cop-ocracy could totally fuck this up. The burglaries *and* the murders."

"Not to mention fuck *us* up, while the lunatic who killed at least one person, and probably two, heads for Timbuktu."

"The Flying Wedge," he stood up and stretched. "Hey, if there's volunteer fire departments, why not volunteer detectives?"

Dinah Rowan found with relief that her black pants still fit. Between Mudge's desserts and Lydia's soups, she'd wondered–yanking them off their hanger–if the elastic would still go over her hips. Good! These pants had to get her through both the wake tonight and the funeral Monday. Leo would go ballistic when she told him she'd be taking half the morning off. Wouldn't you just know, he'd fume, Al Pope'd have to be buried smack in the middle of a work day! What's wrong with the weekend?

The delay caused by the autopsy was working out OK for the family. The Pope girls had all stayed on Cape, racking up husbands and kids, but the boys were scattered over hither and yon. One in California, one in Hawaii last she'd heard, one up north of Boston . . . and every one a success. Some folks said the reason Al had moved back here was so as to be a big fish in a small pond again, instead of overshadowed by his younger brothers.

According to Maria, they were all coming home for his funeral.

Dinah held up two T-shirts and debated: black or white?

Some folks had remarked at Terri's wedding last year that it was a funny thing how the Pope girls got married and stayed married, while the boys couldn't hang onto a single wife among the four of 'em. Why did that surprise anybody? In Dinah's experience, men just never knew what they wanted. Or, to put it another way, they kept tripping over their expectations. Take poor James: a string of broken engagements, still shopped around at church functions as an eligible bachelor, unwilling to break his mother's heart by coming out of the closet. Jack, the globe-trotting playboy, chose the old Hollywood revolving-door strategy of weddings and annulments. At least Al had the common sense to avoid vows along with commitments.

Yeah, and look where he ended up.

White, she decided. Save the black for Monday.

Dinah refused to be drawn into customers' speculations as to who'd whacked Al on the head and chucked him in the pond. She thrived in both her lines of work by leaving that kind of thing to the professionals. Let sleeping dogs lie, that was her policy. Live and let live.

Al, now, was just the opposite. He'd taken the view that he knew best about most things, and duty required him to enlighten others. Dinah–and Leo, too–had told him to put a cork in it while he was at the Back End. She suspected that was why he never became a regular. Shutting up wasn't in Al Pope's repertoire. Between his big mouth and his endless running after women, Dinah would have said he led a high-risk life.

Would have said, but didn't. The cops hadn't asked her. No wonder they were still chasing their tails looking for somebody to arrest.

That ought to please the sniper who'd shot at her in the woods.

Shoes. Somewhere in this closet was a pair of low heels. She'd only worn them twice. Too fancy for most Quansett events. Worth digging out to say good-by to Al Pope?

Once Helen Wills told her Kevin Kelly had found Al's pistol in a nearby bush, recently fired, there was no doubt in Dinah's mind who was the target. That was the up side to small-town living, was having a feel for your neighbors. Who flared up under stress and who hunkered down. Who would take the risk of confirming your suspicions so as to warn you to keep them to yourself. Not that Dinah needed warning. Both of her jobs constantly exposed her (like it or not) to touchy secrets. The secret-keepers relied (like it or not) on her discretion. In this case, somebody must have panicked. Dinah got the sniper's message loud and clear. It could only be one of two people. She'd sent a coded reply that should reach them both: Back off! I'll stay cool as long as you do.

So that was settled. Nothing to worry about.

She dumped the shoes out of their box. Unrolled their tissue wrappings. Held them up. Voted them down. At the wake she'd be standing. Save these for the funeral. Tonight was a night for flats.

Nothing to worry about, except Lydia.

The trouble with discretion was she couldn't tell Lydia things were cool. The others–Sue, Wally, the Ward kids–didn't concern her. Lydia, though, being new around here, and smart, and curious, might be seen as a loose cannon. That danger hadn't struck Dinah until this afternoon, when the cops grabbed Mudge, and Lydia went off in a corner with Edgar Rowdey and Dave Whatsit from the Times, and came out radiating trouble.

What to do? Nothing had occurred to her at the time. That was the down side to small-town living: you got lazy. Stuck in a rut. Until the road twists, and dumps you in a minefield.

A minefield? Hah! More like a tempest in a teapot. Come on, Dinah! What kind of trouble is Lydia Vivaldi going to make? Leo's sous-chef? With no connections in Quansett, no background, no clout, no friends or relations? She's no threat to anybody, herself included. That is, long as she don't go opening any can of worms. Which you can let her know when the opportunity comes up. Right? No problem.

Dinah padded across the carpet in stocking feet. Checked her bedside clock. Four-ten.

Lydia was bound to be at Al's wake tonight. Most likely an opportunity would come up there. Something casual that wouldn't ruffle any feathers. Slip her a note? Take her out to the car for a chat? Invite her to supper afterwards?

Two hours. Plenty of time to think of something.

Chapter Thirty

Mudge came down the ladder from Lydia's loft with good news. His cousin Charlene was working the evening shift in Wareham. If they left now, they could catch her on dinner break and be back in time for the wake.

"Wareham?" Pocketing her cell phone, Lydia recalled the one order she'd been given by both Pete Altman and Helen Wills. "Isn't that, like, on the mainland?"

He nodded. "I can go in the truck if you want."

"No way."

Could the cops arrest a person just for crossing the Cape Cod Canal? Unlikely. Would they have checkpoints set up at the bridges? Very, very unlikely.

Would Sherlock Holmes miss a key interview and stay at Baker Street, would Miss Marple sit home knitting in St. Mary Mead, because the police said not to leave the area?

She stuck a note on Edgar Rowdey's door saying if she wasn't here at six, don't wait. In the Morris, Mudge turned on the radio. He refused to tell her anything about Cousin Charlene or why he had to see her. Although Lydia understood his reasoning, she felt miffed. Before the Flying Wedge tackled any more detective jobs, they'd better get it clear who was Holmes and who was Watson.

He read directions off a slip of paper which her keen investigator's eye identified as a page from her bedside pad. That suggested he hadn't been to their destination before. Meaning, either Mudge and Charlene weren't close, or they usually met somewhere else. Mashpee? Probably, if she belonged to the same Wampanoag tribe as his father. If she lived on the mainland and came over sometimes to visit, that would fit with giving him the ring as an early birthday present. You wouldn't want to mail such a handsome gift; you'd want to present it in person. Especially if you didn't expect to be on the Cape for his actual birthday.

Good, Lydia! Next question: Did Charlene know the ring was stolen?

They crossed the Rubicon: green water flecked with white-caps, like a chipped celadon plate. From the highway they turned and turned again into a cluster of nineteenth-century brick ware-houses. Mudge navigated them down an alley to a long garage with corrugated metal doors. Painted on the nearest door, in fading red capitals, was LUX LIMO.

An arrow underneath directed them to a smaller door. Three small vans, two English taxicabs, and a lone black Cadillac parked outside the garage wore the LUX LIMO logo.

"You want to wait here?" asked Mudge.

"No, I don't."

Lydia followed him inside. This tiny lobby must be the wait-ing room: brown carpet, plaid sofa, end table stacked with maga-zines. On the garage side, the top half of a dutch door stood open to an office. Mudge dinged a brass bell on a shelf.

A woman appeared, tossing back a cascade of frosted dark hair. "Hey, Mudge!"

"Hey, Charlene."

They hugged each other through the open half-door. Lydia pegged Charlene as a decade or more older than Mudge–around her own age, although Charlene's cheerfully settled, almost matronly air echoed Cynthia Ropes. There was nothing matronly, however, about her low-cut flowered blouse. A gold locket hung just above her cleavage; amber chandelier earrings twinkled through her wavy hair. No wedding or engagement ring. There were long, elaborate silver rings on both her middle fingers, and an ornate silver band with a small amber stone on her right thumb. Charlene, Lydia guessed, liked rings, and men.

Mudge introduced them. Charlene's voice was husky–a smoker's alto. "Good timing. I'm off in a couple minutes. You guys want coffee or anything? Coke? We got everything."

"Orange Dry?" said Mudge.

"Water?" said Lydia.

A minute later, Charlene set two plastic cups on the door shelf. Five minutes later, she bumped the door open with her hips and carried in a plastic box of salad, a handful of paper napkins, and a can of Diet Pepsi. Her white skirt ended six inches above her knees, showing off long bronzed legs. Shapely toes, painted crimson to match her fingernails, peeped from the straps of white spike heels. Wow, thought Lydia. Then: Why? Who's around here to appreciate her? And, What kind of work can she do dolled up like that?

"Hey, baby." She sat next to Mudge on the sofa; squeezed his shoulders. "How's it going?"

"Not bad, mostly."

"Your dad OK? You don't mind if I eat."

"No, go ahead. Yeah, he's good. Your mom?"

"Just fine. Kids've been driving us buggy. School ends next week. Lydia," she turned, "you got kids?"

"Nope. Not yet."

"No rush, huh?" Charlene chuckled. "So what brings you two all the way out here?"

Mudge shot Lydia a look that suggested he'd be glad if she took a self-guided tour of Lux Limo. Lydia ignored it. She was as curious as Charlene to hear what he'd say.

"I think we better talk about this outside." Mudge stood up.

"OK." A lilt in her voice suggested Charlene was humoring him. "Hold this."

She handed him her salad, leaned through the door and fished out a key, called to someone inside, then led the way to the parking lot. Lydia followed her and Mudge to the black Cadillac. Charlene opened the back door. "Step into my office."

In Lydia's opinion, this was a big improvement over the Lux Limo waiting room. She sank into a soft leather seat beside Charlene. Mudge pulled down a jump seat opposite. "Cool car. What year is it?"

"1976 Fleetwood Formal 75. They only made 834 of these, with the window where you can shut out the chauffeur. We've got five of 'em." She opened an armrest between her and Lydia, revealing a telephone. "You can't actually call anybody, but it looks classy."

"Charlene," Mudge rested his elbows on his knees. "You know that ring you gave me."

"Your birthday present. Sure. You like it?"

"I love it, but it got me in some trouble. Turns out, it came from a heist."

"No!" Her shock sounded genuine. "Baby, you kidding me?"

He explained. She listened, shaking her head slowly. Whatever Charlene's job was, Lydia figured, it must involve some level of performing. Right now she was performing–punctuating Mudge's story with small gestures and exclamations. But Lydia's impression was that under her act, Charlene truly was amazed and outraged.

When Mudge finished, her head shook more vigorously. "I'll kill him," she said. "I am just so embarrassed, I swear to god, I'm gonna kill him and then I'm gonna kill myself. Honey, I'm so damn sorry, I don't have words to tell you."

"Can you tell me where you got it?" Mudge asked her.

"I'll take care of it." She took a bite of salad. "Guaranteed. Don't worry about a thing!"

"It's kind of gone past that, Charlene." He leaned toward her. "I know you didn't mean to mess me up, and I don't want to mess you up, either. You were really sweet to give me such a great birthday present. But here's the thing. Aside from these burglaries, you probably heard there's an unsolved murder. Well, I was the one who found the body. I pulled the guy out of Leo's frog pond and did CPR. But he was dead. So the cops are like all over me. Like I'm the number one suspect for everything."

"Oh, honey!"

"That's why I came up here, is because I need your help. To track that ring from Ed Roberts' house to me."

Charlene took a long, thoughtful swig of Diet Pepsi. "Damn!" she said at last. "But the cops don't have anything on you, right? You told them you found it in the parking lot."

"I told you. They know I made that up."

"They can't prove it, though. As long as you don't crack, they can't touch you." She sat back triumphantly.

"Didn't you hear what I said? They know I lied about the ring. So they figure I must be lying about the murder, too. I mean it, Charlene. This is serious."

"Well, I can't just– There's other people involved here besides you, sweetheart. I tell you what." She took his nearest hand in both of hers. "Let me feel things out. Check out the lay of the land, you know? I've got to get back to work pretty quick here, anyways. You go on home, OK? and I'll call you tonight. Or tomorrow. Soon as I can."

"Bad idea." Lydia intervened for the first time. "You ever watch TV, Charlene? Or movies?"

"Sure." She was patting Mudge's hand.

"What always, always happens to the person who has crucial information and says I can't tell you right now, but I'll tell you later?"

Mudge made a choking noise and drew his free hand across his throat.

Charlene sat back again, trying to make light of it. She teased him: "This is a friend of yours?"

"Yeah. She is." He wasn't smiling.

"Hmm. Well. OK. Lydia, right? Baby, can I talk to Lydia alone for just a second?"

Mudge hesitated, then got out of the car. Charlene forked salad into her mouth as he crossed the pavement. Lydia watched him disappear behind the yellow Morris, which stood out in this lot like the first flame on a pile of charcoal.

"He's a wonderful kid," said Charlene.

"Yup," Lydia agreed.

"I've known him since he was born." She closed her plastic salad box. "This is a fucking mess. What's that saying about good deeds always get punished? Anyways. Did he tell you why I gave him that ring?"

"Only that it was an early birthday present. He didn't even say it came from you."

"Bless his heart!" Charlene sighed. "I really should get back to work. I've got three cars coming in like any second. So here's the deal, OK? I'll tell you about that damn ring if you'll do something for me. Actually two things. One: whatever you tell the cops, it has to come from you, not Mudge. If they connect it back to me–" She drew her own finger across her throat. "And two, I don't want to come off like a total shit and hurt his feelings, so you gotta work out some nice way to tell him. OK?" She held out her hand.

"OK." Lydia shook it.

Charlene began with her job. She was a dispatcher for Lux Limo, which provided chauffeured transportation in southeastern New England, mostly to and from the Boston and Providence airports. Although two-thirds of their trips began or ended on Cape Cod, it was cheaper to run the business out of Wareham. The dispatchers rotated shifts, taking reservations, setting up pick-ups and drop-offs. Their main contact with the drivers was by phone. They also logged in each vehicle when it came in for maintenance.

Friendly relations were in everyone's best interest. Sometimes a dispatcher and a driver would grow more than friendly, but management frowned on that. Flirtations were common. Many drivers scheduled their maintenance visits for when a particular dispatcher was on duty. Sometimes they brought gifts–flowers, candy, jewelry–which the dispatchers usually shared with each other, like tips.

What did you do with a gold ring?

Charlene told the guy she couldn't keep it unless he was her boyfriend, which, face facts, he wasn't. He refused to take it back. She dropped it in her pocket, where she found it again later that night. Mudge's dad and his girlfriend were over for dinner with his sister (Charlene's mother) and her family. The subject of birthdays came up, specifically Mudge's. Lincoln's girlfriend stated there would be no party or cake in her home. That upset Charlene so much that she went straight upstairs and wrapped the ring in sparkly paper with a big white bow, and handed it to her uncle to give to Mudge with her love and best wishes.

They agreed Lincoln Miles's girlfriend was a bitch, and it was a damn good thing Mudge had other women in his life who appreciated him. Then Lydia asked Charlene who'd given her the ring.

Her head tipped back in a throaty chuckle. "I'm not telling you that!"

"Why not? You think he stole it?"

"Hey, we're done here. You got a cigarette?"

"No," said Lydia. "You don't even like this guy. Right? But you'd rather save him from getting caught than save Mudge from getting screwed?"

"Nobody's getting screwed. Or saved. I don't want cops in my life, OK? Look," she pointed out the window, "here he comes."

She reached for the door handle. Lydia grabbed her arm. "Charlene, if you want Mudge to join this conversation, that's up to you, but if I were you I'd listen for one more second. Here's the deal. Tell me who gave you that ring. I'll phone an anonymous tip to a friend of mine, he'll tell a cop friend of his, and nobody will ever connect it with you or Mudge."

"Forget it. This guy's not stupid. Anybody comes after him?–he'll know."

"Well then . . . " Lydia talked on, hoping her racing brain would stay one step ahead of her mouth. "How about we make a bet? I'll write some names on a piece of paper. With Quansett addresses. After we leave here, you look them up in your dispatch records. I'm betting that your guy, or somebody in Lux Limo, picked up these folks sometime in the past few weeks. If that's what you find, you call me and say yes. If not, call and say no. Either way, I'll take it from there, no connection to you. But keep in mind, if it's no, then you lose, because Mudge stays Suspect Number One."

Charlene waved to him through the glass. "OK. That I can do."

They got out of the car–Charlene making a show of kidding around with Mudge, then of craving a nicotine fix before she returned to work. Lydia was glad to be ignored. She was still reeling from the shock of having just solved (was it possible?) the Quansett burglary case. She also needed to remember fast who the other victims were besides Ed Roberts.

In the end she asked Mudge, while Charlene went inside for cigarettes.

"Why? You're not dumping this on her?"

"What I'm trying to do," Lydia retorted, "is haul both your

asses out of it."

He made a list of names and streets on the back of his driving directions. "Did she tell you who she got the ring from?"

"Ask her."

Lydia guessed, correctly, that he wouldn't. What was that saying about beating a dead horse? Charlene blew smoke rings at Mudge and reminisced about their grandparents. She insisted she was going to find him another birthday present, the best ever. He insisted no present could be better than seeing her today. Lydia, meanwhile, jotted her phone number at the bottom of the list, and slipped it to Charlene when she hugged them both good-by.

In the car, Mudge wanted to know immediately what he'd missed. Lydia promised to brief him as soon as they found the Sagamore Bridge.

"So?" he demanded at the first Cape Cod sign.

She'd reviewed the situation while she drove, and it hadn't changed. "Score another one for the Flying Wedge. I think we've solved the burglaries."

"Solved the burglaries?" Mudge whistled. "Prodigious! How?"

"Well, it's not definite yet. Charlene's checking something, and then we'll know."

"Does *she* know? She's not– You don't think she's part of it? She can't be!"

"No," Lydia assured him. "Except on the edges, by accident. She wants to stay out of it. Since it looks like the burglars are guys she works with."

"Oh, man. Lux Limo? Shit!" Mudge clasped his hands behind his head. "You mean, like–what? They drive Ed Roberts to Logan, and once he's on the plane, they come back and steal all his stuff?"

"That's my plausible scenario."

There were plenty of details still up in the air. Mudge agreed with Lydia's theory. His only gripe was that if she and Charlene hadn't left him out of the loop, he could have nosed around the office and filled in most of the blanks by now. Lydia countered that they'd only gone to Wareham so he could straighten things out with Charlene. For her safety as well as theirs, they would follow the plan: wait for her call, then phone a tip to Dave Wheeler to forward anonymously to Pete Altman. Filling in blanks was up to the cops and robbers.

"Yeah, well." Mudge wasn't convinced. "I get what you're saying. But that sucks! We do the work and Altman gets the credit? What good is that?"

"It gets us off the hook and him back on the murder case," Lydia retorted. "We don't want the credit, Mudge! We're chefs! Remember? We want people to pay us tons of money to cook them gourmet dinners and then disappear so they can shine in front of their guests. How can that work if they think we're detectives, searching their house for clues?"

"Still." He slumped down in his seat. "It isn't fair! The cops have had this thing for weeks. We're on it for like two hours and–pffw!" He mimed a slam dunk. "If we stayed on it, it'd be wrapped by tomorrow. What are they gonna do with it? Keep on barking up the wrong tree. Right? Drug connection! Temporary construction workers! Give me a fucking break."

Lydia sighed. Part of her agreed with Mudge. Part of her resented his forcing her to play the grown-up, the straight man, Wendy to his Peter Pan. Part of her recognized that there was only one option here, and neither his feelings nor hers made any difference.

"Three things," she said. "One, the cops can't screw it up if we drop it in Pete Altman's lap. Two, that's assuming we've got anything, which we don't know yet. Three, last but not least: Charlene. If we're in it, so is she–like a goldfish in a piranha tank."

There wasn't much else to say. Mudge turned up the radio and stared out the window. Lydia focused on the road. She wondered if the Lone Ranger had ever looked back wistfully as he rode off, longing to stay till he could be sure things really did come out OK.

During the Ken Boose era, Wally Hicks used to spend hours in his eyrie. He enjoyed watching Quansett through his two eagle eyes, even when it was snoozing. And then his Pirandello blog took time and thought. Sometimes he didn't get around to the day's webcam stills until just before closing.

Since Wednesday, when he'd become the Frigate's senior employee, he hadn't managed a single scan-and-discard session.

So you could say it was thanks to Roosevelt Sherman that Edgar Rowdey fell in love with CodCast.net.

Ignorance, reflected Wally, is bliss. The technology–uppermost when he'd showed off his set-up to Dave Wheeler–meant nothing to Edgar. Whereas Dave had graciously refrained from remarking that even his pocket camera had better resolution than Wally's webcams, Edgar simply marveled that from here you could invisibly watch Fred Jones raise the top on his convertible, or look in Louise French's window.

He was equally charmed by the stills. What a miracle, to page back in time! Wally (who was beginning to share the New York Times Book Review's regard for this man) asked if there was any particular day he'd like to see. Edgar said hummy hummy hoo, how about the beginning of this week? Say, Monday through Thursday? No problem, replied Wally magnanimously.

Before they came upstairs he'd flipped the Open sign to Closed and locked the front door. The boss wouldn't mind. The more favors the Frigate could do for the future star of his grand opening, the happier Rosey would be. From happiness grew gratitude. Already Wally's sights had shifted from scallops at Swan River Seafood to swordfish at Mattakeese Wharf.

They sat side by side at the desk, balding white head and graying ponytail. At first Edgar peered intently from one screen to the other like a great blue heron stalking minnows. Minnows was all he'd catch here, Wally suspected. As a long-time local, Edgar no doubt recognized more cars than he did himself. Still, cars going in the driveway, cars coming out the driveway, cars parking, cars passing by–who cared? Even to Wally, this demonstration was a yawn. He showed Edgar how to watch the images as a slide show, and excused himself to go down and reopen the shop.

Half a dozen customers came and went. Upstairs, Edgar hadn't stirred, except to jot notes on a scrap of paper. Buns of steel, Wally thought with admiration. Big asset for a writer.

"What'd you find?"

"Hm. Well. One would be hard put to name a soul in town who doesn't pass under your cameras." Edgar stretched back in Wally's multi-adjustable chair. "And that's just Monday."

"You through here, then?"

"Oh no. Just getting started."

Tuesday came and went, as did Wally. Onward through Wednesday. Halfway into Thursday, Gromit lurched to his feet and trotted toward the door. There were only two people he welcomed like that.

"Hey there, boy!" Rosey Sherman bent to tousle his ears. "How's tricks?"

Wally waited until he had the man's full attention before he spoke. "Rosey. You still want to talk to Edgar Rowdey?"

"Sure do."

"He's upstairs."

"Well, hot damn!" Rosey didn't even pause to ask how Wally had pulled off this coup. He charged for the door with the zip that had made him famous on the football field.

Only a keen concern for his future kept Wally from following. They've got a deal to make, he counseled himself. Don't think about CodCast.net in alien hands. Think about a dinner-jacketed waiter at Chillingworth refilling your champagne glass as he serves your lobster thermidor.

Chapter Thirty-One

Safe in his car, parked at the front end of the Back End's lot, Edgar Rowdey sighed.

He'd escaped from Roosevelt Sherman as fast as courtesy allowed. Much as he adored the Frigate, now was not the time for a fencing match with its new proprietor. Not with a killer at large, a police investigation looming like Damocles's sword, and just two hours till the wake.

Now was the time to fill in missing pieces.

Tact forbade telling Lydia that Helen Wills's scenario had struck him as worse than plausible. As the detective herself had quipped, you only had to know Alistair to want to kill him. His staying alive for this long was a testament to his friends' patience and sanity. Lydia (she implied), having met him just a week ago, might not be so patient; and who could vouch for her sanity? Nobody on the Cape. Nobody in Cambridge, either. Was Mr. Rowdey aware that she'd walked out on her rental without notice? And was Leo aware (Detective Wills wondered) that no Lydia Vivaldi, Liz Valentine, or Lynn Vail could be found in Legal Seafood's employment records?

That didn't make her a murderer, needless to remark. Edgar knew perfectly well that Detective Wills knew perfectly well her dicoveries didn't justify an arrest, much less a prosecution. What they did justify was keeping the bloodhounds hot on Lydia's trail. Where there are media, wheels must visibly turn.

Really, the more he saw of the legal system, the more it reminded him of the blackberry jungle behind his house. Over the years its prickly tentacles had sprawled in all directions, beyond the reach of fences or pruning shears. One might wish for greater order, fewer brambles, more berries; but the only choice was to take it or leave it–accept it as is, thorns and all, or burn it down.

The Commonwealth of Massachusetts was paying Helen Wills and her henchpeople to find a culprit whom a Barnstable County court would convict of murder. Edgar's task was simpler: to lift the cloud of suspicion and fear that hung over his friends.

The suspicion was irksome; the fear, alas, was (in his view) realistic. Edgar could think of several routes by which a miscreant might have got hold of Alistair Pope's pistol. He could think of several explanations for the shots in the woods. However! Steal Alistair's pistol, fire it where the police were sure to be called, and then drop it in a bush? For that he could conjure up only one plausible scenario, and it didn't bode well for Lydia.

Edgar adjusted his glasses and climbed out of the car.

Thanks to Wally Hicks, he now had his own list of "persons of interest" (Mrs. Wills's quaint phrase) who'd popped up near the Back End for no apparent reason in the days before Alistair was killed. Next: separate the sheep from the goats. Discreetly–it wouldn't do to become a POI himself on the wrong list.

Edgar's target was Sparkle, the only shop in this cluster of offices and boutiques with a rear-facing window.

For a jewelry store it was modest: one thickly carpeted off-white room, waist-high glass cases along the sides, a cylindrical glass display near the center. A bell jangled when he entered. A woman emerged from a curtained doorway whom he'd seen occasionally around town. Slightly stout, in a floral Lilly Pulitzer dress, she looked more Chatham or Osterville than Quansett. Her wavy blonde coif didn't stir as she approached.

"Welcome! Is there anything special I can help you with?"

Edgar arranged his left hand on the nearest case. "Hmm . . . "

"Oh my goodness! Look at your wonderful rings!"

Elise, it emerged, was a fan of West African jewelry. Sadly, her passion was not shared by her customers. Most of them sought more traditional items: a diamond solitaire, a gold bracelet–

"Hmm. Yes. Absolutely. My friends." Edgar chose dithering as the best way to cast a wide net–not knowing what stories his POIs might have told. "One of those grand celebrations, you know, pool our resources and so forth, what do you give the person who has everything sort of thing? Clock ticking, really must come to grips. I wonder, do you recall seeing any of them? If they leaned toward anything particular?"

"Oh," Eloise said blankly. "We get so many people . . ."

"An executive type, the older girl. Tall, in her thirties. Dark hair pulled back? The younger one is more T-shirt and shorts, I'm afraid."

"Aha. The first one, I believe so. In a tailored gray suit, black pumps, rather severe?"

"Oh yes. Absolutely."

"A birthday gift for her brother, wasn't it? The football player. She was most interested in our shockproof watches, back here by the window."

From the watch display, one had a full view of the Back End's facade and frog pond. Edgar's pulse quickened, although this was what he'd expected. Helen Wills would park on the street and find an inconspicuous way to check who was lunching at Leo's before she went in. So he'd surmised from spotting her cruiser out front at 1:12 PM on Monday. Sue, less cautious, would drive right up to Leo's door. Her car the webcam had caught as it turned the corner, at 6:51 AM on Tuesday. (At least, he assumed that battered wedge of Toyota was Sue's car.)

Wild horses, Edgar suspected, couldn't drag the men on his list into Sparkle. Still, one must be thorough. He described them. No, said Elise, no pony-tail and cane. No camera and Red Sox jacket.

Any men at all interested in watches these past few days?

Oh, well, of course. Those who came with their wives; what else could they look at? One other . . . Wednesday, wasn't it? Fiftyish, on the heavy side, ruddy of complexion and scant of hair. Red canvas trousers, polo shirt, and boating shoes. Was he from their group?

"Hm." Edgar felt curiously reluctant to claim Ed Roberts as even a fictional friend. "Most helpful. So good of you, Elise."

He was halfway out the door when she added, "Well, and then– Oh, dear, what's his name? Not to say that he, that you– But he's a football player, too."

"You mean, Roosevelt Sherman?"

"That's it." She nodded. "Came in with his little boy. They bought a stopwatch."

"A stopwatch," said Edgar. "How very interesting."

Wallace Hicks found himself flipping back and forth like a windshield wiper about Alistair Pope's wake. The best way to mark that evil sonofabitch's passing was to ignore it–just go on selling books like he never existed. Yet how could he ignore the mounting momentum of his mission?

Rosey Sherman tipped the karmic scale.

He didn't say why he'd decided to close the Frigate early. To attend the wake? Not likely. Wally doubted he'd ever met Pope. His guess was the Shermans had other fish to fry, but closing the store would count as a gesture of respect, if anyone was counting.

Nor did the man likely suspect what ripples his decision was sending through the cosmos. Suppose somebody should come by here tonight and find the lights off, the door locked. Maybe she'd realize it wasn't so smart to shoot off your big mouth–

Now don't get all het up again, Hicks! She was drunk. Trying to be a poet. Showing off. You can't trust a damn thing she said.

Like he cared, anyhow. They were both adults. She'd been around; so what? So had he. Alistair Pope or some bartender in Bourne or the man in the moon, what difference did it make who she screwed?

Well, it might matter to her. Give that a little consideration, Hicks. If her last lover was dead, in fact murdered, that could throw any woman off her game. Fill her with contrary urges. Like, get laid again real quick and then back off. Ambivalence: strong emotions pulling in opposite directions. Especially a woman of an impulsive nature. Impulse was the wind that blew her here, and might just as well bring her back.

Or not. If she was still in shock. Drinking to cover it up. Not knowing which way to turn. Or who to trust.

A caring friend showing up at the key moment might make all the difference. Pull her back from the brink of . . . well, who knew what might befall a shook-up woman groping for comfort?

"What was he after?"

Wally swiveled. Rosey Sherman had finished closing out the register and stood with his arms folded.

"What? Oh. Edgar Rowdey?" He tied off the window-blind cord. "Well, I don't know that he was after anything particular. He'd heard about the webcams, was all he said, and could I show him around."

They collected their belongings, and Gromit, and moved toward the door. "Will he do the book signing?"

Rosey smiled as he flicked off the lights. "He didn't say no."

He never does, thought Wally. Part of his legend. But hey. Not my job to step in between Quansett's two biggest celebrities.

"You heard anything from Sue?" Rosey inquired.

"Nope." Wally's cane pulverized a clamshell. "Not a peep."

"Looks like we lost ourselves a hand. Well, easy come, easy go. What do you think about that kid, the cashier at Leo's? Mudge?"

Easy come, easy go? Over a ringing in his ears Wally said, "You mean who the cops picked up today on burglary charges?"

That stopped the man in his tracks. He wanted an explanation; Wally supplied it. Half the customers who'd passed through the Frigate this afternoon had remarked on the Back End's latest turn of events. As you'd know, thought Wally, if you'd stick around your own shop.

Rosey leaned against his SUV, shaking his head in disbelief. "Damn! Last thing I wanted to mess with tonight."

"You mean, at the wake?"

"Nah. Family barbecue. You going over? Pay your respects?"

"I might stop in."

Rosey took out his keys. "What the hell. We've got time yet." Wally, still startled by what had just come out of his own mouth, recognized that his boss had changed subjects again. "My dad used to say, You catch more flies with honey than with vinegar. And if that don't work"–he clicked open the locks–"make 'em an offer they can't refuse."

As Rosey patched out in a cloud of clamshell dust, Wally

retrieved his key to the Frigate. Sufficient unto the boss are the problems thereof. He had his own evening to arrange. A man about to culminate an eighteen-year mission had best do it in style. Take a real shower, not a rinse-off in the Airstream. Wash the hair. Put on clean clothes. Maybe a splash of aftershave. Respect for the occasion.

The long-awaited day of reckoning! Well, evening of reckoning. Stay real, Hicks. Ascending the karmic peak doesn't mean forgetting the other notches on your belt.

For instance, why not take along any belongings that somebody left behind who might not come back for them? That denim jacket–no point letting it collect dust. Overdue for the laundry anyhow. Ring around the collar, black streaks down the front. Piece of paper in a pocket. Forwarding address? Crumpled, but worth checking. Nope, this was a note. Scrawled in pencil on the ripped-off back of an envelope. Smeared to semi-legibility by whoever'd wadded it into a ball. *You dick-brain Casanova piece of shit!* Me? Damn! *Who do you think you're fooling, scumbag?* No, can't be me. *Touch her again & I swear I'll kill you both. YES fuck-head I mean NOW!!!*

Whew! Wally shook his scorched fingers. Thrilling as it was to imagine some mad rival attacking him over Sue, he didn't believe it. You don't win the girl by staying out of sight, much less by sticking a note in her pocket.

Who'd hurled this threat at whom? Wally had no clue. Nor what it was doing in Sue's jacket. Some mysteries, he reflected, a wise man doesn't try to decipher.

Still, replacing the note where he'd found it, he felt a twinge of envy for the Casanova who'd provoked such passionate jealousy.

Lydia Vivaldi thought she looked pretty damn good. She'd discovered a black sundress in the bottom of her duffel bag and a steam iron in the linen closet. Add sandals, a scarf, and some bangles and you had a perfectly respectable outfit for a wake. A touch of mascara and lipstick . . . The green streaks in her hair hadn't stayed as bright as the package promised. That was OK, though. They'd made their point in Cambridge. Here she didn't need them. In fact, out of consideration for Alistair's memory, she removed two earrings.

Edgar stood waiting for her at the foot of his porch steps, still in the jeans and yellow sweater he'd worn to lunch. Poor man–she hoped he hadn't hung around the house all afternoon for fear of being late.

"Hul-lo," he greeted her cheerfully.

"How was your day?"

"Slow as the fabled tortoise, but progressing."

"I invited Mudge to join us," she leaned against the lamppost, "but he's peopled out."

"You found him."

"He's sprung. We went to Wareham." Lydia summarized their adventures. "Now I'm just waiting for a call back from Charlene, to find out what we've hooked."

"Excellent!" said Edgar. "You are a woman of remarkable talents."

"Remarkable luck, you mean," said Lydia. "This was your idea."

"And when you hear from Charlene–?"

"My phone'll go off in the middle of the wake, I'm sure, confirming what a total Philistine I am, and if our luck holds, I'll have to run outside and call Dave Wheeler to ask him to call Detective Altman, so he can wrap up the burglaries and phase back into the murder investigation before Hell on Wheels comes on duty Monday. Assuming there's any cell reception."

"Mercy," murmured Edgar.

"Justice," Lydia corrected.

"She understands, does she, that caution is essential?"

"Charlene? Oh yeah. More than anybody. She works with these guys."

Caroline and Carlo's silver Mustang made the turn off Main Street. Edgar waved to them across the triangular green. Lydia shifted her purse on her shoulder. In it, her phone rang.

He gestured at her to take the call. She stepped onto the porch, out of earshot. Caroline, at the wheel, lifted an inquiring eyebrow. Edgar climbed into the back seat beside Carlo and asked how the opera was progressing. Carlo groaned. Caroline leaned around to pat his arm and said actually it was picking up. Although Act One kept expanding in spite of their best efforts–if it wasn't the long-winded contralto, it was the rivals' meeting on the train–they'd had a breakthrough with the hero's leitmotif. She for one could see light at the end of the tunnel.

"Sorry." Lydia opened the passenger door. "That was kind of an emergency."

Her intensity moved Edgar to ask, "Do you need more time?"

"Nope." She got in. "I need to find somebody who I hope is at the wake."

They proceeded in cramped silence back onto Main Street.

"Cell phones," mused Carlo. "How did we ever manage without them?"

"Some of us still do," Edgar returned.

"That's right," said Caroline. "You're a holdout. Edgar, you dinosaur. You Luddite."

"Not at all. If I ever lack interruptions when I'm trying to work, sleep, and so forth, I'll go straight out and buy one."

"So," Lydia half-turned to look at him, "why do you think the person who killed Alistair took his phone?"

"I'm sure I don't know."

"If it was Edgar," said Carlo, "he was desperate to try one without his friends finding out, so he made a call and then chucked it in the pond. To save face."

"There must have been something on it, don't you think?" said Caroline. "An incriminating message?"

"Like, a threat?" asked Lydia. "That the cops would recognize as X's motive?"

"Or a phone number. Carlo, should I take 132 or stay on Willow?"

"Stay on Willow, to North, to West Main."

"They keep messages, do they? Like an answering machine?" asked Edgar. "And phone numbers?"

"Right," said Lydia. "Your calling record, and also your personal phone book–that's the numbers you input because you use them a lot."

"You think North is quicker than Main?"

"Oh, yes."

"This calling record–what form does it take?"

"A list of the last six or eight numbers you've made calls to and had calls from. Incoming, outgoing, and missed. Unless you delete them."

"But do as you like, Caroline."

"Well, then, Caroline's got it, don't you think? X must have made a call to Alistair–or had one from Alistair–that would betray him to the police."

"A red flag," Carlo agreed. "If not herring."

"Which X didn't trust Alistair to delete," said Caroline, "either because he didn't recognize it as a threat–"

"–or because he did," Carlo completed.

"It could have been a message," added Lydia, "or even just a number that didn't belong on his phone."

"What kind of number would that be?" Carlo wondered.

"Somebody he wasn't supposed to know? A competing film-maker? A drug dealer?"

"Perhaps multiple calls to or from the same number," said Edgar. "That's what always gives them away on television."

A sex hotline?

"'Professor Plum, although you say you barely knew Miss Scarlet, I see you called her at home on June fourth, fifth, eighth, and tenth.'"

No way. Dinah wouldn't kill Alistair! Never mind her strong arm with a cleaver, or her short temper. They'd been friends since, what? Grade school?

Caroline chuckled. "Elementary, my dear Rowdey."

OK, he was pushy that way. Maybe more of a Casanova than his dwindling attractions could support. But he'd apparently been getting enough not to need a professional.

"To us," said Edgar, "if not the police."

Anyhow, didn't Dinah say she only took clients from off Cape?

"Thanks to our classical education," said Carlo.

No, not exactly. She'd said she avoided local clients because they were too risky. Which could mean she'd had a problem at some point–a guy whose voice she recognized, or who recognized hers. Alistair?

"Now if only the Exmouth police department's 21st-century computers are so efficient," said Caroline.

"As us Luddites," said Carlo.

"In our great gas hog of a car," said Edgar.

Cars already lined the street in front of the funeral home. Lydia had vaguely pictured a pillared mansion along the lines of Tara in *Gone with the Wind*, but this was New England's version: a large, comfortable-looking two-story white house with chimneys and dormers, where you could imagine a long-ago merchant's or minister's family playing tag on the wide lawn. Caroline pulled in across the street, in front of a pizza parlor where she and Carlo and Leo had agreed they would all meet for supper afterwards.

Lydia fell in behind her as they walked toward the open front door. As usual, she was impressed by both Caroline's cheerful practicality and her tastefully exotic clothes: for Alistair's wake, a black mandarin jacket embroidered with birds and flowers, over an arrangement of silk panels that fluttered like a skirt, not quite hiding black trousers underneath. She'd have felt dowdy by contrast, except that even Carlo's handsome charcoal suit looked dowdy next to Caroline. And then there was Edgar, nonchalant in his yellow sweater, jeans, and sneakers.

Smoke rose from a cluster of people standing a stone's throw away in the driveway. Even funeral homes, apparently, had banned cigarettes. Hard on the bereaved–at this of all times you'd want a puff of comfort.

They joined the line inside. It began in the lobby, with guest books to sign, then snaked down a few steps to the formally old-fashioned main room. Those heads at the far end, appearing and disappearing behind visitors, must be Alistair's family. Lydia didn't see Dinah, or Dave Wheeler.

"When we get up there, will you introduce me?" she whispered to Edgar.

"Oh, heavens," he murmured back. "I don't know more than half of them. Anyhow, they can't care who we are. So many hands to shake!"

"Caroline doubts most of this crowd ever met Alistair," Carlo added softly. "Sensation-seekers, I'm afraid."

Edgar's eyebrow went up. "Well, I for one have no intention of going anywhere near the casket."

That gave Lydia's stomach a jolt. What could be more repellent than seeing dead Alistair framed in white satin, his army jacket replaced by a suit, his waxy cheeks and blue lips colorized to the pink of health? She wished Edgar hadn't reminded her about the casket. Now she couldn't help scanning the room for it–wondering in spite of herself what the undertakers had done with that stringy hair and erratic comb-over, and the bashed-in spot on his head.

No. Worse than that. They'd had an autopsy to cope with.

Enough! Stick with the living, Lydia. There's Leo up front. Working the line? From here he was a glimpse of bristly white hair and a bony dark-blue shoulder, shifting in and out of sight between other silhouettes she vaguely recognized from work.

The line had stopped. That might be thanks to Dinah, talking to Alistair's family members. She'd be the person to make introductions. Or maybe not. What could she say? I want you to meet your brother's last seduction target? The top suspect in your son's murder?

Not for long, Lydia vowed. If I could move Edgar's Rube Goldberg plan this far along in one afternoon, I'm sure not hanging around waiting for the cops to collect enough reasons to arrest me on Monday.

She checked her cell phone. No reception.

Three minutes, she decided. If we're still barely moving, and Dave hasn't shown up, go find a place to call him. Then ask Dinah how well she really knew Alistair.

Outside the funeral home the afternoon shadows lengthened. Cigarettes were stubbed out in the sand-filled decorative urn beside the driveway. The younger brother of Alistair Pope's father wondered when they'd junked the cast-iron jockey who'd stood on that spot when Grampa died. His wife said she still couldn't believe it about poor Al. No, they all agreed. What a shock. And no word from the cops yet who did it, said Alistair's oldest sister. Probably nobody, said her mother-in-law. Easy to slip and fall into a pond. Her daughter said they wouldn't call it a murder unless they were sure, and who had a breath mint? Alistair's cousin Pat, offering a roll of Life Savers, said considering how Al chased after women (not to speak ill of the dead), he was lucky this hadn't happened sooner. Her husband, also named Pat, said he hoped they hadn't junked the iron jockey. Those old statues were worth a nice chunk of change.

Wallace Hicks completed his third circuit around the neighborhood. No sign of Sue's car. He preferred not to go in there before she arrived. Since every fiber of his being would rather not go in at all, and once he did, every fiber of his being would be needed for his mission, he preferred to catch her out here. Supply whatever comfort was required. (He'd stowed a pint of Wild Turkey under the seat.) Then leave it to karma whether he'd escort her in, or make a solo entrance, or chuck the whole thing.

He'd noticed a second cluster of smokers on the side patio. Delsey and her New York buddies. This bunch was more furtive–like they shared a guilty secret, something to giggle about. One of them kept flashing a silver hip flask. All in black, like they never wore anything else, which maybe they didn't. The funny thing was, Wally could equally well picture Alistair at the center of either group.

He pulled into the lot across the street. A man could only take so many whiffs of spicy tomato sauce before opting to wait at Rosa's Pizza and Mexican.

She was drunk, Hicks. Blabbering nonsense. Making up rhymes for her silly song.

Still.

If you accepted that Sue had in fact slept with Alistair Pope, why shouldn't she think she knew who whacked him?

Wally ordered a slice with extra cheese and pepperoni.

Maybe she didn't even know what she thought. Ideas had a tendency to bubble up in Sue's brain and flow right on out of her mouth. Maybe she'd seen Caroline or Carlo do something that sparked her unconscious suspicions. Or overheard Rosey Sherman say something confessional. A little far-fetched, but not impossible.

Then there was Lydia.

OK, sure, the sous-chef's job. The cat fight at Leo's. How could Sue help hating the newcomer who'd waltzed into town and elbowed her out? Still. Just because she'd got a chip on her shoulder didn't mean she was wrong.

Put Alistair Pope in between those two, and you had an explanation for the note.

The girl at the counter asked what he wanted to drink. Water, Wally meant to reply. Water? At a moment like this? Step up to the plate, Hicks! He ordered a Moosehead.

Beer in one hand and his pizza in the other, Wally chose a small table with a view of the parking lot.

Suppose that once upon a time Sue had a fling with Alistair Pope. Lydia arrives in Quansett. Alistair shows an interest. Does Lydia know that Sue has switched to Wally? No. How could she? She's too busy stealing Sue's job behind her back. Until one day she makes a serious pass at Alistair, and he admits he's still holding a torch for Sue.

Lydia flips out. Hell hath no fury like a woman scorned!

Brilliant! Everything fit perfectly. Well, almost. Hard to imagine Alistair Pope as Casanova. Easy, though, to imagine somebody–anybody who knew him–calling him a dick-brain piece of shit.

Not Sue, of course. She might think that, but she didn't care enough about Alistair to threaten him. Anyway, if she wrote the note, how did it get in her pocket? You could argue she'd changed her mind, but only if you didn't know her. Sue wasn't the type to pull punches. Or, far as that went, to vent her fury on the back of an envelope. If she wanted you to do something, or stop doing something, she'd get right in your face.

No. Lydia wrote the note to Alistair, who threw it away, and Sue grabbed it as proof of her own superior sex appeal.

Chewing the last bits of cheese off his pizza crust, Wally contemplated this picture. Nice detective work, Hicks! Now, what are you gonna do about it? Give the note back to Sue? Let her keep it to remember Alistair by, when the cops might regard it as the key to his murder?

That incident in the woods. It wasn't him or Sue who'd fired those shots, and he'd bet a waterfront seafood dinner it wasn't Dinah.

Even if you opposed the capitalist police state, you didn't want to shield a crazy jealous woman who was running around at large in your town, carrying a violent grudge against a friend you'd given shelter. What if she couldn't find Sue and decided to shoot up the Airstream? Or torch the Frigate? Or poison Gromit?

On the other hand, you wouldn't want to piss off the aforementioned friend by taking something from her jacket and handing it over to the cops. Not if you ever hoped to get lucky again.

It ain't rocket science, Hicks. Drink your beer, wait till Sue shows up, and leave the rest to karma.

Chapter Thirty-Two

"Edgar," said Caroline, "how is your snake coming along?"

Lydia wondered if it was this receiving line that made her ask. In the past two minutes it had barely crawled. It was also losing its serpentine form. As guests who'd greeted the Pope family emerged into the empty side of the room, many of them didn't leave, but clustered in conversations–with each other, new arrivals, or friends still waiting in line.

"Oh, well. So much afoot lately, I haven't gone near it in weeks."

A memory stirred. "Is that those rocks alongside the magnolia tree?"

Carlo prodded Edgar to explain. "What did Alistair name it?"

"Nidhogg. My gardener turned up a number of nice rocks last year, and I thought, instead of a border or whatnot, why not make a snake? Slithering down the slope from the cottage, half hidden in the grass."

"Like a real snake," said Carlo.

"Invisible and dangerous," said Caroline. "Lydia, watch your ankles."

Edgar continued: "Alistair insisted on calling it Nidhogg after the serpent that gnaws the roots of Yggdrasil the great tree that holds up the world."

"The magnolia tree?" said Lydia.

Caroline nodded. "Norse mythology."

"But really, it's just a snake," said Edgar. "If I can find it a head."

"Here come the smokers," said Carlo. Through a french door near the middle of the parlor appeared an androgynous trio in black jackets and black leggings.

"Time for me to go try my phone call again," said Lydia.

She could see a patio outside the open door which showed promise for cell reception. As she walked toward it, a familiar voice called her name.

Cynthia and Raymond Ropes once again looked like waiters, standing in line in the same navy-blue suits they'd worn last Sunday. Lydia stopped to shake hands.

Cynthia asked how she was liking her job. Lydia asked what she thought of Trader Joe's. Raymond gazed into space. Lydia asked if they'd heard anything more from Alistair's office.

"No," said Cynthia. "I was just wondering if one of those," pointing at the smokers, "might be the girl who called us. Raymond, what was her name?"

He answered without looking at them: "Delsey."

"Delsey. Have you met her?"

"No," said Lydia. "But I meant to ask you. You said Alistair sent you flowers, with a note that sounded like he thought something was fishy about DeAnne's accident? What did it say?"

Raymond Ropes swiveled. "It's still on our fridge. I can tell you every word." Folding his arms. "'To the parents of DeAnne–a lovely, vibrant girl. Snatched from her life too soon by a ruthless unseen hand. With deep regret and sympathy. Alistair Pope.' Funny way to put it, but no question what he meant."

Damn! Not the clue she'd hoped for. In Lydia's opinion, there was plenty of question what Alistair meant. In fact, written from one Catholic to another, it sounded more like a dig at God than a hint at murder.

"Aha. Well. Good to see you–"

"That's not the only thing." Raymond Ropes wasn't ready to let go so fast. "When his assistant called, that Delsey? She had some questions he gave her. Remember, Cyn?"

"About the police. Yes. I was the one who talked to her," she told Lydia. "She said Alistair wanted to know what they covered with us. And, did we have a record of the interview?"

"A transcript," Raymond amplified.

"Or a tape," said Cynthia. "I guess they have to make one, by law."

"Do you?" asked Lydia.

"Oh, no. I never heard of the police giving a tape to the suspects!"

"Subjects, Cynthia. Not suspects."

"What exactly did Delsey, or Alistair, want to know?" Lydia pursued.

"Of course. Oh, goodness. Let me think."

"How they found her, that's what he was most interested in," put in Raymond. "Our poor little girl."

Lydia reviewed the chronology. Caroline, Carlo, and the film crew leave for the Whistling Pig–everyone but DeAnne. And Alistair, who waits for her to finish tidying, but finally goes without her. Helen Wills stops by to see if they're still shooting, discovers DeAnne's body, and calls Kevin Kelly as the local beat cop. He starts the same process he'll later follow with Alistair: checks her vital signs, reports to HQ and secures the scene. Whoever assigns detectives–one from the state troopers, one from the Exmouth police force–taps Helen Wills, probably because she's there.

"Did Detective Wills stay at the studio after she found DeAnne?" Lydia asked.

Raymond Ropes was rubbing his hands, cracking his knuckles. "I believe so. We didn't learn about . . . the news, or anything, until quite a while after."

"She must have stayed," said his wife. "Remember? She said she tried CPR, but death was instantaneous. Bang, right on her head. She didn't suffer. Thank God for that."

Every response Lydia could think of sounded equally trite, so she said nothing. The line crept forward. How bizarre was it to be standing here at Alistair's wake talking about DeAnne's death? Not so bizarre, really. What was bizarre was that one and then two members of this ordinary community had died suddenly, violently, and now hundreds of other ordinary people had come out on a fine Spring evening to honor the inscrutable irony of life and death.

"They were very thorough, both of them, I'll say that," testified Raymond Ropes.

"That's what Delsey wanted to know," said Cynthia. "What questions they asked us. We said, You name it! Did DeAnne like working there? Sure. She was an easy-going girl. Was it part of her job to go up ladders? Not usually. Mostly typing and filing. Did she always dress up for work? No, that was for the movie. Alistair Pope told her he couldn't promise anything, but he wanted to get some–what do they call it?"

"Film," said Raymond.

"Footage," said Lydia at the same time.

"Right. Just in case. And then, Did DeAnne have a boyfriend? Now, that I thought was kind of pushy, but I guess he knew it was part of their procedure. That's what the detective said. They have to check possible motives, in case any suspicion comes up of foul play."

"Did DeAnne have a boyfriend?"

Cynthia glanced up at her husband.

"No," stated Raymond. "She wouldn't have hidden it from us. She told us everything."

"There might have been someone she was interested in," Cynthia compromised. "Who she'd just met, and liked, but she didn't know if anything would come of it."

DeAnne's father folded his arms again. "She was excited about the movie, that's all."

Well well! thought Lydia. So DeAnne was sneaking around with some new guy she didn't want her parents prying into. Who? A crewman? Alistair himself? Somebody on the film, or why would his assistant ask if the cops were investigating her love life?

Next question: Why *were* the cops investigating her love life? What did they find at the scene, or later, that pointed to a romance?

"If she did have a boyfriend," said Cynthia, "he'd have come forward. Called us, or the police, or introduced himself at her funeral."

Or been yanked out of hiding by the detectives, thought Lydia. Given how fast they closed the case, whatever they turned up on him must not have implicated him in her death.

Unless . . .

Helen Wills was an old friend of Alistair's. If he were DeAnne's mystery man, might she have cut him a break?

No, that didn't compute. Even if she'd do him such a huge

favor, and could slip it past her partner, Alistair wouldn't have had to ask Delsey to call the Ropeses to find out if he was off the hook.

"Did any suspicion come up of foul play?" Lydia asked. "You said the detectives were thorough. How hard did they look into that?"

Raymond said, "They didn't have to look very hard to rule it out. Did DeAnne have any enemies? Of course not. Anybody who'd want to hurt her? Give me a break! She was twenty-two years old, living at home, for god's sake! Never in any kind of trouble–no drugs, sex, booze, wild friends, never harmed anybody in her whole life. Now, that's not to say it was just an accident–"

Lydia could feel him gathering momentum for another blast at Carlo and Caroline. Since they were standing ten yards away, she hurried to stop him.

His wife was quicker. "She asked about that. Delsey? Alistair wondered if they suspected foul play. He knew nobody had any reason to hurt DeAnne, but–well, like you, Lydia. I guess he thought they shouldn't cross it off the list without making sure."

"What did you tell her?"

"Well, just what Raymond said. They looked into it and ruled it out."

Shivers ran up Lydia's spine. Alistair wanted to know if the police suspected DeAnne was murdered. Why not ask Helen Wills? Why go behind her back and have his assistant check with the victim's parents? Old friends or not, evidently Alistair had shared Edgar Rowdey's view that none but her nearest and dearest could call Mrs. Wills a forthcoming woman.

"Oh, look," said Cynthia. "We're finally moving."

"I've got to go," said Lydia.

She found a spot on the patio where her phone worked. Dave Wheeler still had his answering machine on. Again she left an urgent message for him to call her. It wasn't just the receiving line that was finally moving.

Edgar, Carlo, and Caroline had almost reached the french doors. Carlo was describing a baseball game. Edgar turned to

Lydia: "Any luck?"

She shook her head. "What if he doesn't call me back? Do we keep going on our own?"

He raised his eyebrows and sighed.

"One piece of good news," Caroline told her. "It's a closed casket."

They resumed their baseball discussion. Lydia retreated into her own turbulent thoughts. At the next pause, she posed a general question.

"Did Alistair ever say anything to any of you about DeAnne Ropes's death? Like, if he had doubts about the police investigation, or was it definitely an accident?"

"Not to me," said Carlo.

"Nor me," said Caroline.

"Hm," said Edgar.

They waited.

"Not per se. He did seem . . . well, bothered."

"Bothered?" said Caroline.

"When we were counting frogs. Of course we were all bothered, you not least, dear. Alistair as you know took everything personally, but losing someone on his film set– He sounded almost angry. As if he were the target. I assumed he must be afraid of a lawsuit. Self-absorbed soul that he was."

"And now?" asked Carlo.

"In light of subsequent events, perhaps he suspected something was amiss."

The line moved forward three more feet. Carlo nudged Caroline. "There's Delsey," he pointed at the french doors. "And that young man who brought you the bagel."

Lydia glanced over to see what Delsey looked like. Thinner and trendier than she'd pictured: black leggings and mini-dress, minimalist make-up, skeptically narrowed eyes. Not Alistair's type, she'd have thought, except that his type kept expanding the more she learned about him.

Edgar murmured a question. Lydia tuned back in. What made her ask if Alistair had been concerned about DeAnne's death?

She summarized her chat with the Ropeses. "It's funny you

saying he was bothered by it. I practically begged him to tell me anything at all about her, and he wouldn't. Even when I said she was a friend. Like he didn't care, or he didn't want to be sucked back into it."

"Perhaps he didn't," Edgar surmised, "once whatever bothered him was resolved."

They were past the doors now, approaching the front of the line. Lydia didn't see Dinah or Leo. Carlo and Caroline were silent, girding for the imminent exchange of pleasantries and condolences. *There will be time,* thought Lydia. How does that go? *To prepare a face to meet the faces that you meet.*

Between the backs of the hand-shakers ahead of them, faces were appearing that in one feature or another resembled Alistair.

There will be time to murder and create.

"Edgar, do you think he might have had an idea who killed her?"

But Edgar had stopped listening. His eyes were fixed on the Pope family, and his expression–a mixture of alarm and dread–suggested he wished himself anywhere but here. When he spoke, it was pure reflex:

"Oh, who knows?"

Ten more minutes. Or the end of this beer.

Wally Hicks checked his watch again. He was nearly through his second beer and his fourth time extension. All that remained of his three pizza slices were stiff chunks of crust on an oil-stained paper plate. You had to keep ordering every once in a while if you wanted to keep the table. By now he was about ready to let it go. Face it, Hicks: this may not be your big night after all.

That old Clash song had been yammering in his head for half an hour: *Should I stay or should I go?* He'd tried to switch to a less agitated tune, like for instance Tom Petty's *The waiting is the hardest part*, but his brain just flipped right back. It knew what he was thinking: *If I go there will be trouble; If I stay it will be double.*

When he'd told Roosevelt Sherman he might stop by the

wake, that wasn't any kind of promise to complete the mission. What about Sue? Hadn't he brought her denim jacket to give back? Didn't he plan to catch up with her out here?–before the question even arose whether to go inside the funeral home?

But then why take a shower and put on his best clothes?

Respect for the occasion. Ha! Celebrate, is more like it. Dance on the bastard's grave. Rub every Pope's nose in the dirt that soon, appropriately, would cover him.

Always tease, tease, tease! That was Al to the life–or Alistair, as he'd rechristened himself once he got semi-famous. He'd made sure the first time he spotted Wally at work to tell Ken Boose how happy Rosemary was. Like saying it loud enough could make it true. While he gazed right past Wally like he'd never seen him before. Ha! Rosie the rebel, happy? Hammered like a square peg into the round hole your damned family dug for her? Husband, house, kids, station wagon. Christmas with his folks, Easter with hers. Happy? Give me a fucking break! Rosemary Pope had grander dreams: Macchu Pichu. Serengeti. Taj Mahal. Christmas snorkeling on the Great Barrier Reef, Easter skiing in the Grand Tetons. And not in any damn station wagon, either. Their magic carpet would be an Airstream Argosy 22, which they joyfully agreed was the finest vehicle on earth.

When he finally acquired one, Wallace Hicks set out alone on the adventures they'd spent a year planning together. He never called or wrote to her. Never made any attempt to win her back. Karma had brought them together, the prodigal son and his mother's home health aide. Somehow, karma would reunite them.

And now here she was, just a hundred yards away. If he had X-ray vision he could look through that wall and see her. Which he was damn glad he didn't, since she'd be smothered by her family, the conspirators who'd strong-armed her out of love into marriage. Two kids, Alistair had smirked: a boy and a girl. Teenagers by now. Ha! Old enough to go to your wake, asshole.

When he'd left Cape Cod Wally meant his departure to be permanent. This place was dead for him. Worse than dead–zombieland. Just thinking about it unleashed dark inner forces that rattled him to the core. In his own eyes and the world's, Wallace Hicks was a good man: upright, generous, mild-mannered, patient, kind to strangers and animals. Put him near a Pope, though, and what might happen?

When you recognized a streak like that in yourself, best to avoid temptation. Wally hadn't meant to cross the bridge. Only there he was, taking the scenic route from Providence to Boston, and really, after eighteen years, what harm could there be in dropping by his old haunts? Say hi to Ken Boose, grab a bite at Leo's, and back on the road.

He was shocked to see how harshly age and running a bookstore had changed Ken. Out of pity, Wally offered to lend a hand. Just for the afternoon.

He still didn't try to see Rosemary. He avoided places they'd gone together. The one time he drove around Forestdale, not exactly looking for her house, he was relieved not to find it. He concentrated on his own life: Inventory. Gromit. Webcams. Pirandello. Only when her brother came in every few weeks, pretending to look for a book, did Wally's insides churn. Try Borders, he advised. But Alistair Pope could no more pass up a chance to make trouble than Gromit could ignore a Frisbee.

A man who looks for trouble is bound to find it.

And so karma had restored harmony to one small corner of the universe.

To rejoice openly, Wally understood, would violate that harmony. So would faking sympathy with the bereaved. Hence the pizza parlor.

On the other hand, he was beginning to feel like an idiot sitting here waiting, slice after slice, beer after beer, to see what came next on the karmic agenda.

Should I stay or should I go now?

Should I stay or should I go now?

Ten more minutes, he decided, and one last beer.

Running the Pope gauntlet wasn't as bad as Lydia expected. There were so many of them that you couldn't tell the players without a program, as Carlo quipped, and nobody expected you to.

Shake a hand, say a few words of sympathy, move on to the next vacant slot, and before you knew it you were through.

"Pizza!" said Edgar immediately.

Caroline and Carlo, though, were blocking their path, chatting with five black-clad New Yorkers.

There was Delsey. Top on my list, thought Lydia.

"Is that your phone?" said Edgar.

Next to top.

On the patio Lydia breathlessly thanked Dave Wheeler for calling back. He'd been asleep, he explained. In case she hadn't noticed, he'd been working the early shift–

"Well, wake up. This is important."

She explained about Charlene and Lux Limos. Dave was grudgingly, yawningly impressed, not just with her news but also with her Rube Goldberg plan to inform Pete Altman. Yes, he understood his role. He'd call Pete right now.

"Let me know what he says, OK?"

"Tomorrow."

"Tonight! Come on, Dave. I work the early shift, too. Plus I just shook hands with Alistair Pope's entire extended family. Pleeease?"

Another yawn. She wondered what (if anything) he was wearing. "I'll see what I can do."

Back inside, Edgar had been shanghaied into Carlo and Caroline's conversation with Delsey and company. He looked as spooked as when they'd reached the front of the line. Although Caroline introduced Lydia to the five New Yorkers, Delsey barely glanced at her. She'd fastened onto Edgar like a tick and wasn't about to be plucked off.

"The last one to see him alive! My god. That's so heartbreaking. What did you talk about?"

"Frogs." Edgar was scanning the room, probably for an exit. "Women. Life and its complications."

"I hope he didn't think those two things go together. Women and complications." Pause. "Did he?"

"Oh, who knows?"

"Well, you must know! It was your conversation." Delsey

appeared to be groping for a balance between charm and archness. "Any particular women? Or all women?"

"I haven't the foggiest notion."

"I've been just so knocked over by the women in your books. I mean, how you do so much with so little." Her smile was pure flattery. "I'm not surprised you were the friend Alistair brought his problems to."

Lydia choked back a guffaw. Caroline's nostrils flared. Carlo inspected his sleeve.

"If he just hadn't waited till too late! You know?"

"Do you think it was a woman who killed him?" Caroline arched an eyebrow at Delsey.

"Oh, god! I don't– What he said. I haven't the foggiest. But all those questions from the cops, who could help but wonder?"

"Do the police think it was a woman?" Carlo contributed.

"Don't ask me!" said Delsey. "I'm sorry if I'm not making sense. I'm totally fried, is the problem. Jet lag, insomnia–"

"She's been here two days," explained the young man standing next to Lydia. "The cops made her come early so they could grill her."

"Luckily I bought your hamster book," Delsey told Edgar. "It's very grounding. I mean that as a compliment."

Lydia shoved in her oar. "I have a question. DeAnne Ropes's parents mentioned you called them? About the film? With questions from Alistair?"

"Oh, god. That was awful. Such sad people! Not their fault; but still."

She turned back to Edgar. Lydia persisted: "Did you know DeAnne? Were you here for the shoot?"

"No and no," said Delsey. "Alistair had this idea it would comfort them that he'd put her in the film. And then while we were talking, he called back. Wanting me to ask–oh, I don't remember. I've got the wife on one line and him on the other–I finally just hung up and told her the phone went dead. Alistair and his ideas! Well, as you know, Mr. Rowdey, better than anybody."

"Who asked you to come here early?" Caroline intervened. "Helen Wills?"

Delsey nodded. "Detective Wills. God, she's exhausting!"

The young man nudged the woman beside him: This is where we came in. Aloud he said, "Nicotine break." They headed toward the french doors, followed by their two other colleagues.

"So many questions!" Delsey steered the rest of their circle back to her fifteen minutes of fame. "Made my job interview look like a walk in the park. And you know Zelda, Ms. Gitmo we call her. I mean I'm totally glad to help. Anything. If it'll help catch Alistair's murderer to ask me where his cell phone went and why no messages on his machine, I'm there. And now of course I've got Zelda breathing down my neck, like drop everything and go pick her up at that little airport, un fucking believable traffic I'm here to tell you, and she's all, Why can't we drive straight to Alistair's and grab his computer and disks and so forth, *and* his cell phone and answering machine? Goddammit, we own that film and everything related to it! Proprietary information! Whew!" Her hands flicked as if to shoo away the conflict.

"What did you tell the cops?" Lydia asked. "Where his cell phone went, and why no messages on his machine?"

"God only knows." Delsey made an expressive face. "I said we'd offered a zillion times to get him an iPhone. Even an answering service. He was always losing calls. Or said he did. Considering it was usually about some deadline he missed, or some woman he didn't want to talk to, I had my doubts. 'Oh, sorry, didn't get your message!' Yeah. Right, Alistair. Whatever."

She paused for breath. "Hey," came a voice behind Edgar and Lydia. "There you all are."

It was Dinah, too massive in her white T-shirt and black pants to miss for long.

"Where've you been?" Caroline inquired. "We lost sight of you."

"Oh, well." Dinah heaved a sigh. "They got the casket in that little room next door, you know? Sealed, but still. Terri and Rosemary wanted company, go sit with him for a bit."

Delsey swiveled. "Alistair? Is here?"

"Well, sure." Dinah stepped into the circle. "Can't skip his own wake."

Caroline asked how Dinah thought the family was doing. Delsey hovered, torn between the casket and her semi-captive audience. Edgar murmured to Lydia that he'd just spotted Leo and would meet them all at the pizza parlor.

Lydia tossed a verbal lasso at Delsey. "You were saying. About Alistair's answering machine? Your boss wants it?"

"Oh, god." Delsey's eyes narrowed. "I had to drive her over there so she could look in the windows. I mean, stiletto heels, both of us, tiptoeing across the lawn. Holding back the bushes to make sure there was nothing left in his office. Really, aside from being ridiculous, it was so sad. Heartbreaking. That huge desk of his, empty. Just a stapler, some paper clips, and his answering machine sitting there like a little black bug."

"Huh," said Dinah with interest. "What kind's he got?"

"Don't ask me! It's teeny," Delsey held her hands a hand's length apart, "shaped like a beetle. I mean it must be twenty years old."

"Oh, no more'n ten," said Dinah. "I got one of those. On sale at Job Lot. Al must've got his the same time. I keep a bunch of 'em around, for my business. Good little gadget. Still works like a charm."

Delsey was glancing again at the door leading to Alistair's casket.

"Shall we?" Carlo asked Caroline.

They made their farewells and departed. Lydia confirmed she'd meet them across the street.

"You know what I like about it," said Dinah.

"Great to meet you." Delsey touched Lydia's arm, then Dinah's, and flew away.

"You can get back your old messages."

Lydia, who had been wondering whether to pursue Delsey or call Dave Wheeler again, swung back to Dinah. "What?"

"Yup. These new fancy ones, push the wrong button and you're screwed. Bye-bye! Erased! This old thing of mine–well, in the first place it's only got two buttons. But if you do hit the wrong one, or the power goes out?–all you do is unplug it and then plug it back in. Presto! There's your whole last batch of messages."

"Unplug it and plug it back in," Lydia repeated incredulously, "and your lost messages come back?"

"Yup. Damn handy's what I say. I could tell you stories . . . but not here." She glanced around as if Alistair or his family might be listening. "Something else I wanted to say, though."

"Can it wait?" Lydia interrupted. "Dinah, I just– I'm sorry, but there's an urgent errand I need to do right now."

Chapter Thirty-Three

The thing must be winding down. More people getting in cars than out of them. And here came those two old codgers, Leo (in a suit for god's sake!) and his pal Edgar Rowdey, walking into Rosa's Pizza and Mexican.

They greeted Wally without inviting him to join them. Staked out the big round table by the window. Rendezvous spot for the Back End crowd? For now, the two of them sat alone, tete a tete, chatting in the hushed voices you'd expect from a pair of old men who'd just been smacked upside the head by mortality.

No more shilly-shallying, Hicks. Time to step up to the plate.

Are you on the bus or off the bus?

After three (or was it four?) beers, he had to concentrate to remember what bus had brought him here, to a formica table in Hyannis, clean and shaved, in his black jeans and embroidered cowboy shirt, hair in a braid down his back instead of its usual ponytail.

The wake. Sue.

Rosemary. Fuck.

There is a–what?–in the affairs of men which if you grab it, carries you on to greatness. Not a bus. A ride? A time?

With the support of his table (after such generous patronage, didn't he have the right?), Wally stood up. OK! Ready!

Now, Hicks, are you going in there or not?

A serious-looking man helped him postpone the decision by coming through the door. Familiar-looking, except for the suit. Charcoal pin-stripes. White shirt, dark blue patterned tie. Military-short brown hair, medium height, stocky build, and a square-cut face like a chain-saw sculpture. A cop?

"Hey." The newcomer held out his hand. "Wally, is it? From

the bookstore?"

His grip could have cracked walnuts. "Captain Wills. How's it going?"

"Chill!" chortled Leo, pushing back his chair. "Finally got too hot for ya down there, eh?"

Greetings were exchanged all around. Yes, Florida sure was hot as heck. Not like Cape Cod. Top-notch conference, though. All kinds of new law-enforcement technology. James Bond stuff–don't hold your breath out here in the boonies. Side trip to Disney World with nephews. Two weeks, yes, too long to be away. Shocking news about Al Pope. Terrible thing for his family. No, hadn't seen them yet. Company for supper–a barbecue, the Shermans, planned by Helen before the tragedy. She'd be here shortly. Couldn't walk out on her guests, even for such old friends as the Popes.

"That's one busy lady, your wife," said Leo. "A human dynamo."

"You're telling me," said Chill Wills. "I'm lucky she could fit me in. Well, better go pay my respects."

Although in a corner of his brain Wally recognized an opportunity to enter the wake in good standing, no amount of logic could prevail over his deep mistrust of cops. He sat down again.

"He's looking too tan and fit to be healthy," said Leo.

"Not for long," said Edgar Rowdey.

"You think it's the suit?" He raised his arms. "Do I look like that?"

If Edgar replied, Wally didn't hear him. His slightly glazed eyes rested on the denim jacket draped on the opposite chair. What kind of cop was Chill Wills? If someone showed him a key piece of evidence in his wife's current case, would he jump on it? Or take the standard lazy-ass route, say this wasn't his jurisdiction and toss it to Kevin Kelly?

Too late now. There he went, loping across the street.

Wally took the note out of the jacket, laid a napkin on a semi-clean section of table and flattened the note on top of it. *You dick-brain Casanova piece of shit!* The pencil was so smeared it looked like *duk-hain*. No way of knowing how long ago Sue put it there, where she got it, or anything, really. Why should it be connected with Alistair Pope? Anybody might have written it to anybody. She might have found it on the Back End floor six months ago, or in a stack of books last week.

Could Rosey Sherman have written it?

Not a side of him Wally had ever seen; but then Wally never watched football.

For sure he'd flatten any man who went after Thea. Not by writing to him, though.

Could someone have written it *to* Rosey?

Just suppose, for the sake of argument, Sue had an ex-lover in Quansett. Suppose he kept haunting the Back End in hopes of rekindling their romance. Over she hops to the Frigate, to join the famous football star. Couldn't a jilted man jump to the wrong conclusion?

Except you'd only have to cross the street to see it was Wally she'd hitched up with; and anyhow, what suicidal nutball would threaten Roosevelt Sherman?

Wally folded up the note in the napkin, for preservation, and put it in his jeans pocket.

Now that he thought of it, where the heck was Sue? No matter how over Alistair she was, you'd think sheer curiosity would bring her here. Aside from respect for the dead and/or morbid interest, it wasn't like her to miss a major public event.

Unless something–or somebody–stopped her.

He twisted unsteadily around toward Leo. "Hey, did you happen to see Sue in there?"

"Sue? No sirree. Did you, Edgar? Funny, now you mention it. Not like her to miss a chance to show off." Leo's bristly white eyebrows wiggled. "Must've took off again. Huh! That was quick. With us she always lasted a couple months. Not that she ever quit griping–"

"What about Lydia?" Wally interrupted. "Was she at the wake?"

"Lydia? Sure," said Leo.

"I would like to have a word with her."

"She should be here any minute," said Edgar.

How could Lydia disappear so fast? Dinah stood in the foyer with her chest heaving and a frown on her face. She'd gone after her as quick as she could–delayed by Al's aunt and uncle Pat coming in the front door, both reeking of cigarette smoke, and then Maria's boy Albert who informed her he was changing his name to Alistair. Sweet. You didn't want to rush that kind of thing. Well, or any of these poor folks. That was the whole point of a wake, for heaven's sake! Anyway, Carlo had told her Lydia would be joining them across the street.

Here among her lifelong neighbors, Dinah had a struggle believing she even needed to warn Lydia to lay low. Now more than ever, she didn't want to think about why someone she knew had fired those shots in the woods. Her two jobs lifted the lid on enough of the human cesspool. Not tonight, dammit! She'd suspected she might feel this way, though, and she'd promised herself to ignore it.

Lydia's urgent errand (Dinah figured) most likely involved a phone call or a female problem. Anything beyond that, she'd need a car. So, one more circuit around the funeral home, say good-by to the Popes, then head for Rosa's.

Directly above where Dinah stood, Lydia leaned on a polished mahogany banister and listened to Mudge's phone ring. An hour ago she'd have shrunk from sneaking up the stairs in a building dedicated to dead bodies. Now her sole concern was privacy, quiet, and cell reception.

Three rings . . . four . . .

"Hey."

"Mudge, thank goodness! It's Lydia."

"Yeah, I know. What's up?"

She could tell from the cacophony behind him that he was in a bar. "Can you come get me at the wake? I just had a breakthrough on the murder case. I need to go do something, right now, before the cops or somebody else figure it out."

Pause. Sigh. "Fifteen minutes?"

They agreed to meet around the corner, so nobody would recognize his truck. Mudge couldn't resist asking why it would be a problem if the cops figured out the murder case. Lydia told him she'd explain on the way.

Now if she could just get off so easy with Edgar, Caroline, and Carlo.

Unfortunately they weren't Rosa's only customers. Leo was here, holding court at the big table, surrounded by Back End regulars. And at a nearby deuce, that hippie clerk from the Frigate.

When he saw her, he rose. Gorgeous cowboy shirt, she noted absently. Looks like the real McCoy. Hope he doesn't have a six-shooter to go with it.

"Lydia Vivaldi!"

She froze.

Glaring straight at her, Wally Hicks reached for his holster.

Not a single useful idea occurred to Lydia. Run? Where? Hide? Behind what? Scream? What's the point?

His hand came up. "Is this yours?" he demanded.

Not a gun, but a balled-up paper napkin. With both hands he unfolded it and thrust it at her.

You dick-brain Casanova piece of shit!

That was as far as Lydia read. "Is this some kind of a sick joke?"

"I'm asking you," Wally returned fiercely, "if you've seen it before."

"No!" said Lydia. "Excuse me."

Trembling with aftershock, she edged around the table to Edgar. "I can't stay. I'm sorry."

His eyebrows went up. "Not on his account, I hope!"

She shook her head. "I've got a ride." She'd intended to tell him more, maybe even ask his advice, but she could feel Wally's eyes on her. "Breakthrough on the Rube Goldberg front. Can I call you when I get home?"

Edgar was watching Wally. "Oh, by all means."

Lydia was spared from further explanation by a buzzing in her purse. She bolted for the door.

"Dave! Hi."

"Are you OK? You sound–"

"Yeah. I do, and I am. Did you talk to Pete Altman?"

From Dave's wide-awake voice, she'd already guessed the

answer. Yes, the two of them had a short but productive meeting. Altman naturally had his doubts at first about some anonymous tipster discovering the clue he'd been waiting for, and naturally he twisted Dave's arm to name his source. But this was a dance they'd done before. In the end, Pete was phone-launching his henchmen toward Wareham while he and Dave finished their beers.

On the not-so-good-news side, Detective Altman had announced a discovery of his own.

"Do you know about a snake on Edgar Rowdey's property that's made of rocks?"

"Wow," said Lydia. "We were just talking about it an hour ago."

"Wow is right," said Dave. "That must be right after the cops found the murder weapon hidden in it."

Pete Altman wouldn't reveal what had prompted them to search Edgar Rowdey's side yard. What they found, at the downhill end of the snake, was a blood-stained fist-sized rock. Yes, the same type of rock as the ones bordering Leo's frog pond and Mudge's campfire. Yes, the same type of blood as Alistair Pope's.

Lydia's stomach felt as though she'd swallowed a rock. "Were there fingerprints?"

"What I told you is all I can say."

"Oh." Reminding herself to breathe. "Nothing about, like, how it got there?"

"Sorry." He sounded like he meant it. "Lydia, you know, if I could tell Pete you were the one who tracked down Lux Limos–"

"But you can't." The brightly lit heads in the restaurant window talked and moved, noiselessly, like a TV with the sound off. "Did he say if they're planning to arrest Edgar, or me, or whoever?"

"No, he didn't."

"OK. Well, I have to go now."

"Where? Lydia, you're not– Do you want me to come over there?"

"No. I'm meeting somebody."

Her thumb on a button erased him. Should she turn off her phone? Could the cops around here track you by your signal? Ha!

Good luck to them, in this land of half-assed reception.

Before her rendezvous with Mudge, she went back into Rosa's Pizza and Mexican. Wally Hicks had apparently left. The big round table was almost full. She asked Edgar to step outside for a second.

Dave's news clearly troubled him. Lydia couldn't remember ever seeing his normally unruffled expression look so ruffled.

"Who knows about the snake?" she asked him. "You, me, Caroline and Carlo, Leo–"

"J.D., my gardener. Alistair of course. My niece, Mirella, but she's in Bhutan."

"So, potentially anybody Alistair wanted to impress with his Norse mythology. Damn! That could be half the Cape."

"Well, and visitors. His New York crew–"

"And first and foremost, whatever women he was seeing. Right?"

"I fear so." Edgar pushed up his glasses. "Unless they find fingerprints, it's a large field."

"With you and me, especially me, way out in front. Pete Altman! Dammit, he was supposed to get me out of this, not deeper in."

"Perhaps he will," said Edgar.

"I'm not holding my breath," said Lydia.

Dinah was beginning to think she'd never get out of this room. The Popes must be counting the minutes until 9 PM, with enough well-wishers still lined up to give the whole family carpal tunnel syndrome. She hadn't followed the media coverage, but it looked like every tourist from Sandwich to Orleans had picked Alistair Pope's wake as the hot event for Saturday, June 10. Jesus, you'd think they were offering free booze.

And here came Chill Wills.

Dinah didn't know Chill as well as Helen–he'd never been much of a socializer, which might account for his nickname. Still, in a big crowd, you look for familiar faces. He spotted her right off and hurried over. Cold hands, she thought as they shook; maybe that's it. Flexing her fingers, she asked if he really expected any-body to believe he'd spent two weeks in Florida just for a cop con-ference. With a tan like that? He said she was the only one so far who'd guessed his secret. Dinah hoped he didn't know how true that was.

Had he been back long? Since this morning. Flew into Boston yesterday, spent the night at his cousin's. And already he'd ditched Helen? Not a chance. She was on her way. She'd sent him out ahead, like the dove from the Ark, so as not to rush their guests. Did Dinah know Roosevelt Sherman?

Ten minutes into that absorbing discussion, Dinah remem-bered she had a chore to do.

She couldn't run, but she walked fast. The smokers out front had gone back inside. The day's warmth was fading along with the light. She peered across the street at Rosa's window. That looked like Leo's bristly silhouette, and Caroline's smooth platinum waves. Hard to identify faces from here.

Turning to make sure she wasn't stepping in front of a car, Dinah got a clear view of Lydia, unmistakable even in a side street half a block away, climbing into Mudge's pickup truck.

Whoever wanted to use the men's room at Rosa's Pizza and Mexican had the good sense to stop banging on the door when Wally resumed puking.

There was something time-transcendant about kneeling with your head over a commode. A deja-vu kind of thing. Strewn along life's path, like park benches, small oases of alcohol-induced clar-ity. Well, maybe not clarity. What Wally distinctly remembered was having passed this way before, and thinking each time that *this* time was one he'd never forget.

That was a comforting thought. Maybe in ten or twenty years he'd forget this one, too.

His back hurt like a sonofabitch. As for his legs, well, maybe he could drive home or maybe he'd have to hitch. His stomach was finally quieting down, anyhow. So it should, being as empty as the Airstream's liquor cabinet.

You'd think ralphing up four (or was it five?) beers would make you sober. Never did, though. Not that Wally had done this enough to generalize. The last time (memories flooding back now) was the night Rosemary told him she didn't want to see him anymore.

That was only two beers.

Clarity: The real reason he hadn't gone into the funeral home was he didn't want to see her. His decision, not hers. She must know he was back on the Cape. Alistair would have told her, if the grapevine didn't. Any day in the past six months she could have stopped in the Frigate. Fine. Now let her stew in her own juice. Let her recall, branded on her turncoat heart, the last words he ever spoke to her: *Be careful what you wish for.*

Gripping the edge of the sink, Wally pulled himself upright. Ow, ow, ow! His face in the mirror startled him: not raddled as he felt. Normal. A face you'd be OK showing to somebody you hadn't seen in eighteen years.

He splashed water on it just in case. Why should he go over there? He was free to go home. Tell the Back End table he'd come down with some kind of stomach bug. Yes! Felt a little queasy when he arrived and figured he'd better wait and see, so as not to pass on any germs to the bereaved.

No. He had never lied to her, and damned if he'd start now. Not even through the grapevine.

He dried his face and hands. Enough shilly-shallying, Hicks. Are you on the bus or off the bus?

He opened the door.

Clarity shattered. The cosmic remote control changed the channel. There she stood, as if she'd been waiting for him. Hair like an osprey's nest, scrapes and smudges all over her face, a gauze pad taped above her right eyebrow, her left arm in a plaster cast and a sling, and her dirty denim jacket on her shoulder.

"Shit!" said Lydia.

"What?" said Mudge, flipping his turn signal.

"Do you know what a peach tree looks like?"

"Nope."

"We have to find a nursery then. Is there one on the way?"

He snorted as if stifling a snicker. "No. Why?"

"That's where Alistair's key is. On a nail halfway up his peach tree."

"O-o-oh. The key. No problem."

They made their turn. Lydia had no idea where they were. From the funeral home Mudge had followed a series of small and medium-sized roads, past farms and developments, over brooks and a highway, alongside woods, fields, ponds, and stone fences. They'd rarely passed another vehicle. That's good, she thought. If this goes wrong, we can't be traced.

"You've broken in here before? Why didn't you tell me?"

"Not broken in." He turned right onto yet another one-lane road. "He was always trying to impress Edgar, you know? After the Rowdeyberry Tarte, he wanted me to help him create some dish at Leo's like that. To put his name up on the menu. I came over one time, before I realized. He showed me around, including the key."

"Pope tarts!" said Lydia. "How could you resist?"

"I know. Popecorn. And my favorite, Alisteriyaki."

And here they were at Alistair's pre-Civil War house. No Mercedes parked on the bare patch of grass that had served him as a driveway. No yellow crime-scene tape or Keep Out signs. Hardly even illegal, then.

Still, Lydia wished the sky didn't stay light so late this time of year.

She also wished Alistair had favored a nestled-in-the-woods approach to landscaping instead of wide empty swathes of lawn dotted with an occasional tree. This wasn't a house you could sneak up on. She'd concluded (and Mudge agreed) the best strategy was semi-openness. Not for the truck–that distinctive vehicle they would park up the street. Together they would walk up the stone path to the front door, like salespeople. This unused entrance was the one spot on his property where Alistair had let tall, thick bushes grow–thick enough, Lydia hoped, to hide them while they slipped around the side to the peach tree. Once they secured the key, and Lydia let herself in, Mudge would return to the front door and walk away. He'd try to find a lookout post with cell reception, since that was their only warning system.

In theory, they shouldn't be interrupted. The Back End crowd was at Rosa's; the Pope family would be greeting well-wishers (including their neighbors, right?) for another hour before moving on to dinner. As for police, Helen Wills had her husband to welcome back; Pete Altman surely would need a lab report and a court order before he could start rounding up suspects. That left the local beat cop, who had plenty of other streets to patrol besides this one.

Five minutes from truck to front door. Ten minutes from door to tree to key. Fifteen minutes to find the answering machine, plug it in, and play the messages. Five more to leave, and another five for a safety margin. They'd be out of here in forty minutes.

Mudge thought she should just grab the machine and go. Lydia preferred her Rube Goldberg plan: play the messages aloud, holding her cell phone over the speaker, with Mudge on the other end. That way she could take notes, he'd have a recording on his phone, and they could leave the evidence here for the cops.

Mudge pulled the truck under the droopiest maple tree on the block. He shot Lydia a grin. "Synchronize watches?"

"You know, that's not a bad idea."

She moved her hand out of his sight so he wouldn't see it trembling. Of all her adventures in the past month, this was the first one that truly frightened her. Those phone messages hadn't erased themselves, and she doubted Alistair had erased them, either. OK, sure; if X knew Dinah's retrieval trick, that machine wouldn't still be here. But what if X was watching the house? How would the person who'd already killed Alistair, and probably DeAnne, plus shot at her and Dinah in the woods, react when she unlocked Alistair's door?

Stop it! she ordered herself. Start down the paranoia path and you'll scare yourself into the waiting handcuffs of Altman, Wills, and company.

Who might show up here at any moment.

She looked at Mudge: that strong, generous, cheerful face. "Ready?"

"Ready."

"Let's go."

They straightened their clothes and hair and stood tall. Encyclopedia Britannica, thought Lydia. Avon Cosmetics. Can I interest you in a vacuum cleaner?

While Mudge pretended to ring the bell, she surreptitiously scanned the neighborhood. "All clear."

To get behind the bushes they had to jump off the front steps. So much for looking like salespeople. Even hugging the wall, there wasn't as much cover as she'd hoped. Around the corner, Mudge beelined for the peach tree–a stone's throw from the house, on the other end from the summer kitchen–while Lydia proceeded toward their target. They were both trying so hard to be inconspicuous that she couldn't tell if he'd found the key or not, until he stood beside her, sliding it into the lock.

"OK! Good luck." He squeezed her elbow.

Lydia slipped through the door.

Edgar Rowdey couldn't help wondering what ill-natured fairy had propelled Sue to Rosa's Pizza and Mexican, of all places, on the night of Alistair Pope's wake, no less, for her big comeback.

Mercifully she hadn't started a fight with Leo in front of his friends, or (worse) pulled up a chair. She'd slung a dizzier-than-usual glance around the restaurant, nodded at her former colleagues and customers, and strolled unsteadily to the counter. Apparently what she wanted was the restroom. Instead of going in, however, she leaned in the doorway.

"Looks like something the cat dragged in," Leo stage-whispered.

Edgar, picturing the half-mice his cats liked to leave on his doormat, shook his head.

Caroline arched an inquiring eyebrow at Carlo.

"Oh, no. Not yet," he answered.

What Sue looked like to Edgar was someone who'd been mugged. There were scrapes on her dirty face and arms, gauze patches on her forehead and legs, Ace bandages on her left knee and right ankle, and a sling on her left arm. Her blue-jean shorts were cut up as well as cut off, and her hair stood out in all directions. None of these in itself (aside from the sling) was remarkable. Her T-shirt, however–sparkling clean white cotton–bore a Red Sox logo and the command *Save a Life–Give Blood.*

Where could she have gotten that but Cape Cod Hospital?

Had Sue, of all people, become one more local crime victim?

Edgar devoutly hoped not. Aside from the implications for her, it would ruin this night for the poor Popes, to have their memorial trumped by a new scandal.

Food began arriving: salads, garlic bread, tortillas, guacamole. The sound of a plaster cast pounding on the restroom door drew everyone's attention away from the table.

Really now! What was going on here? Didn't she think she could hold it any longer?

Leo called: "You got the wrong door! The gingerbread man, that's the little boys' room. Girls' is the one with the skirt."

Caroline pushed back her chair. With a hand on Sue's shoulder she stopped her hammering. For a moment they spoke, too softly to overhear. Then they both went into the ladies' room.

Wally Hicks, Edgar realized. That's who's in the men's. For quite some time, as a matter of fact.

He opened the paperback book in front of him and reexamined the note Wally had dropped when he fled. *You dick-brain Casanova piece of shit! Who do you think you're fooling, scumbag? Touch her again & I swear I'll kill you both. YES fuck-head I mean NOW!!!*

Leo slid a salad in front of him. Edgar closed his book and reached for a chip. One might imagine nothing is connected to anything, he reflected. But our Gordian knot is unraveling. What we need now is an Ariadne to pick up the thread.

Caroline returned to the table, clearly shaken under her soignee facade. "She's hurt," she announced. "Her car crashed this afternoon."

"Jesus Christ," said Leo. "Is she all right?"

"What happened?" asked Carlo.

"She doesn't know. The car went out of control on the Mid-

Cape. Flew off the highway, she says, and somersaulted into a ditch." Caroline sat; drank water. "I got the impression she may have been, well, high. Anyhow, she woke up in an ambulance. The emergency-room people said it's a miracle she wasn't killed."

"Good heavens," said Edgar.

"They wanted to keep her overnight for observation. She doesn't have health insurance. The minute they left her alone, she walked out."

People all around the table tossed in questions: Is she OK to be on her own? How bad was she hurt? Were the cops called? What about the car? Should somebody give her a ride someplace?

The waitress, oblivious, held out two steaming platters: "Who's pepperoni and onion? Sausage, mushroom, and garlic?"

"How did she get here from the hospital?" asked Carlo.

Caroline's left eyebrow made a Nike swoosh. "She hitch-hiked."

Touch her again & I swear I'll kill you both.

"Carlo." Edgar rose. "If it's not too much to ask, would you come outside for a moment and show me how to use your cell phone?"

Chapter Thirty-Four

Alistair Pope's wide country kitchen reeked of stale air and rotting food. Through the closed windows behind her Lydia could see his back yard and the little cottage he'd called the summer kitchen. Plenty of light here, in spite of the low beamed ceiling. There was a corner fireplace at the far end, and a row of appliances and cupboards under the windows. No dirty dishes. He'd have put his breakfast things in the dishwasher before heading to Leo's.

She crossed the bare oak floor to a wall of built-in shelves above a wooden table and chairs. One shelf held a phone, but no answering machine.

Which way to go? She chose the doorway next to the refrigerator. This led to a long dim hall covered in a threadbare faux-oriental runner. Ahead and to her right was the main staircase with its fiddlehead banister, then a double doorway–the living room? Straight ahead, at the far end of the hall, a crack of light outlined the unused front door. To her left, opposite the staircase, was a smaller closed door. She opened it.

Bingo.

The left half of Alistair's office was lined with books. The right half held filing cabinets, a printer, an early-model combination copier and fax machine, shelves of videotapes and DVDs, and a stack of machines to play them. In between literature and technology stood the oak table he'd used as a desk. A few papers were scattered across it, lit by fading sun through the window it faced. An oak desk chair had been moved aside–more than once, judging from the indentations on the hooked rug where it now stood.

On a corner of the table sat a small black oval: the answering machine.

She tiptoed toward it. A red light and a green light glowed

like translucent jellybeans. Thank you, cops, for not turning off the power!

Lydia took her cell phone out of her little purse. Two bars: maybe, maybe not. She called Mudge.

"Hey. Good. We got a connection."

"And I got the machine. I feel like Sir Galahad finding the Holy Grail."

"Prodigious! Ready to record when you are."

"Hang on while I pull the plug and see if this works."

She set her phone on the desk. Popped the cord out of the answering machine. Off went the lights. Lydia pushed the cord back in. The red light came on . . . and the green one, blinking.

Her heart quivered in her chest.

"Looks like we got a message. You all set?"

"Yup. Go for it."

She pressed the green button. The machine whirred. Lydia held her phone over the speaker slots. A burst of static . . . and a voice.

"Al-is-tair." A woman: young, flirtatious. "Where's that clip? Zelda's like ready to snap. I can't hold her off much longer. Call me! I already left like ten messages on your cell. Call me ASAP. I'm serious." *Beep.* "Hi, it's your little brother. Don't forget I'm coming out for Mom's birthday. I'll e-mail you my flights. OK. See you then. Bye." *Beep. Pause.* "Where are you?" A woman: older, huskier. *Pause.* "I'll try your cell." *Beep. Static.* "Hiya! *** up in *** " A soprano, with a bad connection. "*** back around ***" *Beep. Click. Pause. Beep.* "Hey. Listen." A tightly controlled baritone. "We've gotta work this out, man. There's too much at stake. By phone, e-mail, in person, whatever. Ciao." *Beep. Static.* "*** forgot." The soprano again. "I need *** OK? *** Leo. *** later baby!" *Beep. Beep. Click.*

The green light stopped blinking. Lydia spoke into her phone. "Mudge. Did you get all that?"

"Yeah, I think so. Donno how clear it'll be, but– Lydia, what do you think?"

"I think the staticky one was Sue."

"Yeah, me too. Pretty weird." Pause. "Lot of women, huh?"

"Three, right? Sue, and the one who only said a couple words, and that first one sounded like Delsey who worked with him in New York."

"Did you recognize the guy?"

"Not a clue."

"Me neither. He could be work, too."

"Well, I'd better get out of here," said Lydia. "We can replay them in the truck."

Mudge confirmed the coast was clear. Lydia tried to recall if the office door had been ajar or shut. Not that it mattered–the police search team wouldn't remember, or care. Nor would his family, who must be due to come in soon and take away his things.

This was the only chance she'd ever get to see Alistair's house.

She didn't dare take the time to browse through his books and tapes, much less go upstairs, but she did hurry down the hall for a quick look around. The nearest door opened into a small room he'd used for storage, which led into more rooms at the front of the house–the rabbit warren she'd pictured when he brought her here for tea. The double door across the hall was indeed to his living room: a motley collection of antique furniture and throw rugs, around a fireplace big enough to roast a pig.

Which president did he say had visited here? Grant? No. Wilson?

Gone less than a week, and already his stories were fading.

Alistair, she told him silently, you were right, it's a fine house. I'm glad I finally got to see at least this much of it. I'm sorry you're not here to give me the grand tour.

Her shoulder bag vibrated.

"Are you OK?" asked Mudge.

"Sorry." She began retracing her steps. "It's a big house."

"Well, hurry. A car just went by real slow, like they suspect something."

"On my way." Into the hall, around the stairs, past the front door. "Mudge, listen. I'm not sure, but I think I recognized one of the other voices."

"Yeah. I think I did, too."

"That woman who didn't say much?"

No answer.

"Mudge, are you there?"

Silence. Lydia looked at her phone screen. The call had ended.

Her heart thumped. OK. Take a deep breath. They'd lost reception, that's all.

She stepped into the office, where they'd gotten a good connection before. One ring . . . two . . . three . . . four . . . and his recorded voice came on: "This is Mudge. Leave a message."

Houston, we have a problem. Our module is moving through space on her own. No contact with ground control. Either we delay re-entry or fly home by dead reckoning.

She looked out the window to Alistair's parking space and the street. Late June-evening sun was strewing patches of gold across the lawn, gilding the distant treetops. Long shadows streaked trees, grass, bushes, and asphalt. Anybody out there?

Once more she pressed Send. Once more Mudge's phone rang, and rang, and clicked into voice mail.

Houston, we're launching Plan B.

They had agreed that if by any chance something went wrong, Lydia wouldn't come out the same way they'd gone in, but would head for the summer kitchen. Hidden behind that mini-cottage, she could reconnoiter: check out the yard and the street, and if she saw anything unexpected–a car, a cop, a real vacuum-cleaner salesman–either stay put until the threat went away or make a dash for the woods that edged Alistair's property. It would take her longer to circle back to where they'd started, but she'd have cover most of the way.

As she returned her phone to her purse, she heard a metallic click-click.

The back door.

Had she locked it behind her? Yes.

She moved to the half-open office door and listened.

Someone was in the kitchen, walking quietly but not silently on the oak floor. Someone who had a key.

Mudge? Not likely. They'd agreed he would stay at his post.

If that had changed, he'd have called her name when he came in.

It might not be X. It could be a neighbor, a family member, anybody.

Dammit, there was no place to hide in here! Lydia's mind fluttered around the room like a trapped bird. Fling the rug over the desk and crawl under it? Unplug the answering machine and stuff it behind the copier, then try to squeeze between machines?

Any move would make noise, and bring the newcomer straight to her.

The footsteps had reached the hall. Her heart was pounding so loudly she could hardly hear. Did whoever-it-was know she was in the house? If not, maybe they'd keep going–past the office to the living room, or up the stairs.

Staying on the sound-muffling rug, Lydia stepped behind the door.

Closer . . . closer . . . and silence.

Then a flurry of footsteps, and the door flung shut, and confronting her in the little room was Helen Wills.

"Lydia Vivaldi."

Her voice was even, dispassionate, a little angry. Surprised? Lydia couldn't tell.

"Detective." Her throat was so dry she couldn't get out "Wills."

"What are you doing here?"

For once she didn't look like a state trooper. She was dressed for Alistair's wake: black culottes over knee-high black suede boots, and a loose-fitting black sweater with an open V neck, where thin gold chains twinkled.

"Looking around?" With an effort, Lydia swallowed. "Alistair wanted me to see his house."

"Oh." Helen Wills tossed her head: *Yeah. Right*. "How'd you get in?"

"His spare key."

She held out her hand. "Give it to me."

They'd agreed Mudge should keep it, in case of emergency. Where was Mudge? Would he have gauged this as a situation calling for rescue or flight?

"I don't know where I put it." Lydia pretended to search her purse. "I must have left it in the kitchen."

The detective didn't bother to go look, or even to check Lydia's purse. "I'm going to have to take you in."

"For what? I didn't break and enter. I was invited. There's no yellow tape."

"How about, for the murder of Alistair Pope?"

Helen Wills rested a hand on her hip. For the first time Lydia noticed the bulge under her sweater.

"That's–" Her throat had gone dry again. "That's crazy."

"I don't think so. And I believe any jury on Cape Cod will agree with me."

This is wrong, wrong, wrong! insisted a voice in Lydia's head. How can she arrest you? In civilian clothes? With no partner or backup? Plus she's off duty until Monday, for Pete's sake!

"What are *you* doing here?" she blurted.

Unexpectedly, Helen Wills answered. "Call it a professional reflex. I was at the wake. Saw you take off with Mudge. We like to keep an eye on persons of interest, especially who might want to leave the area. So I followed you." Her other hand pushed back a strand of hair that had escaped from its barrette. "We've been waiting for you to make your move. And here you are."

"My move?" Lydia fought back a surge of outrage. "This is a move? Wanting to see Alistair's house before his family clears it out?"

"Ha! Like you don't already know this house blindfolded."

"I told you, I never–"

"Like you weren't involved with him up to your ears. And went ballistic when you found out he was cheating on you left and right."

"Cheating on me?" Lydia was still angry and amazed. She also was noticing a red spot on each of Detective Wills's cheeks which belied the flatness of her voice.

"Hey. Not your fault, right? How could you know, when he picked you up off the side of the road, you'd hooked a Casanova? You thought you just got lucky. Fresh over the bridge, and look what drops in your lap."

Lydia missed the withering sarcasm. Her brain had stopped at "Casanova."

How many people in Quansett would pick that word for Alistair Pope?

Seconds ago, all she wanted was to get away. Now she wanted Helen Wills to keep talking.

"How was he a Casanova? I didn't know him that well, much less his love life, but that's pretty harsh. Or, what? You think that's why he was killed?"

"You know damn well that's why he was killed." Her arms folded. "You caught him in the act, didn't you. But you waited till your next date to bust him. What happened under that tree, Lydia? Did he brush you off? What made you so mad you grabbed a rock?"

"This is fairy tales!" Lydia retorted. "What do you think, just because it fits your case, you can make up any story you want?"

Part of her was furious. Good: furious was what Detective Wills expected. The trick was to hide her own inner detective–the part of her that was piecing together the rushed police investigation of DeAnne's fall, the unfiled report on the Morris's slashed tires, the plausible scenario tested on Edgar Rowdey, and the murder weapon suddenly turning up a stone's throw from her cottage.

"How do you know who Alistair was seeing, or when, or anything else?"

Helen Wills snapped back: "I'm a detective, in case you didn't notice."

"Then go do some detecting! Find the real killer!"

"I'm way ahead of you. I know every move Alistair Pope made last week. His New York trip, lunch at Leo's, who he talked to on the phone, what drugstore he bought toothpaste. Also whose DNA was on the sheets in his bedroom."

"Not mine!"

"No." Again she pushed back a fallen strand of hair. "Your rival. Leo's other kitchen help."

"Dinah?" Lydia gasped.

"Please! What's-her-name. Sue."

It was the "what's-her-name" that clinched it. Helen Wills

took her vocation much too seriously to forget the name of a central figure in a murder case. Least of all one she'd just driven home from a revel in the rhododendrons.

Can't she hear herself? Lydia wondered in alarm. How long can we do this? Any second now she'll see through my straight-man act, and then what?

Since that wasn't a point she was willing to reach, she kept going.

"Sue and Alistair? But what about Wally, from the Frigate? Her hot date in the woods?"

A professional shrug. "Relationships, fidelity, not my issue. The lab gives me an ID, I don't ask 'What about Wally from the Frigate?' I ask 'When was she in the victim's home? Where did she go besides his bed and bathroom?"

Mudge. Who should have sounded the alarm. Whose phone was cut off. By Helen Wills?

Don't go there, Lydia.

"When *was* she here?" Play to her ego, vanity, jealousy, whatever provokes her to talk. "Was this, like, a major love affair?"

"Hah! More like a hit-and-run. Monday night, maybe Tuesday? We're tracking her other movements to narrow it down. What it looks like, is he let her stay in the summer kitchen. She got lonely, or horny, and sneaked into the house. While he was asleep? or who knows, maybe she made him an offer he couldn't refuse. Anyhow, there's traces of her all over the place. Like he didn't know how to get rid of her, so he gave up and split. To Leo's for lunch," she nodded at Lydia, "where he found another hot ticket to bring home and chase her out."

She doesn't care about my straight-man act, Lydia realized. In this drama, she's already cast the parts. I may be her Other Woman, AKA the jealous killer, but at least I didn't leave tangible evidence. Sue she has proof that Alistair fucked, so Sue she has to explain away. Find her a suitably small role in the grand epic: the secret romance of Alistair and Helen.

Yuck! Alistair and Helen?

This straight, humorless, neat-as-a-nun state trooper coiled in sweaty passion with that overweight, slovenly, self-absorbed filmmaker?

One thing Lydia had learned in the past month, though: When it comes to romances, you just never fucking know.

"Then wouldn't Wally be the obvious suspect? If he and Sue were a couple, and he found out she had a fling–"

"Wally got her on the rebound," she interrupted. "After Alistair kicked her out. Nice try, but no cigar."

"It makes more sense than me killing him," Lydia retorted. "I just broke up with somebody. I wasn't even interested in Alistair."

"He was interested in you, though, wasn't he."

Cold olive-green eyes gazed at her with the flat malevolence of a venomous snake. Tiny moths of fear fluttered around Lydia's insides.

"The new girl in town. Nothing personal. You could have been anybody."

Her glance flicked to the window. No one in sight, from where Lydia stood.

"A fresh face, that's all. If you'd come onto him, he'd have backed off. That was what attracted him, was the challenge."

It struck Lydia with a jolt that the detective must have followed her here with a plan. If it was to arrest her, why hadn't she done that?

Where the hell was Mudge?

"Fairy tales," she repeated.

"Sure," said Helen Wills.

She couldn't have shot him. Could she? While he was standing here on a residential street, in the middle of a phone conversation?

"Since of course you weren't interested. That's why you kept sneaking off with him. Right? To prove how totally not interested you were by making out with him. In the Back End parking lot; does that jog your memory? Under the tree? Any damn place you could get your hands on him?"

Two options, Lydia: show your cards, or keep bluffing.

"He told me he wasn't seeing anybody! Anyhow, what's the big deal? Guys pull that crap all the time in restaurants–feel up the waitress, grab a kiss. Goes with the territory. If you want a motive for murder–you just said Sue was screwing him and he kicked her out. Why aren't you harassing her?"

"Don't worry about Sue." Helen Wills rubbed her hands together as if to warm them up. "She's got her own destiny to deal with. Sure, she's a slut, but hey. Who just broke into the victim's house?" She reached under her sweater. "Who's responsible for his death? You."

Never having had a gun pointed at her before, Lydia could only gape. What was that wicked thing? A pistol? Standard police issue, or a personal favorite of Detective Wills? She couldn't wrap her brain around it. Her only conscious thought was astonishment that something so small–smaller than Alistair Pope's answering machine–had the power to fill her with terror.

Not just the gun. The eyes that were aiming its short barrel fixed her with such icy hatred that her whole body shivered.

"Let's go."

I can't move, thought Lydia. I can't talk. I'm frozen to this spot, and she's going to kill me.

Then a voice came from the kitchen.

"Helen?"

For two paralyzed seconds Lydia heard Alistair, returning to save his house from being shot to smithereens. Three more seconds told her no, and it wasn't Mudge, either.

The gun wobbled, as Helen Wills stepped sideways to half-face the door. Then it steadied again with its evil eye on Lydia.

Footsteps in the hall.

Helen's thumb moved. Lydia saw from the tensing of her jaw that she was preparing to fire.

"In here!" she cried, and threw herself against the book-shelves.

One loud explosive crack, then a tinkling crash as a window pane shattered onto the desk.

The door flung open. A man in a dark-gray suit hurled himself on Helen Wills.

"Jesus Christ!" He grabbed her arm. "What the hell?"

"Get her!" Helen ordered. "Stop her!"

Lydia was stumbling to her feet, looking frantically for a gap to escape through.

"Quick! She's trying to get away!"

"Stop! You! Don't move!" the newcomer commanded.

Lydia stopped. The man stood between her and Helen Wills, blocking the door. He didn't have a visible weapon, and he was barely as tall as the detective, but his muscular build told her she wouldn't get past him.

"Captain Wills, state police," he snapped at her. "Stay where you are."

Lydia raised her hands. "She tried to kill me!"

"What the hell's going on here?" Chill Wills asked his wife.

Helen wiped her forehead on the back of her arm. You fucking phony! thought Lydia–pretending you're worn out by cop work, when really you're trying to distract him from the gun in your other hand.

"Meet Alistair's killer," she told him. "Lydia Vivaldi, AKA Liz Valentine, AKA Lynn Vail."

"Bullshit!" Lydia retorted.

He held up his hand for silence.

"I followed her here from the wake," Helen continued. "Pete called me on the way–they just found the murder weapon in her front yard. I was taking her in, but when she heard you, she made a run for it."

Chill Wills had the face of a poker player. "How do you know she killed Alistair?"

She answered with an intimate smile that turned Lydia's stomach. "My job, Chilly. While you were off in Florida, I was connecting the dots." She folded her arms, hiding the gun. "They were lovers. She just started working at Leo's. Left a trail of fake ID from here to Boston. She didn't realize he had other irons in the fire. Confronted him under the Elephant Tree, and–wham."

"That's not true!" Lydia erupted. This time he didn't stop her. "I know you guys are married, and I'm sorry, but she's been screwing Alistair since before I got here. He started hitting on me, and she flipped out."

"Ha! What crap."

"She tried every trick in the book to keep him–slashed my tires, shot at me in the woods behind the post office– I think she killed DeAnne Ropes, too, and whitewashed it."

Chill Wills held up both hands before his wife could speak. "Hold it. Where'd you get that idea?"

"I used to work with DeAnne. She wouldn't fall off a ladder by accident." What to say and what to skip? "She sent me a post-card last month–all excited, like she'd met a guy. During the film shoot. It had to be Alistair. And two days later, she was dead."

"Phooey. That's worthless."

"You were here, right? You know how fast they closed that case?"

"Yeah. Good efficient police work," Chill Wills nodded. "Not just Helen. Bob Scanlan's a damn fine detective."

"And I'm not," said Lydia. "But DeAnne was a damn fine carpenter. And I don't believe any more than her parents that she just, whoops!"

Helen Wills put her left hand on her husband's arm. "Let's wrap this up, Chill. We're wasting time. If she wants to make up stories, let her do it at the station, on the record. I didn't even get to the wake yet, did you? I don't want to miss seeing Maria, and the family."

He gave her a long, unreadable look. Then his right hand reached across his chest and patted her hand. "Why don't you go on ahead?"

"No." It sounded so abrupt that she added, "I want us to go together. Naturally."

"Well, somebody's got to take this young lady in. It's your collar, Helen, no question; but if we both go to the station, won't you miss the wake?"

She clasped his fingers. "I didn't drive all the way over here to quit before the job's done."

If Fletcher were here, thought Lydia, he'd describe this couple's dynamic as alpha female and a beta male. She fervently hoped Chill wouldn't back down. No way was she willing to be left alone in his wife's lethal hands. Too bad he was so clearly a traditional cop. No way would this man yield to the pleas of a young lady, as he'd quaintly put it. Least of all a murder suspect.

Dammit, why hadn't either one of them brought back-up? How could this be legal?

And where the hell was Mudge? They couldn't both have missed him. Had he been handed over to the back-up and whisked off to West Exmouth?

Chill Wills squeezed his wife's hand. Then he half-turned toward her, and his fingers slid into the V neck of her sweater.

Oh, please! Lydia cringed. Not in front of the suspect!

But Helen too was shrinking from his touch. Here came his index finger, wrapped in gold chains. And dangling from one chain, an engraved gold earring.

"Where'd you get this?" His other arm slid around her back.

Pause. "I don't know. I don't remember." Pause. "I've had it forever."

"Think." The odd-shaped gold loop was no bigger than his finger nail.

"From my grandmother? No . . . Maria. That's right. When I was in her wedding. A bridesmaid's present. We all got them."

"Nice try," said Chill Wills without emotion, "but no cigar."

Helen stood perfectly still, encircled by his arm.

"Alistair's earring," breathed Lydia.

"This is the mate," he said in the same matter-of-fact tone. "Alistair's earring was in her jewel box, wrapped in tissue paper. It's more discolored," he explained to them both. "Probably from the blood when it was torn out of his ear."

He let the earring and chain fall onto her black sweater.

"You went through my jewel box?" Helen sounded stunned, incredulous.

"I went through the whole house."

"Why?"

A little frown puckered his forehead, as if the question surprised him. "Well . . . I guess, kind of a knee-jerk reaction, after fifteen years on the force."

"But . . . why? What were you looking for? I mean– Chilly, it's been so good since you got back. Better than good. Hasn't it?"

"Mm," he agreed. "Like a whole new start. Like you were

suddenly a different person." His arm let go of her waist. He still didn't look at her. "I knew something was up. I just didn't know what."

Catching his hand, Helen stepped back to where she could meet his eyes. "I realized how much I love you. That's all. Being gone for two weeks– I missed you, Chilly."

Now he was looking at her. "You missed Alistair."

"Oh, come on. You know me better than that."

"Now he's gone, I'm all you got. I know you well enough to give you credit for playing what cards are in your hand."

She shook her head angrily. "That's so– How can you say that? You know I'm exhausted. Working like a galley slave on this investigation, plus getting the house ready–" She brought his hand to her lips. "The earring, you're right, I should have connected. I thought it was mine. I forgot about Maria giving them out–I mean, how many years ago? How would I know Alistair got one, too? But you're right, I shouldn't have just put it away without checking."

"Bullshit!" Lydia exploded. "You've been lying about that earring since last week."

"You shut up!"

Chill's eyes slid over Lydia as if she were part of the office furniture. "Helen," he said earnestly, "we need to get straight here. OK? Are we together on that?"

She seized the key word. "Yes. We're together."

"There's no time for games. The earring, your thing with Alistair, you gotta let go. Quit with the excuses. That young fellow who was outside has probably called HQ, got a squad car on the way over."

"He can't," she cut in triumphantly. "I took his phone."

"I gave him mine," said Chill Wills. "My point is, skip it. You had an affair with Alistair; we both know that. Cut to the chase. The $64 question."

Helen looked him in the eyes. "I didn't kill him."

"Yes she damn well did!" said Lydia.

They both ignored her. "The question is, what's Pete Altman going to find?" said Chill. "A lot of circumstantial evidence.

Right?"

"All pointing straight at her." Helen nodded at Lydia. "The grapevine's already got it. How she came here on the rebound, grabbed onto Alistair, found out he was cheating on her, and went berserk. Met him under the Elephant Tree and bashed his head in. Ran back into Leo's so quick, nobody noticed she was gone."

"That was her, not me!" Lydia wished she'd been quicker to recognize the puzzle pieces Helen was tossing out. She wished she had Edgar Rowdey to help assemble them. Most of all she wished she could get a word in edgewise without sounding like a bratty little sister. "She must have tailed him all week, to find out why he'd lost interest in her. And once she saw him with me, ambushed him under the tree. Making me the scapegoat."

"You can see, she's so obsessed, she's got herself convinced the whole world is out to get her. Including me."

"She *is* out to get me," Lydia told Chill. "She shot at me in the woods with Alistair's pistol. She would have killed me right here if you didn't show up in the nick of time."

"Jesus Christ," Chill was shaking his head.

He and his wife still blocked Lydia's path to the door, but they'd moved apart. Helen stood half facing each of them, with her arms folded and the gun tucked out of sight. What Chill might be carrying under his suit jacket Lydia had no idea.

"Last time I saw Al Pope, he was a fat geek. All the way through high school. He changes his name to Alistair and now he's a babe magnet? Helen! What the hell happened?"

"Damned if I know." She sighed ruefully, making light of it.

"Talk to me."

"What can I say? I ran into him at our reunion last summer, Maria's and mine. He tagged along for a drink. Still the same old Fat Albert, only with a comb-over. I hoped he'd go away, but Maria wanted to hear about his films, and he did have some funny stories. You're right, he really had changed. Into this grown-up, Alistair. I mean, the last kid who ever got picked for the team, and now he's a big cheese, running around New York with famous actors and network executives, and it's him doing us a favor, buying us beers at Bobby Byrne's."

Whatever her feelings about all this, then or now, Helen Wills wasn't showing them. Lydia suspected she too was asking herself: What to include? What to leave out?

"Somehow we decided to go take a walk on the beach. And it started raining, and he put his jacket around me, and, well, I guess I'd had a couple too many beers. The rest," she shrugged, "was just a regular mess."

Chill looked at her for several seconds without speaking. "Well," he said at last. "Where does that leave us?"

Again Helen met his eyes. "Together."

"You think?"

"I do. At least I hope," she amended. "I've been really really stupid, and if you don't want to forgive me, I can understand that. It doesn't change the bottom line, though. You're my husband. For better or worse, till death us do part. I mean, there's no way it'll ever get any worse than this, right? After what we've been through, we deserve to enjoy the best yet to come."

Chill thrust his hands into his pockets and glanced around the room as if he'd forgotten he was in Alistair Pope's office. Lydia would have given her Morris Minor to know what he was thinking.

"So what's your plan?" he asked Helen. "Take this young lady down to HQ?"

"We can try. I'm not sure we can do it." Her shoulders stirred. "She's heard so much. And she's such a troublemaker . . ."

Her arms were unfolding. "You think she might try something?" asked Chill.

Lydia felt paralyzed with fear. It was all she could do to speak, much less move. "The cops are on the way." Barely a croak.

Again they ignored her. "I do," Helen nodded.

"Like, escape?" One hand came out of Chill's pocket, flashing a glint of metal.

"Like attack the two arresting officers."

Time somehow managed to speed up and slow down simultaneously. Several events took place in no clear order: Helen Wills's arm flung out, there was an explosive crack, Chill's arm jerked up and then down, another explosion, something fell noisily behind

Lydia, both of Helen's hands flew high in the air, and she collapsed onto the rug. A pistol bounced across the wooden floor into the bookcases.

Lydia staggered and grabbed the oak chair.

Chill dropped to his knees beside his wife.

"Are you OK?"

Who was asking whom? Lydia didn't know. Nor did she know the answer.

Chill's hands slid under Helen, gently lifting her shoulders. Her hair had escaped from its clip and tangled in his fingers. He pulled one hand out to shake it loose. A patch of the rug beside them turned red.

Lydia managed to sit on the chair.

"Are you OK?"

That pale rough-hewn face a yard away from hers must mean Chill Wills was speaking to her. "Yeah," said Lydia. "I think so. Are you OK?"

"Yeah." Wet streaks on his cheeks–sweat? Tears? "You got a phone? Call 911. They'll be on their way–but tell them we need an ambulance. Tell them," tears rolled down his face, "an officer's down."

Chapter Thirty-Five

Night had turned Alistair's side yard into a woodcut: flat silver grass, tall black trees. Lydia stood in a crowd of people and vehicles lit up as if by fireworks. Two police cars and an ambulance flashed red-white-and-blue rooftop racks. A fire engine beamed its headlights from the dirt-patch driveway. Every few seconds, Dave Wheeler's camera threw a new section of the scene into brief, bright contrast.

There was Mudge, leaning against his truck parked in the street. Lydia had an idea he and Dave both had spoken to her when she came out of the house, but she couldn't quite remember–as if she'd woken from a dream which was dissipating faster than she could clutch at the fragments. She knew that two police officers had stood beside her while a female firefighter asked her medical questions, then led her back into the kitchen. Detective Pete Altman, rising from the wooden table, looked so tired she almost offered him a hand. Their taped interview was short. Had they made an appointment for tomorrow? Probably. That would be Sunday, her day off. She vaguely recalled writing something on a business card and putting it in her purse. If her escorts had offered to drive her home, she must have said no. Enough cops for one night.

She stepped back to let a crew of firefighters pass. They carried a stretcher covered by a blanket which hid the lumpy shape beneath except for a mat of dark hair hanging down one side.

"You don't want to watch that." A hand on her back: Dave Wheeler.

"Is it Helen Wills?"

"Yes."

"Is she dead?"

"They won't say," he raised his camera and squeezed off a shot, "but it doesn't look good."

"How did you know? To come here. How did everybody get here so fast?"

He lowered the camera. "Edgar Rowdey called me from a pizza parlor in Hyannis. I called Pete Altman. Mudge put out an APB on Chill Wills's Nextel, and you called 911. Pretty amazing. Everything but the cavalry." He patted her arm. "I'll come back in a minute, OK? I gotta work."

"Sure."

Still shooting, Dave followed the stretcher. Lydia went to join Mudge.

He wrapped her in a bear hug, which made her want to bury her head in his shoulder and sob for at least ten minutes. More than a good cry, though, she wanted news.

"Donno," said Mudge. "The cops aren't telling us anything. I think Chill Wills shot his wife. Weren't you there?"

Lydia stayed close against him–recalling that awful afternoon when she and Mudge and Dinah had held each other up beside the frog pond where Alistair's body lay. "Yeah. I guess so. He must have. Can we get out of here?"

She'd been warned by so many cops in the past week not to go anywhere, to call if she remembered anything relevant to the case, et cetera, et cetera, that she'd stopped caring what they might do to her if she ignored their orders. What *could* they do that would be worse than this?

Right, Lydia. That's what Helen Wills thought.

"Are you cold?" asked Mudge, helping her into the truck. "I've got blankets in the back."

"It's just shell shock."

He told her he'd promised to call the Back End group. They'd sounded like they planned to stay at Rosa's for a while yet. Mainly out of concern for her, far as he could tell. Edgar had actually learned how to use a cell phone (Carlo's) so as to sound the alarm when he realized she and Mudge might be in danger.

"Wow. Now that's friendship." Lydia felt warmer already. "How did he know?"

"You got me. I sure didn't have a clue." Mudge was apologetic. "Detective Wills comes screeching up here in her cruiser, says she heard there's trouble, won't listen to me, just takes my phone and says Don't move till I come out. I kind of wondered why she needed mine when she's got a Nextel, but you know how she is. Was. That bulldozer cop attitude."

"Yeah." Lydia shuddered. "Well, she'd been lying to so many people for so long."

"They wouldn't give it back, either. Since it was still on her when they took her away. I told Detective Altman to be careful because it's got important information. But we'll have to use yours to call Carlo."

She handed him her phone when they came to a Stop sign. Lydia wasn't ready yet to face another round of questions. She did, though, agree to a rendezvous at Rosa's. Outvoting the part of her that wanted to go straight home and curl up like a porcupine was the part that urgently needed company.

"What about Chill?" she asked Mudge. "Same thing when he showed up?"

"Exact opposite. He asked me where Helen was, where you were, he gave me his Nextel, and said Tell headquarters to send backup, pronto."

"He must have seen her leave the wake, and followed her," said Lydia. "I wonder why."

"Well, she made such a big deal about not missing it," Mudge said. "They'd just had Rosey Sherman's family over for a cookout. She practically pushed them out the door."

Lydia was impressed. "How'd you find that out?"

In spite of his efforts to be sympathetically grave, Mudge looked so pleased with himself he was almost smirking. "He called me! I was kind of afraid to tell you. Rosey Sherman offered me a job!"

"A job!" Her heart sank. "What kind of a job?"

"Selling books. We had this whole, like, strategy conference. How it'll help me save for college, and juice up my resume– Don't worry, I'm not quitting Leo's." He gave her another one-armed hug. "And guess what! *We* have a job. He wants the Flying

Wedge to cater the Frigate's grand reopening on Fourth of July."

Good news, Lydia recognized, though she couldn't feel it. Sitting beside him on the truck's high seat, she gazed out at houses and trees, porch lights winking through a screen of branches, and marveled that so many people could live so close to the late Alistair Pope's house without suspecting a thing. What a shock when they opened tomorrow's paper! Or checked the website tonight (assuming the Cape Cod Times had a website). Like that poem about that painting of the fall of Icarus–everybody going about their ordinary business, oblivious to the boy in the corner plunging to his death.

She wondered where Chill Wills was now. She'd only caught glimpses of him after they left the house–once with a police escort like hers, once through the kitchen windows. He'd already recovered his self-control and his poker face. A knee-jerk reflex, presumably, after fifteen years on the force. How would it go for him? Would his buddies treat him with respect, a hero obliged to use his weapon in the line of duty? Or would they throw him in jail for shooting a fellow officer?

May the force be with you, Chill. May this be the end of a long uphill struggle, not a tumble from the sky on melted wings.

She realized Mudge had stopped talking–probably because he could see she wasn't listening.

"Are you OK?" he asked.

"Yeah." She shivered. "Sorry. I'm fine. Really."

"What were you thinking about?"

Lydia managed a ghost of a grin. "How glad I am there weren't any TV cameras."

The big round table at Rosa's Pizza and Mexican surprised her by looking the same as when she'd left. Caroline and Leo beckoned Lydia and Mudge to seats. Most of the Back End customers had gone home, but Edgar was still here, and Carlo of course, and Dinah, and two or three regulars. They'd long ago finished the food phase and settled into drinking.

"Hear hear!" Leo raised his beer glass.

"Hear what?" Lydia asked him.

"You heard what happened?" asked Mudge.

"You're here! You're here!" Leo declared. "That's what I said. What I meant."

"Here we go again," quipped Dinah.

Carlo edged past Mudge and Lydia to stand at the counter. "What can I get you to drink? Or eat? Have you had any dinner?"

"Pizza!" said Mudge. "And a Coke."

After a brief round of ritual arguing over who would pay, a pizza was ordered. Carlo brought over a Coke for Mudge, a Rolling Rock and a glass for Lydia, and a pitcher of water.

"Now!" said Caroline. "Tell us all! We know Edgar put two and two together and got Carlo to help him call the Cape Cod Times, but where did you go?"

Lydia left it to Mudge to describe their quest. Leo interrupted to ask why they didn't just phone the police to go pick up Alistair's answering machine. Mudge said they had reasons not to trust the police. Leo asked what reasons.

Mudge looked inquiringly at Lydia.

When she didn't answer immediately, Edgar did. "Honestly, Leo! I've already given you at least two. Mind like a sieve!"

"That note of Wally's, for one," said Caroline. "Edgar just told you that's why he made the phone call. He realized when Wally jumped on Lydia about it that it must be the same note Alistair found on his door." She turned to Lydia. "The day he invited you for tea."

"Oh my god," said Lydia. "How'd you know, Edgar? What did it say? I didn't even read it."

In a dry tone he recited the message. "You mentioned Alistair was shocked when he saw it–crumpled it up and tossed it away. As who wouldn't? And then, not to speak ill, but he did have a habit of bending the truth. He'd complained when we were counting frogs that he was up to his neck in women trouble. That, I thought, was a more likely source of your note than a neighbor with a crisis."

"Well, you were right. Helen Wills wrote him that note. They'd been having an affair–"

"Helen and Alistair?" Caroline's eyebrows arched.

"You can't be serious!" huffed Leo. "Alistair Pope and Helen Wills? She's a married woman! And a state trooper!"

"Will you let her finish?" Carlo interposed.

Lydia figured if they were going to do a running commentary, she'd go ahead and throw the first bombshell. "That's why she killed him. To stop him from leaving her."

Her last words were drowned out. Alistair's killer was Helen Wills? Good lord! He'd been murdered by the detective investigating his death? X was a state trooper? Who'd been cheating on her husband all the time he was away? Shameful! Even before that? For how long? Damn! You just couldn't trust anybody anymore! What on earth was she thinking? What did she plan to do when Chill came home from Florida?

"Don't ask me," said Lydia.

"Isn't it obvious?" said Leo. "Like the female praying mantis. Get rid of him!"

"Oh, now," said Carlo.

"I wonder if she even had a plan," said Caroline. "Edgar, what do you think?"

"I'm sure I don't know." Edgar pushed up his glasses. "I suppose she hoped she'd have gotten far enough with Alistair by then so she could trade up, as you might say. Divorce Chill and marry Alistair."

"Heavens! Not very realistic of her," Caroline observed.

"You can say that again," Leo agreed. "After he's dodged the ball and chain for, what? Forty-five years? I could have told her. Don't hold your breath!"

Mudge contributed: "Maybe Alistair saw that's what she wanted. And thought he better quick trade up himself. From her to Lydia."

"By way of Sue," said Lydia. "Helen Wills told me Sue's DNA was in his bed and all over his house."

That got everybody talking at once again. For Lydia their debate creepily echoed her own with Helen Wills. She tuned it out, until Leo trumpeted over the others: "When did she tell you that?"

"Shortly before she was shot."

Another bombshell. Finishing her beer, Lydia waited for the

dust to settle. By then she'd regained enough composure to tell the whole story again. It took longer this time. For one thing, the pizza arrived, so she alternated talking with eating and listening. For another, answering Pete Altman's questions had been a lot easier than breaking bad news to friends who knew the participants, in some cases since birth, and for whom (except for one) violent death was so rare and horrifying as to be scarcely conceivable.

"Well, if the paramedics had the blanket over her, that's all she wrote," said Leo gloomily. "Covering her face? No question."

"Poor Chill," Caroline sighed.

Mudge was holding Lydia's hand in both of his. "What else could he do? He had to save you, when he saw how she'd set you up."

"Well, and save Helen, too, in a sense," Carlo added. "Alistair she attacked in a fury and left to die, but she didn't out-and-out kill him. As long as there was that shred of ambiguity–"

"She could still hope to survive," Caroline completed. "Reel herself back in. Rejoin humanity. Save her marriage."

"But not if she shot an innocent person in cold blood. Then she'd be doomed, and Chill along with her. To get her off the hook, he'd have to perjure himself. A small price to pay, in her view, but not his. Once he sold his soul, lost his honor, what would he have left? Nothing but her."

"Helen damnation," declared Leo.

Dinah snickered. One of the regulars crossed himself.

Mudge offered Lydia another slice of pizza. She shook her head. She was thinking of Chill Wills's expressionless face as he desperately weighed his wife's assurances, gauged her plans, and offered her what small chance he could to change course.

Mudge slid a small wedge onto her plate anyway. "Eat," he murmured. "You'll feel better."

"What about DeAnne, though?" Caroline asked.

Dinah spoke up. "Good question. If Helen was already a murderer when she whacked Al, why pussyfoot around? With him or Lydia. Might as well hang for a sheep as a lamb, right?"

Lydia was chewing. Mudge offered, "She must have thought nobody would find out."

"Still," said Carlo. "Once a person crosses that line . . . "

"Lydia," said Caroline, "what made you think Helen had killed DeAnne? Or, anyhow, caused her death."

"Well, for starters, I knew DeAnne." Lydia nibbled cheese off her finger. "I'd worked with her, I'd lived with her, and the pieces didn't add up. Stay behind to clean house instead of joining the party? No way! Climb a ladder in clogs, alone, to take down a heavy curtain that wasn't even her job?"

Carlo amplified: "But what reason did Helen have to attack her? If Alistair hadn't actually made a conquest. Why go to such an extreme?"

"Maybe she didn't do it on purpose. I mean, this must be when she first realized he was cooling off the great romance. Right? If she saw him with DeAnne, doing his touchy-feely thing?–maybe she just lost it. Gave the ladder a push, like, to scare her. Warn her off."

"Or him," said Edgar.

"What?" demanded Leo.

"Him," Edgar repeated. "Alistair. Is that not simple enough for you? Helen might have pushed DeAnne off her ladder as a warning to Alistair. That he'd better–what's the phrase?–keep the faith."

Another regular spoke up. "How'd she ever think she'd get away with it? Bob Scanlan's no pushover."

Leo and Dinah groaned.

"She almost did," said Carlo. "She was quite a sharp detective herself."

"Yeah," said Dinah. "Sharp like my fish knife, that cuts both ways."

A new thought stirred Lydia. "Edgar. You always thought DeAnne's fall was fishy. When Dave Wheeler asked you why, you said, her shoes. What did you mean? Didn't she wear clogs much around here? She did in Cambridge, although never to climb a ladder."

"Nor did she this time." Edgar swirled the dregs of his drink. "Carlo. Do you remember how you described coming in and seeing her on the floor?"

He nodded. "Lying all crumpled by the ladder. Her head against the fountain, and her poor little shoes–"

"Like slippers beside a bed!" Caroline exclaimed. "Oh my heavens. Set there neatly as if she'd just stepped out of them. Edgar, that's it, isn't it? She took them off!"

"Mm," said Edgar, sucking an ice cube.

Mudge's eyes widened. "She went up the ladder barefoot?"

"Duh!" Lydia shook her head. "I can't believe I missed that!"

"You weren't here," Dinah pointed out.

"We all missed it." Carlo looked stricken. "We believed Helen. That she stopped by to watch the filming, and there was DeAnne's body, and she called Kevin Kelly, and then came to find us at the Pig."

"In point of fact," Edgar said, "she stopped by looking for Alistair. Very likely they had a date, and he didn't show up, not for the first time, and she got the message. The bloom was off the rose."

"For him," said Carlo. "Not for her."

"That would be why DeAnne stayed behind at the studio," Caroline realized. "To flirt with Alistair. When he joined us, late, he said she was still there cleaning up. We didn't give it a thought at the time. Helen must have peeked in a window and seen them together."

"Possibly," said Edgar, "although one would expect her then to go after Alistair rather than lurk in wait for DeAnne. Who knows? We can assume Helen was upset. She may have jumped to conclusions. She could have seen Alistair leaving as she drove up, and looked inside, and there was DeAnne. Aha! The cause of her troubles."

"So, what?" said Dinah. "She runs in, hollers Hands off my man, and shoves the ladder?"

"Did she wait to see if–?" Mudge started, but didn't finish.

"Who knows?" Edgar repeated.

"No one who was there has lived to tell the tale," Leo intoned.

For a moment they were all silent. Then Dinah said grimly, "That's my fault. Dammit."

A Back End bad joke? Leo thought so. "Oh, sure. Hog all

the credit. What are you, one of those wannabe terrorists? No bombs, just a camera phone? 'I did it! That was me that blew up the Brooklyn Bridge!'"

"Shut up, Leo."

"What do you mean?" Carlo asked her.

"At the wake." Dinah's elbow was on the table, her chin in her hand. "It was me who told Chill Wills to go after his wife."

Everyone waited a moment to see if she would continue. Then Mudge asked, "Why?"

"I saw her pull a one-eighty and take off after you two." Her hand was half covering her mouth; Lydia had to strain to hear her words. "I was getting onto her by then, and so was Chill. I ran into him outside the funeral parlor–" Dinah leaned back, shrugged, took a long breath. "Somebody had to do something."

Caroline spoke first. "Dinah, are you saying you knew Helen had killed Alistair?"

"Not *knew*. I just kinda put two and two together. Like Lydia said. I went to school with Helen, and Chill. The pieces didn't add up."

Leo folded his arms. "Now, dammit all! You're telling me, you've been coming to work in my restaurant every day, serving meals to my customers, knowing who killed Alistair Pope, and you never said a word to me?"

"You got wax in your ears, Leo? I just said, I didn't *know*. And if I did, so what? You're not exactly a stranger in these parts. You wanted to, you coulda figured it out."

Lydia wasn't in the mood to listen to a standard workday squabble. "Dinah," she cut off Leo's retort. "Your pieces that didn't add up–is one of them our sniper in the woods?"

"Yup. That had to be Helen. Who else coulda got her hands on Al's pistol? Her or Chill, but I found out later he wasn't back yet. She must've lifted it when her team searched his house."

"Why did she shoot at you?" Carlo asked her.

"She was shooting at me," said Lydia. "Warning me to stop snooping around her case."

"Oh, no," said Dinah. "She knew I was getting suspicious. She sent me a message, and I sent her one back."

"I don't think so. I'm the one she just tried to kill."

Caroline cut in. "Two birds with one stone. What unexpected luck for her."

"Three," said Edgar. "Don't forget Sue."

There was a series of gasps around the circle. Lydia glanced in alarm at stunned faces.

"Jesus Mary and Joseph." One of the regulars smacked his hand on the table so the glasses rattled.

"God damn son-of-a-bitch," said the other. "Sue's car accident."

"Accident my ass," said Dinah.

Wallace Hicks thanked his lucky stars he'd brought along his crystal-headed stick. Adrenalin had carried him through the drive from Rosa's Pizza and Mexican to Jim's Jiffy Auto Repair. Needs must when duty calls, as someone or other famously said. Whatever your personal feelings might be about a woman driver who never bothered to check her oil, with the result that her engine seized up at 65 miles an hour on the Mid-Cape Highway and flipped the car off the road with her in it, you still had a gentleman's obligation to aid a damsel in distress. You made the phone calls, you drove her to the mechanic's, you interpreted between her and Jim. You advised her not to yell at him. Could he help it if there wasn't enough left of her rusty old Toyota to salvage? You asked her who exactly she had in mind suing, considering the accident was technically–well, let's just say it was nobody's fault. You explained that just because she didn't have medical insurance didn't mean a court would order someone else to pay for her pain, costs, and inconvenience. And then you leaned gratefully on your stick while Jim showed her the ladies' room.

Wally's stomach had calmed down. He was still too dizzy to dare take anything for the headache forming like a thunderstorm behind his eyes. Soon. When he got back to the Frigate. Pop whatever was in the Airstream's first-aid kit and sleep it off.

He could see now the wake would have been the worst possible place to speak to Rosemary. With her brother's dead body lying nearby in a coffin? With her large, aggressive family swarming all over her, who'd pried her away from her one true love? The same loyalty they'd wielded like a crowbar eighteen years ago would have stopped any meaningful reunion tonight. Really, he was damn lucky Sue came along when she did.

Poor kid. No car, no job, no money, no common sense to speak of, and now a ton of medical bills.

Not your problem, Hicks. That kind of girl always lands on her feet.

Still, if she needed a place to stay for a couple nights, what could he do? Leave her standing on the side of the road with her arm in a cast and her thumb out? After she already hitched from Cape Cod Hospital to Alistair Pope's wake to find him?

On their way to the mechanic's she'd gotten huffy when he asked if she really and truly did crash her car. No, no, of course he believed her. He was just–relieved. Relieved? Because somebody you supposedly cared about got smashed up in a wreck? Thanks a lot! No, no, he assured her again. Relieved to know she hadn't skipped Alistair's wake on purpose. Like, out of any sense of, well, let's say, guilt.

Sue guffawed at that. Guilt? For screwing him? Making him happy? What's wrong with that?

Nothing, Wally replied. Unless you got, you know, mad at him, or jealous, or . . .

When she realized what he was hinting at, she laughed so hard her stitches almost popped. Jesus P. Christ, Wally! I didn't kill him! What are you, nuts? Here I been thinking maybe *you* killed him. Like to avenge my honor, you know?

They both had a good chuckle about that. Wally felt lightened inside, although his stomach was lurching again. Lightened, reassured, but not a hundred percent convinced. Was that just him? He doubted it. There must be quite a few people in Quansett who wouldn't rest easy until the cops found out who did kill Alistair Pope.

Lucky for them all this case was in the hands of Detective Helen Wills and not Officer Kevin Kelly.

What he needed was a Coke. Kill two birds with one stone:

Settle your stomach, and strip the corrosion off your battery. They'd have a vending machine at the mechanic's. Fix him right up.

Unless Sue came home with him afterwards. Then he'd be awake half the night. Maybe not, though, with so much of her in bandages.

Gromit sure would be tickled to see her again.

Wally leaned on his stick and hoped he'd had the forethought to stock a major painkiller in that first-aid kit.

A long, audible yawn issued from Edgar Rowdey. With his chair tilted back from the table, he stretched out his arms like a giant condor.

"Time for your nap, old fella?" Leo inquired solicitously.

Edgar righted his chair. "I must be off. Soon. When anyone's driving to Quansett."

"Are we boring you?" Caroline arched an eyebrow.

"Oh, no," he yawned again. "Things to do and whatnot."

How could he be so nonchalant? He didn't appear to care one bit who it was Helen had shot at. Slightly irritated, Lydia asked if he thought she or Dinah or Sue was the most likely target. She could see his answer coming before his mouth reopened: "I'm sure I have no idea."

Unbelievable! From the man who'd supplied half the ideas in this case? More than half. In fact, looking back, she couldn't imagine how it could have been solved without him.

She was about to point this out when a yawn of her own stopped her. Suddenly she was exhausted. Her watch said only an hour and a half had passed since she and Mudge left Alistair's wake for his house. Amazing! It felt like a week.

She looked around and realized they'd outlasted Rosa's other customers. Occasional shouts of conversation and car doors slamming suggested the wake must be over, the funeral parlor closing for the night. *There will be time*, she thought. *Time to murder and create*. Maybe even create some normal peace and quiet, until the tourist hordes pour over the bridge.

Carlo was helping Dinah to her feet. Caroline stood with her usual grace and brushed off the sleeve of her embroidered Chinese jacket. Leo was chivvying Edgar about something or other. There would be time tomorrow, and for the rest of the summer, to ask everyone here any question she liked. Time to listen to a new theory or piece of gossip from each Back End customer, as Detective Altman launched his investigation, and Detective Scanlan returned at long last from his vacation, and the Lux Limo burglary gang was rounded up–

"Mudge!" Lydia almost knocked over her chair. "Have you heard from Charlene?"

He nodded and moved closer, so they wouldn't be heard. "She called me while you were talking to the cops. She's good. Nothing's happened yet. She was like glued to the phone all day, thinking there'd be a raid. Once she heard a siren and she ran out and locked herself in the Caddy. I guess it takes a while, though. Setting up? Like, getting court orders, and planting undercover guys?"

"Did she tell you that?"

"Nah," he grinned. "Your buddy Dave from the Times. He didn't want her to worry. Or more like, he don't know about Charlene, but he didn't want *you* to worry."

Whoops, thought Lydia. And here I just ran out on him at Alistair's without so much as a *ciao*.

They drifted with the others into the parking lot. Dave Wheeler would have to wait. Right now, Lydia wanted a word with Dinah.

She caught her opening her car door. "Can I ask you something?"

"Sure."

"What else put you onto Helen Wills?"

Dinah's broad mouth creased in a smile. "You already guessed, didn't you."

"Your other job?"

"Bingo." Dinah leaned against the car; folded her arms. "Who should I get a call from, maybe six months ago, but Chill Wills. He was traveling, so they didn't know he was from here, and he sure's heck didn't know it was me! I only took him the once. Shook me up but good. Not, you know, but what he said about his marriage. It was bad, he knew that, but he damn sure didn't want to know why. Now, Chill never was a connecting kinda guy. Nobody ever thought him and Helen would make it down the aisle, much less . . . Still. I coulda told him right then, I mean it was plain as the nose on your face, she'd got herself a back-door man. But hey. He's fixed on keeping his head in the sand? Not my business."

"You didn't know then it was Alistair."

"No fuckin' way. Al was like the class dork, you know? Beats the hell out of me how they hooked up."

Lydia told her.

"Damn," said Dinah. "I always did hate those reunions."

Behind them, the rest of the group was dispersing. Edgar climbed into the back seat of Caroline and Carlo's Mustang. Carlo waved inquiringly at Lydia. She saw Mudge waiting by his truck, and waved at Carlo to go on without her.

As they chugged onto Route 28, Mudge asked if she wanted to stop by the Rusty Umbrella. Lydia said not tonight. She felt too wired to sleep and too wiped out to stay awake. She felt like Odysseus after Scylla and Charybdis: glad to be sailing onward, sorry for the lives lost, wondering what further adventures lay between here and home.

Home! Where she could take off her mourning clothes, then lie on her loft bed gazing up at her skylight full of stars until consciousness departed.

"So," Mudge said cautiously when they stopped at the Willow Street light. "What do you think?"

"About . . . ?"

"You know. Everything."

Lydia shot him a watery grin. "I think you're a brilliant chef, even if you don't know it yet, and Edgar Rowdey is a brilliant detective, even if he doesn't know it yet, and Rosey Sherman is brilliant for picking Edgar to sign books and you to work at the Frigate and us to cater his grand opening. And I'm incredibly lucky to be here. And that's all the thinking I'm going to do until tomorrow."

28608826R00194

Made in the USA
Lexington, KY
22 December 2013